SoulSource

12/28/02

Merry Christmas Dad! I hope you find this to be a good read.

May our gracious Father grant you power by His Spirit to live as if Jesus died yesterday, rose today, and is coming back tomorrow.

Love,

Marc

SoulSource

Had He Come to America Now!

Stan Howard

Writer's Showcase
San Jose New York Lincoln Shanghai

SoulSource
Had He Come to America Now!

Writer's Showcase
an imprint of iUniverse.com, Inc.

For information address:
iUniverse.com, Inc.
5220 S 16th, Ste. 200
Lincoln, NE 68512
www.iuniverse.com

All Scripture quotations are translated or paraphrased by the author.

ISBN: 0-595-19204-1

Printed in the United States of America

This book is dedicated to my elegant wife,
THERESA

First the crank, then the cam,
then the full blown combustion in the head.

Preface

Most excellent, Genevieve, greetings. As you know, the major headline events surrounding the appearance of Jesus from the northwest suburb of Buffalo Grove, including the controversial signs and wonders he performed in and around Chicago in the space of three-and-a-half years were not carried out in a corner. Others have sought to write an account of everything that has happened and I too having gathered all the necessary records, tape-recorded conversations as well as the sworn affidavits of eyewitnesses felt it would be prudent having investigated everything carefully from the beginning to present my own compendium, laid out for you in chronological order so that you might know the exact truth about all that you have been taught.

The sources from which I have borrowed have not been edited to appease any particular religious sect within the North American subculture or beyond. This finding is written in the same street language from which it was taken. Everything has been preserved; some of which sensitive readers may find indecorous. Certainly this account will shock the sensibilities of militant fundamentalists as well as confront the authoritarianism of America's religious elite, just as Jesus' words provoked Jewish nobility a few short years ago, when they issued from his mouth. But again, not a sentence has been embellished nor romanticized; I've simply allowed the well attested data surrounding these public events to speak for themselves.

This true story took place in the City of Chicago while Harry the renowned architect and builder was in his second term as the City's Mayor and Pilot was governor of Illinois. Jesus was born into the home of poor Jews living in Skokie by a miraculous conception and virgin birth to a young girl named Mary. He was introduced by a baptizer named, Jack prior to his public appearance just as the prophets foretold and maintained a mission consistent with their predictions that was primarily directed to the Jewish populace of suburban Chicago.

The copious prophetic material, of which you are aware, finds its fulfillment in the actual historical appearance by Jesus to a specific geographic location along with his ties to the Jewish temple cult that was centered in the Great City and inextricably linked to the larger story of redemptive history. Because of the enormous written length needed to cover all the aspects of prophetic fulfillment, this retelling must ignore some historical data that leads up to and envelops the Christ event being described. Otherwise the finding is complete and recorded just exactly as it occurred.

I commend this carefully researched version with its special handling of geography and calendar dates to a world readership since Jesus stood upon an overpass spanning the old and new beltways and himself declared, "a time is coming and has in fact already arrived in which genuine God-seekers will race to him neither on this stretch of highway, nor in route to Jerusalem, for God is posting radar to catch people everywhere who come to him running wide open according to the rules." The conventions of Judaism were already crumbling as he drove our streets and those relevant to this story have been largely abolished. We are limited here in our retelling by time and space whereas The Great Story Teller is not. May you not be harmed by the vortex, lady Genevieve, but rather caught up and swept along by the calms of its inner eye. Perhaps you will be dropped off at a port more favorable than that from which you were snatched.

Acknowledgements

With special thanks to the following:

ROB MURRAY of Tiger, Georgia, who introduced me to DON & JEAN BROWER of Severn, Maryland. The net you all laid might have been obvious to other birds!

NATE, SARAH AND STEPHEN, my children and daily joy, who share my faith in this story.

BOB JONES of Calgary Canada, for your incarnate touch and counsel. Nursery magic is still softly spoken and passed along by the likes of the Skin Horse. Thanks for the stitches you bore, Bob.

DR. P. DOUGLAS McINTOSH of Lilburn, Georgia, for showing me the power of observation. You may never know the full impression you made by faithfully teaching God's word, little by little and year after year. Thanks for the foundations and good virtues you modeled to so many of us.

NANCY J. TIENVIERI for your leadership, spirituality, unusual integrity and good friendship. Thanks, Nancy for pouring over a manuscript laden with errors, and in desperate need of stylistic help. Any distasteful items that remain are owing to my own bullheadedness. I am especially appreciative for the way you found time to edit this book during a difficult season in your own personal life. Your kindness and selfless regard is an inspiration to me.

DR. KENNETH E. BAILEY for your parabolic insights, without which this book would be impoverished. I wish I could think of a higher compliment to pay for all the literary treasure I have gleaned from your studies in the gospel of St. Luke.

AL ANDREWS of Franklin, Tennessee for your singular word of empowerment while sitting with other warriors on a mountain top outside Denver. You are a man to be reckoned with, Al.

DR. DAN ALLENDER for the tour you offered me into the interior of a soul. This book would be about as interesting as washing dishes without exposure to many of your ideas. Some of them have been gratefully adopted.

DR. LARRY CRABB for your passionate dedication to the health of the Church. I am also indebted to you for ideas drawn from your writings (too numerous to recount), that I have thought about and wrestled with over the years.

These must also be mentioned:

Steve and Cindy, Dave and Becky, Gary and Joeline, Tim and Sharon, Ron and Jane, Stacy and Rhonda, Danny, John Paul, Eric and Mary Jo, Pam, Doug & Sandy, Pete & Martha Taylor, Jim & Cindy Peterson, Paul & Jeanette Doetsch, Jimmy Beckett and John Diacou, Harold & Betty Anderson, Tom & Marlene Ashby, John & Linda Thurman, Todd & Sharon Olson, Dick & Chris Schmidt, Richard & DeLane Hall, Dale Jones, Gary & Nancy Gilles, John & Sally Filipiak, Ian & Annette

Granville, Glenn & Helga Vicent, Rob & Geri Sullivan, Don & Linda Montgomery, Lew & Gina Hubbard, Wells Lovett, the old Chestnut Hill crowd in Atlanta, the Owensboro Tuesday prayer group: David, Malcomb, Bob, Dave and Neil. Thanks finally to the families of Stone Mountain Community Church, the Chicago Singles—you know who you are! And a special kiss to Chris & Connie McCoy.

Prologue

Summons issued from a realm not governed by time, nor plotted in distance and space. The voice of a trumpet piercing the four winds in search of their pilots. In the same instance a great one–marvelous in appearance–arrived with legions in his company.

Michael hovered above a sea of glass several meters thick that glistened and traced out in a fascinating shape, the ends of which lay hidden beyond vanishing points where orthogonal lines meld with infinity. As he lowered prostrate to the surface, his feet softly docked while lifting him upright. His massive wings lengthened perfectly parallel before being pulled along side creating an awesome posture. The size and strength of this archangel is enormous. He is older than the seas and earth but younger than eternity that surrounds him. His wisdom is deeply layered and his faithfulness fierce and dependable like the character of his superior. With energy and joy he executes each order as if it were his first.

Following his Lord's command, Michael rose up effortlessly and immediately disappeared into the stars as though he had passed through a door hinged somewhere in the expanse. As Michael carried out a detailed cosmos plan for the day, Quinn, an attending angel without any capacity for fear, except that due his Lord, escorted his Majesty to closed chambers where he would be joined for a special summit.

"Can't you just tell me why you have to be away and how long you will be gone?" asked Quinn.

"Sure," he said, "I can help you with part of that. We'll be on the surface several man hours while they're dark."

"O.K., but which side?" asked Quinn.

"Their west," he sighed.

"Any particular city? I mean I just know you're going to one of those cities; you always do when you go," said Quinn with an exasperated voice.

"That's yet to be determined," he said.

"Can't you tell even me?" he pleaded as they reached the vast falls that stand at the top of the channel where galaxies tumble into a bottomless boil feeding the expanse.

"In time," he responded.

As the Lord's closing was imminent, Quinn ventured one last question in desperation, "Will it really require three of you?"

Smiling, he responded, "Three of us, Quinn. I'll expect your usual good job. Go now and release the shining ones in the north. Commence code word: *Jerusalem*. And remind them to stay low and keep moving."

"Stay low and keep moving," answered Quinn with a quizzical look on his face, "what in these realms does that mean?"

"I overheard a Marine use the expression once and I liked it," he said.

"A Marine!" exclaimed Quinn, "what's this place coming to?"

"I said I like the expression, Quinn." The mighty angel was familiar with the kind tone, but the gravity of his voice was also unmistakable, and before the last syllable was issued, Quinn lay low and in profuse agreement. "Carry on," he said. "And Oh, Quinn, you're blushing."

The Lord vanished in an instant and then reappeared as quickly in the great throne room of heaven. Others were already seated in chambers with a space open on the right and part of the great center throne that stood in the middle. There was a rainbow around the throne that was brilliant in appearance and twenty-four other thrones circled it round about and they were occupied by twenty-four elders. Before the throne lay an enormous sea of smooth crystal glass with seven lamps burning with fire as well as four living creatures full of eyes in front and behind and each different and wonderful in appearance.

"No use using their expressions with the angels," said one present, "they just don't get it."

"Yes, Quinn was totally baffled by that one," said the Lord. The elders and living creatures were holding solemn abeyance when their Lord's arrival lifted them to attention and further oblations of worship. Suddenly the Lord burst into uproarious laughter and remarked, "Well, we certainly meant dress rehearsal didn't we?" The Lord looked upon two others who had already suited themselves with Polo shirts, loose fitting khakis and boat shoes. The Lord ordered denim jeans, a white T, a lightweight button down shirt as well as a pair of trainer tennis shoes. As he sat down, he asked, "who ordered up the water and glasses?"

"I think their glass is appropriate in view of the age," said another. "They've come a long way since the animal skins of Abram's day. This is just a little taste of the upcoming human event." The elders and living creatures were totally bewildered and speechless because of the posture, dress and North American idiom that flowed between them.

Without a signal seats were taken and silence fell over the room except for the voice of the one unto whom all homage is due. "Lucifer never tires of his rampage. His expulsion from these heights has incited his great fury. And his rage burns for want of glory. Woe indeed to those in the world who bear our image, for his wrath would swallow them alive."

"Yes, all wise God," they said, "and all your counsel will be established. All of your decrees will find their fulfillment according to your righteous will. May it be carried out on earth just as it is here in heaven."

"But what of man?" he asked, "what shall be done for Adam?"

The Lord moved about a pavement of sapphire elevated above a mezzanine that was lined with myriads upon myriads of angels that cannot be counted for number and who cry to Him day and night, "separate, separate, separate is the Lord God, the Last Word." Then with a flutter of wings creating drumming thunder, they fall to their faces and worship in a swelling chorus that is deafening to mortals.

"The devastation of Sodom will not do. That was temporary and remedial," he said. "Adam's problem runs deep and from generation to generation it is the same. A red man cannot change his skin's color, nor can a tiger reverse his stripes. They are helpless without our intervention."

For the benefit of the elders, the Lord began rehearsing events of human history's recent past. As He spoke, life size characters including their actions and communications were manifested in exact detail before them. "Crime, suffering and destruction have continued escalating," he said while pointing out several noticeable spikes, "especially since the period of their great war. This would be according to the count of Julian and the 1940's," he concluded.

"Yes," the elders agreed. "And the Holocaust associated with it will remain the epitome of human atrocity in perpetuity."

Then, in grave response, he said, "until there's light!"

After a moment, he continued speaking by noting that the sufferings of this human drama were but the birth pangs of things to come. "Rumblings of the end are already discerned by the wise of the earth," he said. "Adam thirsts for the wrong things. He covets, cannot obtain and so he murders. His sons have not understood the path of peace.

And this is all very grievous. The time is approaching the unfolding of our plan laid out in eternity past that will soon work itself out in human history."

Then, from beneath an altar the voices of souls were heard, pleading to know how long.

"The time is fast approaching," he said, "the culmination of all things is at hand. Rest." The Lord concluded his address by saying, "eternity is always and equally present before us. Let's drop in on them as before, in the days of Lot, and see if they have involved themselves in everything contained in the reports."

Following dismissals from the great throne room, the Lord concluded another message at a different location within the heavenly city by calling upon Anthony to direct legions of seraphs who had gathered in the open expanse to hear his word. The Lord's presence brought light into a place already filled with light. His brilliance is constant, undiluted and equal, filling every space. The glory of his majesty filled the temple and as the smoke rose from that place, the thresholds trembled and all the foundations shook in acknowledgment of his presence.

As two stepped forward and joined him at center, others fell down and cried out in worship as smoke kept filling the expanse. Seraphs of renowned strength and unlimited numbers flanked their sides and strode magnanimously before and behind in procession as they made their passage through the Temple-Court, down the corridor called 'Beautiful' that leads to the open expanse and beyond the outer gate. The three rose high above heaven's epicenter and appeared as one. The foundations of the universe were laid bare. A glance below at the heavenly city showed itself magnificent—a constantly imploding constellation radiant with light.

"As before, I think it would be wise for us to remain legitimate and try hard to accommodate ourselves to them while we're on the surface," the Lord said.

"Shall it be Chicago?" they asked.

"Yes," he said, and with a nod three men stepped up to the curb on Lakeshore Drive in front of Monroe harbor to signal a cab.

"They call this the 'Windy City,'" remarked the one.

"Is that a political or atmospheric observation?" asked another.

"The two of you are really entering into this aren't you?" observed the Lord.

"Just trying to stay 'legit' and take in a little of the local color," they answered together.

"By the way, what's with the Rolex?" asked one from behind and smiling.

"Quinn ordered this up for me. He had a hunch we were coming to Chicago. He is always concerned for my bearing and class while I'm abroad like this. I told him the Rolex really didn't fit into the look I was after, but I didn't want to crush his spirit entirely. Turning down the tux was a terrible grief to him. He was convinced we were up to something political and would spend a lot of time wining and dining with their great ones," he said, returning the smile to the one behind and winking. A cab slowed to a stop at their feet while the last vestiges of light looked west leaving the three standing in shadows that were thrown over them by the towering multi-story buildings. The skyscrapers created a range of aggregate rock along the gold coast.

"Wonder what will go on up in those crevices tonight," he asked rhetorically, but in a convinced kind of way. Changing the subject he asked, "Can you believe these little fellahs lay out ten bills for one of these?" He placed his elbows on the roof of the waiting cab and turned the watch on his wrist as he observed the traffic and scanned the city's skyline. "They're hungry for glory. Never been terribly content to reflect it. If they can't attain it, they seek to buy it; and if they can't afford it, they grow dark and destructive. The sinister one has carefully laid out a descending spiral and how he loves to ride them down its slopes. But Adam benefits from his shame. It's always been easier for him to walk in it, stand in it, and sit in it, than to get up and come home," he said compassionately.

"The cravings of his flesh," began another, "all seem so desperately just, until it begins to eat at the things that are vital, leaving his soul so mutilated that he's no longer recognizable."

"Yes," the third man agreed, "a prophet among them now has summarized the prevailing attitude well when he said, 'always deprived, but never depraved.'"

"Yes, it's time to deal with this coronary disease," the Lord concluded.

"Any time gentlemen, the meter's running," shouted the cabbie, "This isn't exactly a pick up zone you know!"

"O.K., Dave, sorry for the inconvenience." they said.

"Hey, how do you know me?" asked the cabbie as he adjusted his glasses and squinted into the rear view mirror. "Are you the three I picked up two weeks ago in front of Twin Anchors singing and barking at the moon," he kept searching as they piled into the back seat. "Boy you guys were tanked up!"

"Different trio, Dave," they said.

"O.K., O.K., trio, threesome—uno, dos, tress, there were three of 'em, "holding up three fingers, "and they were barking at the moon. So how do you know me?"

"Let's get over on State and head down to about 35th," they directed while ignoring his question.

"Yea, the Tech Institute," said Dave.

"Pretty close," said a voice from the rear, "drop us off a few blocks west of the expressway."

After several minutes, the cabbie broke a still silence by asking, "So, ya Trio fellahs, ya gonna take in a game? The Yankees are in town for a series."

"Reckon not," they said, "We've seen this game before."

"Reckon not!" whispered the three among themselves and chuckling. "Now we're getting 'legit.'"

"Hey, you guys are real celebrities, so you've seen this game before huh?" asked the cabbie.

"Yea, Dave, it's a real thriller for the religiously committed. The Sox are down three runs in the bottom of the ninth, load the bases and hit into a double play leaving runners on the corners, but it's not over until..."

"Yea, yea, until the fat lady sings," interjected Dave.

"Those are not my words, Dave," said one of the men from the back seat.

"Ohhh," Dave muttered sarcastically, "How in the scratch else ya gonna finish a sentence like that?"

"Dave, a lot of desperate and unfortunate things including sentences like that get finished on the last day. Let's just stick with what happened and allow me to finish the story," he insisted.

"With what happened!" Dave interrupted again, "For the love of checkers, the game isn't even over!"

"Dave, just keep your eye on the road, we don't want you to get hurt. Anyway, just when the bleachers begin to empty, the Sox get a walk, then they get a base hit on an in field error—the Yankee's short stop juggles the ball and all of the sudden they're back in the game. At this juncture, Carbiener steps up to the plate with two out, an empty look on his face and spitting tobacco juice until you wonder if he's got any saliva left. He scratches the box with his cleats like a war horse hungry for battle, takes the first pitch, a slider low and outside and belts a grand slam to right field—right over the bill board! The Sox will win this game by two runs—7 to 5."

"Yea, well you ought to seek out a bookie with that kind of information," said Dave.

"How long have you been driving, Dave?" asked one of the men as he passed him a twenty dollar bill.

"Oh, not long." Dave stammered as they handed him another twenty. "I guess I've been laid off from the steel mill about three years now." Hands from the back seat produce several more fresh twenties as Dave relates that he has two girls to feed and the wife doesn't bring in much.

"How is Carol Ann doing since surgery? I'll bet Kathryn and Elizabeth are glad to have her back home," they said, while handing Dave more twenty dollar bills.

The three men stared out the windows taking in the sights, including a liquor store hold up and shooting while Dave nervously asked, "What do you know about my Kathryn and Elizabeth? Do you hand out dough to everybody?"

"Nope," they said, "there's an uneven distribution of resources on the planet and it's a big problem. Just wanted to help you out a little in the short run."

"Who are you guys? What do you want from me?"

"Typical response, Dave," they said. "We don't want your possessions—just your heart."

"My heart," Dave said squirming. "My heart! Now you guys are blame bold hitting the streets looking for a donor. Look, my blood's no good, I'm weak, full of cholesterol, I take more meds than…"

"Relax, Dave," they said, "it's not our intention to harm you, we're just along for the ride. But yes, Kathryn and Elizabeth talk to us on a pretty regular basis," as they handed Dave another group of twenties.

"Well, what do they talk to you about? Are they in some kind of trouble?" asked Dave in a shaky voice.

"Oh no, nothing like that. They just talk to me and generally ask for a few things related to your work and safety and Carol Ann's recovery," he said.

"You guys are doctors aren't you!" exclaimed Dave.

"That's right—we are in a sense," they said.

"I mean, that's why all the money—right? You want your money. This is sadistic as hell."

"Oh, you're greatly mistaken about that, Dave. Sadistic doesn't even begin to describe the place," they said.

"You guys do you're own collections! Look you all did a great job on Carol Ann. How did you find me on a night like this? It's the bills—I'll pay you—I just need a little more time," Dave said hysterically.

"C'mon relax, Dave, you can let us out at the next block," they said. The cab pulled to the curb and as the last man exited, he turned back to Dave and handed him more cash. "Dave, here's all you need for the balance of Carol Ann's surgery. Why don't you turn in early tonight and go home to be with your family."

Dave turned his eyes to heaven and prayed, "Dear, God thank you—thank you!"

One of the men drew his attention and said, "Dave, your welcome." As the cab pulled away, the Sox radio announcer offered the play by play of the bottom of the ninth. Dave leaned forward, turned up the volume and made his way north toward home.

"Boy, he was intense," they said among themselves. The three men walked along streets between 35th and Pershing Road and noticed an eight-year-old Black youth shooting baskets in a side lot. The hoop was bent, had a ragged net and nailed to a utility pole, that stared down on a large grass worn area they call 'The Lane.' As the three men approached the boy, he began to back up and was overcome with fear. "Hello, son," they said, "we're just passing through the neighborhood to have a look at the condition of things here."

"Mister, I don't do drugs and I don't have any money. Are you going to take my ball?" asked the boy.

"Oh, we're not here to take what is yours," they said.

"Then why are you in our hood?" asked the boy.

"Like we said, just checking things out young, Adam," replied the three.

"My name's not Adam," said the boy.

"We know. Say, what's this attached to your leg?" they asked.

"I'll never be able to play real basketball on a team or anything," said the boy.

"Mind if I take a shot?" one of the men asked.

"Will you bring it back?" winced the boy.

"Sure, let me see if I can swish it from mid-court," he said. Then, bending his knees slightly, and taking a careful look at the basket he pushed a shot with a perfect arch toward the basket, but it hit the rim on the left side and bounced onto the grass that was drenched with summer's dew.

While one of the men retrieved the ball, the boy remarked, "Don't feel bad, a lot of great players miss from out here. My brother's friend Scottie is one of the best in the hood and he's only made it once or twice that I can remember."

As they bent down for a closer look at the boy's leg brace, one of the men fondled the little boy's ear; while speaking tenderly to him and said, "You know, there are things more important than baskets that folks miss in life. Seems to me, the most important things in life require childlike trust."

"Did you think that you would make that basket from mid-court?" asked the boy.

"Well, did you believe that I would?" he replied with a chuckle. As he began to remove the brace from the boy's leg, he asked him, "What do you believe about this brace?"

"I believe it's a pain," said the boy. "Are you guys doctors or something? My mama said some people from the Health Department were coming this week."

"I guess you could say, we're doctors," they said. "Young Adam, I'm going to fix your leg so that you can play on that team you've been dreaming about. Do you believe I can fix this problem?"

"Well," said the boy, "Mama told me that nobody at Cook County could fix it. Are you better than those doctors?" asked the boy.

"We are from above," they said. "Now I'm going to remove this last pin and brace. If you believe, take off that support shoe and run toward the basket for a lay-up."

"Yes sir," said the boy, as he leaped to his feet running. But, before he reached the basket, he began leaping, crying and screaming for joy, "Mama, Mama, I can run! I can run! Mama, hurry and come!" As the boy ran around the house shouting hysterically, his mother stepped out the back door looking for her son and noticed three men moving away from the back lot toward the next block with a basketball under the arm of one.

Nearly a block away, the three passed and dribbled the basketball among themselves as they jogged down the street and sidewalks dodging sporadic traffic.

Meanwhile, the boy who was nearly out of breath tried to explain to his mother what had happened while she sobbed with joy. "Mama, Mama, three doctors from above were here and they fixed my leg for no money. They just asked me if I believed they could—that's it! They just asked me if I believed. He took off my brace and I felt it all Mama! I felt it fix! He really did it! It was His hand, I know it was His hand!"

"I believe you baby," cried his mother.

The boy jumped up, looking for his ball and said, "Mama, you're gonna see the jump shot I've been telling you about. Where's the ball? Did they take my ball?"

"One of the men had a ball under his arm as they walked away child," said the mother, "but I'll get you another one."

"They'll bring it back, they were good men Mama," he said.

At that moment from another street nearly four blocks away, one of the men predicted, "Off the billboard, through the alley, under the truck, up the slide, nothing but net." He bent His knees slightly, took a careful look at the basket and pushed the ball forward with perfect speed toward the bill board. In a moment, the ball came flying through an alley with incredible velocity past a group of teens involved in a drug exchange who were terrorized by its close brush between their faces, flew up the slide and swished through the metal rim in the boy's back lot.

"Nice shot," two of them remarked in unison while lifting their gaze. "You do all things well."

"Mama, look! look! It's my ball—that's my ball! Did you see that? I know you saw that! Do you believe it Mama?!" asked her son with all astonishment and wonder.

"Yes, baby I believe, she stammered with fear, "I always believed." The mother buried her face on his small shoulders and squeezed the boy until it hurt for her joy could not be held back. At that time the boy's older brother and two friends walked in from the alley and found the leg brace laying on the ground. The boy raised up from his mother's arms and walked toward his brother.

"Ricky!" they exclaimed, "What has happened to you?"

Meanwhile the three men continued their trek in and out of cabs and neighborhoods, passing crack houses that backed up to the Stevenson near Loomis and later stepping into the poverty at Cabrini housing. Passing along they witnessed a car theft, then turned up an alley and surprised a man who had robbed and brutalized an individual at gun point. The gunman threatened the three with his weapon when one of them made a face that caused him to crumble to his knees and lose consciousness.

"Hey," said the others humorously, "I thought we were going to blend in?"

"Yes," he replied, "but that one was about to make a loud noise." Together they helped the trembling victim to his feet and retrieved the money that had been stolen.

"Easy now, we're not going to harm you," as they held the man who was gasping but speechless. "Here you are Adam, I believe these papers belong to you and here are a few more to help your family," they said while each of them drew new currency from their pockets. Mysteriously, the gaping wound that had been opened beneath the man's left eye was closed and completely eliminated by the gentle brush of one of the men's hands.

"Now then, let's catch a cab and move on back over toward the lake and see if we can find some ice cream—we can sit down and I'll have some things to say," sighed the one to the others.

The three moved away from the traumatized man who scrambled to the corner of the building and fled like a deer that had been loosed from a trap into the underbrush of the dark forest from which he came. Upon catching a cab they made their way back to the area of the Shedd Aquarium. After purchasing ice cream, the men filed behind others who were boarding a boat for a ride along the Gold Coast. Just ahead stood a young mother haggling with her three small children about how they would spend the few dollars they had scraped together for their trip downtown from Calumet City.

"We can't ride the boat and get ice cream too," she said in a scolding tone.

"But mommy, those men have ice cream. I don't want to ride the boat, I want ice cream," insisted six-year-old Wendy.

"Mom, I know you're not giving in to that," warned her oldest son, Calvin. "Every time we go somewhere she lights up and you cave in."

"How about you, Wilson. What do you want, ice cream or a boat ride?" she asked while looking for an unanimous vote.

"He doesn't count Mom," whined Calvin, "he's too little and if you mention ice cream again you know which one he'll choose."

"Oh, God, help me, I can't do this alone," she said welting up with tears and marching onto the boat alone.

"See what you've done, Wendy!" Calvin screamed. "Mom works extra to get a few more dollars for gas and you screw it all up by arguing over ice cream. No you enjoy this ride or you're in trouble."

"No, you're in trouble if you touch me," Wendy whispered with all the courage she could muster. Then taking young Wilson by the arm she led him aboard and snuggled close to her mother. After a few minutes Calvin walked aboard and grudgingly sat down next to his sister.

"Children," came a voice sounding from behind their shoulders, "anybody for cookies and cream?" asked a man with kind eyes who stood with arms extended and offering four waffle cones with double dips to a family with long faces. "We heard your cry for help," he said. "Please enjoy. They're on us," nodding back to his companions and distributing cones to hungry hands.

"You heard my cry?" asked Jean trying on a new composure.

"Yes, your cries are always heard," he said in a soft statement of fact, then returning to his place.

"Mom, did you thank them for the cones?" asked Wendy as she stared back at them with appreciation in her eyes.

Jean turned toward the bow and drew tissue from her jacket, when Calvin snapped Wendy from her infatuation and said, "turn around girl. You're not supposed to stare at people, they're probably trying to set us up for something."

"Oh, Calvin, you are always suspicious whenever somebody's good to us," Wendy said as she turned back and began licking her favorite ice cream that was quickly changing form.

From the rear of the boat, the three men took in the sights, pointed out the contours of Lake Michigan, Burnham's lakefront design and reflected on the architectural quality of the period. After some time, the mood changed and with solemn gravity they began to relate among themselves their deep love for Adam.

"His sin is offensive," one began, "but we can't give him up. He will die under the first terms. It's now time to finish the plan we laid out before the foundation of the world. The everlasting terms. His guilt and shame must be carried by another; one perfect, innocent and willing.

There is no other way. The Evil One will work hard to force a compromise of the terms. But it stands written in order to be fulfilled, 'He will nip you on the heel, but you will shatter his head.' Let's be going." Upon finishing their cones, and without being noticed, one of the three loosed a gold Rolex from his wrist and dropped it into a handbag that belonged to a woman who had boarded with three children. They then stepped silently over the starboard side of the boat onto the water and walked several paces into the darkness before beginning a gradual ascent that led invisibly into the stars.

Chapter I

"Joey, will you please sit down and stop pacing the floor?" Mary pleaded in a concerned manner from the living room sofa while rubbing together her stocking feet.

"Sit down and stop pacing the floor." Joey replied with mild sarcasm and thoroughly exasperated. "What do you want me to say? What would you say for crying out loud? I guess I just need to hear it straight," his back to Mary and staring at the wall paper as though he were melting into it, then dropping his head and placing both hands on the door jambs before him inquired, "So you weren't seeing Earl while I was with my unit in Nam?"

"Joey, how could you think that?" Mary managed through tears.

"I mean this stuff of an afternoon visit from a guy named Gabriel who claims to be a messenger from God—an angel for crying out loud—is just more than I can swallow. This is front page cock-and-bull material and you're asking me to believe this dream. And he didn't touch you, just shows up for afternoon tea and poof—you're pregnant! I guess stranger things have happened, I just can't remember when," quipped Joey as he turned and joined Mary on the sofa where she sat sobbing. Joey placed his arm around Mary, threw his head back on the old cloth sofa, closed his eyes and tried to forget about time and anything rational. Mary's sobbing turned to a restful purr as she lay against Joey's chest and in moments fell into a listless sleep. Joey, still awake but now staring at the ceiling and trying to relax his over-taxed mind by seeking out that mental compartment that provided him a place for quiet reflective thought. The ceiling with its brown nicotine stains and plaster swirls laid down by craftsmen of past generations were no longer visible. Cobwebs that used to spark petty controversy over whose turn it was to brush them down vanished. The ceiling had become a large screen in the imagination of his mind. Even the laughter and screams of small children playing in the corridor of the apartment flat faded into the background as Joey mused upon the events of recent weeks. Stranger things have happened, whispered Joey's unconscious self to anyone listening. Let's see, Mary's aunt Liz has been pregnant for several months and Zack's not exactly a whippersnapper any longer. Now Mary's been struck. Good grief, how am I going to tell her? Mary it's over; go find the father. Mary I'm sorry, but I wasn't in on this. Or baby let's stay friends and....

Joey's musings were suddenly interrupted by a clear and distinct voice from somewhere within. "Joseph," the voice announced, "Do not be afraid to take Mary as your wife. She has become pregnant by the power of the Holy Spirit. You will name the boy 'Jesus' because he will save his people from their sins."

"Something big is happening. Do you trust me, Joey? Do you trust me, Joey?" continued the voice, but it was no longer coming from within, but beside him, in his arms. Mary continued to whisper and invite his response, "Do you trust me, Joey?"

Now flinching and reaching for consciousness, Joey began pressing his face with the palms of his hands and slowly pulling them until his fingertips reached his chin. He lowered his head, looked to Mary with tenderness in his eyes and said, "I want to, Mary, with all my heart, I want to."

With tears flowing, Mary asked, "You don't want an abortion, too, do you?"

"Of course not!" said Joey, "Of course I don't want that for you."

"Well, that's what everyone else is telling me," said Mary with tightness in her throat. "Even Lori is insisting that I go through with it and get my life back on track before I'm nineteen."

"Well, let me tell you about Lori," when the door bell rang and interrupted his thought. "Are you expecting anyone?" Joey asked with surprise in his voice.

"Not unless it's the social worker Lori booked for me," said Mary.

"Social worker!" Joey scowled while pacing to the door. "Who gave her the authority to call on a social worker for us?"

"Go easy, Joey," coached Mary as she dried tears from her eyes.

"Yea, I'll go easy," Joey said, opening the door, "until she steps in front of this train. I've had it with her obnoxious, controlling, in your face advice about issues for which she hasn't the slightest knowledge, experience or ability to...Whatever you're selling, we don't want any," said Joey, nearly spitting the words into the face of the woman standing squarely before him.

"And you must be Mary," said the social worker as she brushed past Joey and made her way across the short foyer to the living area. "My name is Cathy with the Illinois Department of Social Services," she said, flashing her credentials before her. "I've brought along the release forms and some literature regarding the procedure. We need to move quickly. You are getting very late. Mary, are you listening to me? Didn't you hear from your friend Lori? We are prepared to help you. There are offices with trained professionals who counsel and help young women like yourself find contingents and plan for your future—it's your only choice."

"But I don't want an abortion," said Mary, "besides, it's illegal."

"Let us worry about what's legal. I know it's a difficult consideration but after reading the literature, statistics and stories from girls your age—well, I think the financial stress alone would be more than mom or dad could bear. Aren't they both working? Isn't this their apartment? Mary, you're still at home. How will you provide for this baby, the food, medical, clothing—the cost of living in Skokie isn't getting any cheaper," Cathy said, concluding her speech with a manipulative tone.

"Joey and I think we can make it with the baby," Mary said timidly, staring at the floor.

"So, Joey, you're the father?" asked Cathy.

"Well kind of, I guess in a way," said Joey.

"Hmm, I see," Cathy said condescendingly, "Certainly you can appreciate the difficulties this pregnancy presents. I'll expect your full cooperation. Look, I've already booked an appointment for Mary next week," said Cathy, while indicating a date in her planner the first week in 1968. She underlined it for Joey's benefit with a red felt pen. "This is a safe, fast procedure and will get you started off on the right foot for the new year. Mary will need to arrive before 7:00 AM for prep work. Here's the address for our clinic," she said, handing Joey a business card and opening the door to depart. "You're making the right choice. I'll drop by after the procedure for a little follow up work. Mary, I'd like to have that appointment alone with you," she said, ignoring Joey.

Shutting the door, Joey muttered to himself, "Yea, we'll see you next week—over my dead body!"

"I'm not going through with it, Joey," Mary insisted.

"I don't want you to either! Just let me think," said Joey.

"You're pacing again," Mary said smiling.

"Listen, I'm going to get some things. Can you pull together some stuff, maybe a suitcase? We're driving to Morton. You're going to meet the friends I told you about. I think they can help." Dropping to his knees before her, "Mary, you're going to have the baby," Joey said confidently as he stroked her glistening black hair.

"Oh, Joey, I knew you were in there," said Mary leaping forward and hugging Joey's neck.

"We'll go down for a few weeks until the baby comes. Everything will be fine. We can drop down to Decatur and see my parents, I'll help dad with the press that needs to be overhauled and take care of some local census information mom mentioned," said Joey. "Listen, I'll be back around three," while kissing Mary on the forehead and rising to his feet. "That will give you a couple of hours to get ready and don't you dare walk to the lot without me. We've gotten about four inches of snow and the sidewalks to this dump are covered in ice as usual."

As Joey departed, Mary began to shift to her feet when she felt something warm flowing down both of her legs. Grasping the waist of her slacks with both hands, she rushed fearfully to the bathroom and sat down only to realize that she had wet her pants. She began laughing hysterically which turned to a song to her baby as she showered and found dry clothes and packed a bag for the trip ahead.

Shortly before three o'clock, Joey pulled off Golf into the apartment complex near Old Orchard. "Man, this traffic is the pits," he murmured to himself as he maneuvered his small pickup truck through narrow passages created by stalled cars still stranded from last week's snow storm. "C'mon Mary be ready, we've got to beat feet if we're going to make it out of here before rush hour," he said to himself. Parking next to the side entrance, Joey sprang to the door and gathered bags from Mary who had been waiting and looking out for his arrival. "Way to move baby," said Joey with a sigh of relief. "Now don't move, I'll be right back to help you out." Joey half walked and half skated to the truck while making his way to the back and raising the hatch on the camper lid.

"Hey, when are you guys going to put down your coffee and deal with this ice," he shouted at two maintenance men who were passing by to the next unit. Ignoring Joey, except for a hand signal, they walked on while he stowed bags, packages and extra clothing beneath the lid. Returning for Mary, Joey poured the last cup of coffee into his thermal cup, locked up the apartment and escorted Mary down the walk and helped seat her comfortably in the cab with pillows and extra blankets. "Sweetie, did you leave the folks a note," asked Joey as he gently repositioned Mary's leg away from the floor shift.

"Yes, Joey, I left the note, tied up the kitchen trash, folded the laundry and thawed out dinner for Mom and Dad."

"Whoa, what did you thaw out," Joey asked in a knowing kind of tone, "I mean maybe we should stay. Was it more of that delicious potato soup with the flour lumps and little green things added for color. Now that was absolutely burpable. Let's see, when was it, Sunday dinner three weeks ago and I can still taste it. Think of the mileage folks could strain out on a regular diet of that gook. Can you see it: A new breakthrough in frugal dining for those on a tight leash. Feed your kids one tablespoon of mom's popping potato soup and you'll not have to eat again for a month. The little woman should definitely submit that one to one of those fancy French magazines that features a corner section of exquisite cuisine for those on a budget of say less than twenty dollars a week. List it under foods with low carbs but high octane, that should grab 'em."

"Joey," Mary said chuckling, "Mom makes good soup and you shouldn't make fun because they can't afford better. I happen to like mom's potato soup."

"Yea, I've watched you woof it down. Have you ever seen a coon hound sucking up chicken gravy? You inhale the stuff. I'm just worried about what its doing to the little guy," petting Mary's stomach, "he probably spends his afternoon doing dips from your rib cage every time you eat that stuff. He'll be a regular superman," Joey continued.

"Oh, he'll be more than that," said Mary, "but it won't be on account of mom's soup. I'm going to nap funny man. Don't wake me up unless you see a truck stop offering homemade potato soup."

"Don't hold me to it," said Joey as he headed to Dempster. I'll see if you're ready for a rest stop after we get down the Tristate a ways."

Several miles passed and as Joey and Mary skirted O'Hare on the east, three men who were passengers aboard a 747 that originated in Kuwait taxied to the gate for the unboarding of passengers.

"Enjoy your stay in Chicago," said the stewardess as she handed three men their packages that had been placed in a cabinet near the front of the cabin.

"And you likewise madam," and they each nodded in appreciation. Following the mass flow to the main terminal, the three men stopped and ordered double mochas and each produced a cellular phone and began making arrangements for transportation and connections around Chicago. Without a word between themselves, the three men almost in unison placed phones in their pockets and made their way outside where a black Mercedes limo awaited them.

"Greetings gentlemen," said the driver, "You're right on time. Are these your only personals?" The driver placed three small packages in an interior safe that opened from the floor of the trunk.

"Yes, Gordon that will be all for the safe. We will hold our satchels. Please prepare our service and fruit, and may we be going?" they asked

"All is waiting as you requested. By your leave gentlemen," as the driver opened the door and invited his passengers to take their seats. Once inside, the driver proceeded out of the terminal area and onto the

Kennedy Expressway to downtown Chicago while the three passengers nibbled fruit and whipped cream from crystal goblets. Each of the men wore full length black wool coats with black gloves and accessories, dark matching suits, white tailored shirts with hand made silk ties that appeared brushed with soft colors of green and pale red. After the last morsel was coaxed up the wall of the inside glass by his work with a spoon, the man in the center cradled it, then dropped both it and the spoon to the bottom of the dish, placed it aside and began rehearsing their plans aloud as the others listened in agreement.

"Following our 4:30 meeting with the Mayor's office, we'll fan out and inquire about the sighting from local sources," said Ruel as he faced his associates from an opposite seat. "Breverard, you work Michigan Avenue and remember anybody and everybody is fair game. Talk to merchants, newspaper sales, the guy in the alley, anyone who knows anything about this star. Somebody has seen it as we have. I want to know the time, place, date, what they were eating, who they were with, you know the drill—stand 'em up and shake 'em down. Claude, you stay with Gordon and take the Dan Ryan towards Hammond until you get stalled. You will get stalled. Get off and do a complete finding. I don't care who you have to collar, I want something solid. Remember, keep one eye in the sky. Also, your astronomer's maps and compasses are all included and recently calibrated. I'll be traveling to Skokie from City Hall checking out synagogues and talking to merchants. Let's synchronize our watches on my mark—Ready. Three, two, mark. Everyone rendezvous at the Planetarium at 8:00 P.M. We'll compare notes and debrief on our way out of town." With that each of the men placed their right fists together, stretching their arms full length from their seats and shouted together, "unto the King!" Minutes later speakers in the passenger cabin alerted the men that they were exiting the Kennedy at Ohio and would be arriving at City Hall in minutes.

"Yes officer," Joey said. "I realize I was pushing it a bit. My fiancé is real uncomfortable with this pregnancy, she's due in a few weeks, her first! I'm trying to get her to Morton so…."

"Yea, well Morton's a piece from here, now slow it down or you'll be following me over to Kankakee for a little R & R. You were a good eight miles over the limit."

"Yes sir, officer," Joey groveled, "I'm much obliged for…"

"Don't be thanking me boy, the State of Illinois thanks me twice a month. Now go on and get your foot up off that pedal. And just a word of personal advice; do right and marry that girl."

"Yes, sir, we're working on that," Joey said weakly.

"Kids don't have any blasted sense of responsibility anymore," grumbled officer Meyer as he paced back to his cruiser.

"Whew, a little too much potato soup, I mean octane," grinned Mary.

"Alright chosen one, let's not get carried away," chimed Joey, "You might want to make a rest stop soon. Just remember who's driving."

"Yes sir, captain," said Mary. By the way, is this truck bumpy or is it the road? I feel like I've been riding a camel, bumpity bump, bumpity bump, there's definitely a rhythm."

"C'mon, Mary, this is the great State of Illinois, The Land of Lincoln; couldn't be the roads with a heritage like that and the taxes we pay now could it? Our tags ought to read something like, 'Illinois—The Holy Land.' Sure it's the potholes alright and I'm going to have to have this truck realigned when we get back. There are only two seasons in this state…"

"You say it all the time," Mary interrupted and smiling fondly, winter and road repair."

"Yep, and this is the only place you can go and experience them both at the same time!" concluded Joey.

"Are we getting close? I need to go to the rest room," Mary said in obvious discomfort.

"Yes, there's a rest area just up the road, maybe five to six miles max. How are you doing honey? You know this trip may not have been such a good idea after all."

"I'll be O.K.," said Mary as she readjusted and placed her head against Joey's shoulder, "Let's just get there soon." Both of them were silent as they traveled together, but Mary was sure contractions had begun for her, however they were supposed to feel. "Maybe I can get some relief and feel better after a little walk outside this truck," she thought to herself. "I'll not bother Joey with more worry right now."

Joey pulled into the rest area and Mary released the latch on the passenger side door before the truck came to a complete stop. "Easy lady," said Joey, "Let me come around and help. The last thing you need to do is fall down in this snow."

"O.K., O.K., O.K., but lets go," said Mary. Joey braced her left elbow in the palm of his left hand and with his right arm held her waist as they made there way to the foyer.

"See you in a minute dear, I'm going to have a look at this map," said Joey as Mary made her way into the ladies' room. Minutes passed as Joey traced the remainder of their trip down I-55 to Bloomington, then I-74 over to Morton. We shouldn't be long Joey thought to himself. Another hour or hour and fifteen tops. We'll kick back with Ed and Sally and catch up on old times. Joey began to move away from the map and toward the front doors when he overheard two truck drivers commenting on a grid lock down north of Bloomington at 51 and I-55. A semi-truck had overturned and the trailer obstructed the westbound lanes. "That's nothing," Joey thought to himself, "They'll have that taken care of in no time." Brushing the thought aside, he turned toward Mary who was just coming out of the rest room. "Ready to mount that Camel?" asked Joey.

"Oh, don't remind me," said Mary frowning.

"Look, I know its been a tough trip but we're almost there. I'd say we'll pull in at the Klein's in one hour," Joey assured her pointing at his watch.

"I feel some better, just pray that these contractions don't grow any stronger," said Mary.

"Contractions!" Joey shouted through his teeth and folding his body. "I thought you were five weeks away from delivery. For crying out loud Mary, what am I going to do?"

"What are you going to do?" Mary asked in astonishment. "Help me to the truck, I think I'm O.K."

"Maybe you're just having cramps or something," suggested Joey. "Say, did you dip into that soup before leaving home?"

"C'mon Joey, don't get me started, I don't need to laugh right now."

"Alright, you just sit tight and I'll have you on a soft couch at the Klein's before you can say potato soup."

They pulled back onto I-55 and joined a string of vehicles traveling the speed limit at about 8:00 P.M. Mary was restless and still experiencing contractions. "Joey, are we getting close?" she asked.

"Honey, we just got on the road. Like I said, maybe another hour. Can't you relax?"

"No, I really can't in this little cab. You said this was a three hour drive. Haven't we already been on the road three hours?"

"No honey, I said that I could drive this in three hours. Allow me to remind my little peach that we've stopped at just about every rest area, truck stop and gas station between here and Chicago!"

"You're a patient man darling. By the way, do you know Ed and Sally's house address there in Morton? Does Morton have a hospital?"

"No hospitals in Morton, but Peoria is just a skip away on the Interstate. We've got time to worry about that. You're not due for weeks. Ed and Sally moved, but they won't be hard to find. Morton's not a large town and I'll call as soon as we get in."

"I don't know Joey. I think my water broke back at home."

"You're what? Is that a joke? I mean is that serious?" asked Joey.

"I'm O.K. Joey, I'm scared. I've never done this. I wish mom were here, she would know what to do."

"I wish somebody up ahead knew what to do," commented Joey in a very deflated voice. "Welcome to Park City folks! Can you even believe your eyeballs? That's got to be a five hundred mile back up. Frog sweat! Just look at us! Do you think these people know you're about to have a baby right here in the cab of this truck."

"Easy Joey, I'll be O.K. We'll make it through this on God's timetable," Mary reassured him.

At exactly 8:00 P.M. sharp, Gordon pulled the limo into a parking lot close to the Planetarium, got out and opened the passenger doors as Breverard and Claude climbed in and took their seats on the rear cushion. Closing the doors, the driver assumed the wheel and made passage over to the Eisenhower and on to the west suburbs as Ruel directed. "Well, gentlemen, let's have our usual and hear from one another's findings," said Ruel while reaching into a small freezer that was sunk into the center console and producing chocolate fudge bars for each of them. "Handkerchiefs, gentlemen. Enjoy."

"Magi Ruel, if I didn't know better I'd say we've come to the wrong city. I spoke with 26 people of virtually every walk of life and their story matches that of the folks at City Hall. The star phenomenon is unheard of," said Claude licking chocolate from his knuckles.

"Same here, master," confirmed Breverard. "These people look at me like I'm from another planet. I mention star, scepter or king and they start talking about Hans Solo, Spock and space travel. They are totally in the dark about the star we seek."

"Shouldn't surprise us," said Ruel. "The sacred book maintains that it is the brillance of God to camouflage a matter, but it is the brillance of rulers to uncover a matter. Apathy, arrogance or both I suppose. Our inquiry sure piqued the Mayor's interest. Awful strange fellow and clearly paranoid about the notion of a king. But, otherwise, I got the same reaction as you from folks in Skokie. Everybody's ready to cut a deal but no time for star gazers. The locals are always asleep when something big is breaking right under their noses. As one of their own poets has said, 'let sleeping dogs lie.' We'll be outside the City's aura soon and will have a better look at the heavens. I'm confident that we will recover its passage and find our way to the place it indicates." Upon closing their eyes and resting their heads against the seating, Ruel paged Gordon and reminded him to remain on course and alert them when they had reached their destination just south of DeKalb near Shabbona Lake.

"What time is it now, dear?" Mary asked yawning and rising up from a blanket roll in Joey's lap.

"Just after 10:00, baby. By the way, can you believe how patient I'm being. Do you know what a great guy I am. I mean while you slept, I've started the motor and heater as needed, crept along on this tarmac with the stealth of a Navy Seal and have taken out several key enemy positions that were entrenched along that embankment and waiting in ambush for us. You don't mess with G.I. Joe. There goes the last of their cursed air arsenal that I blew from the sky back near the underpass. We pulled out from the camouflage, locked on him with a SAM and I waved him goodbye while I rocked you in my lap."

As a wrecker pulled away with twisted rubber and steel from the crash site traveling east, Mary playfully remarked, "That looks more like the cab of a semi-truck to me, honey. I'm sure glad you weren't injured in all that battle," she said while pinching his ribs. "Do all guys blow up stuff while they wait in traffic jams?"

"Real men do, baby. Others just work on grocery lists."

"Well, I'm glad I've got a real man."

"Hey, what do you know, we're moving, moving, moving and just under forty minutes to Morton, thirty if we crank it," said Joey shifting the transmission to second gear with great enthusiasm and readjusting in his seat.

"Oh, let's not crank it," said Mary. "I don't want to go all the way back to Kankakee and start over. By the way, have you noticed the brilliance of that star overhead? It seems so low. I know I've seen that star before. It was at mom's. Gee, that is really strange." Mary continued staring out the windshield, straining to look up from the dash and in front of the rear view mirror.

"You know if you stay there long you might get frozen in that position. I have to agree with you though, it appears mighty low. You know, if I didn't know better, I'd say its following us. No, can't be. I've tried watching stars while on the road before, as soon as you change direction, they drop out of sight or move to the left or right."

"That's my point, Leonardo…"

"You mean, Divinci."

"No, and thanks for jogging my memory, Copernicus. This one's staying right behind us," Mary said with amazing wonder.

Joey drove along in silence, yawning and sipping from a Styrofoam cup the last dribble of the cold coffee left over from a previous rest stop. Mary stared ahead, mesmerized by the snowflakes that raced to the windshield, only to have their purity and beauty shattered upon the glass, mix with road slush, then quickly carried away by the busy work of two tireless wiper blades and forgotten. Mary's thoughts carried her back to a time in her early childhood when her family lived in south Skokie and Grandfather Cohen was a regular guest at their dinner table following morning services at Shul. I'll never forget Granddad's story of the star, Mary dreamed to herself. It will be great and glorious, his raspy voice would rattle on as mom's homemade challah loaves filled every space of the room with an aroma that said they were hers alone. The star will signal Shiloh and rest there as a testimony. The scepter will not depart from Judah.

"I wish I could remember all of it," Mary said, breaking the silence that had felt so warm and peaceful.

"All of what, babe?" inquired Joey.

"Joey, this star is his. It's definitely his star."

"Yes, I know Mary. I had a visitor today myself," he said to her astonishment. "I can't explain it but a man spoke to me today—one I didn't see but there is no question in my mind that it was a messenger from God. That's got to be the first time I've been called Joseph since I was circumcised."

"Joey, why didn't you say something? What did he sound like? So you didn't actually see him! When did it…"

"Mary, I believe. I've thought and prayed and thought and prayed and the only thing I can conclude is that we are caught up in something bigger than life. I just have no idea how things are going to unfold from here on out, but we'll trust him together for guidance."

"So, he just shows up in your dream and knocks on the wall of your cranium and 'poof,' you're convinced," Mary said chuckling aloud. "Oh, Joey, I hate to change the subject, but I'm feeling it again, and it's…Joooeey, oh, please help me! O.K., I think I'm O.K. Oh, that hurt. Joey, this gift is coming early. I can feel it."

"Well, look here's the Morton exit, we've been running on fumes for fifteen miles. Let me get some gas, make a phone call and see if we can rush you over to a hospital in Peoria."

As Joey pulled the truck under the canopy for fuel, Mary remarked that she was feeling much better and felt it was premature to go to the hospital. "Joey, I think my body has been in a kink for so many hours that something inside got twisted. Oh, that hurt."

"Are you sure," Joey asked with deep concern in his eyes.

"Yes, I really think so. I'm fine. Besides, I'm too early for delivery. The baby will be much better if I can hang on for a few more weeks," Mary assured him as the pump nozzle released signaling a full tank. "Let's go ahead and call Ed and Sally. By the way do they have pretzels in there, I'm starved."

"Look, I'm going to pull off of this island and park near that semi under the light. Keep things locked up. I'll leave the truck running for heat, make the call and be right back."

Joey stamped the snow from his boots as he stepped into the restaurant side of the truck stop. Pulling down a phone book he began searching the directory for Klein. "Alright, nothing to it," he said aloud while placing a quarter into the slot and dialing the local number. After two rings an obnoxious, dreadful tone came over the receiver followed by a message indicating that the number had been disconnected.

"Disconnected!" Joey shouted in disbelief. Retrieving the quarter from the dish, he dialed the number again only to be greeted with the same trumpeting report. "Frog sweat! How can that be," Joey wondered aloud. Moving from the phone booth, he peeked outside and found his truck safely purring in the cold. "Great Scott," Joey breathed to himself, "that star has definitely moved," as he looked east. Turning to the counter behind him, Joey asked an attendant if he could look at a copy of the phone book covering the greater Peoria area. Paging through the directory, Joey grew more frustrated as he couldn't locate a name or initial combination that looked anything close to Ed or Sally Klein. "Good night, even a blind sow will turn up an acorn every once in awhile. Where are you at Ed? Mister, here's your book." Dialing again, Joey connected with an operator and asked for a Morton listing for Ed and Sally Klein. "What do you mean unlisted. There has to be a way to reach them!"

"I'm sorry," the voice said followed by a disconnection and dial tone.

Controlling himself, Joey turned and asked, "by the way, what do you get for a room for one night?"

"Sorry fellah, you won't find a room between Peoria and Bloomington this entire weekend," he said matter of factly. "CAT has brought in some emergency workers to get them through a crisis this strike has created, there's a political convention of some kind in Peoria and there just aren't any rooms available. I'm sorry. If you're desperate, you might find something on your way to Springfield, but that would be a ways."

"Well, I'm desperate," Joey said in retort. "Look, this isn't your fault. I'm sorry for snapping, but I've got a…, well my girlfriend is going to have a baby in another month, we're from Chicago here to stay with friends that I can't seem to locate and I just have to get a room for her."

"I'm sorry bud. I'd give you any room in the house at this hour, if there was one available. I've had to turn away several of our usual drivers to sleep in their trucks because of this."

"Well, thanks anyway," said Joey. "Say, let me get a couple bags of those pretzels," as he laid down two singles.

"There's your change," Dave said, drawing from his cigarette and sliding the register drawer back in place with his only arm. As the man turned and pulled pretzels from the snack tree, he tried to console Joey who was obviously young, inexperienced and worried. "Coffee's on the house bud. Help yourself—it's a fresh pot."

"Not right now," he said appreciatively. Turning from the counter, Joey began a fresh soliloquy, "This is just outstanding! Murphy's law, number 23…" Catching himself in mid-sentence, Joey was reminded of a poem from the Psalter, number 23 and began expressing his thanks to God for his promises to watch over and provide for him, Mary and the baby.

Stepping out of the cafe, Joey pulled the hood up from his inner sweater and zipped up his outer jacket as he made his way to the remote lot. His small pick-up was now hidden from view by a semi that had pulled along side with a load of cattle. Joey approached the cab from the right and oblique. Opening the driver's side door, he gently tossed the pretzels in the direction of Mary without looking in and lowered the door glass about half way with no intention of sitting down. As he shut the door he continued talking through the open window with his forearms folded over one another and resting upon the roof of the cab. "Mary, I'm sorry that took me so long. You're not going to believe the predicament we're in. I can't seem to find Ed and Sally's number, operator says it's unlisted, this place is packed to the gills and there's not a motel room between here and Iowa. Mary, you've got a right to be a little peeved. I'm disappointed in myself too," he said remorsefully. "I should have never started down here without calling ahead. Look, I'll think of something. Can't you say anything?" he asked.

Joey lowered his eyes to peek in on Mary to read her expression, when he found the cab empty.

Startled, Joey turned his head from the driver's door and noticed the bottom weather strip of the rear hatch protruding above the shell's lid like the flag on a mail box. Something inside his chest was flashing, 'delivery!' He immediately walked to the back and found Mary lying on her back amidst tools, bags and two heavy bails of straw that he always carried for additional weight during winter months. "Oh, baby," Joey cried. "How did you get back here?"

"Joey," Mary said in agony, "I'm having my baby! Please help me!" Mary had placed each of her elbows upon the bails of straw and created room to pull her knees closer to her breast. As another semi pulled near loaded with logs, Mary's cries of pain were muffled by the sound of a Cummings droning in the cold winter air. "Joey, these contractions are at least two minutes apart. Please hold me!"

"Hang on honey," screamed Joey as he lowered the lid and raced around the lot shouting, "Somebody help, I'm having a baby! Hurry, somebody help! Mary's definitely having a baby!"

Two truckers walking from the cafe in the direction of Joey heard his cry for help and ran to assist a young man who was nearly hysterical.

"Hey, slow down. What's going on?" asked a trucker as he caught Joey's arm.

"Mary's having a baby in the back of my truck. She needs help!"

"Let's have a look," said Jerry. Opening the lid, a new burst of diesel rushed in to fill the space as Joey crawled aboard and began pulling extra clothing from a bag near the gate. "Pap, get up in the truck and bring me those blankets from the sleeper. And grab both of the pillows too," said Jerry. "What's your name son?"

"My name's Joey and this is Mary who continued to squirm in pain."

"My name's Jerry and this is my dad, Ben. We're up from Whitesville, Kentucky, with a load of cattle. Now we're no hand with a woman, but we've pulled many a calf from the hind of a heifer. You take these pillows and cushion things as best you can while me and Pap gather up some help. Nature's going to take its course son. You just hold that girl real tight until we get back." Ben gently lowered the shell lid and cut a plug from a fresh twist of Mammoth Cave while Jerry scouted the lot and cafe for someone who could further assist them.

Another wave of contractions fell upon Mary who was fully dilated and as the spent surf rippled away, she cried in great agony that could be heard outside while she pushed out her baby onto layers of undergarments and T-shirts that had been carefully laid before her. Joey held Mary who was sobbing with joy and shaking from the penetrating cold.

"Oh, quickly gather him Joey and place him here next to me. What time is it?" she asked in broken syllables and quivering voice. "I'm exhausted. I'm starved. I'm a mess."

"Your absolutely beautiful," Joey said. "And look at this little man. Mary, he's gorgeous."

"Oh, he's so precious. I want to feed him." Mary snuggled with the baby as Joey maneuvered in the bed of the truck and was helped to exit by Jerry and Ben who had now returned with a nurse coming home from night shift at a Peoria hospital.

"This is Nadine," Jerry said as he quickly introduced her to Joey.

"Help me up, I've got to have a look at her," said Nadine crawling into the space Joey had just vacated. "This little girl is nearly asleep. Poor thing is exhausted. You just rest hon." Dangling her keys to the outside she ordered anyone listening, "here, go to the back seat of that blue Goat and get the clean laundry from the basket. I'm going to need more towels.

Someone get me some hot water in a clean container. Now hurry! And close that lid; it's an ice box in here!"

Joey stood outside the truck talking rapidly with truckers about the events of the last hour, while the C.B. air waves began to fill up with talk of a star phenomenon reported hovering above a truck stop on the north side of Morton. While more trucks pulled off of I-74 to get a closer look, one rig heading down state on route 121 with a load of sheep swears that he witnessed a group of angels singing in the heaven's night. The trucker's apparition was answered with profanity, laughter and ridicule. But he stopped his rig near the Mackinaw bridge and stared in holy consternation while mindlessly feeding his snack sandwich and celery to sheep through slots in the trailer.

Back at the truck stop, several truck drivers stood beneath the star with Joey, sipping coffee at the rear of his pick-up, when Nadine emerged from the shell, motioned for Joey and related that Mary and Jesus were going to be fine. "She's an extraordinary girl, Joey. She delivered her baby without anyone's help," said Nadine. "What will you name him?" she asked.

Without hesitation, Joey said that his name is Jesus. "Isn't he wonderful?" he asked proudly.

At that moment Jerry directed his dad to pull their rig down wind. "Pap, get up in there and move this herd down around the next light pole, this place smells like a stable."

Others began moving away from the area as Nadine spoke with Joey about getting Mary and the baby over to her place until they could locate their friends. "You can just follow me home for the night, what's left of it. Mary and the baby are fine but will need to see their pediatrician in the next day or so," Nadine insisted.

"Well look, I don't know what to say. Sure. I mean that's awful generous of you. What's a p.d. electrician? Do they wire bones? Anything broke you're not telling me about? I mean I can handle it."

"No silly, they take care of newborns and children," Nadine chided.

"Oh cool, I could use one of those myself after a night like this," Joey remarked.

"You guys," said Nadine shaking her head while leading them away, "go have a kid and tell me about it!"

Four days later Joey was standing in Ed and Sally's garage warming the truck and packing the rear with clothes items, disposable diapers and personals. Mary was in the living room saying good bye to her new friend, while bouncing the baby on her shoulder after feeding him. "Mary, we've hardly been introduced. Are you sure you have to go back so soon?" pleaded Sally, "Ed's on vacation and we have no plans for the entire week."

"You and Ed have been so generous. You're hospitality and kindness exceeds even Joey's tendency to exaggerate. Maybe your family can drive up and be our guests soon," invited Mary. "We really need to spend some time with Joey's mom and dad before returning to Chicago."

While the men waited upon Mary, Ed drew his new driver from the golf bag and handed it to Joey for feel, when a black Mercedes stretch limo pulled into Ed's driveway. "He'll never drag that thing out of the road," observed Joey.

"Yea, probably lost. Never see a limo like that around here," continued Ed. Instead of turning the unwieldy vehicle around, the chauffeur turned off the engine, got out and opened the passenger doors. Upon opening the doors, he proceeded to the trunk and selected a new key from his wallet that would fit a compartment inside. In the meantime, three stunningly dressed men donned in black stepped out of the car in single file from the same side and were handed gifts from Gordon who remained stationary.

"Anybody you know, Ed?" asked Joey.

"No way," Ed said in total amazement. The men approached the house and were greeted by Ed and Joey who were now emerging from the garage. "Good morning, gentlemen," said Ed. "Hey listen, before you go and get all creased, messed up and everything, we didn't order anything with that kind of price tag. Who are you looking for, maybe I can help?"

"We have come from a far and wish to share your joy," said Ruel with a beaming smile that revealed several gold fillings.

"Did he say they've been through a fire?" Joey whispered to Ed with sincerity.

"Well, wait just a minute fellahs," said Ed as he ran ahead and cut them off at his front porch. "Folks around these parts generally call and make appointments before showing up, don't they, Joey?" said Ed humorously, but now firmly as he looked into the eyes of the three.

"Edward, we are king-makers and only wish to present our gifts to the child of the star. We must not be delayed. Yes, he is under your roof, but he is the king of all. We will not harm you, only allow us to present our gifts and we will be gone," insisted Ruel.

"What's going on, Joey?" asked Ed, "How does this guy know my name and that there is a baby inside?"

"Stranger things have happened, Ed, I just can't remember when," answered Joey from beneath a grin. "I think we should get out of the way and let his plan run its course," Joey said.

"His plan?" asked Ed stepping aside. "These guys look like Mafia!"

Ed and Joey followed the three men into the house as Gordon appeased a traffic officer and attempted to make explanation for the small crowd that was forming out in front of Ed's house. Once inside,

Ruel, Breverard and Claude fanned out in the living room, bowed low three times in unison and expressed to Mary their great joy regarding the infant Jesus. Each of the men approached the baby with their gift and laid it at his feet as they expressed wishes of blessedness with the greatest reverence and awe, although their words were whispered and not entirely intelligible. Following their brief visit, the men thanked the couples profusely and walked to their transportation in single file. Without lifting their heads or acknowledging the audience, they disappeared into the interior which was shut up by Gordon and drove quietly away. Turning at the next block, Ruel directed Gordon to change course and not travel back through Chicago in their trek east. "Our New York connection will have to be altered," he said soberly, "I have been duly warned about that Mayor."

Three weeks later after arriving home and settling back into some kind of routine, Mary and Joey were wed in her sister's living room with Jesus asleep in a plastic portable crib on the floor. The couple spent their first morning alone as husband and wife at Joey's Buffalo Grove apartment located on Trace off Dundee Road. Time was spent arranging furniture and allocating space that was in scarce supply. "This is a real honeymoon darling. I'm beat," said Joey. "I vote for a break and a fresh pot of coffee. Any takers? How about it Mary?"

Picking Jesus up from the crib, Mary asked Joey to turn the volume up on the radio. "Have you heard this story before?" she asked. Mary and Joey listened in silent rage at the report of a developing story involving a pediatrician down state in the community of Morton who had been indicted on charges of nine counts of murder. Each of the children were under two years of age and had died from a complicated serum of poison that was still being traced. Autopsies were incomplete, but all evidence was pointing to a single practice according to local authorities. "Joey," Mary said in hysteria, "that was the pediatrician recommended to us! Thank God we couldn't meet that schedule."

"That sorry coward slaughtered nine innocent babies!" Joey screamed to the top of his lungs. "Every Ph D of Electrician in town ought to march over there, tie him to the back of a truck and drag him in the street just to save face."

Chapter 2

Mary hurried about the kitchen just like every other school morning, fixing lunches, marking bags, pouring juice, frying eggs and nibbling from plates she served her family who disposed of the food as quickly as it arrived at the table.

"Mom, can I have another swimming pool egg? Mine just did that vanishing thing again. Now you see it, now you don't," said Jesus.

"Yes, it vanished behind the sports page with his face and all you can hear is that nasty coon hound slurp he's patented," said Mary as she playfully put her knee in Joey's side while holding a skillet and spatula in either hand.

"Yea, I'm a regular hound dog, kids." Joey bawled playfully and sounded like a black and tan scratching at the base of a tree in a distant river bottom.

"Jesus, take this," Mary said after a minute as she handed him a fresh plate. "Put some distance between yourself and this critter and see if you can get that down before your bus comes. You and Jimmy have to be at the stop in ten minutes. C'mon, Jimmy, deal with that hair as I asked and get moving, you're both going to be late."

"O.K. mom," Jimmy said as he whisked down the last of his juice and ran to the bathroom for a comb. "Man if I get any better looking the girls just won't be able to stand it," Jimmy said aloud as he stared into the mirror.

"C'mon Jimmy, I'll race you to the stop," said Jesus.

"Easy through that door," shouted Joey with firmness. "The next one to take out that screen will pay for it and I mean it this time."

"Loud bark with no bite," Mary said as she dropped into a chair next to her husband.

"Do you think it's a whirlwind in everybody's house on school mornings or are we just totally undisciplined?" she asked sipping from fresh coffee. "I just don't think I can handle one more demand, Mary said, brushing her hair back from her forehead with a free hand. "O.K. enough pity party right?"

"Oh, I thought I'd let you air that out a minute longer," Joey said smiling. "I know it's been tough trying to keep up with three kids, the house, accounting and a zillion other things moms do.... Well, speaking of angels, there's little miss, Sarah." He spied his daughter who was peeking back from a corner in the hall.

"Good morning, princess," Mary greeted. Joey slid from his chair to the floor and took up the posture of the familiar trolley and quickly crawled over to offer Sarah a ride to the table. "Free rides today for pretty girls," Joey coaxed.

"Daddy you always give free rides," as she straddled his back with her blanket and held on for the ride across the foyer to the breakfast room.

"O.K., we're coming into the station," said Joey as Mary helped Sarah into her lap for a tight hug.

"Oh, you give the best hugs," admired Mary. "Are you ready for breakfast? How much can a three-year old eat?"

"Oh, I'm hungry mommy. Can I have cereal?" Sarah pouted.

"In a snap if you ask with a smile, otherwise it could be awhile..." Mary drew out the last words slowly and sounded as though they were crawling out from the bottom of a drum.

"What do you know, Sarah, your mom's a poet and didn't know it, she can make it rhyme every time," Joey sang as he stroked Sarah's soft black goose down.

"O.K., up in the booster, sweet girl." Mary said, while helping Sarah to a new height at her side.

Mary assisted Sarah while Joey looked over blueprints for the cabinetry that had been ordered for several condominiums being constructed at an exclusive Inverness development. "I'm going to have to hire more cabinet makers if we continue taking on these kind of orders—I'm swamped." Joey admitted. "Look at the count on some of these units, and we get to install them!" Laughing aloud he proceeded, "The bucks are great, but when do you ever find time to spend it." Joey spread out several layers of plans across one end of the table and continued looking for possible errors.

"How is Jesus working out?" Mary asked. "Is he helping lift the load?"

"He's terrific with dimensions and smaller cuts, but there's only so much a twelve-year-old can handle. Three quarter inch plywood sheets are too heavy for him at this stage, and it's unrealistic to ask him to help load finished sets; those pieces are all I and another man can handle. I'll just keep pouring over resumes. Finding quality tradesmen is more difficult than searching for a needle in a hay stack. We'd been better off training from within and teaching apprentices how to do it our way."

Mary stepped away from the table and returned with a calendar and coffee refill that she placed on top of Joey's prints. "You know Passover is next weekend. The Goldsteins want to room near us. The kids can play in the pool at the hotel and we can relax a bit."

"Hotel!" Joey said with surprise.

"Their treat—they insisted. And it's just blocks from the new synagogue," Mary said.

"Bret and Linda," he thought with a loving sigh, "what can I say—they're great. Alright, I mean yes, let's do it! Well, I've got to scoot," kissing Mary on the head and blowing another to Sarah. "See you tonight my beauties. Oh great, did the boys forget their lunches again?" asked Joey as he scooped up plans and grabbed his usual mini-cooler.

"Don't worry, I'm going out to drop off the box of leaven items; I'll be in that direction and can visit the school on the way," Mary volunteered. "Supper's at six sweetheart. Read my lips," she continued, "Be late and no cake."

"No cake," countered Joey with a wry smile, "and no mall."

"O.K. wise guy. Remember, I love you," she said as Joey opened the door and stepped into the garage.

"I love you too, baby. I'll try really hard to be here for dinner," and closed the door.

The automatic opener muscled the big door to its loft, as the sun's rays broke in forcing shadows to their corners and spotlighting a glistening red Chevy Blazer standing silent as a steed awaiting its captain. Joey walked to the front of the garage and looked out onto the neighborhood while breathing in the fresh April air laced with the scent of Mary's lilacs carried over the roof from the back side of their suburban home. Overcome with the reality of three healthy children, a wife that feigns description because of her sheer beauty and gift of encouragement, who also doubles as the company accountant, bills finally being paid on time and a company and household that recently stepped ashore from a river of red ink that used to carry them along its punishing rapids was just more than he could contain.

"What a gift life is!" Joey shouted to a string of starlings that had gathered in the neighbor's lawn. Joey smiled to watch them patrol back and forth in staggered column in search of straggling crawlers seeking their return to dark caverns before the shade cast by the house retreated to the porch.

"Thanks for holding onto us, God," Joey said to himself as he pulled keys from his pocket and wandered back in his mind to leaner times. "How in the scratch did we even eat back then, his monologue continued, Mary must have produced more tasty tricks with Mr. Potato than Betty Crocker has recipes for everything else combined. With the single exception of the soup. And a certain queasiness sent a signal up his inside abdominal cavity that made him physically shudder. That girl has been tighter than bark on a tree with our money, but it has sure paid off." Turning from his position of meditation, Joey mounted his truck and grinned with satisfaction to hear the muffler echo back a steady neigh that said it was ready for blacktop. As the beast grew under him, Joey released the brake, pushed in a tape of Johnny Rivers' greatest hits and meandered out of the subdivision onto Lake Cook for another painstaking drive to the shop over in Northbrook.

"Governor, it's the Mayor's office—Chicago—secure line #2," announced Brenda, a busty brunette with a reputation for late night adventures and secret rendezvous with those in high political office.

"What is it, Harry?" the governor hissed with loathsome disgust while laying aside a new 8-step manual to leadership success he had recently purchased. "You're interrupting an important meeting."

"Easy Mr. P.," he said while pulling his executive chair forward with the heels of his feet and snatching the cigar from his mouth, "and start showing me a little respect before I find a way to leak out last weekend's Vegas episode to the local sharks. Your re-election bid will shrivel up quicker than a hot dog in a microwave once word leaks out about your fling with that lust thirsty nag you call a woman. What was her name?" Harry's sarcastic interrogation continued, "Let's see if I can make out the notes my paparazzi attached to these explicit photographs. Oh yes, Kelly Mansfield, and wife of our friend the Senator from Colorado no less," continued the voice over a phone line that connected two offices red with mahogany and smelling of tans. Upon the respective walls hung identical credentials from the University of Illinois and Harvard with the exception of the names of the recipients. "How will it smell in the ears of our good citizens here in the State when they learn their trusted Governor, who dethroned an incumbent mind you with similar but less weighty allegations, has himself stepped into the same pile? They tell me caked manure is pretty hard to scrape off one's boots."

"You light weight son of a wench woman, don't threaten me with that straw," the Governor shot back.

"Governor it might be straw," the Mayor couldn't control his belly laughs, "but like we Black folks up at this end of the State say, 'it sho do burn mighty good!' Tax payers in this State are already on tilt following your proposal to complete those nuclear power plants. If they find out how you've been squandering their hard earned money, well, shoot-fire—Illinois may not need nuclear energy anymore. My guess is we'll have all the heat we need for years to come."

"You're a real comic, Harry," said the Governor in a slow blood boiling voice. "You're old man would sit up in his grave if he could hear this cheap talk from the mouth of his boy. By the way, does Chicago still smell as bad as when you're old man was running—I mean—raping the City? Can't imagine a little concrete and a mere six feet of dirt doing much to leach the stench emanating from his rotting corpse."

"Oh, that's good Governor," Harry interrupted while laughing aloud.

"Now you listen to me," the Governor continued, while leafing through his manual, and of course always feeling more confident when separated from an antagonist by a hundred miles or more, "I don't know who your sewer gremlins photographed, but I can't be bothered with threats made by little people like you."

"Mr. P. I'm trying to be awful patient. The photos in today's mail, those in the white envelope on the corner of your desk, are copies of those I'm holding and reveal more of your tongues than anything else, but the frontals are all here and I'm fairly confident that if this fell on the streets of this windy city and got swept along with some of the other stench you mentioned, well, I'm just afraid it would make a lot of people real sick. What do you think, Governor?"

"Harry, you know I can't endorse the kind of plans you've concocted," said the Governor as he ripped open an envelope on the other end of the line and began paging through several 5X7 color photographs that featured himself and Mrs. Mansfield. "The whole thing is outrageous," he continued, "why does everything have to be so outlandish. How did you scam Washington appropriations to even consider such a thing—there's not that much pork in the entire State of Iowa," said the Governor as the heat grew up his collar. "Don't even answer that," he quickly recovered while slamming the photos on the desk top, "I don't even want to know!"

"Listen Mr. P.," Harry said firmly, "You just be on hand for the gala at the end of the month and I'll make some remarks without committing you to anything. Just smile like an opossum eating persimmons, nod at appropriate times and you go home with the copies and negatives. Let a little man worry about building the big airport. Good bye, Mr. P. See you near the end of the month."

Joey laid in his recliner rehearsing last night's Pesah meal—a near disaster. His kepah was finally recovered after literally hours of search. Sarah had found that it made an attractive table cloth for her doll house tea party. Jesus dropped the roasted eggs on the hardwood floor and the salt water ended up in the wrong glasses thanks to Jimmy. Joey was still perplexed by little Jack's unexpected arrival at their table. It was agreed that he would spend the night, but Aunt Liz dropped him off about an hour early which was unusual. After Joey poured a couple of ounces of wine to satisfy the tradition for Elijah's glass, Jack stepped through their front door, dropped his things and joined them at the table. Last night's closing hymn: 'L'Shana Haba-a,' was still melodious in his ears when a horn sounded from the front, driving Joey's feet to the floor, and drawing his recliner back to its full upright position.

"Joey, can you see Aunt Liz? She's here to drop off Jack's tooth brush and swim suit," Mary shouted from the master bath as she continued spreading a film of base coat onto her cheeks.

"I'm there," Joey assured her, walking to the door. "I'll run a little interference but don't leave me hanging too long," he insisted. Joey pushed open the door with his right arm as the boys pressed through the opening at full throttle; brushing Joey's arm with the tops of their heads, they bound into the front yard like spring calves, leaping to greet Aunt Liz.

"Hi, Liz," Joey greeted as he walked toward her. "Let me take Jack's bags," he said, and bowed low for a kiss that fell on his eye.

"These boys live to see one another," observed Liz.

"Oh, no question," Joey agreed, "these pups definitely eat from the same dish. By the way, is Zack going to make it back for Passover? Mary tells me he's had a humdinger of a fishing trip."

"Yes, he got in Wednesday and we spent the early afternoon rearranging the freezer to accommodate about seventy-five pounds of Walleye. 'Chicken of Lake Erie,' he calls it."

"Whoa," Joey said with surprise, "that's quite a catch!"

"I agreed to go along two years ago but I promised it would be my last. We put in at Luna Pier, just north of Toledo there in southern Michigan, you know the place, he's had you and the boys along. Well, we were at least 45 minutes in choppy water in route to Sister Island or some such place, and I've never gotten so green in all my born days. I'll spare you the graphic detail but it wasn't pretty. I think I vomited from one end of Lake Erie to the other. Joey, it was dreadful, the bagel bits and what little juice I ever drink, well, it was all there and easily identified. Zack still brings it up to me, says he didn't get any fish because I fed them so well. I think it was the choppy water and east wind and I told him so. The planer boards were not even visible most of the time. To top it off the motor failed but the kindness of God brought a Mister Close and his family near and they towed us in for which I'll be eternally grateful. His lovely wife held my hand and tried to comfort me the best one could, given the miserable conditions. I mailed them a card as soon as I got back and thanked them for their trouble. But you know full well what a rickety craft that is he calls a boat—'Miss Doolittle,' he calls her. Says it's because of the boat's personality and the little Johnson that propels her. Now have you ever heard that kind of talk from a grown man? Attributing personality traits to a bucket of warped cedar and fiberglass!"

"Not exactly," Joey began.

"Well, I've all but concluded that he's spent so much time with her that he's become emotionally bonded in some sick pathological way. What do you think, Joey, you're a man? I mean is it possible for him to spend so much time on the water, that he just begins to think differently—you know, come up with a whole new value structure."

"Well, I don't know, Liz, but maybe we could," when Joey yielded to a new line of argument."

"It's weird, Joey, the way he pampers that boat. Why, he flaunts it too. Right there laminated and taped to the dash is a comic that tells the whole story, 'Wanted: Woman who can cook, cut bait, and has her own boat and motor. Send picture of the boat and motor.' I don't guess I have to tell you what sits out on the driveway all winter, no sir, not little Miss Dolittle, or the truck that pulls her, but my poor little Chevy. Just look at her, the poor thing has suffered a lot of abuse. Doesn't her bumper just seem sad to you? But, Joey the thing I just can't hardly deal with is the way he eats those fish—those Walleye. Why, you'd think he'd never been fed in his life when he sits down to a mess of 'em. And he sops up the grease and cracker crumbs from the platter like a great dog of some kind."

"Well, that part I can understand," Joey said with his mind only partially engaged while searching for Mary with the other. From behind his back he motioned for Jesus and James to see if they could find what was keeping, Mary.

The boys started to the porch when the door opened and out stepped a woman of extraordinary beauty followed by Sarah in close tow.

"Aunt Liz," Mary chimed and bowed to kiss her.

"How's my lovely?" asked Liz. "And what on earth is this in my bag," she asked playfully, while looking into Sarah's eyes.

"Let me see," said Sarah in an excited voice. Liz extended her arms and offered Sarah a new book and a fresh box of colors.

"Thank you, Aunt Wiz," she said in a tiny voice.

"And be sure to remind mom and dad that they're washable," as Sarah ran to dad grinning with pleasure. I've packed some little gifts for the boys along with Jack's things. Maybe they will slow down long enough this weekend to open them."

"Liz, you are so thoughtful," said Mary.

Joey backed up to the rear of the Blazer, lifted a heel that caught the bumper's ledge and quietly admired his lovely bride as she and Liz talked. Mostly Liz. The fringe of Mary's black silk crown moved gently with the early evening air and was elegantly folded behind her ears like leaves of a rare anthology marking one's favorite poems. Her large brown eyes were harbor lights that signaled port and safety. His eyes followed the graceful curves of her face and neck. Hopelessly infatuated since the day they met, he danced with her somewhere in a ballroom, his face brushing the soft fuzz of her cheek while pecking lips with a gentle touch of his own. Joey breathed in a burst of Mary's vanilla perfume that had waltzed in his direction and as his chest swelled to take it all in, so did the sharp pain he so carefully concealed.

Dropping his foot and making reentry to the planet, Joey turned on the balls of his feet and yelled for the boys in the direction of their last sighting. In a moment faint war cries from the back yard proceeded the assault of three little Airborne Rangers, packing enough nerf and plastic arsenal to fend off a formidable enemy of their kind.

"Alright men," Joey played, "into the Huey attack helicopter—stay low and keep moving!" pointing to the open door of the family's vehicle. "Hurry," he said, "we've got to get Mom out of this blazing LZ before she becomes a casualty." Each of the boys slapped high fives to one another as they climbed aboard. "Hey, no frags on the chopper," Joey said while he picked pine cones from reluctant hands. "Man, if one of these were to go off in here, it would take more than a vacuum to clean it up."

"Oh, 'Uncle Joey,' you are so funny," chuckled young Jack.

"Hey, I'm just glad you got to see me," Joey said smiling. Petting Jack on the knee, he double checked seat belts and prepared the carrier for Sarah. "Come to Daddy, princess." Sarah strolled to the vehicle with a certain awareness due her title carrying, Molly, markers and a book in one hand and a sandwich baggie of animal crackers in the other.

"Everything is rolled up, turned down, unplugged, squared away, locked and ready for inspection sir," Mary smiled in Joey's direction while leaving Liz to join them.

"Sweetie, you bring back some of the most pleasant memories of my life when you do that! Boy, I miss Parris Island, my Drill Instructors, the sand fleas, the heat, the chow....Uuurraahhh," he shouted, with a blood curdling yell that sent Liz searching for her keys and turned the head of a neighbor who was pushing a lawn mower a couple of doors down.

"Joey, stop that! You're embarrassing me," said Mary.

"It's a male thing, honey," he said, while closing her door and waving good-bye to Aunt Liz.

"Dad, do the 'ahuga' yell again," demanded Jimmy.

"No, we've got to cool it guys, got ourselves an officer on deck."

"Awww," they said together.

"C'mon, cheer up guys, maybe you can help Sarah with connecting lines on the way down."

Joey was pumping the accelerator a little more than needed, when Mary asked, "You're not letting go of this are you, Joey?"

"Oh, Mary, I was just having a little fun," he said softly as the boys involved themselves in fresh war strategy.

"I know, but I've asked you many times not to holler out that, that obnoxious noise, especially in our neighborhood. You actually frightened Aunt Liz and there is no telling what the Boyles think. 'There goes the Jew sounding off again.'" She aped Mrs. Boyle. "I'm sorry for that last remark, Joey." Mary apologized with a sincerity that touched him. "Your humor is usually in good taste," she continued, "and you bring me far more laughter than tears. I'm sorry if I've over reacted."

"I'm sorry too," Joey admitted as he headed down Lake Cook to 53. "Let's not sabotage a great weekend. I shouldn't have crossed that line. I remember how you felt the last time I let it rip out front of the synagogue after that boring, well let's say, that meaningfully extended time of exegetical survey of the entire Torah. Now that was totally justified, your petrification notwithstanding."

"O.K. Joey, just promise me you'll save it for fishing trips and the great out doors."

Mary turned to check on the kids when her nose nearly touched Jesus', who said, "I love you, Mom."

"Well, that's always a pleasant surprise," kissing her son on the forehead. "I love you, too," she said while staring back into eyes that always appeared deep and beautiful.

"How long before we get there?" he asked.

"About an hour," Joey said, while glancing at his watch.

"O.K.," said Jesus.

"By the way, did I ever tell you guys that my wife is madly in love with me?" teased Joey and squeezing Mary's hand.

"For obvious reasons," they said in rote harmony.

"He gets this way when he's away from the shop," said Jesus, pushing Joey's hat forward playfully."

"Easy now. Remember, I'm internationally unknown," as he adjusted the rearview mirror mimicking the head movements of a model and straightening his cap.

"Nap time for mom, kids," Mary winked, then crowded the passenger side door. Resting her head on a pillow, she continued speaking in the direction of the roof, "he will be singing next."

"Yep, nothing brings the Blues out of me quite like Chicago traffic," he said.

"Oh no, he's going to do it, Mom!" the boys squealed.

"Let me see if I can produce the right inflection," Joey said, while clearing his throat,

"Weeellll, I went down south just to see my baby, bumb, bumb, bippity bumb, bumb. Weeellll, I went down south just to see my girl, bumb, bumb, bippity bumb, bumb. Weeellll, I went down south just to see my baby, went down south just to see my giiirrlll, WooaahhaWooaahh,

But she was running around, running around, Ooold coon dog Blue, Oooha Awooaah. Now I'm bluer than blue for old Blue, yes, I'm bluer than blue for old Blue.

Bluer than blue, for old Blue, yes I'm bluer than blue for old Blue."

Joey began the same stanza when Sarah's book slipped from her fingers to the floor, she having been rocked to sleep by the steady bounce and humming mud treads beneath her carriage. The boys continued peaceful elimination rounds with a board game while Joey shifted from song to sales, purchasing, rearranging and adding on to his ever expanding company.

Following the larger Seder meal, they concluded Sabbath with songs at the synagogue among family and friends. Afterwards, Joey and Mary drove back to their room, changed into swim suits and made their way to the hot tub on the lower level. "Are you sure Jesus will be O.K.," Mary asked, while Joey lit elevator buttons in hopes of finding an empty carriage traveling south.

"Oh sure," he said. Goldstein said he would bring Jesus along when they come."

"I've never seen Jesus so locked onto a reading before. The Exodus passages, well, it was like he was digesting it or something," she observed.

"Yea, that's marvelous," Joey agreed. "Jesus has always pursued God and taken issues of personal spirituality very seriously. Thanks to your involvement with him, honey."

"Yours, too, Joey," said Mary as they walked onto the elevator with the other children. In a moment the doors opened and the family stepped into the pool area, dropping personals and towels on vacant chairs that marked their parcel of indoor beach. Jack and Jimmy were corrected by a life guard before they could get wet and admonished not to run. Sarah joined her mom and dad at the hot tub and they each lost ballast until their chins rested upon the warm churning water. "Ladies," Joey began a speech or toast, "only fools sit around camp fires sucking down cheap beer, slapping mosquitoes in sultry humidity with one hand, and their mates back with the other while trying to convince themselves that it don't get any better than this. The desperate red necks ain't never been stranded with gorgeous women in a swimming hole like this," he said, sipping from a tall fruit tea on ice.

"That's right, dear, and aren't you glad I rescued you from all that futility."

"Yes, I'm indeed the lucky one." Joey played, while tickling Mary with his toes.

The next morning Mary led early risers through a breakfast buffet downstairs. While gathering juice and a bumper chair for Sarah, Jesus approached Mary and asked permission to join Rabbis whom he espied beyond a partition of garden plants and trees.

"Mom, may I sit with the Teachers and continue a discussion we broke off last night?" asked Jesus.

"Well, I don't know. Did you not spend enough time with them last night? I'm not sure they would appreciate you inviting yourself to their table. I mean look at them, they are obviously deeply involved in business."

"Yes," Jesus said, "but I too must be about my Father's business." Mary looked at Jesus, not bewildered, but with eyes that were unconsciously resisting his intellectual, moral and even physical development. "It's important that I see them, Mother." Jesus said while waiting upon a nod.

"Sure, Jesus," she said without any particular expression. "Come to the room soon, should we finish before you." Mary sat down and mindlessly picked at a bran muffin while she turned the years over in her mind. How long will I have him, God? Oh, Blessed One, her silent prayer began, please keep him under your watchful care. Protect him from snares laid before him and strengthen him for the journey ahead. Make him powerful in word and deed and may you be magnified through him. Hasten the day of the kingdom he speaks about and gather to yourself the precious tribes of your inheritance. Amen.

Joey purposefully bumped the edge of the table as he sat down and the children began their fun pointing out the more salient features of his face including disheveled hair, sleep wrinkles and barbed whiskers.

"Good morning, darlings," Joey announced. "You too, boys," he said squinting his eyes and putting on a face. "I'll have you two standing tall before the good Rabbi if you keep up that disrespectful talk and making fun of my appearance."

"Daddy, drink your coffee and feed that frog in your throat," Jimmy continued.

"He's a chip off the old block," Mary remarked. "How did you sleep?" she asked.

"Like a log."

"You mean a frog on a log," Mary corrected while reminding him of his nocturnal croaking habit.

"Where's Jesus?" Joey changed the subject, "I didn't see him in line when I came through."

"It took him all of about two minutes to identify the Rabbis and find a seat at their table." Mary said while pushing her nose in their direction.

"Oh, yea I see them," Joey said coming alive. "What's up; did they invite him over?"

"No," Mary said, "he initiated it, but they sure seem to be caught up in something heavy. Their jaws haven't slowed down since he arrived over there."

"Well, this is just a piece of a larger story. Awful peculiar though, an adolescent carrying right on with them. I wouldn't know the first thing about what to even say around them. I mean how do you begin a theological discussion with a Rabbi without asking something real stupid."

"Oh, Joey," said Mary, "I've always enjoyed reading with you and some of your thoughts on Isaiah have been precious to me."

"Yea, but these guys run theological circles around folks like us. I wonder what they're talking about. I mean Jesus about crawled onto the lid of that table a moment ago. Always was a feisty little guy when it came to truth. Well, I've got a truck to load and a room to square away. It's time to make like a sheep herder and get the flock out of here," he said crowing with the boys, who felt that one was getting a little over worn too. "You know the problem with kids today is that they don't appreciate class, you know anything vintage like." Joey's voice trailed behind him as he and the boys walked back to the room.

Mary moved with unusual sloth while she gathered spent cups and plates and spoke with Sarah until it was obvious she really had nothing to say. Taking one final look at Jesus, she turned in the direction of the elevator and hid from view beneath a canopy. While staring at him from her place, she was emotionally gripped when she observed his lips freeze in what appeared mid-sentence and his eyes turn to catch her brooding. Startled and embarrassed, she took Sarah's hand and began a conversation in flight about totally disconnected thoughts.

Minutes later, Jesus joined his family and helped tote bags and luggage to the elevator for final descent. Once in the parking lot, Phil and Gwen, other life long friends attending the meetings asked if Jesus could ride back to Palatine with them.

"Mary," said Gwen, "we can drop Jesus off at your place on our way home. Danny hardly got to see him and wanted to show him a new game he recently purchased."

"Well, I guess that will be fine. Jesus really does need to come along soon, however; he has lots of homework that's unfinished."

"Awesome," said Danny with an excited voice, I'll go back inside and get him. Mary and Joey said good-bye to others who had formed a small crowd in the lot, then pulled out of the city onto the Kennedy for their trip home. Meanwhile, Danny approached his folks with misty eyes and said, "I guess they took Jesus after all. He isn't at the pool or anywhere."

"What do you think, Gwen?" asked Phil.

"I don't know unless they were confused and thought we left without him." There were a lot of people standing around. Let's check the lobby again. If he's not there, it's my hunch he hooked back up with his family after we talked with Joey."

"Danny, did you actually speak with Jesus and invite him to ride home with us?" Gwen asked.

"Well, no, not really. I was just asking for permission."

"Well, that settles it," said Phil, "Jesus found his mom and dad before we did and they probably assumed we missed one another and so they drove on home with him. Let's take a look anyway before we go." After a while, the Bauers emerged from the hotel and departed without Jesus.

Nearly forty minutes later Joey pulled through a traffic pile up that delayed them. As the flow resumed and lanes were once again selected, a Caravan with dark tinted glass pulled along side Joey and the woman on the passenger side was pointing with her finger and gesturing in a quizzical way. Joey nodded and smiled at Gwen while Mary napped and the cars broke stride with Phil falling in behind Joey. Minutes later, Joey exited at 53 and pulled in to get gas. Phil, who was also on empty followed behind.

"Hey, Phil," said Joey, "long time no see."

"Yeah, not long enough pal," he said grinning.

"Say, what if we take Jesus from here and save you the drive over," offered Joey.

"What do you mean? You nodded while on the road—I mean we didn't hook up with Jesus. We thought he was with you," said Phil.

"Are you serious," asked Mary in a petrified voice, "C'mon, Joey, we've got to get back down there and find him," while clawing for the cellular phone.

"You sure you didn't see him with, Yohanans?" Joey asked in a controlled manner.

"No way," said Phil, "I was standing right there when their family pulled away. Jesus wasn't with them. Boy, I'm terribly sorry for this mix up."

"Can you give Mary and the kids a ride home?" asked Joey.

"No way," Mary interrupted, "Let's get moving—he may be in trouble!"

"I've got your gas; get out of here," said Phil, and Joey bootlegged around the pumps and climbed back on the expressway south.

"Stay calm, dear," Joey reassured Mary, as she pressed disconnect and placed the phone in her lap shaking her head in disbelief.

"How could this happen. He's probably frightened to death. Where would he go from there, Joey? Do you think he would try to walk home?" Mary asked.

"He's got the determination, but he's smarter than that. Jack, did you say you saw him at the pool."

"Yes sir. He got out and said he had some things to do. I thought he was going back to the room," said Jack.

"Well, we've got the wind on our backs. I'd say we'll be there in 20 minutes," Joey calculated.

"Just don't get pulled over, honey, we don't need another delay right now," Mary pleaded.

For hours Jesus sat in the company of Hebrew scholars who were mesmerized and held spellbound by the youth's wisdom and comprehensive knowledge of the Torah. Two elders from the group stepped aside and while scratching their heads admitted that they had never encountered anything like this.

"One minute he's politely run ahead of me in a discussion of epic repetition in the Hebrew sentence and the next thing I know he's somehow brought that all around and begins correcting my view of several critical glosses in the Pentateuch. He made a fascinating case for the preeminence of worship over work, based upon the garden narrative in Genesis, and something I'd like to explore with him further," said Rabbi Kaufmann.

"No question, the boy is well advanced and has been tutored in a strict regiment of study. I wonder who his father is? Do we know which synagogue he attends?" asked Mr. Pearlman.

Arriving at the hotel, Mary leaped from the vehicle as quickly as it stopped and ran to the counter spilling out a description of a young lad to ladies who had already gathered the information from an earlier phone conversation. Joey pulled up the rear with the kids, looking in adjoining lots and building corners that might hide his young man. In a short time, they crossed paths with Mary and elected to drive back to the synagogue and worship center.

"It's several blocks," Mary said.

"But it's a logical place to look," Joey agreed.

Back in the car, they were just minutes to Locust near LaSalle. They entered the doors on the auditorium side and poured through the lower level feeling more lost than the one they sought. Mary pushed opened doors to a conference area and beheld her son sitting at the table with elders and teachers of the Law who were fascinated with the insights and answers of the young prodigy.

"Jesus," Mary scolded, with emotional relief. "Joey and I have searched everywhere for you! Why have you treated us this way?" Several men quickly rose to their feet as Mary reached the table. She pulled tears from the corners of her eyes with open palms while leading Jesus from their company with a free hand.

"Sorry to close your meeting. I mean I'm glad we found Jesus," Joey said as he nearly tripped over a chair that caught his knee. Jimmy, Jack and Sarah burst into laughter, needing to shed some emotional anxiety of their own. "Alright," said Joey's beat red face. "Let's get moving and see if we can spare Jesus some words."

"You've an extraordinary lad, sir. Your own understanding of the sacred canon must be profound indeed. Perhaps we might have the pleasure of a visit with you soon," one of the men remarked.

"Yes sir, well that was a very wise and righteous statement. You gentlemen are also profound cannons," Joey said appreciatively. While he herded the children in the direction of the passage, the elders looked at one another with perplexity, wondering at the nuance and slippery subtleties couched beneath his words.

When Joey arrived outside, Mary and Jesus were releasing one another from a tight hug. "Mom, you more than anyone else must know that I have to care for my Father's business," Jesus concluded.

"I'm starved to death," Joey teased while searching Mary's face for any familiar sign.

"Oh, can we get ice cream, Daddy?" they all pleaded.

"Only if mom says so," Joey said in a false sheepish way.

"Oh, I don't know how we could possibly have time for that," Mary played the role beautifully.

"Alright!" said Jesus emphasizing each syllable, "I know where there's some great cookies and cream down by Shedd Aquarium!"

"Shedd Aquarium," said Joey, "that's miles from here. When were you ever down there anyway. I was thinking of maybe some kosher dogs on the way home."

"Sure wish I had a man who would take risks," Mary said taking the kid's side.

"Yea dad, you grew up watching too much, Clint," said Jimmy. "They didn't have ice cream back then. He pretty much lived in a desert, seldom shaved and ate cigars."

"Cool," said Jack.

"Today's man," Jimmy continued, "guys like Segal live in the city (nobody knows exactly where), jumps from buildings, hurts only bad men and stops for a cone just about every day."

"Say all that again boy," Joey said seriously as they all piled in and made route to Shedd Aquarium.

Some great years passed. School days turned to work schedules for the boys while Sarah married her love from college and moved downtown near Lincoln Park. Mary sat alone on the bench quietly watching yearling squirrels run figure eights up tall oaks with their mates. Acorn cuttings and notes from Dan Hartman fell like intermittent rain upon leaves about to complete their dance of days. They were already showing signs of a season—green—turning into colors of orange, yellow and red. Bright reds, those were his favorites, Mary remembered. What I wouldn't give to relive an Autumn day with him and listen with my head in his lap as I often did on the big porch during our annual trip to my favorite bed and breakfast there in Boston. He would talk on in his way of wind and earth, fire and rain and God. She wept for the emptiness she felt, never dreaming that loneliness could feel so black and overwhelming and incurable. Rising from her place she repositioned a vase of early mums beneath his name on the stone.

"I love you, Joey," she whispered, " we'll all be home soon." She stepped away as gently, but with different stride than years before.

Mary pulled into the drive along side of Jesus' mini-van and went into the house for a cool glass of tea.

"Jesus, how about joining me for a glass of tea?" Mary asked.

"Sure, that sounds great," and he joined her at the breakfast table. "You've been out to the cemetery, haven't you?" Jesus asked.

"Yes, it's so peaceful there," Mary said while lighting a memorial candle just like she did on every anniversary date, "but it all comes rushing back." Mary burst into tears that became a bawl and Jesus rose to hold her in his arms. Remarkably, she quieted soon, dabbed her eyes, then pulled a pitcher from the refrigerator and poured tea over tall glasses of ice.

"Jesus, I know you could run the shop. Doesn't anything interest you? Why do you keep procrastinating? You will be thirty this year," Mary said. "I'm sorry," she continued, "Jesus, I'm just scared."

"Mom, you have to trust the Father. Keep up your abandoned-control trust. It has to be greater now than it's ever been. It's alright to be afraid. Remember how we've prayed? Look, the time has arrived. The kingdom of God is at the very door. I'm going to begin calling on men and women soon, everyone to repent and believe the extraordinary message. I'm leaving, Mom. All of my things are already in the van, but you are not alone," said Jesus.

"I've known this, Jesus. I want you to go. His will must be fulfilled. He has shown me how desperately we need you. Go and be strong for him," she said. "But give me just one minute." Mary crossed the foyer to the rear of the house and returned with a shallow box that she placed on the table. Removing the lid, she lifted a woven hooded sweater that had been the subject of many late hour's work.

"Mom," Jesus said affectionately, "you made this yourself. It's beautiful and cotton too!"

"You need plenty of warm clothing around these parts," she said with pleasure.

"You're terrific, Mother. It will be cherished, I promise you. Look, I'll see you from time to time, but I'll be on my own. All that I've focused upon and prepared for is ready for launch." Jesus finished his tea while verbally finalizing some details that would move ownership of the business and prepare Mary for future income and a modest retirement. Jesus and Mary embraced one another in a long hug before he backed the van from the drive and departed. Although he saw his mother on occasion, he never returned to that address.

Chapter 3

Prophetstown is a small farming community out I-88 west just beyond Sterling and Rock Falls. This is where Jack made his home in the vast wilderness of cornfields that ran for miles in any direction. Jack left from under his parent's roof during his early 20's and though he was seldom seen, those who knew his family often joked about who contributed to him the more dominant genes. His father, Zack had far more hair on his upper torso than he did his head. He was a man of medium height with a thick 26 inch neck and literally built like an English Bulldog. Folks in his Chicago suburb nicknamed him "Magilla Gorilla" after an old cartoon series. His hands were thickly calloused as well as his entire outer shell. His wrinkled hide hung loose to a frame that had endured many years of exposure to the elements. Zack loved roofing, second only to fishing and treated his work more as an art than dreaded labor. He was one of only a few men who could confidently work an 8/12 pitch without toe support; his upper body balanced his lumbering walk as he kept knuckles low and his chin parallel to the deck below. Zack never owned a conveyor or air tools but could lay down 30 pound felt and a square of shingles quicker than any who did. He was an even tempered man of few words, liked his lunch packed deep, dealt mostly in cash, and seldom had a problem with customers tardy with payments.

Liz was equally stout in her own right and could easily tote five gallon pails of roofing nails to the top of a ladder in her early days, assisting Zack when Jack was young. She had plenty of soft places and was still the jewel of Zack's eye after all their forty years of marriage. Elizabeth's gift was verbosity with velocity as Zack would secretly put it, and only secretly. "If Johnson ever stalls," he would carry on, "I could make it to port with her mouth in the water as a prop," although he was never directly quoted. Liz could sure spin yarn. She made a decent wage selling encyclopedias after Jack entered school. She would always make her stock presentation followed by a remarkably effective closure—"These would make a wonderful resource for your family; would you like to buy a set or would you like for me to read for you the first volume?" Liz was a piece of work. She and Zack were admirably suited for one another and besides the infrequent flare ups ignited by discussion of his perceived mistress, "Miss Doolittle," kindness generally prevailed.

Jack closed the door on the lean-to and stepped out onto a path near a field of freshly shelled corn that laid off the quarter mile to the front of the property. He drew a large handkerchief from his coveralls, folded it in the form of a parachute, turned it upside down with corners tied and filled it's lap with about a cup of wild seed he had previously gathered and mixed. Pulling down a towel spent, he replaced it with a fresh sleeve, attaching it to the end of a wire which hung from a limb that was heavily visited by species of smaller birds. Crows stood arrogantly aloof among the limbs of a tall walnut scoffing at most everything below while the moan of beagles crept out of a distant hollow, now loud, then faint, depending upon their circuit with a cottontail.

Al and Edie had been generous to provide him with a bed and place to disciple young men who had come to him for instruction in his ascetic ways. The first year he was a tenant, Jack roofed the Strassfeld's house and smaller buildings that sprinkled the farm in trade for shelter and the isolation he sought. Food was always free and generously supplied. Edie made sure of it.

"Edie," Jack would brag to her face, "there aren't any ovens in all of Chicago raising biscuits this morning quite as good as yours." And Jack could sure put down a plate of 'em, ladled with her blackberry jam drawn from briars right there on the place or else the dark sorghum molasses brought up from relatives in the South. It was always a secret bet with the kids which he'd choose on a given morning. They all had to be called down more than once for staring at Jack's eating habits.

"Daddy," young Andrew would ask, "can you put a whole one of mama's biscuits in your mouth and swallow it in one gulp like Uncle Jack?"

"Don't reckon I'd want to try that son," Jack remembered the way Al considered the comparison, "and I'm also confident I wouldn't want to arm wrestle the man. You just pay attention to them grits," Al directed his son back to his own plate, "and let a working man tend to his trough."

Al and Jack insulated the shed he called home, ran a flu through the roof for the wood stove and trenched in a single strand of current and a water line from a nearby barn with the neighbor's trenching machine for roofing trade.

Life was quiet on the back side of the Strassfeld property. Their children were pleasurable, respected his privacy and considered Jack an uncle, though there was no blood relationship between them. While many folks were suspicious of Jack and knew he was extremely eccentric, the Strassfelds knew him as a man with a kind heart, brilliant with stories about God and stronger than a mule. In fact, it's a matter of record that a large crowd at the annual Bar-B-Que witnessed Jack out pull a young mule by several feet the first year or two he was around, each of them harnessed and dragging a sled loaded with 16 inch blocks under the lights during the main event.

Jack was reluctant to involve himself in competition of any kind, but Al had already coaxed him into the arena by entering him in the annual wood splitting contest—one that really had been no contest at all for several years since Tom Sparrow, a tall muscular middle aged man, had held the cherished champion's title to this event for at least a decade. Tom was a big strapping man who was thick all over and tougher than a pine knot. The locals knew him by several nick names including, "Buzz Saw," "Buster," but most generally as "Terrible—T." It wasn't that Tom was a bad person or anything; in fact, he was considered gentle by most everyone except the man who made the unfortunate and distasteful remark before his wife, Sandi one day. Tom just had a nasty habit of making splinters of most any variety of standing timber that he came into contact with and was more committed to wood with an axe than a border collie with sheep. Large or small he had a reputation for reducing trees to kindling in short order. Exaggerated stories typeset on a coffee table at the local diner circulated reports that Tom could reduce a 30 inch white oak to a mountain of toothpicks in just a day or two.

Jack didn't put a great deal of stock in the local news. He stepped up toe to toe with Terrible, gave him a manly shake, and at the sound of a 38 caliber cap, the two of them sprinted to equal piles of hardwood with a double bladed axe in hand to see who could build the biggest stack of split quarters before the five minute halt sounded by the air horn on Murray's Dodge. At the horn, Tom fell to his knees with his chin on the butt of his axe handle exhausted from the cardiac overload and smiled up at Jack who had stepped over, locked palms and helped lift him to his feet.

Tom looked back at his pile that was dwarfed by the new champion's. "Well Jack," he said amid hoots and cheers for both contestants, "let me get you and me a quart of tea apiece. That was a right serious little workout."

"Yes," Jack agreed, "not even Al ever worked me that hard."

"Oh yeah?" asked Tom grinning. "He's coy, clever as a red fox, or did Edie put you up to this?" The two left their blades while swapping stories of Al with him now walking between them and they joined others for a little reception at a nearby picnic table.

Jack placed back the fond recollection with the many other treasured photos he'd taken of the area and kept stored in his heart. Turning back after a few more minutes walk he waited for Wes, an eight year old mix, who was a frequent visitor to his bunkhouse. While taking pause in the heat of the Indian Summer, he noted the many cords of wood he had recently split and lay beneath a slip roof away from the west to cure for winter. The outbuildings wore fresh paint and the pumpkins and butternuts, now beginning to bare, were about all that was left in the acre garden. Jack had already winterized the tiller that rest against a locust post in the fence row with a galvanized tub over its head that served as an umbrella. It's tines would not dig again until spring, he mused while wondering how many miles he had followed her between rows of table vegetables. 'Peggy' he called her, to the Strassfeld children's delight because of the way he kept cadence behind her like a man with a pegged leg. Jack was the first to assign a name to an inanimate object on their farm. "Oh," he would tease, "if only you had met little Miss Dolittle." Mention of the boat always brought belly laughs from all as a raft of stories remembered came alive in Technicolor while picking silver queen, snap beans or whatever else was due.

Wes caught up with Jack and made his familiar turns around his boots while scratching his head on exposed cord laces. The cat was white and shy of most anyone but Jack. He saved it as a kitten from the jaws of an adult shepherd that had sniffed out the litter.

"Wes, I reckon I'll be heading out for a few days," said Jack enjoying his play with the dialect picked up from the local soil. "Got right smart a walk ahead of me but should be back around in a fortnight." Wes licked his paw as Jack briefed his friend on his plans. The two stood alone on the path and strangely content—both of them understanding providence a little better than most.

Up ahead Al stepped out onto the back stoop, sat down and began lacing his Wolverines. "Where are you headed so early, Jack?" he asked. "I've not seen you in a coon's age, boy. Thought I'd have to step down in a mite and see if I could stir you up. You've made yourself plumb scarce."

"I've been plenty busy," Jack returned, "Reckon we've missed one another coming and going. By the way, what kind of yield did the corn bring?" asked Jack. "That was a mighty loud crop."

"Oh, just a tolerable like, just tolerable," said Al methodically. "Maybe a hundred bushels," jutting his head toward an early International two ton with grain sides still sitting in the field under the combine's auger. "I didn't run enough 'monia' under it and the old Gleaner leaves plenty for the deer and pheasants as you well know."

"Al, I'm heading over to the City for a few days, could run into a couple of weeks actually. Just wanted you to know not to look for me and maybe ask Edie to put a stop on the gravy train."

"You mean Moline or the big 'en," asked Al as he placed a pinch of snuff between his bottom lip and gum.

"Chicago, Al."

"What's going on in Chicago? You ain't been back in those parts in quite a spell. You gonna see Jesus ya had out here before? It were real good of him to make that extree trip over to Southern States for the diesel and nitrate we was shy the tractor and side dressing of that sweet corn. That boy was sure whipped and he went right on over yonder straight away and picked it up in his own van. You bring that back to him, Jack, and tell him we still talk of him."

"I'll be sure. The time is approaching," Jack said in a grim kind of manner.

"Reckon so, Jack," Al nodded without fully understanding his friend. "Look, I can carry ya over as far as Dixon. I've got some belts and a couple of sprockets to pick up."

"Thanks, Al. I'd be much obliged."

Just days later, Jack stood nearly waist deep in the DesPlaines River across the road from the Palwaukee Airport. A handful of people lined the banks as Jack's voice carried over and forewarned them of God's impending wrath.

"Hey this guy has a pretty nasty message," remarked George. "He's scaring the hell out of those kids from Great Lakes. C'mon Nate, you can't be serious about this poppycock, let's blow this place."

Nate lowered the window on his driver side and began removing his tie. "I told you that you didn't have to come along. No, I've thought about this for a long time. You've listened to the times he's been on radio. He makes a lot of sense. Aren't you looking for the kingdom of God?" Nate asked. George ignored his question while pulling the last of his milk shake aggressively through a straw.

"Look," George asked in desperation, "what in the scratch are you going to tell your colleagues at Northwestern. You'll be the laughing stock if they find out you're into this nuttiness. O.K., O.K. you don't need to rehearse it all now. Can you just hurry it up? I have to be filling teeth in 20 minutes." Nate stepped out of his BMW, dropped his coat and tie in the seat and proceeded to the river's edge. Slipping off his shoes, he fixed his eyes on Jack and stepped into the cold water without noticing the temperature or the mud that rose up to his ankles. Wading to him, Jack addressed him in an even tone but one that made his heart race.

"Sir, do you come in repentance?" asked Jack. "And are you prepared to evidence the fruit?"

"Yes I am," said Nate. "I want to be cleansed the way you've taught and prepare myself for the Messiah."

"Nate," Jack began, "I'm just splashing you with water, but he is coming soon who will immerse you in the Holy Spirit and fire." Jack poured water over a new convert's head while his disciples lifted others from beneath the surface.

"Mister," Nate said sincerely, "bathe my hands and arms and back also."

"Go on," Jack said as he splashed him again, "and make a difference."

While Nate stepped onto the bank and retrieved his towel, Jack began a fresh burst of scathing rebuke directed at doctors of the law who had often come to mock and ridicule his message.

"Who told you deceivers to run from judgment?" Jack's voice bellowed through the fog warning lighter freights to pull aside. "And don't tell me about your ancestry for God is able from this river gravel to raise up children to Abraham. You're a nest of adders. How will you escape the judgment of God?" Two young sailors joined Jack following Nate's ascent and admitted their desire for baptism as they related how powerfully they were impacted by a message he delivered weeks earlier outside of Gate Three at the Naval Training Center. "Be content with you're wages, put away falsehood and honor your superiors," Jack admonished. He then slid his arms under theirs, one on each side of him; and while cradling their heads, he bent down and pushed them both beneath the water.

While the young men waded ashore, Jack's eye caught sight of a familiar face that changed his countenance. River water passed on either side of Jack's legs. The two concrete pilings were sunk in solid depths, forever stationary, supporting a bridge about to be crossed. Jesus kicked off his boat shoes and laid aside his shirt before joining Jack.

"Bart, Thad, he's here," Jack announced to his disciples. "Get a good look, men. He is the Lamb of God who will clear out and cancel the world's sins." As the cousins faced one another in the water, Jack said, "It's been awhile, Jesus. We've all wondered."

"You know it's never been my time table, Jack. The time has arrived. I'm beginning my Father's work in earnest."

"You know, Jesus, you ought to be the one doing this for me. Besides, this river is filthy," he said with a serious smile that was familiar to Jesus.

"You're a man of propriety and your motives are pure, Jack. Let it be, for we must completely satisfy all righteousness," said Jesus. When Jesus came up from the waters, a voice thundered, "this is my beloved son who bears my seal of absolute pleasure." In that moment, Jesus saw heaven ripped open and the Holy Spirit roll down upon him in the form of a dove.

"Bart, did you hear the voice?" asked Jack.

"Of course I did," he said, "that was truly majestic."

"Blasted jets from Glenview showing off!" said a Jewish legal expert. "It's against the law."

When Jesus reached the river's edge, he turned back to Jack and said, "I've missed you Jack. It's hardball from here on out. You're no stalk blowing in the wind, big boy. Don't let go of your confidence." Jesus then gathered his things and walked south on Milwaukee.

As he passed over the gravel driveway apron and onto the easement, a solid white government vehicle was signaling to turn in at the river's bank.

"It's about time the Mayor's goons showed up," said a Jewish Chazzan. Two large athletic looking men stepped along side of parked vehicles and joined Jewish leaders a short distance from Jack.

"Where have you been?" asked a small Jewish man authoritatively. "They could have easily been gone by now," he scolded.

"Look, Rab, the line at the little French eatery down the street here was a bit longer than usual. But to tell you the truth, I seldom get in a hurry for Heebs."

"You two just do as you're told," passing an envelope, "and pick up the large hairy one! Do you have County shields? Don't make any mistakes. The mayor wants him put away this time."

"We know full and quacking well what the mayor wants," said the second thud sarcastically. "Now you girls get on out of our way and we'll do our job. By the way, aren't you supposed to be burning incense somewhere at this hour?"

The small gathering had diminished when Jack, Bart and others stepped out of the River. Somehow, Jack didn't sense that those remaining were on hand for acts of contrition. As Bart began to pull off his sopping shoes, two men blind sided him with a penetrating blow to the ribs, forcing out his wind and buckling him to his knees. Jewish leaders looked on from a car while they raised Bart to his feet and directed him to take his beach ball and go home. Flashing County shields, they advised Jack that he had violated a public bathing ordinance that would cost him a trip downtown. While one of the men erected a fresh sign, Bart, who was still gasping for air asked, "Jack, what's going on, can they do this?"

"Its O.K. Bart, I'll be fine. Take the others and I'll be along after I finish up with their trivia." Slipping cuffs on Jack, they roughed him unnecessarily to the back seat and pulled away from his sanctuary like bushmen out of the Amazon with an exotic catch.

On the way to Cook County jail, the driver stabbed through the mesh cage that divided the compartments with cruel words aimed at tormenting Jack.

"So you're the hairy gorilla with the big mouth. The Mayor is still awfully steamed about your little slip with WGN. He doesn't think the whole world needs to be privy to the frequent trips he makes with his brother's wife. You don't seem to be happy with much of anything on the planet."

"You keep running your mouth," said the other, "and we'll see if we can remedy that problem." As the driver passed under I-294, his partner took a hit of coke from a supply they had recently confiscated in a drug bust.

"Hey, Martin," he said, "let's blow off the afternoon at Sonia's place and check him in at precinct later tonight. He can stay in the cage tucked away in her garage and might even have time to dry out a bit. Besides I don't want too much time to pass. The little woman will forget all about the favor she owes us for our blinking real big over the weekend."

Lonny called up dispatch and related that they would likely be several hours walking the river bank in search of their suspect who had resisted arrest and crossed the river. "Look," Lonny spoke into the receiver confidently, "I'm sure we'll find him. Don't look for us on the radio—we'll check in when we wrap this up."

The plain clothes detoured and surfaced later in Oak Brook at a condo off of Spring Road. Martin pulled into an open bay in the two car garage, lowered the door and stepped inside unannounced. "Think we should leave him cuffed?" Martin asked, when Sonia stepped into the kitchen, not even startled, and stood wanton under a loose blouse tied at the waste with a revealing skirt.

"A man's got to keep his priorities straight," said Lonny. "I'm going to be tied up for awhile myself, but if I get free I'll check in on his circulation."

"Back so soon boys?" she played and was obviously under the influence of something intoxicating which was evidenced by her slur as well as the smell of open bourbon.

Martin lit up a fresh smoke, grabbed a cold beer from the refrigerator and flipped on the tube while Lonny and Sonia snuggled and giggled, dropping intimates while staggering to the back room. After nearly four hours of nap and play, the two men emerged from the unit, showered, nearly sober and ready to get back on the clock. They pulled into precinct with Jack and booked him on several false charges including assaulting an officer of the law.

"I didn't touch these men," Jack said to the jailer, "they'd be a couple of sore welts if I ever took a mind to—I'll tell you that." The jailor released Jack from his cuffs after the officers departed and placed him in a block with twenty others in low security.

Chapter 4

Jesus parked his worn Chevy Astro at a rest area along I-44 outside Springfield, Missouri, just before 9 P.M. He pulled out a road atlas and began calculating distance and time to Phoenix, tracing the main arteries with a yellow highlighter. Hunger pains were growing strong after three days without food, but his spirit was compelled to ignore their groans and press on with renewed vigor. He drove on in the night, but a few hours before daylight he was overcome with sleep and being low on gas, he decided to exit the interstate about halfway between Tulsa and Oklahoma City where he found a filling station and parked at the pumps until morning.

Just before 7 A.M. the service station owner awakened his customer with raps to the glass with the butt of a screw driver on the driver's side door where a man's head lay soundly asleep. Jesus opened his eyes and read upside down the name Pat that was ironed to his shirt on a football shaped patch just above his Winstons. The red letters stood in bold relief at his first light and against the dark blue utility shirt. Pat walked to the front and unlocked the office door and switched on the pumps after he was sure he had roused a new patron from sleep. Jesus stepped out of the van and began filling the tank with fuel when Pat hollered above a depleted compressor that was trying desperately to make up losses from the previous night, "Say you're a ways from home aren't you mister?" while glancing at the Illinois tags.

"Yes, its already been quite a trip," admitted Jesus, "but I've got miles to go before I sleep."

"He writes great poetry doesn't he," said Pat, who had drawn near and asked to check the fluid levels.

"Yes, he did, some of my favorite," Jesus said. "I think the oil is O.K., but I've been hearing some roaring whenever I apply the brakes."

"Appointments aren't due for another hour; after that I'll be busier than a cat covering up tracks on a tin roof," Pat said with a country smile. "I'd be happy to pull the wheels and have a look. It sounds like your pads are gone."

"Is that serious?" asked Jesus.

"Yeah, unfortunately by the time you hear the growl, it's too late. It's a serious warning that you're about out of brakes," said Pat.

"Well, I guess we'd better have a look," said Jesus. Pat guided him into the bay, then directed Jesus to a fresh pot of coffee while he positioned arms of the rack to touch only the frame, then hoisted the van to a height above his head. After a few pops with a hub cap tool and whines from an air gun, Pat called Jesus into the shop and pointed out some deep grooves that had been cut into the front rotors by hungry rivets that had patiently waited for pads to grow slim.

"Your rear drums are also just weeks away from kissing metal," said Pat with an honest expression.

"Is that pretty costly?" asked Jesus.

"Yeah, it will take some more, but if I put new pads on top of these canyons, you'll be right back in six weeks time. I guarantee it."

"So, it's like they say, 'you can pay me now or you can pay me later,'" Jesus remarked. After staring at tie rods and ball joints for a moment, Jesus asked, "So you feel sure it needs that kind of overhaul, I mean turning the rotors as you said, the whole shot?"

"It's a must. I see this all the time. Folks sometimes ignore stripping it all down and starting with everything new, but I can assure you, they're just putting a band aid on a serious problem. Only a fool would ever consider putting new pads over these scoured rotors. This way you preserve both the pads and the rotors. Pete will be along shortly. He can run the rotors and drums over to Gipes to be turned, the pads can be ordered up and you'll be back on the road by 9:00 or 9:30."

"How much are we looking at spending all total," asked Jesus.

"Your calipers and wheel cylinders are in good shape; I think we can keep it around 'a hundred fifty' and change," said Pat

Jesus eventually picked up I-40 out of Oklahoma City and spent the day in further pursuit of a call he intended to answer. Passing through the upper block of Texas, he picked up a hitchhiker who was standing on an entrance ramp with his thumb in the air.

"Thanks for stopping; hey, I'm safe," said the young man. "Boy is it tough to get a ride from anybody these days."

"Well, pleased to meet you, Safe; My name's 'Danger,'" Jesus said, smiling while easing back onto the highway."

"Cool," said the wanderer in an unsteady voice that was detectable.

"Hey relax," said Jesus, "I was just carrying on with you. By the way, what is your name?"

"My name's Kenny," he said.

"Hi, Kenny, my name's Jesus. So where are you headed from here?"

"Oh, I'm heading over to Vegas for a few days, shoot a wad, stay up night and day until I'm broke, psychotic or both; and then, Oh, I don't know for sure, maybe head over to L.A. or somewhere. I dropped out of college just a few hours short of a degree, told the old man I was leaving, wanted what was coming to me; and I've been on the road pretty much enjoying myself ever since."

"Well, I'm pleased to have your company," said Jesus.

"Where you from, Jesus?" asked Kenny as he fumbled with a pack of cigarettes, looking for a smoke.

"I'm from the Chicago area, northwest suburbs."

"Yeah, I thought I recognized that Midwest accent, clear and articulate," while lighting up, "I'm from just north of you at Madison. Boy howdy, this is big country out here isn't it," shouted Kenny while responding to the billboards that boasted about the humongous size of everything from hamburgers that would scarcely fit on a plate, and the dinosaur size Longhorns that provided the meat to vast areas of ranch, with sprawling homes that could house a neighborhood. "You've not seen big," shouted Kenny while he reminded anyone within earshot that water wasn't scarce around the Great Lakes; he made Jesus laugh aloud.

"Yeah, you're right about that, Kenny, we definitely hold the trump cards in that category." Pondering man's appetite, he continued, "you are gods—sons of the Almighty, but you will die like everybody else and be buried right along side all the other princes."

"Hey, that's a nice blend of something existential and extra-terrestrial; is that Nietzsche?" asked Kenny trying to repeat a phrase or two. "Does that mean anything?" he asked.

"Man most usually involves himself in doing something he feels competent about," Jesus began. "It makes him feel needed and secure. Sports competition, politics and war are a few of his specialties. But there is something about the notion of dancing that frightens him. It makes him feel wanted and out of control. It's not the moral issues that are bothersome, not a reaction to the selfish sensuality that is sometimes associated with it. Dancing is an art form and can even be a means of worship. It's individualized and though steps can be memorized, one still has to get out on the floor and move through them with a partner in their own personalized style."

"Whoa, now wait a minute dude, I've had a few hours of philosophy, but it didn't involve a lesson in dancing," said Kenny.

"Comparatively speaking, few people dance," Jesus said, " and a fewer number dance with God. The ones who do are often misunderstood or harshly criticized. Folks who dance before God are excited about his glory and so they twist and shout with all their might. Michals we live beside or possibly work with cannot endure the joy and festive celebration. They ridicule and despise dancers in their hearts and insist they're making fools of themselves. It's not a foolish thing to dance with God. It is glorious. There is something oily and invigorating about it. Dancers are alive with emotion if the great book of poems teach us anything, and in touch with God at a level few experience."

"O.K., O.K., I see where this is going," Kenny buzzed with interest, "you're into some of that Utah movement with the crystals and channelers—is there really anything to that?"

"Poles apart," Jesus paused, "People who dance are a little scary to be around. They are festive, unpredictable, a bit more poetic than scientific, lost more in the wonder of God than trying to figure out angles and make life work on their own. God calls people to dance with him in life in spite of all that is wrong around them. Of course people don't know the steps. Andrew Murray's book of dance will not help. He wants you to follow his lead as he spins you toward glory and waltz's you toward a vision for beauty. Much of life is the story of his courtship with adulterers and murderers who celebrate his forgiveness, seems those are the only ones who really dance, as well as inviting the Michals around to kick up their heels and join in."

"Michals?" Kenny grunted.

"There are a number of macros in force around us," Jesus continued talking as he pointed to a beautiful herd of wild horses not too far from the road, "big whopper size truths or realities that tend to color and inform human experience."

"I'm with you homie, bigger than Texas," Kenny injected while flicking his cigarette out the window and scratching around for another.

"Glory is a huge backdrop," Jesus smiled, "that has always remained on the stage of human history. The cast has changed over the centuries, but God's glory has not changed nor diminished. While considering the great throng of men and women who have walked life's stage and passed before the camera of time, it's interesting to note that some have been wicked and some have been righteous. But each had their moment, no matter the circumstances, their opportunity to dance with God."

"You know I always used to ridicule those people who flocked to a guru, but I'm beginning to understand the process," said Kenny, "this is definitely not Philosophy 101. Did you just sit out here with the Indians and Billy Jack and meditate until this stuff came to you? I mean this stuff is pretty heavy."

"Glory is like that," said Jesus. "In fact glory is best described as something weighty. Figuratively, the word could be used to describe an impressive or worthy person. It can also mean beauty, that which is swelling, praise worthy or brilliant in some way. If we add color to the word, it will require analogies because it's really too big to define and too illusive for words. There is an element in which glory surprises people. Have you ever had cold water thrown into your face unexpectantly? Or how about the hooker staring at costly jewels in a velvet box held by a redeemer prince who snapped the lid closed just to hear her scream with surprise."

"I saw that film!" said Kenny.

"Glory or beauty calls forth awe, it enlarges something inside of us," Jesus taught on, "It prompts a thank-you from people. Pictures are helpful. Glory is a father conversing with his son, Kenny. Glory is fresh summer air after a thunderstorm has passed through and pushed out the humidity. The air is crisp and clean and a rainbow stretches its great arch across the sky. Glory is a husband and wife walking hand in hand along a beach in shallow breakers at sunset. Glory is a young person making difficult value choices that are unpopular with friends. Glory is Niagara Falls spilling over in quiet thunder. Glory is a night fallen on vacant Canadian hills. In dense blackness, one can look into the heavens and mark all her constellations. Glory is something way outside the normal that leaves the eyes wide and the mouth dropped. Just try taking in the Grand Canyon with even a wide angled lens. The sight leaves people motionless and their gratitude says, join in! You see Kenny, there is something inside people that wants to step right into the picture—to be immersed, as a vital and necessary piece; to become the very color rolled up in a sunset, then burst forth at dawn and run the circuit with the bright ball as he steps out of his chamber to revel in a new day. One will soon summarize the longing and make intercession that stupefies, 'I in you and you in me and they in us.'"

"Man this is hard to get my hands around. I'd like to think about some of these concepts again. Can you believe I've carried a little pocket recorder in this backpack until just a week or two ago. I pawned it to buy a bus ticket," said Kenny.

"So, dad's bucks didn't go too far I take it?" asked Jesus.

"Nope," Kenny admitted while flicking a cigarette butt out the window and spitting for emphasis. "I was a fool," he said, while evaluating every signal in Jesus' nonverbal feedback. "I've never admitted that to anybody before now, but I'm tired of lying and running from one town to the next, just a step ahead of utter exhaustion."

"It's hard to get up and go home," Jesus said, "all men and women struggle with it. I'm just sorry they get their mouths chock full of chocolate cake before they realize there isn't any milk out here in a place like this—just steers and manure to shovel. They got any milk in Wisconsin, Kenny? The glory is in my Father's house, there is a celebration going on there in your honor—I'd like to invite you to the dance."

Kenny was staring ahead deep in thought but also nodding back at the monologue that was revealing something awfully powerful about his recent past. Jesus spoke toward him while watching the road, "Man wants to touch glory, but he's also afraid of it. It's a strange paradox. Even though glory can be seen in a number of beautiful pictures, there is the awesome glory before which all of this pales. The glory of God descending upon a mountain top that overlooks a huge peninsula. His is the glory! His makes the earth and the hearts of all its inhabitants quake with fear because his is tied to his very nature and when he unveils it, everything else becomes distant shadows. God's glory leaves men transfixed in bewilderment, like novice climbers who encounter majesty at the summit of a mountain peak. One wonders what to do—what to do but pitch tent and stay for as long as you can. But a man fell from that pinnacle once and it paralyzed him. The great climber is now a glorious ruin and so the push, pull continues with his sons. They want to go up, but the evil tragedy has melted their courage."

"I know about that," said Kenny seriously, "why do you think we struggle with that?"

"Evil is not as old as glory, but it has been around for a long time," Jesus responded. "Seers allude to a mighty angel who once traversed even greater heights, but he grew in blind arrogance until he promised to ascend far away to the north and dethrone the Most High. He was summarily condemned and subsequently banished, but with no small fight. Unfortunately, evil was unleashed and polluted the order. Since he can't tamper with God's glory, he seeks to stamp out, mar and disfigure the glory of God in men and women who have been made in his image and likeness. Listening to evening news anchors, reading the local paper or just driving around the cities you mentioned earlier makes one aware at once that he and his legions are getting the job done."

"It's tragic how dark one can grow. He plants a seed of suspicion—"God is not good." After the husk falls away and its meat rots beneath the soul, something poisonous sprouts that soon covers the once beautiful edifice with brambles and thorns. The story is told of a great painter, and alleges to be true, in which he began a large oil on the face of a recently prepared canvas, then personally entered the streets in search of a man to sit among several of his officers. Stumbling upon the most handsome, angelic person he had ever seen, they agreed for a wage and the painter soon established the centerpiece that would hinge the others. Work progressed slowly, other projects were demanded of the painter; but the day finally came in which he needed a subject to sit for a traitor he wished to place next to the royalty at center. Again, search was made for the most degenerate, haggard person that he could find. The painter uncovered such a man in the square; one who was dark, beaten up by life, vulgar and cynical. He began to dialogue with the individual in hopes of fixing a wage for his possible sitting, when the man interrupted the painter and said, 'but don't you recognize me, man? It was I who sat for the Prince!'

"Kenny, there are many others who never develop a vision or taste for beauty and so they also grow dark and destructive. They cooperate with evil and are enemies of the sign. Their god is their belly and the only glory they know is in shame. They walk in the lowlands and stay comfortably clear of the risky heights."

As they neared the New Mexico boarder, Kenny asked Jesus to pull to the shoulder and let him out. "I know this is strange, Mister. It's strange, Jesus, but I just feel real deep that I want to go home," Kenny said. "I wasn't really going to Vegas anyway. I don't know where I was going. It's just real strange. Listen, thanks for the lift. I'm going home. I've made up my mind, I'm going home. I'm going back to see if dad will talk with me." Jesus waited with the van idling until Kenny crossed the median and took up an eastward path, then pulled away with a prayer. Kenny stopped beneath an overpass, just a quarter of a mile down the road. The shade felt especially refreshing beneath the skirt of that bridge—a refuge from the punishing heat. He sat down and opened his back pack to retrieve the remainder of his cheese crackers. There he found several dollars wrapped in a poem.

ragged scarf

A son walked out just yesterday; how can it be explained?
No thanks, no kiss, no sorrow, just calloused words and heart.
Said I won't be back tomorrow, you've held me back too long.
Gotta go—they're waiting, gonna make it on my own.

And the wind was cold that morning as dad peered down the lane.
A son fading in the distance—huh, that's my scarf flapping like a mane.

Turning from the window, there he liked to pray.
It was different now, all is still; what can I say?
Memories rushing in and crowding out my prayer—
Gotta stay and wait on God, it's more than I can bear.

Laughter in the city rose as darkness fell.
C'mon boy we've waited, let's run and gather hell.
The pain felt good and then it hurt, as it all began to swell;
I wanna get back, the wound's too deep, nothing left to even sell.

Busted, broken, begging now, it's all been lost and more
Someone whispers c'mon home and heal the heart you tore.
Throughout the night he ran alone, miles until dawn,
Hoping just a servant as he stepped up on the lawn.

Stopping by the window, there he liked to pray,
Someone in the distance, an old scarf badly frayed.
Holding back his tears, never saw him run so hard—
And falling on his knees to embrace a son so marred.

And the wind was cold that morning as dad sat in the lane.
A son lost—now safe at last, my prayers and scarf held fast.

"Anybody home?" Jesus asked while he gave the desk buzzer a push or two. The clock on the wall said it was 6 P.M. and Jesus thought it could be about right. A middle aged Indian woman opened a door from the hall behind the counter and was unable to persuade her daughter to remain with the others in front of a blaring television. Jesus had pulled in at a dive near Albuquerque that was seriously dilapidated but didn't appear to be taking on water from the rain outdoors.

"Can I help you?" asked Carmella as their eyes momentarily met.

"Yes, I'd like a room," Jesus said, "do you have any vacancies?"

"Any what?" asked Carmella. "They tell me this place hasn't been half full since the big blast at White Sands back in the 40's."

"Yes, that was a big one," admitted Jesus, "but just the birth pangs I suppose."

"I suppose," agreed Carmella as she directed Jesus to fill out some general information and collected rate.

"What's your name, sweetie?" asked Jesus stretching over the counter for a smile.

"Oh, that's my little Joy," said Carmella in a bit of a dejected tone. "Something that's always in short supply around here."

"Why do you suppose that is?" asked Jesus.

"What's that? You mean the chronic depression? That's just from being us," she said. "Maybe you know a little about that," she continued while observing his darker complexion and trying to make a guess about his race. "Indians, Hispanics, Arabs, it don't matter. We all might as well been cursed. I guess everybody got their signals crossed when they stepped out of that ark they talk about," said Carmella.

"Yeah, the flood didn't wash away everything," Jesus said, adding to her remark. "By the way, something is being done about that," he assured her.

"Don't hold your breath on Washington," she said passing him a key.

"Carmella," Jesus asked, "What would it take in the short run to experience a little more joy?"

"Just a lot of damn money," she shouted. It was very obvious that she was at her breaking point. "Everything is in short supply around here. The kids haven't seen their dad in three weeks; I get to work night and day and can only hope to nap between…Look I'm sorry for all this steam," she said with real tears forming in her eyes, "you've got your own problems."

"I care, Carmella," said Jesus. "I take comfort in knowing that folks are leaving the land of the dying and going to the land of the living one day." As Carmella gained composure and apologized again for the seepage of rage, Jesus placed his fingertips upon the knuckles of her clinched fist as it lay on the counter. "Carmella, you're angry at God over some huge disappointments. You ever talked to him about it? I don't suppose I'd wish your circumstances on anyone, but you're letting them stand in the way of a relationship with him. That's what he wants with you. Wherever the bars are you'll find a prisoner, Carmella. Contentment is a slim key," Jesus said as he slid the metal stamping into his pocket, "but it can open some massive doors to freedom. You'll feel for it and find it when you search for him, with all your heart. What father after all would not hear the heart-cries of his daughter—unthinkable! Love and enjoy God—that's a real straight line that no one can twist. File all your important desires beneath it, for if you seek first his kingdom and justice all those things will be generously supplied," Jesus concluded and lifted his hand from hers. "Listen," said Jesus, stepping away, "thanks for the room and keep up the Joy," as he blew the little one a kiss.

Jesus grabbed a quick shower and crossed the street for doughnuts before going to bed. "Just give me a couple of each and stop at two dozen," Jesus said. The man taped down the lid on a large box and handed them to Jesus who had prepaid. The alarm sounded at 3:00 A.M. and he staggered to the bathroom to brush his teeth and pull his hair back into some kind of shape. After pulling the duffle bag closed, he lifted the unopened box of doughnuts from a shelf and stopped by the front office that lay quietly still. Jesus set the box down on the back side of the counter with a note appended to the lid along with a pencil drawing of her daughter Joy that showed an uncanny resemblance. The note was signed, 'your friend, Jesus.'

Back on the road, Jesus was nearly eight hours through Flagstaff and on to Phoenix. He left route 17 just above Phoenix and made his way over to Fountain Hills to the home of Terry and Carol Shank. It was after 11:00 A.M. when Jesus pulled into their cul-de-sac. Carol was tending plants when a light blue van pulled along the front curb a length or two ahead of the mail carrier's lane.

"Terry," Carol shouted, "It's Jesus, he's here." Carol ran the length of the drive and gave Jesus a full bear hug, that forced his knapsack to the ground. He held her tightly across the shoulders as they exchanged words. Terry was up in a moment and they repeated the ritual.

"Man, why don't you drag that thing you call a car in off of the road. There's plenty of room in the drive," Terry said.

"Oh, you don't want that on your nice drive," Jesus said, "that van's worse than a dog about marking its territory."

"Joey left you with a whole repertoire of river talk," Terry laughed, "now didn't he boy," and he twisted Jesus' ear until he squealed.

"Don't hurt the boy, Terry," ordered Carol and she meant it.

"That's it, lay into him with a belt Carol. He don't have any learning about how to bring in a guest," said Jesus pointing in fun from behind Carol who had physically come between them.

"I'm going to get everyone tea," Carol said, as a playful scowl directed at her husband retreated from her face.

As she stepped away, Jesus hugged Terry's side, looked into his eyes and said, "boy, you better behave yourself or she'll be on you like white on rice."

"I only wish," said Terry as he picked up Jesus' bag, "why that woman's so mean she has to hold a gun to her head when she shaves in the morning just so she don't cut her own throat."

Once inside the foyer, Jesus passed Carol her favorite fresh ground bean.

"Is this it kid?" asked Terry, who was playing floor hockey with Jesus' knapsack. "We thought you would be here for a few weeks."

"Oh, I've got another van following with my clothes," said Jesus, "by the way, that bag shouldn't have been brought in," he said panicking, "Can't you smell it? A bloody road kill I found along the way. I can see its seeping through the fabric." The prank caught Terry off guard, who looked carefully at the floor, but wasn't lost on Carol, who howled in satisfaction that he had been caught for a change."

Laughter followed them into a sunken sitting area that was plush with fine furniture and elegantly decorated. "Carol, you have such a fine hand with your home, everything is beautiful," Jesus complimented.

"Terry's new territory with Century has been better than we expected," Carol admitted.

"She means, Terry's newly arraigned sentence," her husband corrected, then added, "My boss brought us out here from Chicago and promised me a gravy position, managing sales for most all the southwest, then boom, the hammer drops, reality sets in and I haven't stop running since we got here. How I miss Rolling Meadows, the pool and working at the Merchandise Mart."

"Yes your back yard was a garden. I still have pleasant memories of your wedding there," said Jesus.

"By the way," continued Terry who was obviously airing out, "the boss is the ugliest one human being I've ever laid eyes on. Now am I exaggerating?" he asked Carol who couldn't contain herself and made an obvious affirming vote with poorly suppressed sputters and grunts. "I mean his nose is where you would expect to find his mouth—the guy looks like a carp or something worse. I'm telling you the truth, I've never seen the man's teeth. And when you're sitting at your desk and he stands over you and you have to look up at that thing, the little whiskers and everything, it's all there—I'm telling you its bad. The guy is so ugly his family has to tie a chop to his neck so the dog will play with him."

"Well Jesus, I've talked about myself long enough, you talk about me for a while," said Terry.

"On second thought, lets change the subject," Carol suggested. "So what's happening in Chicago?" she asked. "Have you seen Jack, Bart, Thad, any of the others recently?"

"The outlook for Jack has never been good," Jesus answered. "He's never been guilty of mixing words as you know. He was escorted away from the river the other day by the same kind of deputies that booked Daniel last year. I didn't like the feel of things."

"Well that doesn't sound good at all," admitted Terry.

"But, they've locked him up before and usually not for long. He's a scrapper, he'll do fine," said Carol. "Well look, my stomach says its time to eat. Which one of you handsome men want to escort me to the car. I'm not cooking and I've been waiting days for us all to sit down and visit."

"Say, I'm sorry to spoil your plans, but I'm here on business of sorts," said Jesus apologetically.

"That's what I like about you Jesus," said Terry, "real straight forward and ambiguous. O.K., we've been her before; we're available; how can we help?"

"I just need a place to park the van," he said.

"I like the plan," Carol said, "real simple. So is that it? I mean there's an extra space in the garage. What kind of storage time are we looking at Jesus?"

"I'm not sure at this point, maybe a month or longer. You two go eat, I need to spend some time alone. I'm sorry I won't be available this evening either. How about if I take a rain check on the lunch. We'll try to do dinner when I return—my treat."

Jesus stepped out of the Shank's home and crossed the rear patio shortly after 2:00 A.M. and walked out of Phoenix in a southeast direction.

Jesus periodically rested, but abstained from food and water throughout the duration of his desert experience. His time was spent in prayer and meditation interspersed with long walks to nowhere in particular.

* * * *

Bart and Andrew settled up with one another and made correct change for Simon, laying a fountain drink, grinders and fries at the edge of his desk. "Simon, are you going to stop long enough to eat?" asked Andrew.

"Forget it," said Bart, "the boy is still trying to net minnows."

"Yeah, we'll see who's crying when I take my little minnow bucket to the bank this Friday," said Simon as he removed a headset and rubbed eyes that had been frozen to a monitor for hours. "Blasted market has been locked up for weeks! I wish it would just break and send me some early retirement."

"Simon, I told you we should have stayed in commodities with the real men," Andrew added.

"Commodities!" Bart had to repeat himself since his last bite was going down when the word came up, "commodities—do you want me to choke on this sandwich? Another month in soybeans and you'd been delivering pizzas for a living."

"You know Bart, you're absolutely disgusting when you chew and try to be funny at the same time. You remind me of a clown trying to blow bubbles with peanut butter. Now you two get out of my office before I call some government bureau and file harassment charges," said Simon.

"Now, now Simon," said Bart with friendly sarcasm, "what has upset us so today? All the big fish off spawning somewhere?"

"Knock it off Bart, I'm in no mood for it," said Simon firmly. "I've been cold calling until I'm blue in the face, dropped fifty bucks on a bum list from a rookie scam artist who is probably sucking down cold ones over at the sports bar while I support his habit. I'm serious guys, I've got to find a way out of this."

Andrew, who had heard the same moans and groans many times before changed the subject and asked, "Well Simon, what did you think of Bart's story? I mean Jesus, the baptism, Jack's role, and everything?"

"It's him Simon," Bart affirmed.

"Yeah, yeah, I've thought about what you said," pushing his food aside and lighting up a cigar. "Hey, pull that door Drew," Simon said, then continued, "Sure it fits, but what about your friend Jack. Was he into something over his head. I mean I know they hate Jews, but we don't pay our friendly government servants to go about arresting law abiding citizens for no reason."

"These weren't your typical friendly government servants," said Bart rubbing sore ribs. "So, what do you want me to do, just jump on the fire truck and parade through town with you?" asked Simon.

"You make up your own mind Simon. I say it all fits. Jack showed me first hand how the writings point to him. Are you coming to the meeting Simon?" asked Andrew, "it's tonight at 7:00. Here's the phone number if you want to come. Just tell them you're my brother, they can give you directions."

"Well, I've got a client waiting on me," said Bart, "Can you see the tip of that rod bending?" as he simulated reeling in a fish and ribbing Simon.

"By the way, Jesus is out of town," said Andrew.

"He's probably backing off," Simon torted.

"No way," snapped Andrew, "he'll be along when he's ready."

* * * *

After spending several days walking between I-10 and the San Pedro, he crossed the river and passed north of Mammoth through the Aravaipa wilderness and looked to Safford. "Whoever penned, 'The desert is an ocean with its life underground,' had certainly spent time here," Jesus thought to himself. Cholla cactus fixed like ocean coral stood beside the brittlebush and ocotillos, that looked to be craving the mention of such waters. The land was teaming with life, no less than one would find in a forest out east, just harder to see. Small finch played before Jesus, where he stopped to rest on red dirt. He lifted his eyes and caught glimpse of an eagle gliding gracefully through the midmorning air. Locking onto a colorful ribbon that pushed gently along the floor, she raced through the aisles of a distant department with unsheathed knives that glistened under the fluorescents. Slamming them down on the counter, she clutched the bolt, and stepping it off with a cloth rule, she judged its length. The seamstress might have cut a new pattern but the stirring by Jesus sent her aloft to work elsewhere.

Three more days journey brought Jesus to an evening in Klondyke. He knelt in the Aravaipa Creek as the sun began to set and splashed water onto a face still pulsating with heat. A ladder back woodpecker seeking refuge lit nearby. "Tov," Jesus uttered while admiring it's color and characteristic movements. His fast and surroundings spoke to him of dependency and his intestines cried to be filled with even some sand. There are no opportunities in the desert but there are also few distractions. One's inadequacies are brilliantly mirrored by equally abject resources. Jesus' eyes followed the markings of the beautiful bird that hung on a limb like a framed piece of art, when suddenly something black backlit the picture. Jesus refocused upon the breast of a magnificent stallion saddled by an older man with a kindly voice.

"Say mister, you're going to get cool in this canyon tonight with those wet trousers. I'd be happy to carry you up to a ridge."

"I'd be grateful for the lift," Jesus said in a confident manner while looking into the horseman's eyes. Jesus willingly climbed onto the back of the horse and held with his hands the lavishly upholstered rim of the upper rear saddle.

After the horse crossed the creek bed, the man asked, "So, what's your name? You on some kind of survival training? I don't believe I've seen you in these parts before?"

"My name is Jesus."

"Jesus," the horseman repeated but not for clarification. "Jesus, now that's a nice name," a sinister voice fumed from the same mouth. "It's been hotter than a firecracker all day, hasn't it? And I'll bet you're starved to death. You've been out here forty days and squandered away Yom Kippur in a desert," he said while laughing hideously. In a moment, the desert's tranquility was invaded by a blowing wind that brought a cold front into the region out of nowhere. The storm began shaking the ground with lightening bolts and claps of thunder. As a blinding rain fell upon them, a large pack of black dogs—sleek, oily, and ravenous ran ahead of them in tall grass that bent in the wind and was unnatural for the area. "Fools. The stupid fools don't know anything about hell, but they'll find out soon enough," he said, holding the brim of his hat. "You know, if you're the big Texan you say you are, you could make pork tenderloin of these cliffs."

"It is recorded," Jesus said, "It takes more than just food to keep man alive—he must digest every word that comes out of God's mouth."

"Well, Jesus, I hate to rain on your little picnic, but I'm not here to review the decrees, talk about theological tossed salad or any other cerebral pickle loaf. I want you out of my way," he said matter of factly through seething rage.

"The title deed to this place is in the hand of the landlord," Jesus said.

In that moment the horse was goaded, and it lifted its head in a shriek that sounded like something prehistoric; and as its mane fell back to its place, their dialogue continued atop the Sears Tower. Night had already fallen upon Chicago. Jesus dismounted the beast while the dark horse walked about the building's lid pawing loose stone and snorting at one he instinctively knew to be an enemy. Visibility was clear for miles in any direction. The man made lights and travel arteries appeared to Jesus as a flat, one dimensional work.

"It's in the record, it's in the record," said the evil one sarcastically, now hanging upside down like a bat from one of the tower's pinnacle uprights, "it's also in the record that certain angels," he stopped and spit mucus to the roof below, then continued, "care about your very hangnails. If you're really the son of God, then step off this ledge and prove it. Michael or some other rookie will catch you before you drop an inch."

"It's also written," said Jesus, "that one should not trifle with God."

"Alright, enough of this moralizing. Listen to me! I'm going to cut through the ages and lay out my terms. You fall down and worship me and everything you see on both sides of this sphere will be transferred to you immediately. Don't be a fool, Jesus," he said in blinded rage and convinced that he had persuaded him. "Think of the glory," as he dropped down to his side extending his hands to greet him.

"Get lost, Satan! For it is written: you will worship the Lord your God and attend to him alone."

In the blink of an eye, Jesus stood beneath a clear Arizona sky, filled with stars that shouted back at a horseman who galloped away screaming, "let the fool pay!"

A familiar voice came from behind him, when men approached and confessed, "Lord, we are at your disposal. The next time we meet," said a mighty one, "I'll bind him with a chain and reduce that nag to dog food."

"This is just the beginning," Jesus answered them, "and there can be no interference. Everything will be cared for in time. Let's move out of here. I want to be in Chicago by Sabbath."

It was nearly 9:00 A.M. when Jesus rang the door bell for the second time. After a moment, he went to the rear of the house and located an entry key under the grill. He let himself inside and went immediately to the refrigerator and found a piece of fruit. While savoring the juices of a sweet apple, Jesus loaded a machine with soiled laundry, began the cycle and returned to the refrigerator and pulled out left over vegetables that he slapped in the microwave. Before the minute timer had signaled the time spent, Jesus opened the door and made short work emptying the contents. After a hot shower and double shampoo, Jesus cleaned out some remaining tuna salad, filled the dishwasher, then left his hosts two crisp twenty dollar bills with a note: Terry and Carol, I'm sorry you missed me—smiles. I'm good for the rain check, have a date to the golden arches on me. I'll be in touch. Love, Jesus.

Jesus stopped at a truck stop in Bolingbrook just before twilight on Saturday morning for a shower, change of clothes and last fill up before completing the final leg home to Chicago's north suburbs.

"Would you like a doughnut with that coffee?" asked the clerk.

"Yes, I believe I will. Can I buy you one?" he asked in reply.

"No thanks, I'm on a diet," returning his change.

"Yeah, well drink lots of fluids," he said, nodding good-bye. Jesus left the Tristate at Willow and carried 45 to the corner of Dundee where he stopped for a paper and coffee. Major headlines continued to carry details of the developing story in which the Veteran's Hospital, Hines as well as the Shriner's Crippled Children's Hospital on Oak Park were both nearly leveled and many lost their lives as the result of simultaneous midnight blasts that shook area suburbs. The entire Country was enraged by the merciless, outrageous and cowardice act.

A beautiful young Hindu girl offered Jesus a refill as he finished the news and turned briefly to the religious section. Listings and advertisements of virtually every flavor were pasted to the page making appeal to the conscience of the masses to join them in self discovery of one form or another. The Hub was far and away the most dominate organization but was itself splintered into a handful of factions that were spread worldwide.

Jesus rolled up the paper and set it aside with a tip. He arrived at the synagogue in Buffalo Grove a few minutes before 10:00 A.M. and surprised his mother who was walking ahead to shacharit and conversing with a friend.

"Jesus!" Mary said with pride, "Aren't you a pleasant surprise. Now you've lost some weight since you've been away."

"So good to see you, too, mother," kissing her on the cheek.

"Jesus, this is my friend, Florence. She just transferred here from New York and is staying with me while she seeks a place of her own."

"Hello, Jesus," Florence greeted, "I've heard many wonderful things about you. I must admit, your mother has been such a treasure that I haven't searched terribly hard for that apartment of my own."

"It sounds like the company has been good for both of you," Jesus observed. As they approached the entrance a familiar usher greeted Jesus with a beaming smile and asked if he would be willing to assist in the Sabbath readings.

Jesus sat with Mary and Florence while candles were lit and seats filled to near capacity. The ark rest against the east wall between Daniel's glass where the Torah was being lifted from its place. Following a word of welcome and song, an attendant invited Jesus forward to read from the holy Scroll. Jesus ignored many of the traditions, moved to the right of the baal koreh, found his place in the prophet Isaiah where he read of an anointed one who would preach the gospel to the poor. The Scripture spoke of one who would release captives, provide sight to the blind, set free the discouraged and speak boldly of God's favor. After Jesus completed the reading, he pulled a stool from the musician's corner, placed it at center stage and sat down. For a few moments he allowed his eyes to slowly scan the synagogue as he surveyed the faces of strangers as well as families that he had known from the days of his youth. While remarks were being whispered among friends in the audience, praising his eloquence and rehearsing short vignettes about miraculous stories that circulated mostly around north Chicago, Jesus broke the silence with several sentences directed at their complacency.

"Today," Jesus began, "this Scripture has been fulfilled right here in this room. But hasn't it become proverbial, 'doctor come home?' Many of you are wanting to see the signs and wonders you've only heard about. I tell you the truth, people always honor a prophet except in his own neighborhood." As the room began to churn with foaming waves, Jesus continued, "Let me tell you something. There were many desperate widows during the time of Elijah when there was widespread famine and the skies were not permitted to rain, but he paid a visit to only one of them and she was from way out of state. You might be interested to know as well that there were many who suffered incurable disease during the days of Elisha, but only one was healed and he happened to be a…"

Jesus' remarks were cut off by the angry cries of the audience, some of whom were beginning to rise from their seats.

"We've changed your diapers, and you would come back and shame us!" cried a woman from the near front. Others moved toward him shouting that he should be thrown out. As angry worshipers pressed the front and knocking down the curtain covering aron hakodesh, Jesus backed to the rear of the building through an exit to the outside. He stood on the deck overlooking a ravine that ran along the back of the property among a throng who shouted, "throw the ungrateful traitor over the rail."

"Make it look like an accident," another whispered while wrenching a loose piece of pine rail with his hands. Jesus, turned into the frenzied crowd and walked casually through their midst back through the exit and down a corridor that led to the side lot. He drove to Fort Sheridan, drew out a cotton hooded sweater from the back of the van and found a place to sit under a grove of trees next to the golf course overlooking the lake and spent the remainder of the day in solitude.

Pretense, he rolled the word over in his mind before taking a nap. They pretend that all is fine, that there is no ache in their souls and that relationships satisfy. They pretend that their lives are in tact and that they are pleased with God. They pretend to be their brother's keeper, but are scared to death of one another. The only thing they are authentic about is their hypocrisy. Now there's a category in which they take home all the Oscars, he continued meditating. It's a small wonder that the synagogue has become an event, rather than people who celebrate history's greatest events.

Jesus laid on his side and fell off to sleep under the gaze of sea gulls that nervously fluttered about the beach sorting drift and looking for anything edible.

Chapter 5

The temperature at the Waukegan bank read 15 degrees, but it felt like 15 below with the cutting wind careening off the lake. Jesus turned off Belvidere onto Jackson in hopes of picking up an efficiency for a day or two.

"Been here before sailor?" she snarled. It was a private owned complex of less than twenty units, and she lived overhead with a retired Naval officer whom she supported with a slim income.

"No, this is my first visit," said Jesus.

"You impressed with his can collection?" she asked, being aware of the conspicuous sight but unconscious of the odor that filled the little office. "The jock would have been smart to buy stock in Old Style. He gets all kinds of exercise walking the path he's worn between the couch and refrigerator—double time during Monday night football. The slack back puts down three to four cartons a day between ESPN and the girly channels, then sleeps until it's time for another bottle." The empty cans stacked in drums at the end of the counter gave evidence that it was time to pay a visit to the aluminum recycling warehouse.

Crushing out another cigarette, she began a tirade that sounded like it was memorized, drawn from recruit pick-up day, and deeply intentional. "I'll need your service number and the name of your company commander. You people think you can come in here on Fridays, pull sinks off the walls and swing from light fixtures with your girl friends all weekend! Listen to me, I've already got word from your brass," she said leaning over the counter for emphasis; "That kind of drill is history. You trash the place and I trash the Commander with court documents and he trashes your weekend. You got the arithmetic on that sailor?"

"Sorry ma'am, but I'm not in the military. I'm just looking for a place to spend a night or two."

"Yea, well how many times have you told that one?" as she looked again at his short locks. I've heard about all the scuttlebutt, sea gibberish and prattle-bull the Navy has to offer. Let me see some I.D. or you can swim back to post with the rest of those squid for the night," she rudely quipped referring to a group of young men and women crossing in front of her on the side walk outside. The woman gathered Jesus' drivers license and bank check in hands scarred from previous bouts with Popeye. There wasn't any real doubt in Jesus' mind who the reigning champ was in this weight division. "Buffalo Grove huh?" she said with apparent doubt. "This better check out son. I've got one savage collections agent you won't want to meet. Her name is, Mo. She's got the jaws of a pipe vise with four stout legs; she's always hungry and stands about this tall," measuring with her free hand to about her waist without lifting the fountain pen with the other. "And let me have a plate of plastic for damage deposit."

"Anything else?" Jesus asked as he collected his I.D., "I'm going down to the laundry in a bit; can I pick anything up for you while I'm out?" The woman was silent as she pulled a key from a drawer, skipped it across the counter top and excused herself without a word.

Jesus dropped a few personal items off at a room that was grossly overdue for just some basic cleaning, locked up and drove to a nearby restaurant for soup and salad. Afterwards he made a visit to a Laundromat where he caught up on some reading while playing cake walk with patrons who timed and positioned their baskets near washers and clothing dryers that were in scarce supply.

"Look 'boot,'" announced a broad shouldered salt who looked to have some years but no rank. "The flipping frosted deluxe dryer number four has my name on it," he said while drawing from a butt and slamming his fist above the glass for emphasis. The sailor's eyes were nearly shut as they strained to shield the smoke rising from a dangling cigarette that danced between his lips and syllables, then concluded, "and if you step in front of me again, I'll dribble you're young civilian links through those doors to the lot outside."

"Sorry about the mix up," Jesus said, "I guess I got in a bit of a hurry." He wished to wrap up the weeklies and be at the synagogue before the sun set. The big man with tattoos up and down each arm stepped up to number four and started unloading damp clothing onto the floor. The bear looked to be tearing away bark and reaching for comb. His T-shirt was a little short and jeans hung low, revealing cleavage in the rear and a belly that was regularly satisfied. One of the last items snatched out was a hand woven sweater lovingly crafted by his mother. Jesus often wore the covering and cherished it as a gift. The man laughed like an immature adolescent and placed it around his neck while jeering at Jesus. Hazard was flashing in Jesus' mind while he considered how to diffuse a ticking bomb.

"Should have figured—a Jew freak. Always stepping ahead to get ahead. Look Jew boy," raising his right hand and slapping Jesus across the face with his left, "caught you looking didn't I? Do you want to see it again?" he scowled. Jesus balanced himself on one knee and adrenaline flowed through his veins while his eyes scouted a convenient exit. Surprisingly his adversary backed away and he quickly gathered his belongings in a towel and proceeded to the door amidst sheep too immobilized with fear or apathy to intervene. As Jesus reached the door, his sweater fell to his feet—a matted ball that had been flung from the rear. "Go on, Jew boy," he laughed and raved, "go get your daddy!"

"Forgive them Father," Jesus whispered, picking up his sweater and walking to the van.

The next morning Jesus drove to the Temple of Aaron Synagogue where he had been invited to teach. He arrived early and greeted Rabbi Samuel Hirsch upon entering. While they exchanged pleasantries in the narthex of the building, the choir wrapped up a brief rehearsal of L'Ha Dodi and others as doors opened inviting worshippers to empty the lobby. Rabbi Hirsch completed a reading from the Torah and invited Jesus forward when he was immediately confronted by a man whose eyes bulged from their sockets; he exploded with assaulting remarks.

"I know you," he screamed and laughed with shrill tones that hurt the ear, "you've come here to kill us—the separate one of God!" Jesus stepped down from the platform smartly with a foreboding look that ordered the man's attention. Many in the audience were physically shaken and their sensibilities shocked by the circus like atmosphere that had invaded their hallowed house. "Go back to Buffalo Grove where you belong," the man insisted while urinating in his pants, thus defiling the entire service.

"Shut up and release him," Jesus ordered; and with one brisk command, the man well known in the community was cast to the floor, momentarily wreathing before he let out a shriek and lay still as a corpse. "Help him up," Jesus said, and a couple of men assisted him to a chair as he began with some fresh movements

A synagogue official tried to speak over the chatter of the crowd who were reeling from the demonstration of power that had just been displayed before their eyes. Having no luck, he cleared pedestrian traffic and provided Jesus passage down a corridor on the side of the building. Jesus was visited that afternoon by several people who learned of his whereabouts and was only able to leave Waukegan after great resistance.

"Please stay with us," an elderly couple asked as he loaded his van near the door to his unit. We want to hear you teach next Sabbath," they insisted.

"I have other communities to visit," Jesus said, "I'm here for the purpose of spreading the most wonderful news—it's all about the kingdom of God!"

Jesus checked out of his room a day early, dropped off the key and asked his host to keep the extra day's rate already charged to him. "Have you been down to Lake Forest lately?" Jesus asked.

"Now who in the scratch can afford to get a cup of ice water in Lake Forest," she said, and breaking a wrinkled smile for the first time.

"You ever been romanced, Lucy?" Jesus asked, having caught her name from the shouting overhead.

"You're way too young for me slim." Lucy continued loitering with a dust cloth and worrying over shelves that hadn't been disturbed in years. Jesus had struck a cord deep inside her breast that ached and longed to be strummed by someone who cared. Years pent up in an asylum filled with routine madness had conditioned her not to expect much from life.

"I just wanted to put a thought in your head," ignoring the remark, "maybe we could take the few bucks, split a plate at this place in Deerfield—by the way, they serve awesome Latte," as he pushed the name to her on a piece of scrap. "Then maybe drive up to Lake Forest, put on some extra wraps and enjoy a peaceful walk through the neighborhood together and over to the Lake. Those folks have plenty of money and many of them are the finest neighbors you'd find anywhere, but they don't own the most important things. You know, Lucy," he continued conversation with a woman who was trying to walk; he could see steps coming alive in her eyes, "ownership is small. Think of the things in life you can enjoy and when you're done you don't have to clean it, wax it, repair it, lock it up and defend it."

"Well, that's quite a mouthful sailor," she said nervously, not knowing quite how to respond.

"Lucy, I already told you that I'm not a sailor," Jesus said chuckling and trying to entice her to come out. "Am I tattooed from head to toe? Is the back of my neck that red?" She too began to laugh at Jesus' playfulness. "You know as well as I do that those guys are legendary for the sewage that flows out of their mouths. I got an ear full from one of their finest just last night. Said he was going to pick me up by my ankles and use me for a posthole digger if I didn't get out of dryer number four. You would have thought I'd bunked down in his rack, drank his last beer or committed some other sacrilege. Lucy, I think the guy lived on a diet of 'woof-cookies' sprinkled with gun powder—he sure had a mean bark. He even threatened to dribble me out the door for a slam dunk. He was big enough, but I don't think he could reach the rim with me so long as that spare is wrapped around his waist."

"You come back Jesus," she said leaning over the counter and bouncing like Jell-O with laughter, "I'll remember you. I've got another unit or two over here on the other side that's in better shape than where you were last night," and the hysteria started again as she just couldn't put away the images just drawn and how pathetically real they fit her own husband. Jesus waited in the parking lot for a woman nearly twice his age who was churning inside like a sixteen–year–old.

After several minutes he thought to pull away when he saw a small 'CLOSED' sign, red letters and all caps, go up on the entrance window. Jesus stepped out of the van and was quick to open the door on the passenger side the way a bell hop serves a woman of prestige. He then ran to escort Lucy to an afternoon of relaxation and discovery. Jesus dropped Lucy off back at her place before dark and encouraged her to stay alive with some final remarks.

"It's like you said, Lucy, 'he'll either shape up or ship out.'"

"I sure hope he shapes up. I know this sounds stupid, but I loved him once. He was a good man, but what am I saying, you've already heard all this," said Lucy.

"All glory fades, Lucy. Scientists stumbled upon entropy some years ago and put it into a formula of sorts which they call the second law of thermo-dynamics. Everything we looked at today is at some stage of deterioration. And unfortunately human relationships undergo a similar process. Do you remember the early years with your husband Lucy? You sat down somewhere to an absolutely beautiful and romantic dinner, maybe a banquet the Navy hosted, the finest in dinning, no kids, the conversation was sweet and tender; he asked if he could butter you another roll. You remember don't you, Lucy?" asked Jesus without a hint of manipulation. "In moments like that," Jesus continued, "folks feel like they are experiencing heaven on earth. But Moses came down from Sinai and found that the people had quickly corrupted themselves, I'll descend somewhere and find faithless followers," which she didn't quite understand, "and you left the diner only to rise in the morning with bad breath, kids to raise, bills to pay and everything needing to be fixed." Lucy may not have been pretty by human standards, but she had a soft heart beneath a hardened mask and an inquisitive mind that delighted Jesus.

"So what do people do when the glory fades," she asked, "I mean, you already said that stuff would fade. How does one handle those kind of let downs?"

"Some folks like your husband give up. They say, 'I've trawled this cement out for the last time, now I'm going to mess things up real good. I'm going to run through it before the crowd does,' and that can get pretty ugly. I call it a desperate but willful effort to destroy one's own soul."

"O.K.," said Lucy, "I've seen three clowns do this routine, but why is it so purposeful?"

Jesus related, "Because most folks don't know how to handle sorrow. Don't watch the sun set—pull the shade! Don't watch the candle flicker—blow it out! Don't read the epilogue—rip it out! You see fading glory is like driving home from that wonderful date. It makes you anticipate when it will happen again, and since people do not want to see glory fade, they choose not to anticipate it. I'll grow dead and angry they admit or insist that my spouse do something humanly impossible like freeze the frame, and they'll pay if they don't!"

"Well, I don't understand all of that, Jesus, but I think I get most of it. I'm just sorry life has to be this way," she said.

"Sorrow and suffering are things most folks don't understand too well," Jesus said concluding the conversation. "Rather than live with seasons of sorrow and grow closer to God through suffering, we demand heaven on earth. We insist that God deal with us on our terms. Cain was the father of that philosophy."

"Well, Jesus, you're a gentleman and a scholar," said Lucy extending her hand to shake.

"And you, Lucy, are quite the lady," Jesus said admiringly while kissing her scarred knuckles.

"Goodbye, Jesus, and thanks for a wonderful afternoon."

"The pleasure was all mine," Jesus admitted while walking her to the door.

"You come back around when you're up this way. We've got lots that we could talk about."

"Yes," said Jesus departing, "and kick up those heels in the meantime." Jesus pulled away from the units and headed back toward Chicago.

Weeks later, Jesus placed a phone call to Peter and Jill's place whose number was drawn from a list previously given him by Andrew.

"Hello," greeted a soft feminine voice on the other end of the line.

"Hi," my name is Jesus; is Simon or Jill available?"

"This is Jill speaking, what a wonderful surprise Jesus! Are you going to be able to join us for the meeting—I mean your meeting this evening?" she asked.

"Yes, I'd very much like to be there. My plans have changed and I'm available to be on hand. Jill, let me thank you now for the preparations you've made. Andrew has already told me about your enthusiasm." Jill related specific directions to Jesus, got off the phone and returned to the back of the house to assist Simon's mother who had become ill.

Jesus made his way south on 94 to the Edens and then over to Evanston to the house of Simon and Jill. Simon answered the door and invited Jesus into their home.

"Here, let me take that coat," said Simon feeling a little coy which was totally out of character, and pulling a hanger from the entry foyer. Jesus placed a shopping bag on the floor and removed his coat and scarf, handing them to his host.

"Now, these must be the two young men Andrew spoke of," Jesus said, pointing to Simon's boys.

"Yes," said Simon, "this is David and Jonathan. I have to tell you, they love one another like their name sakes. I credit Jill with that side of their development."

"Well David and Jonathan, let's see what we've got here in this bag." The three and six- year-old's eyes lit up with fire at the hint of a gift, and they didn't waste any time crawling into Jesus' lap who had already taken a seat on the sofa. "What's coming up this month?" asked Jesus.

"Hanukkah," said David, "But, Jonathan doesn't know how to say it yet." Jonathan leaped from Jesus' lap and ran to the kitchen, retrieving a colored picture of a menorah and food items from the refrigerator door, then raced back and took up his former position. The name Jonathan was scratched across the top of a page brought home from synagogue. The complicated lines of hieroglyphics could only be deciphered by dad and mom.

"We're pretty sure Jonathan will one day work for the Pentagon in areas of cryptology," remarked Simon.

"Yes indeed," Jesus said admiringly, "this is real special work." Jesus let Jonathan hold his art piece while David assisted in drawing out packages from the bag. The first item out was a little heavy for David, but he managed to raise the bottle of wine from the floor and pass it off to dad.

"Excellent taste, Jesus," said Simon, as he examined the label of the white chardonnay, "and now for the good stuff, right boys?"

"Yeah," they said almost together, while touching their top and bottom teeth in a little nervous chatter.

"What is it, Sir?" David asked.

"Oh, you're going to have to tell me," said Jesus mimicking his Aunt Liz.

"Oh cool," said David, which always brought Jonathan to a point of attention, "Lego's!"

"Well, not hardly" said dad, who had stooped low to help interpret things. "Wow," said Simon, "Jesus, did you make these connecting blocks? These are really neat. You had to have put many hours into a project like this."

"They do require some time," Jesus admitted, "but I enjoy making them. They were taken from a pattern handed down by my mom's parents. I can't tell you how many sets I've made. Look boys, Jesus continued, "If you share and put both sets together, you will have just enough for a house and barn. Mom and dad can finish it out with toy animals of your choosing."

Jesus rose to his feet as Jill entered the living room and introduced herself. "Jesus, it is so good to finally meet you," extending her hand, "Bart has already shared so much about you and we can't wait to hear first hand of your plans. Isn't that right dear?" Simon was basically drifting along at his wife's whim and it was not hard to detect his air of disinterest.

"Yeah, Jesus," Drew tells me things about you that are just right out of this world. You probably know more about his acquaintances and the meetings than I do. This Jack guy they recently put away is one of his closest friends. Do you know anything about him?"

"Yes. Plenty," said Jesus.

"Well, the whole thing sounds a little bazaar to me, but he's my brother and so I cut him a little slack."

"What do you do for others?" asked Jesus rather seriously. Simon was feeling a little uncomfortable in his own living room and was relieved to hear the door bell chime.

"Jesus," Jill whispered, "never mind Simon, he's a little edgy about me hosting this meeting. Did Simon tell you that his mom is here with us for a few days. She flew in from Minneapolis yesterday and wanted to help with the reception and all, but she came down with a fever that I'm afraid has put her in bed for the evening."

"Do you mind if I see her?" asked Jesus.

"No, of course not," said Jill, "let me just pull this dish off of the stove, or maybe Simon could show you back. Simon," Jill hollered over the guests and gaining his audience, "can you show Jesus back to see Mom?" It was hard to know which Simon was more reluctant to do, pull off from door duty and assist Jesus or ignore Jesus and keep up the pasted grin at the foyer.

"Yes, I'm right along," he said as Bart stepped into the house and pointed at Jesus with excitement. "Hey Bart," growled Simon, "You mind assisting these folks while I introduce Jesus to my Mom? Jill has gone to lu lu land and forgotten all about the fact that Mom's sick. She definitely doesn't need any guests right now."

"O.K. Simon, I've got you covered," said Bart in a discouraged voice. "The guy is always peeved about something," he thought to himself.

Meanwhile, Simon tapped on the door to the guest suite, "Mom, can I offer you some water?" he asked through the door. "There's someone here, Jill," he paused but an instant, "I mean Jill and I would like for you to meet."

"Certainly," her voice broke with a cough.

"Mom, this is Jesus you've heard about," said Simon as he and Jesus stepped into the room. "Jesus, this is mom, Miriam."

"I'm pleased to meet you, Miriam," said Jesus.

"Oh, the pleasure is all mine. I've heard all about you. Please forgive my laziness, I don't know the last time I felt this bad."

"I'm sorry," said Jesus.

"Mom, it's about time for another round of meds," said Simon, "let me help you tilt your head and see if you can get a few more tablets down." Before Simon could open the bottle, Jesus had moved from the foot of the bed to along the side and took her limp arm in his hand.

Simon was offended at Jesus' bedside manner; but before he could formulate a sentence of tactful protestation, Jesus remarked, "Miriam, I'm going to go back out front with the other guests. Your fever has been removed. Jill could use your help in the kitchen and I know how much you enjoy serving in that way." Miriam felt immediate relief and as Jesus stepped into the hall she told Simon that she was ready to get up from the bed.

"But, Mom," Simon said, "you had a 102 degree temperature just 15 minutes ago! You're not going anywhere. Now let me get a thermometer."

"Honey, I feel like a new woman," she mumbled with her tongue holding the mercury stick.

"I don't even believe this," said Simon, "and this is the only thermometer in the house. This can't be right. It says you are right on the pickle, and I must say you feel as cool as a cucumber."

Jesus arrived back at the front of the house and mixed with guests who had been invited to an informational meeting designed to offer exposure to his ministry and how others might become involved. As folks took seats around vegetable trays and drinks, Bart gathered a note or two of introduction and was about to rise to his feet when Simon, who stood with the overflow in the adjoining foyer, announced that Andrew had been delayed.

In his absence, Simon opened his mouth and began relating his own interpretation of the event. "Drew called earlier," he began, "and said he would be along as soon as possible. Now many of you already know Jesus or have perhaps heard about him by now. Drew invited you all here in hopes of figuring out a way to organize a movement that would best facilitate Jesus' business plan."

Simon looked into the faces of men and women who were perplexed by the sudden shift in ministry direction. Drew had been previously advising a very different approach during earlier times of meeting. While taking momentary pause, Simon's mind spooled off the five M's that he felt marked most religious upstarts. He just never dreamed that one would birth in his own home. "You begin with a *man*," he thought, "who dreams about a *movement* and so he concocts a plan to push the *mission*, while attracting a team to complete the *ministry* only in time to leave a *monument*. "Drew won't tell you this," Simon lifted his voice, "but these kind of things require a lot of money. Contributions for this fund raiser can be left with Bart."

Bart was shifting in his seat and wondering how to pull up the stick on a craft that was obviously out of control when a demon possessed woman stood up and startled everyone by pointing at Jesus and repeatedly shouting, "You are the Son of God. You are the Son of God. You are certainly the Son of God!"

"Be silent," Jesus commanded her and she fell to her seat as though her feet had been kicked out from beneath her; and while her lips continued to move, no sound was uttered. Hair stood up on the back of Simon's neck as Carol, a familiar family friend, related to Jesus that she had recently passed out and was picked up for dead following a lapse with her insulin. Jesus extended his hand, touched Carol and assured her that her pancreas was now totally functional. Another man was inspired to relate his all consuming bout with dialysis. Jesus stood up and approached Arnold, while another woman whispered to her friend that she was going home to get her husband who was prepared to undergo radiation treatment in the next few days. Simon stepped out of the foyer and pulled Jill into the kitchen.

"Jill, this is getting entirely out of hand," said Simon. "What kind of scam is this? Who's holding the account on this operation? There's big money in this, but I can't put up with the showboating."

"Simon, will you ever believe?" Jill tenderly asked. "This wasn't Drew's idea. I'm the one who organized this reception and the last thing any of us intended was for it to turn into some kind of a fund raiser. Sweetheart, at least look at him. Please listen to him."

"Look, I'm going to make a few calls, this is already getting a lot later than you said."

"Good things are happening, Simon. Please stay."

Simon grumbled, "Wait until the wine and infatuation wears off. You know how unstable some of those people are and they're as gullible as a barefoot mountain woman with a satellite dish. Bring out the next item for sale! No, I'm going to the office for the night!" Simon walked out the back door of his house mumbling to himself, "this guy is going to screw around and mess up my entire life."

* * * *

At daybreak, Jesus left a reluctant crowd and drove to the City. He surfaced at Grant Park near Buckingham Fountain around lunch time and began walking a tight circle and teaching in a style like one's professor. He had a very definite greed about his subject but was controlled and relied primarily upon the force of vocabulary which was understandable but daring. It was an unusually warm day for the end of February. Several joggers ran along Lakeshore Drive. Mounted park police were wary but kind and nonintrusive. Simon and Andrew cabbed over from Michigan Avenue by Drew's furtive efforts and grabbed dogs and a cylinder of drink from a mobile vendor. As they walked along the park's perimeter and discussed business, Simon lifted an ear and turned his brother closer to the messenger with a slight nod of his head the way a trained horse is guided with loose reins.

"For crying out loud, does this guy ever get tired!" Simon exclaimed, and surprised to find Jesus lecturing a sizable crowd who sat on the grass. Jill said the house didn't clear until early this morning. Drew, I thought I'd seen it all—even been to an all night drug store, but this guy can push a string, rewind history and back down the E.P.A. I'm not kidding. The man's got an intolerance for sickness and sin that would make the A.C.L.U. look like one huge concession! You'd had to have seen my living room for yourself."

"Yeah," said Andrew ignoring Simon's skepticism, "he's one person who might actually work harder than you." The two men moved closer until the audio was clear but stayed on the wings.

"Crisis creates desperation in people," Jesus spoke on, "and desperate people often do wildly reckless, even irrational things. Stories from war fronts of past generations abound. Chesty Puller, who won several medals for valor including the Navy Cross, was once surrounded by enemy forces and isolated in a Korean reservoir. What was his encouragement to his men? 'The enemy is to our north, they are closing in from the south, we are flanked by other red units and the sea. Men, they're not going to get away this time!' "In another vein," Jesus continued, "desperate business deals are struck in which either party puts on a poker face, no expression, just intense perspiration, stakes are higher than they've ever been, one can cut the air—somebody's going for broke. Then in a moment of interlude, even a criminal prays; he looks at the market, considers his creditors, his obligations, it's now or never and he leaps. One common thread about desperate acts of this category is that it feels like mission impossible because one can never be sure of the outcome. Just throw everything and all that you have into the venture, risk absolutely everything to meet the crisis and hope for day. Sounds foolish doesn't it? What if I told you that this is exactly what God requires of each one of you?"

Simon began a second dog and found it convenient to visit a nearby trash barrel and put a little more distance between himself and the speaker but not out of ear shot. "There is a profound crisis associated with God's coming kingdom," Jesus related. "Keep your trainers laced up and your lights on high beam. You people know how to interpret the weather—you've got a local Doppler radar, but why do you struggle to figure out the state of the times? You're confronted with a threatening storm, you will soon appear before a judge and there is danger of condemnation and imprisonment; yes indeed, seize the day! Friends, take stock of the situation and face the facts—when the tempest strikes, I must live."

Jesus lectured on for another 15 or 20 minutes while Andrew and Simon listened from a perch to the story of a man in upper management who wasted his employer's material resources. Jesus described the man's boss as merciful but firm enough to cut him from his hire. The manager's own silence at dismissal underlined his guilt.

"Boy, he sure has an interesting teaching style," Andrew remarked to the mummy standing next to him. "Some of the turns in this story have been absolutely fascinating. Simon, maybe you should get on the phone and dial up some accounts, cut them a handsome deal with no loads under the auspices of our firm so that when they let you go, somebody will buy you lunch. You can take credit for the reductions and just tell them that the market's been so good we wanted to just spread around a little of the butter," he said with a hint of derision.

The wind brought Jesus' words near again, "The boss has basically two alternatives. He can call his clients and tell them that the transactions were all a mistake, that the broker was fired and what he did was unauthorized. However, the client's joy will turn to anger and they are likely to begin doing business with a different firm. His only option is to allow the celebration between this trader and the investors to continue.

You see, friends, the clever knave stepped off the ledge. He took a risk. He went for broke. He bet on the character of his employer and won."

"Yes, that was real clever," admitted Simon, "but he doesn't work for the same Pharaoh that drives us. More bricks, more bricks. What are we building, Drew?"

"Simon, now that's a question that deserves an answer!"

As Simon and Andrew took steps to return to the office, Jesus' concluding remarks could be heard chasing after them, "and if the widow got what she wanted from a shark who was presiding over bankruptcy court, don't you think God can be counted on? And if the man got a table spread from his friend at the most inconvenient of times, don't you think God can be counted on? And if this crook returned from a point of no return by risking everything on the character of his employer, don't you think God will come through for you when you need him most desperately?"

As a cab slowed to receive the two men, Simon remarked, "C'mon, let's get on back. I'll be until midnight wrapping up work the way it is—this market trend is the pits."

About 2 P.M. that same day, Jesus stepped past a receptionist's station that was temporarily abandoned and proceeded down an interior path to Simon's office. "Hey, Jesus!" Simon said in a startled voice, "I didn't get a light from the front. Say that was quite an interesting message you delivered this morning," he continued while wiping beads of perspiration from his brow and returning focus to the monitor before him. "So Jill tells me that you all were real early getting away from the pad—I mean like 6 A.M. early. Oh, here, grab a seat. This office is always filthy." Jesus browsed Simon's office as he talked on beneath a veneer of confidence. "You'd think they could afford some decent help around here,"

Simon continued. "The Polish folks around here can't half talk and it's all surface work."

"They're hearty people," Jesus countered, "the boss ever considered increasing their wage?"

Simon pretended to ignore the remark, then said. "Hey look, Jesus, the market will close in less than an hour. Can you just hang loose? I'll buy you supper later." Jesus stepped up and looked over Simon's shoulder onto the screen of the monitor which Simon found extremely irritating, then sat back down after just a moment, picked up a Crain's and leafed through its pages.

After several minutes had passed with no more sound than the strikes of fingers touching a keyboard, Jesus broke the silence and said, "Simon, you're not deep enough."

Simon who was bearing his normal load of frustration and wearing a little thin, sarcastically mouthed back, "What is this some kind of therapy, personality inventory—what do you want from me?"

"Simon, there at your cursor," Jesus said underlining the particular stock. "Give up the last of your blue chip and buy in at 7,000 shares."

"What! Are you nuts? That stuff hasn't moved for months, besides, that's terribly weak and not predicted to perform." Jesus returned to the magazine and Simon broke open a lap top while masking his calculations. Just minutes before the market closed, Simon began shuffling papers and moving things to a drawer when he quietly turned and placed an order for 7,000 shares at $3.18 a hit. Seconds following the last key stroke finalizing the transaction, the market rolled like a slot machine, while both phones in Simon's office lit with fire. "Yeah, I'm watching it," he said hypnotically while striking keys to sell. "Holy yakking yes, I'm watching it—I'm in deep on this stuff," he shouted and totally oblivious that he had an audience of one. Simon scooted his chair back from the desk and repeated aloud, "I did it, I can't believe I finally did it—yes!" Out of the periphery of his eye he saw Jesus lower a magazine and their eyes met in a weld that would not let go. Simon actually fell to the floor on both knees and said in sincere anguish of emotion, "Don't waste your time with me, Jesus, I'm screwed up from top to bottom."

"I've heard all about you, Simon. From now on you'll be investing in men." As Jesus rose to leave, Simon regained a little composure and found his chair when two other brokers, James and John, slid to his door popping with excitement. "Simon," Jesus spoke from the doorway, with the others listening, "the people of this world are more mentally astute in relation to their own kind than the people of God. They wrestle with crisis as though it were life or death—with far more tenacity. People of God have the arrogant, rather cocky attitude that says, 'I'll live as I please, frolic and tease, we'll have our pie in the sky with the great bye and bye and live happily ever after.' The security they're after can be provided, but it's precisely their ungrateful and lackadaisical attitude that disappoints God. If folks down at the synagogue were as focused, diligent, resourceful, calculating and risk taking, yes even shrewd in their pursuit of eternal matters as people of this world who simply seek personal preservation, well, we'd hear a different message. Simon, I'm going to have to pass on the dinner offer, but I'll catch up with you real soon."

"Whoa, what was that all about?" asked James as Jesus walked away. Simon consolidated information for James while John watched a man walk away whom he knew immediately, that he loved.

Jesus stepped out of a breakfast diner early the next morning and retrieved a newspaper when he was approached by an A.I.D.S. sufferer the waitress tipped with a call placed to her friend's house. She recognized Jesus from some local publicity he was beginning to attract.

"You're him, aren't you? You're Jesus," asked the emaciated young man with a quivering voice.

"My name is Jesus and yours?" he asked with concern in his eyes.

"My name's Joshua," and still wondering about the advisability of his trip out. "Do you deal with our kind?" he asked.

"Is there any other kind?" Jesus asked sincerely while examining the young man with the eyes of a trained physician.

"There's a lot of folks who believe this is some kind of a curse for a detestable practice."

"Many of man's practices are detestable, Joshua," Jesus said looking into his eyes. "Some of them just aren't quite as noticeable or perhaps felt in just the same way." Jesus could tell that the man was in advanced stages of deterioration. "Do you think the folks who went down on the jet out of Detroit last month were any worse culprits than all other sinners?" Jesus asked. Joshua shifted in his shoes, trying to piece together a message of acceptance that was beginning to sieve through. "Or how about the construction accident over in Wilmette, where the boom of the crane fell, killing several workers and pedestrians?" Before Joshua could respond, Jesus continued, "No, but I tell you in the most solemn terms that unless these turn around with remorse," lifting his eyes, "they will all similarly die." Jesus reached out and took both of Joshua's hands in his. Jesus was touched by the frailty beneath his palms that cried for life. "Joshua," Jesus began, "the strong man has been securely strapped down. I cleanse and release you—put away ridiculous cravings and take the plunder I offer; eat it up with your hands!" In that moment, Jesus pushed open the door to the cafe and left Joshua in the hands of a friend inside who knew his name. "Joshua, he said departing, "try the house breakfast potatoes and open biscuits with gravy. It'll pull your strength up. You're fortunate to have a friend like Karen. And by the way, don't broadcast this. Speak to your Rabbi, he'll know how to direct you." Karen and Joshua were several minutes moving out of the entrance, still wondering over his emancipation. Jesus drove out of the City into the corn belt as was his habit and spent the remainder of the day in prayer.

* * * *

Thursday and Friday, March 6th and 7th, Jesus reread the itinerary Bart pulled together that would involve a ministry presentation provided by him at a fine hotel in Wheaton. Jesus was slated to offer the keynote address which would kick off a two day meeting and conclude before the observation of Sabbath on Friday. Rabbis, Jewish professors, as well as several prominent Jewish business men and women from across the State, responded to the well advertised event for which they were not necessarily targeted.

"Right this way," directed one of the hotel employees, responding to questions by new arrivals. Lunch is being served in the atrium. You can pick up name tags and folders that contain meal tickets on the way in. A waiter picked up three ladies and an older gentleman from the end of a line and escorted them to tables.

"Will this be suitable?" the waiter asked.

"Of course not," one of the women snorted with her nose in the air sniffing out the head table.

"Where is the platform?" another one asked.

"The people in charge of hosting this event specifically asked us not to make those set ups," answered the waiter.

"Over here, ladies," said their leader, "you, too, Lawrence, I don't want to miss any of this."

Others filed into the atrium and either made new acquaintances or renewed old ones. Jesus was already seated along the side sipping ice water and visiting with distant relatives from Skokie he had previously heard about but never met. Bart stopped by with Simon who was finding his legs in this new adventure and indicated that they would be out of room very soon at the rate folks were pouring in.

"I just hope the Fire Marshall is off fishing today," said Simon. "This place is packed to the hilt."

"You can say that again," Bart agreed.

"Simon, just give me the nod when you want me to get started," said Jesus.

"Give me just five more minutes while I try to pull a few more of these folks inside," said Simon. Bart followed Simon back to the entrance and they were both astonished at the size of the crowd that had assembled.

"Simon, I know we had a capacity house just with the registrations, but this overflow is unbelievable," remarked Bart.

"That's great," observed Simon. "Maybe we can skim enough off the top to pay for our gas this next week."

"C'mon, Simon, you won't have to work for a couple of years after that catch back in the Winter."

"Just pulling your string kid," said Simon smiling and further assessing the crowd.

Another table was drawn in from the back and set up to accommodate seven formally dressed teachers from a nearby yeshivah who promptly seated themselves near Jesus. It was obvious these men were born scrutinizing the birth canal and critical of the whole laborious process but managed to make a show eight days later, quick for b'rit.

One of the seven, Mr. Frankel, asked a table companion, Rabbi Abraham Pinsker, "who was that who just nodded in our direction?"

"That Rabbi Pinsker is Leonard Geiger, a man of no small importance at the University of Chicago. I must introduce you to him."

"Yes," said the Rabbi, "I am well aware of the name and would very much look forward to a visit with him while I am in the country."

"He's a definite power broker," Samson interrupted from across the table, "he controls everybody and everything in his reach, including the Mayor."

"Yes, and his companion, Herzl Holdheim is an expert in deuteronomic law and rabbinic traditions," said Mordecai from across the table. "Things will get very interesting when this Jesus stops for Q & A."

"Well, that must be him," said Frankel, as Jesus made steps to the center and front.

"And look at these fools tripping over themselves to get to him," said Samson who exaggerated some of the friendlier gestures made to Jesus. The Jewish leadership of this caste had obvious disdain for common Jews and absolutely no tolerance for non-Jews. "God, I thank you," was an often recited prayer, "that you did not create me a woman, a Gentile or a dog."

Musicians took their places behind Jesus as he offered a variation of the Kiddush blessing for the wine that preceded the lunches. Following a rejoinder in chorus led by the musicians, Jesus began welcoming remarks and appropriate thanks directed to those who helped facilitate the meeting including the patient assistance of the hotel staff. Just as Jesus adjusted the mic to begin his remarks, a commotion was heard overhead. Four men stood above the audience on the second floor leaning over the rails with canvas fire hose in hand and attached to a hotel emergency stretcher; they kept their friend steady and lowered him to the lobby level right before Jesus. The commotion this caused in the atrium stirred hotel security who rushed upstairs, avoiding a locked elevator and apprehended the men without incident for questioning in an office downstairs.

The eyes of everyone were fixed on Jesus and even Simon and Bart were trying to predict his next move. Jesus continued his gaze to the second floor and waved off other security who were having no luck penetrating an over crowded exterior wall. Aware of their abandoned-control trust, he said to the paralytic who lay petrified on the stretcher, "Friend," Jesus paused, while surveying the audience, "all your sins are forgiven." There was momentary stillness that literally felt like centuries in passing—centuries that waited for new wine to spill over—a tidal wave toppling theological sandcastles that were not prepared for the unexpected swell but new wine that brought cheer and refreshment to other socials cracked with drought and languishing for springs.

Throughout the room men and women gasped for air, and clinging to drift, they asked one another, "Who can forgive sins, except God? Who does this blasphemer think he is?"

But Jesus, aware of how they felt, said over the mic, "Why is this so difficult for you? Is it easier to say that your sins are cancelled or get up from the stretcher and walk? Here is evidence that I have authority on earth to forgive sins." He turned to the paralyzed man and said, "get up, put the stretcher back where you found it and go home." Immediately the man who had been paralyzed got up from the stretcher glorifying God.

Many in the audience were phobic and awe struck. An accountant who had an office in a wing of the hotel told guests at his table that he knew the paralytic. "Hey, that's George, that's George—I see him almost weekly! The guy fell from a ladder near the second story of his house a few years ago and severed something in the back of his neck. He's been in bed ever since," he admitted.

Many of the sightseers made a hole and followed George to the outside while others continued to swim in the atrium following the aftermath of Jesus' display of authority. Simon joined Jesus down front and wondered aloud if the evening events could be salvaged. "Simon, get with Bart and decide if you want to proceed with the remainder of the program," said Jesus. "My guess is that this crowd may need some time to dry out."

"Yeah, you sure hit them with a blast when you opened that hydrant," Simon said, playing with a pun that still lay coiled on the floor. "How did you stage that, Jesus?" he asked. Jesus handed Simon the hose and asked him to consider it for himself, then walked out of the area but didn't leave the hotel. Simon felt embarrassed and a little bewildered but mostly stung. After a minute or two he found Bart and together they located Barb and Robbie to get their advice on registrations and who they thought they could hold until tomorrow's program. The luncheon was a disaster and leaders of Jesus' company, known as The Way, were cordially advised not to return again.

Matthew was a round man of middle age who owned a C.P.A. firm together with another partner. He pulled his Wall Street up tight under his arm and walked back to his office slowly, trying to make sense of the spectacle. Other merchants, many of whom had past dealings with his practice, passed him without the slightest greeting. They despised the man who had gouged their own bank accounts with inflated costs associated with tax returns and audits they sought from him for hire in years past. Matthew was known to have taken advantage of a number of widows who were cleverly swayed into assigning him larger than normal percentages to execute wills or manage estates and trusts. His hunger for money drove him to build wealthy personal holdings, but something else was also building and all he could think about was his boredom with life. Even the recent purchase of the new Infinity sedan did little to motivate him to spend more time out of the office. Matthew was stuck in a routine that made him feel as though he had descended into his own hell. Alone and separated from his wife and children, who would have nothing to do with him, he threw himself into the one thing he was really good at, generating more money. The truth is, his own partner idled along with weak excuses about his poor productivity while Matthew brought in the lion's share of new business accounts from people in distant concentric circles who knew little about his reputation. Matthew knew his partner was a leach, but he enjoyed his company for midmorning coffee, though he sat like a manikin with a wrinkled smile until Matthew's regularity said it was time to get back to work.

April 15th was only weeks away and so Matthew's office was busier than usual. He pulled client account folders from a stack that was being replenished with fresh ones by a secretary named Linda who worked harder than anyone in the entire office. Matthew's desk squared up to a window so that he could look out to the passageway and break up the number crunching monotony that went on inside. A rap on the glass lifted his attention from a list of itemizations to a man standing outside who had an itemized list of his own. Jesus, he thought to himself and rising from his chair without wondering why he didn't send the secretary around to invite him in; Matthew moved through an office maze constructed of cube partitions and made his way around to meet Jesus who remained outside.

"Boker tov," Matthew greeted with a whimsical smile.

"I guess it's a real twilight zone in there," Jesus remarked and aware that it was after 2:00 P.M.

"Yeah, I guess you're right," said Matthew who was catching up with the clock.

"My name's Jesus," the words tumbled out of Jesus mouth and all Matthew could think of was the epitome of sheer honesty wrapped in impeccability and redundant to the 10th power. Matthew had never met a man who could look right through him, but he had the distinct impression that he was being morally ex-rayed as he stood on the tile with his back against the wall.

"I don't think we have formally met," Matthew said, extending his right hand. "My name's Matthew."

"Pleased to meet you, Matthew," said Jesus as their hands unclasped. Jesus was aware that Matthew sat in the atrium earlier and was still staggering emotionally from the display of power he witnessed by Jesus. "Matthew, do you carry your clubs in your trunk?" Jesus asked.

"As a matter of fact I do," he said.

"The weather's permissible and I've already booked a tee time for the two of us at the Village Links. Do you want to ride over with me?" Matthew didn't even consider the work that needed attention inside until he got on the road and dialed up his partner from a cell phone, having persuaded Jesus to join him in his car.

"Well listen, Jesus," Matthew began, "I mean I just never considered that you might possibly golf. So, what's your handicap?"

"Oh," said Jesus, "would you believe just slightly better than your friend George prior to his new steps."

"Whoa," Matthew cajoled, "now you, I can play with!"

Both men struck near equal tee shots off the 17th and climbed back in the cart with no one behind them. "Yeah," Matthew continued from a previous conversation he himself had initiated, "I make plenty of money, but life's no good."

"Life might improve if you had proper regard for that money, Matthew."

"What are you talking about?" Matthew inquired in a teachable tone.

"There are spiritual laws or axioms that have bearing on our lives and what we do with money tells on us," Jesus said, while pointing in the direction of his ball. "You see, your use of money is a brilliantly lit fibre optic pipeline that feeds back with crystal clarity, the movements, values and spiritual choices of your soul."

"I guess I missed that lesson at synagogue when I was a kid," Matthew said and concluding a remark left off before his chip shot that nearly hit the pin.

"Don't miss it now, Matthew," Jesus said, and Matthew knew he wasn't referring to the ball. "Money is temporal," Jesus spoke on casually while removing the flag, "wrinkled paper that we trade for goods and services. Use it wisely in the short run and by the way, life is a short run. When God settles accounts; if you've been faithful, he'll have some true riches for you—some heavenly responsibilities. If people can't execute with money," Jesus said after sinking a put, "how will they be trusted with anything greater?"

"Well, I happen to love God," Matthew admitted. "In fact I seldom miss services at the synagogue," then adjusted the statement, "well maybe a few Sabbaths during tax season."

"Men pay allegiance with their lips," Jesus said as they moved on to 18, "but they despise God in their hearts. Money is just one obvious indicator of what goes on in those recesses, and you cannot serve God and money."

The following weekend Matthew hosted a party at his place that was attended by a sizeable number of guests, all of whom were of questionable character and basically came to enjoy the generous spread. Matthew lived alone in a sprawling home that had been professionally decorated by an interior designer and was equally matched by a well manicured and generously landscaped lawn which was populated with a variety of trees, shrubs and bulbs that were smiling at Spring.

"The lights are all on and Matthew's at home," Jesus thought to himself as he ascended the steps of the colonial and rung the door bell. Matthew got up from a stool in the kitchen where he had been preparing drinks and walked to the entry to greet his new friend.

"Come right in, Jesus," he said. Matthew was just a big kid waiting to open a gift.

"Say, good to see you, Matthew," as Jesus handed him his putter and a box of Moose Tracks. "You left the putter in my bag and I thought you might enjoy the ice cream."

"Are you kidding!" said Matthew. "Moose Tracks is my absolute favorite and guaranteed to cleanse your colon."

"Only if you down the whole half gallon in one sitting," Jesus said smiling.

"Let me get this into the freezer," Matthew said, erupting with laughter that could be heard through the house and helped break the ice some were feeling who really only knew one another through Matthew. "Come in and mill around, I'll introduce you to some people."

Jesus moved easily among Matthew's guests, sampling cheese balls purchased at the deli, brie, fondue, vegetables; and a variety of wines spread over two large tables. Jesus spoke with men in professions ranging from real estate, attorneys and sales to a retailer and even an owner of a small drywall company.

"Hello, Jesus," said Herman, "I overheard you talking with Matthew earlier. This here is Roy Fienberg." Herman singled out several men standing nearby and continued. "He does insurance sales with his dad and is cracking the books for brokers securities license. Bill here has a semi-trailer full of paper product parked in a leaking warehouse downtown and is looking for someone to buy his 'turn key' operation." Herman was cut off by laughter from those surrounding Jesus as they ran up and down the back of their fellow rogue who was the target of some often obnoxious play over his great dreams but inability to get ahead. "Elvis," Herman continued introductions, pointing with a wine glass, "owns a dry wall business and is the only one of us who really works for a living." As a semi-circle formed, he said, "My name is Gould. My dad and I do real estate under the family name."

"I'm pleased to meet you men," Jesus said and his sincerity was quickly gauged by four hawks who made a practice of reading eyes and who could spot a counterfeit in an instant. "So what's the link with Matthew?" Jesus asked smiling.

"Skip it." Fienberg shouted while spraying everyone in range with a mixture of mulched cheese and crackers that spewed from his mouth, "We'd all be in jail if it weren't for Matthew!" And laughter shook the house bringing Matthew out of the kitchen for a glance to see if anyone had been hurt.

Hours later a few remaining guests scraped a chili mix from the bottom of a crock with corn chips while Clapton played in the background and Jesus wrapped up with a sentence or two. "So we were teeing off again this week at another course and Matthew slices three in a row into the subdivision next door; although I didn't hear any glass."

"Yeah," folks who live around the greens are scared to death of Matthew," Herman remarked.

"Well of course, but folks on the street are scared of you, Gould, at midday," said Matthew. "A day's growth and you look like Jack with his head pushed through a splintered door from blows with a fire axe, screaming, 'It's Johnny!'"

Elvis got up from his seat following the barrage in hopes of not getting hit. "I'm out of here guys," he tried to get his voice to carry over laughter surrounding a familiar joke. "Nice party, Matthew; let's do it again."

"Wow," said Jesus looking at his watch, "I was supposed to be at a wedding in Lincolnshire an hour ago. I guess I can still catch the reception." Jesus cleared a few dishes and apologized for not being able to help tidy the mess. "This isn't my style to eat and run," he said.

"No, get moving, Jesus, you'll be later still," insisted Matthew while taking saucers and cups from his hands.

Jesus stepped out of Matthew's house and was confronted by three orthodox teachers who wasted no time debriefing a detailed report and analysis of what they had witnessed or were suspicious of in Jesus' new program.

"Jesus," one asked, "do you make it a habit boozing it up with rift raft, embezzlers and losers?"

Before another could offer his feed, Jesus cut him off and said, "Healthy people don't need a doctor to make house calls, only those who are sick. I didn't come to invite righteous people to turn to God—only sinners."

"Even Jack taught his followers to fast and pray as we do, but you teach whatever you call your entourage to feast and get drunk," said the older one.

"You're right about part of that!" Jesus said to their surprise. "They won't be fasting while the bridegroom is with them; there will be plenty of time for that later. Now I'm going to tell you syllogists something the folks inside already know, but a detail about which you might need to consult with your local mechanic. No one puts new brake pads onto rotors that have not first been turned," said Jesus, looking into baffled faces and admonishing them to revisit premise 'A'; "otherwise, the new pads are quickly destroyed and you're back where you started. New disc pads have to be placed on freshly ground rotors. Unfortunately, most folks don't want to pay the price for the complete job. 'If it's not broke—they whine—then don't fix it.' They think they're saving money. Gentlemen," Jesus said most solemnly, "don't push the pedal any longer, the old pads are worn completely out and they're going to fail you when you need them most. It's time for a change."

Jesus politely excused himself, but the three turned inward as one related, "I want you two to stay on him like a bad smell! I want to know his every move," Rueben said furiously times, dates, places, everything. And Fritz, you stop by the garage you use and see if there is anything to the mumble jumble he just sprayed out. Geiger wants every detail laid down in order."

Jesus arrived at the Lincolnshire Marriott where the wedding party joined by families and friends swelled with joy and filled the space of the huge reception hall. Jesus met eyes with the newlyweds as they stood with their parents and witnesses for more photographs. Those taken at the synagogue under the chuppah never seem to be enough. Rachel, the bride, was a close and loving niece to Mary who was helping others serve tables through their own catered arrangement authorized by the hotel.

Jesus stepped up from behind Mary, held her elbows in hand and kissed her on the cheek. "You show up at some of the most remarkable times," Mary said. "It is so good to see you sweetheart. How would Joey put it?" she asked with a swag, "reckon it's been a table of time."

"Yes, it's been too long," Jesus agreed. "By the way, Mother, I just wanted to congratulate David and Rachel, but I can't afford to stay long. I'm beat and I've got a schedule this week that's thicker than hair on a dog's back," he said, bringing back some more. In that moment men and women from the drink table approached Mary and reported that they were completely out of wine and without a budget to buy more.

"Out of wine!" Mary said in disbelief. "Is that possible? I mean we had several gallons." Mary walked quickly to the rear in order to verify the report and search for bottles that may have been overlooked. "No, this is all we brought," she said to her own astonishment, with her hand on her forehead and obviously concerned as to what to do. Mary turned around slowly and somehow knew Jesus stood there beside her.

"Jesus," she said, "we are completely out of wine."

"Woman," Jesus said, "what do you want me to do about it? The timing isn't right for this."

Looking into the faces of help, she said, "whatever he tells you to do, just do it without question."

Jesus smiled at the woman as she went back to tables and thought to himself, "she's got the heart of a lioness and somewhere tucked away, the vanity of a peacock. How many of those bottles are back there?" Jesus asked the waiters.

"Several," they said.

"Take them to the kitchen and fill them with water," Jesus told them, "And after you've done that, pour off a glass and give it to the man in charge." Without hesitation or a clue for that matter, the gallon jugs were placed in boxes and moved to the kitchen for filling.

One of the men poured into a glass from a replenished gallon and took it to the waiter in charge of catering. "This is a fresh batch," he said handing him the glass.

"Where did you find this?" the head waiter asked between sips. "This is outstanding! You didn't find the hotel's supply did you?"

"No sir, this is some that Jesus made," said a subordinate.

Without cognitive engagement he turned and said, "No one reserves the best wine until the end. Bring it out and pass it around, they all want new wine." Jesus greeted Mary on his way out and lingering shadows followed him north toward his place of stay just west of Waukegan.

Chapter 6

Milton pulled his pickup into the drive of a small two bedroom bungalow where Jesus stood on the lawn watching laborers at a nearby construction site gather tools and begin to wrap up the day's work. The older section of Hinsdale a few blocks off Ogden was extremely desirable real estate, and Milton was just one more contractor in the hunt for possible tear-downs that would fetch a premium price following demolition and new construction. The building lots were considered to be more valuable than the homes that sat upon them, and Milton just wanted to secure a one year lease while the property sat idle to cover taxes while he finished another job down the street.

"Hi, the name's Milton Watson," he said, greeting Jesus who had walked near.

"Hello, Milton, my name is Jesus. Thanks for meeting me here." Milton surfed through a ring of keys as large as his fist looking for property he owned on The Lane.

"Here we go," he muttered to himself. "Let me walk you through, Jesus and you tell me if this is what you had in mind." The little place would be a tight fit for a family, but Jesus was impressed with the location, and the terms were affordable because of a deal the two men had struck. "Look," said Milton, "there's no air, but the furnace still fires, the refrigerator and stove stay and unless you want me to pull the old sofa out, you can use it too."

"How about this table and chairs?" Jesus asked as they stepped up from the basement and sat down in the kitchen at an old chrome set.

"Oh they stay for sure. My men were supposed to have hauled that out to the street for pick up when they ripped up the carpets. Can you imagine anyone putting carpet down over beautiful oak floors like these? I'd pay more than 15 dollars a square foot to put that down at today's cost. One other thing, Jesus, be sure to watch the overloads on the circuits; this is the old 100 amp. service and it looks like there are still plenty of unused fuses there if you blow any," Milton said, while pointing to the panel and a shelf lined with several odd size screw types. "I don't care if you burn the place down, but the neighbors might," he concluded without expression.

Milton was a man in transition. He still picked up a hammer from time to time but was also trying to keep up with the pace set by new blood who were entering the market. He lifted his glasses from a pouch in his coverall bib and opened a narrow briefcase retrieving a calculator and page of agreement.

"Jesus, I just want to say it again. I'll be knocking this down in 12—18 months if I can stay on schedule. I know I can guarantee you the full year lease. Are you sure I couldn't interest you in new construction on this site later on?"

"Yes, I'm sure," Jesus said again for the third or fourth time since he met Milton. "This is an affluent area," Jesus continued without flattery, "you build a quality home and should have no problem with sales so long as the markets behave."

"Well, I hope you're right," as he witnessed Jesus' signature. "Is that it? Just Jesus?" Milton asked as he examined the contract. "Do you have a last name?"

"Jesus is my only name," he replied.

"By the way," said Milton, "I've worked with folks long enough to size up a man. I don't have time to run down these references and you're not going to hurt this place anyway; just be sure you get my money to me before the fifth of each month. Otherwise, I get all cramped and have to come looking for you and that all takes a lot of time and extra gas. One other thing, Jesus," Milton said concluding his spiel, "You never did tell me exactly what you did for a living."

"I'm the teacher of The Way," Jesus said.

"Yeah?" Milton asked. "Say I've heard about you guys—a Jewish sect or something. Are all the stories true about all that miraculous stuff that shows up in the news from time to time? I mean some of that sounds pretty wild. By the way," Milton continued, "You're lead man really upset the Jewish hierarchy, didn't he? The word I got was that he tore up a synagogue and flogged the snot out of some folks for running a garage sale or some such thing in the place. He's awful bold, I'll give that to him. Didn't that happen right in the middle of one of those Passover deals they make such a hype about? I have to tell you—I stay away from religious fanatics. The wife and I attend a little hub group here in the burbs—just common sense kind of lectures that maximize self expression—you know, mainline doctrine of the Hub."

"Milton," Jesus said, "I know you spend your day working with prints, but have you ever considered God's blueprint on man?" Jesus held up a copy of Scripture and said, "God created man to worship, but he got fanatical about other things."

"Say," Milton said, "I've got another appointment across town in 15 minutes. I'll get a copy of this back to you before the week's end."

"O.K.," said Jesus, "And thanks again for working out a deal on the lease, I think you'll be real happy with the cabinets you selected." Jesus walked out the front door in order to retrieve some cleaning supplies from his van while Milton scampered to his truck.

Jesus didn't let many days pass before he scheduled a meeting with Simon, James and John. His new residence was modestly adorned with plants, furniture pieces picked up from thrift stores, and a conspicuously large three year planner that hung mostly blank and pasted to the living room wall. The center piece of the living room was an oak door Jesus removed from the hinges of an interior closet and set up on concrete blocks for use as a coffee table.

It was late Sunday afternoon when John knocked on the door and Jesus knew by the lightness that it had to be him. John was in his early twenties and fresh out of college with a degree in literature but was making ends meet as an intern at his father's business—the same firm that employed Simon and his brother James up until their resignations. Zeb hated to lose his two sons and the other employees but they were excited about a new teacher and it was no use talking them out of following him. Jesus opened the door and welcomed John into his droll that was presently being freshly swept with early summer breeze. The smell of new cut, tall fescue blended with evaporations from cypress mulch that lay on beds of rhododendrons sifted through tight mesh that had been put in place of winter panes. Their weights hung like long socks of sausage in a smoke house; and no less hidden behind casing, they would grumble and growl when ordered to help open or close for evening draft.

"Well, hello John," Jesus said with a warm smile that made John feel especially affirmed, "You're right on time."

"Hi, Jesus," John said, "So this is you're pad, huh?"

"Yes, come right in and sit down, the others should be along anytime. I'm brewing some tea and will be with you in one moment." John was interested in Jesus and it wouldn't have occurred to him to be anywhere but under his feet.

"Oh, excuse me, John," Jesus said as he made a sudden turn in the kitchen with a hot sauce pan that was destined for a pad on the table top. "Did I splash any on you?"

"Oh no, I'm fine," John said while gawking at Jesus like he'd never seen a real man in his life. "I guess I should have been a little quicker getting out of your way."

"John, do you mind pulling down cookies from the cupboard on the left side of the sink."

"Sure," he said and pretty much just backed himself to the counter while leafing through a novel unlike anything he had ever taken up in his hands.

"John, you can place the cookies on this platter," Jesus said while drawing an old piece of china from a built in corner hutch. Jesus wiped his hands on a kitchen tee and aware of the silence, looked over to assist John whom he now discerned had been invited by a great host to sit for a moment longer in another lofty realm and enjoy the read. "John," Jesus said after a moment, "did you find the cookies, Haus?" John turned to the cupboard as though it was his first directive and found cookies lying on a colorful place mat with the word Bethlehem scrolled across the middle.

"House of Bread," John said, interpreting the word for Jesus.

"That's right, John. Mother picked them up while traveling abroad last year."

"I mean, that's right up there with Morton Salt isn't it?" asked John who was cutting teeth. "Now how does that go, 'when it rains, it pours?' I heard about the incident over at the hotel. Simon said the Mississippi stepped right over and took a bow right there in the place. Jesus," John continued, "I think I know what happened." Jesus paid John attention, but he picked up different leather for whatever reason and returned to a discussion about Jesus' new home. "I mean how did you find anything in the middle of Hinsdale? Better yet, how did you afford it?"

"A contractor owns the place," Jesus began while washing celery and carrots. He says it's a tear-down and just wants to cover the property taxes until he can level it and make it look like the one next door. The guys who took over Joey's old company gave me the lead. Kevin you met once, the man whose infant baby was diagnosed with diabetes lets me have access to the shop and tools after hours and so I moonlight a few sets to keep bread on the table."

"You are resourceful, Jesus. By the way, how is mom getting along these days?"

"I think as well as one can expect. She and Joey were pretty frugal and when I tried to offer her some money recently she related that the house was paid for and she even had some means to help others. She's not opening any new accounts, but she'll be O.K. I do hope she's able to find another woman to share the house. Her friend, Florence, recently moved on and loneliness is one of her great enemies."

As Jesus and John finished trimming a vegetable tray, the sound of Simon's new Pathfinder was his only introduction to Jesus' entrance foyer. "Yes, come right in, Simon," said Jesus while carping in play about where he parked, not hinging the door and leaving his manners in the glove box.

"Relax, Jesus," said Simon, "flattery will get you nowhere with me." Jesus passed through to the living room while rolling his eyes as Simon approached John and began sniffing around his shoulders and the collar of his shirt. After a moment, Simon stepped back and appeared to have identified something rancid, when he asked, "Boy, what's this on the end of your nose? Did you get here early to suck up to the man?" John quickly raised his right hand making passage an inch or two from

Simon's face and falsely scratched around on his head like a young baboon picking for lice. Simon always got caught lunging backward on that move which pleased John and he let him know it. "O.K. boy, try that again," Simon ordered, "I'll bite off your fingertips and spit 'em outside for the squirrels to fuss over."

"No, you're too slow old man," John got in the last word before James knocked on the door and let himself in.

"Jesus," James asked before offering a hello, "where did you find these 'low-lifes'? All they want is your food." James seated himself and began nibbling from a tray in front of the host."

"Hello, James," Jesus said, "Are you sure you and John sprung from the same litter?" James and John shared the same name, but one would never know they were shoots from the same stump by looking at them, the two men were more than shades apart.

"Jesus," said James, "that was the first real compliment I've received this entire day."

"Here we go," said Simon. "Now don't get these two going or we will never accomplish anything." Simon was full of business so long as the plan was clear and his role reasonably well presented and it all appeared to rely on his control. "Jesus," he said, "why don't you sit down over there on the folding chair where we can see you and let's get this meeting under way. I'm anxious to share with you a direction I think this needs to take."

"Something you need to understand about Simon, Jesus," said James, "the boy is wrong about many things but in doubt about nothing."

"You said that right." John voted with him. "He's got a mind like cement. It's all mixed up and thoroughly set."

"Jesus, Jesus, are you growing bored yet?" asked Simon. "These little fellahs have such an underdeveloped sense of humor," he said shaking his head and warning them to stop with his eyes."

"Well," said Jesus taking a seat on a cushion on the floor and backing up to the wall, "let's pray and see if we can get some work done."

Jesus began to pray when James stopped him and asked, "Did you say we would pray for some things to get done or you are going to pray so that we can get some things done?"

"James," Jesus said, "I am going to pray for us as a team. We've got some things to do that can only be accomplished through prayer. Let's be silent for a moment, gentlemen, as I pray and petition God to empower our efforts." Jesus' words and the pause between his remarks and prayer brought an uncomfortableness over the room that was slowly extinguished as the short prayer concluded, "Father, thank you that you always listen when we pray. We want to be about your business. Because of its enormous importance, we ask you to give us clear minds and undistracted focus as we consider plans you seem to be indicating for the coming year. Honor this time for your glory and bring to us your kingdom. Amen."

"Jesus," Simon asked sincerely, "do you pray like that often? I mean nonmemorized stuff?"

"Are you going to teach us to pray like that? Is that part of the plan?" asked James.

"Along the way, men," Jesus answered.

"Will you pray again right now?" asked John. "I just like to hear the way you do it."

The silence and looks by Simon and James told him to wait for another day, but Jesus turned to John and said, "You pray, John."

Simon and James both made huge readjustments in their seats as John began, "Father, thank you that you hear us when we pray. And because it is so important give us focus as we make plans. Honor us this day and make your kingdom come in an undistracted manner."

"Pretty close," Simon said, "Jesus would you like for me to pray?"

"Not at this time," Jesus said, then continued, "friends, I've invited you here for the purpose of building leaders. I've taken on a one year lease at this place and intend to fill the calendar behind your heads. Some of the data will record work we pray to perform daily, and some will contain notes at the end of periods that summarize our time with God and what he did through us. I plan to stick close to Hinsdale for the first year and work with a few. We're going to need more and more helpers as this vision begins to take shape, but the Father will provide them when the time comes. The kingdom will grow like leaven in a lump of dough and proceed until the entire lump is permeated. I want to build into the three of you especially. We're going to lay a foundation that will support the weight of succeeding generations."

"You be the cornerstone, Jesus," John injected at the price of a smart kick by Simon.

Jesus smiled at the insight then continued, "I'm asking you on the front end to clear your schedules, keep commitments lean and above all else, be available. When you go home later tonight, I want you to find some solitude and really count the cost."

"Jesus," Simon said and respecting the gravity, "you can count on me right now, you already know how I feel about the plan. Jill is in on it, too. John, go order pizza in. How are you voting on this, James?"

"Sit back down, John," Jesus demanded, as he closed a manila folder that lay open in his lap. "Simon, you are going to be a challenge." Simon was flattered. "School circle," Jesus breathed aloud and Simon had the distinct impression that he was being invited to listen closely. "Gentlemen, for the next few minutes keep your eyes and ears open and your lips sealed. I had intended to present this another way, but I rather think a story is in order," Jesus began. "When we were small, it was something of a family ritual to sit around our living room Friday evenings following initial Sabbath observance, munch popcorn under candle light and listen to Joey or Mom tell stories from their personal past. Jimmy and I always locked onto Joey's stories about his tour in the Marine Corps with intense interest. I've thought a fair amount about one application in particular. It presents an important value that is in scarce supply and I'm challenging you men to find it, own it, model it for others and participate in it for life."

"Joey tells about a 2:00 A.M. bus ride out of Charleston, S.C.," Jesus continued speaking to three green recruits. "They were in route to a small island off the South Carolina coast. This particular island had but one gate that was manned by well dressed—almost mechanical looking sentries. It was surrounded by swamp, the trees were garland with moss and the sand venerated by all its inhabitants. Joey spoke of how relieved he was to finally arrive after flying most of the day or else waiting around in airports.

"'Ready for a bite to eat and a little shut eye,' he would say, 'we'll probably roll out around 9:00 or 10:00 A.M. after getting in so late, I'll check out the agenda and start being a Marine.'

"Joey talked on about how all his misconceptions suddenly changed when they arrived at the receiving barracks. The driver got off the bus and an eerie feeling drifted down and settled in like poisonous fumes, breaking up the ruckus on board. An oversize D.I. stepped out of the hatch onto the stoop and stood beneath a dim light that grew his silhouette. Everything was perfectly still.

Joey would always pause at this point and tell us, 'already I'm feeling like there might not be any chow for some reason.' The D.I. walked onto the bus and Joey said all he could remember was a neck about the size of uncle Zack's with pulsating jugular pushing fire to the rear.

"'When I give you the word *move*,' the D.I. would scream it out, Simon, and not before—I want everyone of you maggots off my bus and standing on the yellow footprints outside. If there is so much as a word, bodies will be dismantled and my Island will be strewn with human carnage. Now you've got three heartbeats to comply and two of 'em are gone, now move, move, move!'"

"Boy, it sounds like the man was trying to wake up the neighborhood," said James who was totally immersed as the rest.

"Everyone quickly assembled on the footprints facing the receiving barracks, and the D.I. directed their attention to his scarlet and gold sign fastened over the hatch which read: 'Through this portal pass prospects for the United States finest fighting force—United States Marines'—then quickly added, 'and you ain't it ladies!' For the next two hours this angry D.I., with pulsating jugular and a voice inflection unlike anything I've ever heard anywhere else on the planet, told us what he thought of our girl friends, mothers, close kin; he told us about sexual conduct we didn't think was possible, then closed his sermonette with several more choice superlatives and 20—30 reasons why we were going to fail."

"Is all that legal?" asked James, "I mean wasn't somebody indicted for something like that recently?"

"Joey said that he was mortified," Jesus continued, " Strangely enough during week one, the newly assembled platoon was herded over to the grinder and watched a Battalion Graduation Ceremony as his platoon sat on the asphalt deck out of everyone's way. 'These have earned the title,' Joey quoted the D.I., while they watched graduates who'd recently completed third phase, march in perfect cadence before families and friends who had traveled to celebrate on this special day. "You see," Jesus broke into the narrative, "The D.I. wanted to instill vision—the vision that it could be done," then continued Joey's story. "Our new platoon was a motley undisciplined herd by comparison and we would lose a full fourth before graduation. Onion heads, unbloused utilities, soft covers, we weren't much to look at. Following the graduation, our Senior D.I., the one with the wide black belt, turned to us in a firm but fatherly kind of John Wayne tone and said, 'Ladies, there are only two ways off this Island and only two. You either tighten up your little civilian bodies, conform to my Marine Corps standards and graduate with the rest of the platoon or else you leave in a pine box. Are there any questions?' About this time, Sarah had fallen asleep in Mom's lap, but Jimmy and I were just getting warmed up and refills on popcorn."

"I'm sharing this story with you for at least four reasons," Jesus continued speaking into three men who were full of tenacity and used to staring into less interesting monitors for longer periods of times. "Like Marine recruits, God doesn't promise you a rose garden. I'm not telling you the path will be easy. On the contrary, I'm telling you to add up the cost." All three men were doing their best not to interrupt Jesus, but they each wanted desperately to tell him that it was his good fortune to have struck upon three of the most committed individuals he was likely to find, and the one thing that motivated them the most in life was a challenge or for someone to hint that they couldn't stay on task. Simon could stand it no longer and politely solicited that Jesus move to the print key so that they would have a more specific idea about their area of responsibility.

"The next point, Simon, involves rank in the kingdom." It's human nature to pull rank and seniority to leverage position. That may work in the military, but it is not to be heard of among you. The greatest among you will be everyone else's private. Another point I wouldn't want the three of you to miss is the fact that love is a far greater motivator than fear and intimidation. It is true that fear produces results, but only while the boss is watching, right, men? And finally, if Marines are fanatical about being Marines; how are you going to behave as you serve the real Commander in Chief? I'll tell you how—you're going to be on tilt!"

"Joey used to share in all seriousness that every night before they hit the rack on the Island, the D.I. would order someone to pray for the war to continue. "What good is a Marine," the D.I. would shout, "without a war!"

"See there," said James, "and we blamed all of Vietnam's lingerings on Johnson."

"Listen up, James," Jesus said. "Now if a D.I. can motivate recruits to pursue an earthly crown, what can happen when you catch the vision that servanthood is a means of worship! It glorifies God and edifies his people." At that moment, Jesus stepped into the kitchen and returned with a shallow cake pan with an inch or two of water, catching Simon and James scratching up turf like a couple of Banti cock roosters trying to establish pecking order. Jesus said nothing to the men, but bent down to floor level, removed the shoes and socks of the youngest man present and bathed his feet. Two cocks stepped out of the center of the circle and took appropriate roost.

"Jesus," John asked with humility, "may I now wash yours in return?"

"Not at this time," Jesus said and he knew from the looks on their faces that a Definite Intuition of their own had just shouted them down real proper.

"Men," Jesus began to lift their faces, "important people in the Gentile community laud themselves and are considered Benefactors because of their humanitarian efforts or contributions that will benefit the human race. Ask folks in Wilmington what I'm talking about," Jesus said with a wink. "But I don't want you to be like that," he continued. "Your motivation to serve has to stem from a deeper value—a love for God and his kingdom, where all crowns and recognitions to be conferred are temporarily postponed. Men, you're in basic training. It's going to feel like you're on Parris Island some days. Do the paradigm thing they teach you in school and shift your categories around until you make room for what I'm telling you. Fix your eyes on the day of graduation. All your friends will be on hand to celebrate and watch you march in procession. It'll be a great day I promise you that!"

Jesus got up again from his seat, walked to the kitchen and placed two homemade pizzas in the oven and spun the dial to 400 degrees. The others wandered in momentarily and they all secretly knew that they had been baptized into an order that would bond them in a unique way for life. Following the meal and some light talk and wine, both of which cheered their hearts, Jesus excused his brothers to the front entry where night had fallen. Just before Jesus unlatched the door, he pulled down a piece of cardboard from above the passageway which others thought had remained there to cover an unsightly hole, and John was quick to read, 'Through this portal pass prospects for the Kingdom's finest serving force—servants of God, Most High.'

"And you're it," Jesus signed off with a laugh that they felt.

Chapter 7

Nearly a year to the date of lease, Jesus once again stood on the front lawn with Milton who was accompanied by Ronnie, his foreman and a couple of laborers who had brought up a backhoe and an oversize Ford refuse truck destined for County fill. Milton directed his men to reassess the lot and consider the best elevation for the 2700 square foot two story that was coming in place of the much smaller ranch. While Milton spoke to Jesus, Ronnie stepped off setbacks from the center of the street and began calculating side and rear yards.

"Jesus, don't be in too big a hurry," Milton said. "Bruce is finishing up the gas disconnect before we start pulling it down."

"Thanks, Milton," Jesus said, but we've gotten everything out—it's all yours. By the way, how do you intend to take it down?"

"Ronnie and Keith are experts at this and follow a plan all their own. They'll pull some cables through the windows and tie into the load bearing wall. We've already been in the attic sawing up the bottoms of trusses. When we pull the jacks out, the roof system will implode on itself and fall to the ground the way a trap springs when the stumbling block is snatched away. Maybe you've built one as a kid—same principle. After that we clear the sub floor, dig out the basement to fit new dimensions and start a foundation. Knocking it down doesn't take long, but the clean up will last two or three days."

"Yes, foundations are everything," said Jesus, and his foreman was listening.

James and John joined Jesus and Simon after Milton walked away, and they spent a minute or two reminiscing late nights they spent in the house over the past year. Space would fail in the length of a book to describe everything that transpired there in the course of one year including trips, overnighters, good food and lessons drawn from beautiful hidden hardwood to blown fuses of old electrical systems to—treasure, power and human sexuality.

"It doesn't quite seem right to tear it down," John said, and the others agreed.

"Yes," Jesus said, "we spent some good times here but better times are ahead."

Philip, who was another man Jesus had brought on board in the last year, walked out of the house in front of them carrying a sign he had pulled from over the entry door that had several signatures on it. "We're hanging onto this," he shouted in Jesus' direction, and they all gave him a thumbs up.

James just couldn't let the moment slip away without reminding everyone of the night several months past when Simon stomped out of the living room and said he would never be back following a heated exchange between he and Jesus over a decision made to write a sizeable amount of their operating capital to the poor. "Simon," said James, "you were fit to be tied. Jesus, did he ever pay you for busting up that door he stomped to pieces on the living room floor?"

"Yeah, I paid him," said Simon. "Tell him I settled with you on the door, Jesus."

"I never saw a cent," said Jesus, remembering the incident and how he himself had glued it all back together and restationed it on the blocks. "You said you were going to pay for it, but you never seemed to have gotten around to it."

"Well, no use worrying about it now, the whole mess will be parked in a landfill in a day or two—you heard the man," Simon said.

"Yeah, but it's the principle of the thing, Simon," Jesus said smiling. Simon stomped off again, but the steam was mostly show.

"That boy's always been wound up like a top," said James, "he never could take a joke very well." Jesus knew a teaching moment when he saw one but felt that it might be wise to let the locomotive cool down.

Bart and Thad were tying off a pickup load of odd and end furniture when another car pulled up loaded with a fresh platoon of help; the fourth to drop out was Jude. Maggie ran to Jesus and threw an arm around him like an old friend.

"Jesus," she apologized, "we might have been here sooner, but Jude's car wouldn't start and so Siva carried us all the way over to Elgin and got mine. But hey, I've got some friends I want you to meet."

"I'd be pleased to," said Jesus.

Maggie was a Janice Joplin made all over again. Her mannerisms and voice were so similar that strangers would often point out the resemblance to her. Maggie's background was even more colorful in some respects. Although she couldn't sing, she left Chicago at 15 years of age for Woodstock, New York, without a dime; she heard her look alike and wondered if she couldn't possibly sing after all, then made the round trip back hitchhiking a different route. As wild as it all seemed, drifts like that were all in a common week's activities back in those years.

Maggie was not a good neighbor prior to her encounter with Jesus. While at work, her fellow employees referred to her as an absolute witch with a capitol 'B.' She often drove the forklift at the distribution center while intoxicated, laid with men of every sort outdoors during breaks in the summer months, or in a hidden cardboard hold in the winter. Maggie's addictions and disorders would fill several pages in DSM IV, and there were a few of her behaviors for which that manual didn't have categories. She was so vulgar around the dinner table at work that seasoned truck drivers, men who could teach the Navy a new sentence or two, would often remove themselves so as to eat their food without all the graphic elements laid between the bread by Maggie. She spent years building her own machine. Raise the hood on this muscle car, pull back the breather and one could count all her modifications added for greater horsepower. Eight cylinders that mixed debauchery, lude pipes with unspeakable sound, a felonious dual point distributor that fed fire; she was a fuel guzzling sex engine with three ports, a seared head and no kill switch—this woman was on a collision course with absolutely no insurance.

One evening Jesus drove Simon, James and John over to a dark corner in Hammond for a little first hand experience with a spiritual reality he had been seeking to teach them. James insisted during a recent discussion that demons were just a bunch of malarkey. When Jesus pulled off I-80, it was after 2:00 A.M. James grew wide awake and struggled to find vocabulary that would describe the area they entered.

"This is definitely not a coat and tie operation," said James as Jesus pushed his van's gear shift into park. Motorcycles and loiterers littered the dark lot. The haunt was no dream.

Simon asked his leader, "Why didn't you just fly us over to Gaza with our own colors, maybe the star of David sewn to our backs with something like the 'Golan Thieves' embroidered below it. You're not going in there are you, Jesus?"

"No way," he said, "I have a tough enough time in Laundromats. We've got enough distance if I need to pull away; I just wondered if James wanted to go in and grab us some carry out."

"These folks look like they could eat nails and spit tacks," said James. "Why don't you ever see these guys in the day time?"

"Most of them would be locked up if they did what I'm witnessing in daylight hours," said John from pure eyes. After a few minutes a creature crawled out of one of the holes and looked more like a walking billboard for Nazism than anything else. As the door pushed open from behind him, the momentary sight was incredulous as smoke rose up like someone had lifted the lid off a furnace.

"What do you know," said Simon as he looked in the direction of the big man, "Leroy Brown is a real personage."

The leader of the Pagans summoned everyone in the parking lot and they followed him toward Chicago. A woman remained and thought to saddle a Harley behind the plague who owned it, but an argument erupted that turned to blows, and just a few seconds passed before the bludgeoned male victim limped away, having been lanced with a razor and suffering multiple thrust kicks to the face. The woman's powder keg was touched off by the primer and she fought the lot and side of the brick building seeking to inflict more damage. Her ravings sounded like someone seriously ill, but oddly enough, pushing maximum torque.

"O.K. Jesus," Simon said, "I for one see your point. These people can be left to self-destruct." The woman turned from thrashing the wall and faced the van like a heat seeking missile locked onto an enemy target. She sucked down the last contents from a pint she produced and threw it to the ground while taking steps to open the hatch on a load of fresh lamb.

"I think the distance you spoke of earlier has just been reduced by about 50 per cent," James said.

"Yeah, Jesus," said Simon, "and this isn't the time for a school circle; are you going to turn the ignition or wait until that thing comes through the windshield and jumps into your lap?"

Without responding, Jesus drew the keys from the ignition, pulled on the headlights and stepped to the front of the van the same moment Maggie arrived. She honestly looked more like an animal hybrid than anything human and smelled like it for sure.

"Boy, if Joey could have a look at you," Jesus said out loud, "this is a lady who could run a bear up a tree with a switch and he better hope it isn't a sapling—and I don't mean the switch." The woman was numb with alcohol and high from some fresh pot that was part of the ritual inside. She came at Jesus with blood in her eyes and would have carved his flesh, but he stepped aside with a quick move and she kissed the short hood of the van which brought men to erect attention inside with feet about to push out the floorboard and all doors locked and double checked.

"Now this is not even funny," said Simon. "What if she kills him right here and now in this parking lot—who's going to go out there and get the keys?"

"I always wondered where it would happen," James joined in with all seriousness as the woman picked up a brick bat. "I'm going to die right here in Hammond, Indiana, —God have mercy," and he meant it.

"We'll all die with him," John said and they both laid hands on the boy and threatened to put him to sleep if he didn't change his attitude.

Maggie would have lunged repeatedly for she liked to fight, but Jesus was in touch with something internal, something foreign inside of Maggie that she herself was unaware of and had come to regard as who she was—her very person. "What is your name?" Jesus shouted, and the van rocked, but Maggie froze. Jesus didn't repeat himself as he looked inside and identified the inhabitants of a moist worsted nest. Maggie opened her mouth and seven defiant spirits made hasty confession before shaking her violently and screaming away from his stand. Routed enemy fled the mortars that stepped after them by the click of a compass. Maggie fell to the gravel and Jesus motioned for his men to assist him with her to the back seat of the van. Jesus finally had to unlock the door with a key and was only able to persuade them to help under duress that the other cyclists could come floating back in at any moment. They unloaded Maggie's pockets and her limp body at Siva's home back in the Chicago suburbs, a single woman with a huge heart and sincere commitment to rehabilitating others. Siva took an active leadership role in Quest, a single adult group of friends 45 years and up who were bonded mostly through pains of divorce and like circumstances that brought them together like a family. The ride home that evening was an interesting one, but Jesus was not challenged again to specifically validate the real possibility of the cohabitation of demons with humans.

"Jesus," Maggie said, "these are my good buddies Susan and Joan. Siva introduced them to me and I've learned so much about God through them. The devil still comes around once in awhile and reminds me of my past," she continued with head cocked and looking to dodge an illusionary fist, "but I'm doing like you told me and keep reminding him of his future!" And they all laughed.

Jude climbed up on the truck to assist Bart and whispered, "Hey, nice babes, don't you agree. So what's their interest in Jesus?" Bart didn't have a lot of time for Jude and basically brushed him off as someone who had a one track mind involving political subversion. He hated the United States government and viewed the movement spearheaded by Jesus to be the one possible solution to world dominance he hoped would be headed by true Zionists. Jesus was the only teacher he knew who spoke so passionately about a coming kingdom that would one day abolish all human rule and one in which he himself would rule as king. Those lessons Jude stayed up late for and he had his own ideas about where and how he would be situated when that day came.

"Knock it off, Jude," Bart said rather abrasively, "use your head. Those women and others have been supporting this ministry for months. By the way, we'll need to see the books next time we're all together. I think I caught a discrepancy or two during the last verbal account you offered." Jude was known to have drawn money from the petty cash and sometimes significant amounts for car repair and entertainment without accountability to anyone else.

"Clam up, Bart," he said, "the books are as clean as my hands."

"Jude," the voice carried across the lawn, "can you join me for a moment?" asked Jesus. Jude jumped down from the truck and made a condescending remark to Bart on his way out of reach. "Jude, this is Maggie, Susan and Joan and they're all friends of Siva," Jesus said by way of introduction.

"Yeah, I rode in with them from Long Grove awhile ago; you were tied up with the others when we unloaded," said Jude.

"Well, I'm glad you all are already acquainted. Jude, these ladies want to leave some money for the work," Jesus said while excusing himself.

"Ladies, your money is in good hands. Whoa," Jude said while reading the total, "Did you all knock off an armored truck? This is a lot of money!"

"There were a lot of people involved in giving, I mean it wasn't just us," said Maggie.

"That's right," said Susan and Joan, "there are many people who believe in what you all are doing and just want to help out in some tangible way."

Everyone was preparing to leave and Maggie who retained a keen sense of street smarts from earlier days brushed up to Jesus to encourage him but also warned that his message wasn't being well received in certain ranks and maybe even with at least one of his own. "You keep a low ride, Jesus," said the ex-biker, "and turn your head from the wind once in awhile; you never know who's about to run you over from behind."

"Yeah, Maggie," Jesus said talking her lingo, "you stay low and keep moving your own self girl." And their eyes spoke for a moment about casualties of war.

"Bart, why don't you and Jude ride along with James and me. Let Simon drive the truck; they will meet us at O'Hare after he and Matthew drop the things off at the shelter. John, do you have a ride?" Jesus asked.

"No, I'll ride with you," John said, and he crawled in the front between Jesus and Bart. James and Jude took seats in the back and both vehicles backed out onto The Lane and sat momentarily as a wench reeled out the interior walls and brought down the roof with a rumble. No one spoke a word, but there were some internal sighs as memory echoes were flushed out of the place like a covey of quail released from that old oak door. The laughter, tears, struggles and insights would be recorded again. Jesus pulled away with a toot from his horn to Milton, and they jumped on the Tristate from Ogden after a quick stop for more coffee.

Jesus had previously dropped off Bob, his wife, Cheryl and their friend, Doug—all musicians at O'Hare in order to save parking expenses during the two weeks they were in Florida on vacation. Their flight was due back in at 12:30 P.M., and Jesus planned to pick them up on his way back to the northwest suburbs where he would pursue further work. Jesus pulled into a lot at O'Hare and looked at his watch which said they had plenty of time. The vehicle unloaded and Jesus knew that there would be just enough room for three additional passengers and their luggage by the time Simon and Matthew rejoined them. After moving inside, the five checked arrivals only to discover that the flight had been delayed for two hours due to a maintenance problem that forced them to put down in Memphis.

"It wouldn't be a good use of our time to run up to Mt. Prospect and back," said Jesus. "We will wait here until their flight comes in. I'm sorry for the inconvenience, but opportunity surrounds us."

"I'm taking a little walk," said Jude. "Can I get anyone a bite?"

"No thanks," said the others.

"I'm going to catch a little shut eye," said Bart who had been up since 4:00 A.M. with a sick child.

"Yeah I'm hip to that," said James. John found a chair, pulled a paperback from his jacket and continued reading, *A Night to Remember* by Peter Lord. He was fascinated by the dimensions of the Titanic and its virtual indestructibility. But during the course of its maiden voyage, jaws lurking in deep waters gnawed away at the steel until she took on sea bath. John pondered the spiritual parallels when Simon arrived with Matthew and received word from Jesus that they still had another hour wait ahead of them.

"No problem," said Simon while slapping Matthew on the back. "We're starved anyway and being the great servants we are," kicking the bottom of James' propped feet for emphasis, "we're volunteering to treat you lesser slugs to some pizza." Three hungry men jumped to their feet and looked for Simon to lead.

"Aren't you coming along, Jesus?" asked Matthew.

"No, I'd like to just stick around here," he said casually.

"Well, I'll bring you back something," he said. As they walked toward the main terminal for a larger menu, Jesus took up a different seat close to a small vendor off the main concourse.

Simon's eye caught sight of the paperback in John's pocket and he drew it out without his permission. "What kind of ghoulish nightmare are you reading son?" Simon asked. John didn't squabble with him and thought he might even ask him to read it, which would be a miracle because outside of some financial magazines, Simon was strictly visual. If it isn't laid out with far more pictures than text, he wasn't interested.

"That's a tome, Simon, and it's full of words," John said as Simon paged through it. "Just like the man with the yellow hat told his monkey friend, 'words make sentences.'" Simon enjoyed the play so long as there was nothing important at stake, and there wasn't as far as he was concerned so he kept poking at John on their way down an escalator.

"You know, John," not to be outdone by his junior, "like the movie Titanic, this airport has *words* that are unique to it as well. You ever heard the word 'terminal?'" and he shoved him forward down the escalator while holding the back of his shirt, "or how about 'final approach,'" and he grimaced as though someone had fallen from the roof in front of them and splattered onto the floor. Winking to James and Bart who were stoking the fire, Simon asked Matthew if he was sure they had enough money between them to buy pizza for everyone after all.

"I don't know, Simon," Matthew said. "I've lost a goodly number of clients since joining this motley crew, I'm afraid we're going to have to squeeze out at least one mouth until we get paid again. I just don't have *words* to express my deep regret that John will have to go without."

"This little piggy went to market," Simon began but couldn't finish because John had snatched back his book, popped Simon on the head with it which created a general fray that continued to the bar of the food court.

Meanwhile, a jet arrived at a nearby gate but was scheduled to continue its flight to Atlanta after a short layover. A black woman in her mid thirties ran to the little hot dog and pretzel hut near where Jesus sat resting and ordered a large drink to carry back onto the plane. "For crying out loud," she told anyone listening, "how do they expect somebody to get their eight glasses a day the way these airlines ration the stuff. You'd think we were being forced marched to Bataan. I'll bet you there wasn't two ounces in that little plastic cup and I sure didn't know it was legal to package peanuts in bags that small. I embarrassed the life out of the lady when I told her I didn't have any babies traveling with me. Those portions might be enough for the little 80 pound stewardess who served it, but I've got to have some fluids."

Before she could get a straw poked through the lid of the fountain drink, Jesus said, "Give me a drink of that." The woman did a double take that required her to stop, turn around and refocus her eyes on a young man she perceived to be a Jew making demands of her right out in broad daylight.

"Where in the scratch do you Jews get off?" she drew the words out slowly and accented where she pleased. "I just sat in front of two of 'em dressed blacker than me coming in from New York and I could hear their little snickers. 'What's a moan back?'" she retold the joke, "'A trash man in Atlanta directing the driver! Moan back,'" she laughed and told another. "Motea? Motea?" says the little black waitress, and she wasn't laughing as she directed another question to the stranger. "Are you people actually allowed to talk to folks outside your own pedigree?" She took a long draw from the straw, handed it to Jesus and said, "Go ahead. Take a risk; there ain't no telling what I'm carrying."

Jesus took the drink from her hands to her surprise, opened his mouth for her inspection, drew from the straw, gargled for proof and downed it, then said to her, "If you had an understanding of God's gift and who it is who asked you for the pop, you'd be asking me for living water."

"See what I'm talking about?" she almost turned and lectured those nearby. "You blasted Jews are so arrogant. Do you own controlling stock in Pepsi Cola? Well, no! Coca Cola? Well, no! Is your old man the board chairman of a drink company larger than that?" she asked.

Jesus took another drink of her pop and handing it back said, "It has no kick and whoever drinks this stuff will get thirsty again."

"Now that's a big and mighty scientific insight," she said, and this time she did turn to the corridor and repeated Jesus words. "This young man just said that if anyone drinks this pop, they will get thirsty again." Jesus smiled at her brazenness, when she asked, "You learn that at kibbutz as a kid? You even got a dad?" redirecting some of the same slurs that had often come to her in life.

"The water that I'm able to provide for you will leave you completely satisfied. It shoots up in you with fresh fountain springs to eternal life," motioning with his fingers vertical, palm nearly cupped and close to his chest.

"You make good on that one and you'll make a mint, but I don't have to tell a Jew how to make money."

The woman began walking away and Jesus returned to a paper he had been perusing. She turned a few paces away and said, "Mister, important things I'd have to say run a lot deeper than soda pop and I doubt seriously if you've got the intelligence to draw it out—it'll take more than this straw."

Before she could turn back, Jesus stood up, faced her and said, "You're right ma'am, the thoughts of a woman's heart do run deep, but a person of understanding can in fact draw them out. Go get your husband and let's talk about that." Startled, she confessed that she didn't have a husband before she could stop the sentence. "You said that right. You've had five husbands and the one you picked up in Manhattan last night—the one traveling with you is not your own," Jesus said.

The woman drew closer and asked, "Are you a prophet or something like that?" I've heard about your type," she continued evasively but still interested. "I was raised to worship out here and you folks say that there is only one place to worship."

"I wish you could believe this," Jesus said. "There is coming a time soon when it will not matter whether you worship—here, in Atlanta, downtown Chicago or anywhere else for that matter. It is true that salvation comes through the Jews, but the time has arrived in which God is seeking true worshippers—those who worship in spirit and truth, for that's who he's been posting radar for all along. God is spirit and those who worship him must do so in spirit along with the right data."

"Yeah, well I know that the Messiah is coming, even the most liberal hub knows that. And when he appears, he'll clear up all the technical stuff."

"Lady," Jesus said, "I am he."

She was utterly dumbfounded, although she believed him based upon his knowledge of her life. "Mister, you just please stay right here, I don't care if we have to fly standby, my friends have to hear this." The woman turned and ran to the plane as his men returned with food and caught the tail end of the exchange. They were each befuddled that he had been talking to a black woman.

"Here, Jesus," Matthew offered, "I picked you up a sub on the way back."

"I have food you don't know about," said Jesus. "Simon?" he asked, "How many months before farmers begin shelling corn around the

State?" But before he could respond, Jesus said, "You need to understand that the crop is already crisp for shocks."

"Jesus," Bart announced, "Better brace yourself because that woman you just spoke with is headed this way in high gear with her entire family tree."

Chapter 8

The Mayor stepped back into his fifth floor office following verbal blows with aldermen from the southern district who were ballistic after having read press releases that outlined his interest in planting yet another regional airport right in the middle of their wards. Earlier in the year, Harry had projected an electronic template of an elaborate air terminal overlaying it upon a wall map of Chicago during the course of a political dinner. Harry came alive as he keyed the remote, ordering computer software to feed slide after slide into the projection device, marking the proposed site before everyone's view. There had been plenty of talk about the proposed airport but mostly just political talk over drinks late at night. Everyone but Harry knew it was a feasible impossibility, but he dominated the mayoral field among his national counterparts and in fact played in a global league in which only a few were admitted. And there was no argument about that from any sector: north, south, east or west; Harry ruled like a king and his influence was felt well beyond Chicago.

Harry's family history lay buried beneath falsified documents and hearsay that lay deeper than the foundation supporting the Sears Tower. The steep climb to political success was without elevators. And the truth of his upbringing and hardships, had they been known would likely have served to woo the hearts of many who hated him. No one could quite understand his relentless pursuit to cover the region's acreage with expensive concrete mountains imported to the Midwest requiring equal amounts of tax payers' dollars—acres and mountains. But Harry would be horrified for anyone to know of his true origins. The fear made him strong and he courted absolutely anyone who could offer him political and personal advantage. But the honeymoon always ended early in the romance as he had no capacity for intimacy, feelings of loyalty and certainly no tolerance for anyone who could not continue to benefit him in a significant way. Politics was not Harry's first love, but it was the best means he had found to facilitate it. Harry had a penchant for building and the bigger, more outlandish, the better. He once dismantled a 200 foot stone tower, huge in diameter that used to stand down by the Chicago river and moved it to the top of a sizeable high rise because the view from the top was obscured by an adjacent building that was only slightly higher. The mayor billed the entire effort as a kind gesture on his part to unobstruct a draw bridge and provide the citizens a new and affordable mall—"The Harrison" he named it; but everyone near the project understood from the beginning that Harry was designing his own private palace for relaxation and entertainment. The entire top level was an expansive sun roof that provided warmth on winter days and a view of the stars at night. Typically the Mayor wouldn't involve himself in anything low budget; but again, the tower was a personal gift to himself. If other projects didn't crack hundreds of millions, he yawned and preferred to let subordinates shine in smaller spotlights.

Harry earned investiture as Mayor after only a few short years of service as an Alderman. From the beginning, Harry was hauling in far more of the City's share of pork from as far away as Washington. Both of the current U. S. Senators from the State were mere emissaries and the State Representatives were flatware in his hands. Harry's motto simply stated was, "get all you can—can all you get, and poison the rest." Federal dollars that made it through the Mayor's exchange rate generally fared well and translated into more jobs being created which resulted in lower unemployment and area enhancements that were visible and generally desirable. Some of his harbor and break water innovations were the most appreciated, not to mention the coliseum, which the colossal price tag about choked the Nation. But it was the mother of all sports arenas, and sports dominated the minds of Americans—of course, some of the most avid lived right there in the Windy City.

It was Harry's early development that propelled him to the top with atomic like propulsion despite the pull of white resistance that tried to hold him down. He determined one day as an eight year old while sitting alone on a round ten gallon ice water container that he would never look up to anyone for very long if he could ever get out of his present circumstances that were extremely impoverished. Harry was keenly aware of his destitution even as a child. Dark and suicidal thoughts that would visit him again and again throughout life were never allowed to linger long. His gut was already learning how to collaborate with his brain in order to coerce weaker emotions and bring them into submission. This would become the same simple strategy he would also use to govern people—fear and intimidation. In those early years, Harry would jump down from the container after a bout with the blackness and could always affirm himself and redirect his interests by looking upon the city he carved in the dirt where his mother left him to play for 12—16 hours a day. The clay city was incredibly elaborate considering the entire layout was hatched in the mind of a lad who had never been in a town of over ten to fifteen thousand. Harry's metropolis was complete with tunnels, overpasses, parks and lakes that held a few cups of water until it was licked up by a blistering sun that he thought he actually heard laugh at him from time to time. He built a harbor for his boat which was carved by a stranger and one of the few toys he ever possessed. Harry experimented with blinds because of his frustration with the wind that pushed great ripples across his little puddles. He discovered that a harbor would allow his vessels to remain moored and accessible to the imaginary men who boarded them. Harry was never a particularly happy person. He hated the solitude. The sun hardened the clay and Harry hardened his heart day by day.

Harry was born into a family of migrant farmers and his earliest memories included spending entire days waddling half clothed behind his mother in the middle of somebody else's one-thousand acre patch of peppers and other hand picks. He knew what it was to measure the day by watching morning dew evaporate and afternoon sweat run down and soak the back of his mama's sleeveless cotton dress like a gentle water fall. Her black skin glistened and was as soft and beautiful as the same woman laying on a beach basted with coconut oil. But this was no beach, not even in her dreams. From a distance, the family looked like an award stock of Angus with heads low and bellowing blues known only to those who serf in heat. Harry saw far more of the woman's back side than he ever did her face as best he could recall. Now that he was at the headwaters, he vowed never to return to the slough.

Before he was twelve, an uncle who escaped similar sentence talked his folks into a boarding arrangement that would move Harry out east where he could complete high school; Herod then changed his first and last name before pursuing political science at the University of Illinois. The rest of Harry's story is history. Whether it was Eagle Scout (which values he never lived up to), class president or fraternity president, Harry's assiduous nature always landed him in the most important leadership roles in virtually every realm he took an interest. He graduated with the top of his class from Harvard Law School and not because he was such an academic wizard but because of his personal finesse and ability to visually see through problems to solutions for which he was legendary. Harry was offered a teaching fellowship, but respectfully declined, while reasoning with local reporters that his abilities would be better utilized in humble public service. This notion contradicted everything they had come to learn about Harry but such was his style of relating.

"The residents won't stand for it," the aldermen shouted. "This plan is absolutely ludicrous, and wait until we speak with the governor—everyone's aware of the animosity between the two of you and if you continue we're prepared to enlist his support." Harry motioned with his hands and began blowing more smoke than was presently streaming from his cigar as he ever so politely utterly ignored the concerns they aired while leaving them with the false impression that their sentiments had been duly noted and would be considered in upcoming City Council meetings. He knew all along how he and his ad hoc advisory board, which he secretly assembled, would react to their pleas. He could hardly hold a straight face, especially for Willard who he thought more than once to have placed at the bottom of the Illinois River along with some other mutts who had barked up the wrong tree. Harry never listened, but he watched carefully so as to play back the episodes during committee meetings. The room would fill with laughter as he often stood up and pantomimed caricatures of the hated Aldermen in ridiculous and exaggerated ways that made them look like children screaming at the neighborhood bully who wouldn't behave in the sand lot or play by their rules.

"Marie," he called his office manager into their hearing with suckers, "be sure to have Brenda or one of the secretaries transcribe the concerns of each of these men for their individual wards and give them a personal copy. They have brought a number of crucial residential concerns to my attention that I have grossly overlooked.

"Gentlemen," he addressed the three men before walking to his interior office, "Mrs. Pierce will find you seats and someone will be right along to assist you."

"Thank you, Mrs. Pierce, and oh, Marie, I'll need to see you in my office A.S.A.P."

"I'll be right there," Marie said. After a moment, Mrs. Pierce joined the Mayor and began her usual update. "Harry, here is the City Council's calendar as well as the morning's calls, a typed draft of your dinner address at the Ritz…"

"For crying out loud, Pierce—slow down your turbine and do something with that sardine breath," the Mayor made her pause while he studied another calendar and abbreviated notes scribbled from an earlier breakfast. "Alright, go on Pierce, give me the rest of it," he demanded impetuously.

"Leonard Geiger is waiting for your return call," she said without the slightest regard for his insulting and demeaning manner. His rude and often inhumane treatment of men and women alike rose unabated because Harry kept meticulous files on anyone close to him with more intimate and convicting information than they could even imagine. He leaked out notes from his file whenever he felt he needed a little extra intimidation to bring even a seasoned staff back in line. In fact, Harry would not hire staff or pursue a close relationship with anyone until a full background investigation had been conducted that turned up enough mud to qualify them for his administration. Harry adopted the craft from his hated enemy, Leonard Geiger.

"He says it's urgent and would like for you to call him immediately."

"Geiger is a bigger pain than Mr. P. Hemorrhoid ever thought about. He thinks he's got me in his back pocket! The little insignificant, microscopic worthless excuse for a morsel; I'll personally gas the mangy mongrel myself if he hears from me again!" The Mayor's rage was always touched off by the name, 'Leonard Geiger' and it was one of Marie's highest orders to ensure he didn't totally lose emotional control when he vented his incredible wrath toward him around the office. Geiger was the one man who had all the dirt on Harry including his true origins expunged from forgotten files which Geiger could document. Harry's personal files filled with scraps and hearsay he gathered on others was simply spurious mutterings compared to Geiger's scientific reconnaissance exploits. He gained his composure and loosened his tie to allow the blood to circulate freely when he pulled Marie's hands from around his waist and said, "O.K., I'm O.K., I'll be alright. Call the Heeb and tell the cockroach that I've got better things to do than to watch after the young rabbi that's eating away at his ratings." Marie picked up the receiver and Harry quickly emptied it from her hands in a way that hurt her and she cried. "I'll handle that, now dry up and get on back to your desk!"

Harry had a more than passing interest in Jesus, too, but one thing he would find absolutely intolerable was assisting Geiger in pulling him down. In reality, Harry secretly wished that he might see Jesus. He was an extremely superstitious man and the stories he had been hearing around the City and northwest suburbs raised his curiosity.

* * * *

The Passover of the Jews was two weeks past. Jesus and his followers had not stopped since they arrived in Mount Prospect busying themselves with work of every sort but especially the needs of people. Rise early and stay up late was the pattern. Saturday afternoon Jesus brought things to a halt and led them over to a friend's private owned pizzeria for something to eat. Freddie told Jesus anytime he wanted to build his own—just slip in the back, do the health department scrubs, and clean up his mess. Simon and Thad, who were becoming good friends, were more interested in throwing dough at one another than learning the craft of spinning a ball of the stuff until it stretched to the right diameter. Jesus was presently flinging one over his head and trying to teach John the finer points he himself had picked up from the pizza veterans, Terry and Warren, who were brothers to Fred Allegretti. Thad shoveled up the prepared dough's and placed them in the continuous oven while others cleaned up the mess and made their way to tables out front.

"You boys, find drinks and sit down," said Allegretti, who was near 80 and always spoke in a voice that sounded like he was hoarse. "I'll bring these pizzas to you when they're done."

Jesus stepped into the service side of Allegretti's and caught flack immediately from two of Geiger's men who were verbally reprimanding John and had him pinned to the ropes. John was confident but no match for these wolves.

"Jesus," they asked, "why do you train your men to do that which is way out of bounds on the Sabbath?" John stepped back into the fold. They knew Jesus had a reputation for humiliating other experts of Jewish Law, but they were confident of their own theological prowess and came ready to explore any new depths he might choose. Their instruments always read shallow when they were floating dead center above ocean canyons opened by him that couldn't be fathomed with human sonar. Allegretti arrived at the table with two hot pizzas and the four of them began scarping them up the way starved men eat bread.

Jesus had not forgotten about the detectives and while licking tomato paste from his fingers, he turned in his chair and addressed them. His men had seen this routine before and with the exception of John, they hardly paid them mind at all. They ate while Jesus lectured, but in spite of John's physical weariness, he opened a channel, pushed up the slide on his receiver inputs and was ready to record.

"You are men of the Book," Jesus said. "Don't you remember reading in there about what David and his men did when they were famished? He went into the house of God and took the bread, the consecrated bread, gentlemen, bread that only priests were to eat, and he and his men ate it. You see, gentlemen, the son of man is Boss of the Sabbath."

After scribbling another note or two, one agent said to his companion, "This is enough indictment for the day, lets be going, the smell in here is getting to me."

"Yeah," said Simon, "well, don't let that door slam into your back side on the way out." The two legalists glared back at a man who was ready to whip them both."

"That's enough, Simon," Jesus said, and the two men returned to their seats so as to call his bluff. Others of questionable character and well known in the community entered the pizzeria and settled in around Jesus' table.

"Here he goes eating with rift raft again," the annoying drip continued.

"You're the consecrated bread, aren't you, Jesus?" John whispered from his side.

"John," said Jesus rewarding his apperception, "I tell you the truth I am. And if others are willing to sit in the Negev and meditate, they will receive the same comfort you're experiencing. Lift your eyes, for she will come from a distance one evening and join you in your mother's tent." Thad and Simon were still caught up describing how they would spend an afternoon torturing the two while Jesus and John continued an important visit at their seats. "John," Jesus continued, "You must eat my flesh and drink my blood. As it is you have no life in and of yourself. You're looking at the bread of God which comes down out of heaven and gives people life. John, your eyes are pleasantly satisfied for what you see and your ears for what you hear. The one who comes to me will never go hungry and he who believes in me will never get thirsty."

"Jesus, I don't get it," Thad said ending his imaginary tag team with Simon. "These guys are bummed out by the fact that we're not keeping Sabbath regulations as they require, but you tell them a story about David and an incident that involved eating the sacred show bread. What's the connection? You left them with the impression that you are greater than the Law."

"Thad, the entire transaction from the mountain top with Moses was a package. Moses brought down a mighty substance that glowed for awhile and it was true substance. Geiger just cannot comprehend that God has punctured time and stepped aboard. Solely imbued with pure unadulterated truth along with a limitless supply of free dispensing favor—He took on human flesh. That fact blows all the fuses in his dated 100 amp box. He is seeking to defend a code that has run it's intended course.

"Well, that's still about as clear as the DesPlaines River," said Thad respectfully.

Jesus continued while two of his men worked on crust; all the meat had fallen to the floor. "The ten words," Jesus said, "are no more or less significant than the civil and ceremonial laws that proffer them. That's why I justified our Sabbath activity today by appealing to a law not found on the tablets of stone. It's a beautiful and harmonious package; but when its day comes and they're encouraged to open it up and enjoy the gift, they turn up their nose and find the offer reprehensible. I quoted the story from David's experience for two reasons. David saw this moment and rejoiced no less than Abraham. And secondly, I have to take a toy away from them because they are abusing others with it.

The Law and the Prophets ran up until Jack and if you care to trace it through, he is Elijah who was to come.

"God's final appeal to his own justice, his hatred for sin and love for humankind is not the law and never has been. God appeals to the slaughter of the one who is innocent. His love is upheld and his justice is not compromised at the place where two of his greatest passions collide. And one day very soon they will hit head on with such an impact that they will be eternally embedded in one another. The prophet Isaiah speaks explicitly about such a day."

"Still in the dark, Thad?" Simon asked while mimicking a well known sound that recurs in the movie: "The Good, The Bad and The Ugly."

"Simon, why don't you sit up in that chair where we can all see you," Jesus said, "and let me tell you the story of the Good, the Bad and the Ugly. See if you can pick out the players." Jesus had repositioned himself so as to be easily heard by two men at a nearby table who were still taking notes and making castigating comments about others who had also heard of Jesus and wandered in to hear him speak.

"Allegretti," Simon shouted toward the service window, "better put on another pizza, we're going to be here awhile." Simon enjoyed Jesus' stories immensely and couldn't wait to get home at night or from extended trips just to sit with Jill and the boys and retell Jesus' words with his own spin.

"Tucked away in some of my doodlings is a pencil sketch I've just about completed that I think I'll leave untitled," Jesus said.

"Lord," John observed, none of your sketches are titled."

"The centerpiece of the portrait is a loving father," Jesus began. "He is in the foreground of a spacious farm that supports he and his sons very well. His long slender fingers lay like the feathers of a hen upon the shoulders of a boy who kneels at his feet facing him with his head pressed in against his father's body. The smell of his father's garment reminds him of the comfort of home. Standing aside in the shadows is an elder son who awaits the lad's summary judgment."

"What's wrong with the kid?" asked Simon, "the cops after him for something?"

"No, Simon. Jesus just said that the warden was in the shadows; they've already apprehended him." John said jumping ahead with an early interpretation.

Jesus raised his hand in a gesture to go on, "Both of the boys in this portrait have lived their entire lives with ill suspicions about their father. Men, I want you to remember the father in this story as the protector of the limitless favor dispenser; he knows the preciousness of grace. The father is good, but his younger son is bad, to use Simon's allusion. He is the fool par excellence and personifies everything that the Proverbs warn us against. He flies by the seat of his pants, no rules, no fear, better me than you, slice and dice, live for the day only..."

"Pre-Maggie, we've got the picture. Now go on, Jesus, this is getting interesting," Simon said.

"While the father is the protector of the limitless favor dispenser, the younger son is a favor slinger. A squanderer. Inwardly his soul is ravaged by sin which has left things pretty much in shambles. He is angry, resentful and has secretly been praying for his father's death. He will have to go to the dungeon and face starvation in order to find his senses. Finally, we meet a man who can best be described as..."

"Ugly," Thad remarked and cheated a face look to the other table.

"There is something dark about the elder son that is difficult to capture. How do you draw contempt? His is a religious, haughty, self righteous hue that is best portrayed as a shadow. He is somewhat O.K. to an undiscerning eye from the outside, but inside there is a rotten, sulphurous smell of hell that has roasted a heart that hangs dangling on a rotisserie with meat drippings feeding flames that lick the bottom of the grate."

"Wow, Jesus," said Simon, "don't sugar coat this, we can handle it!"

Jesus raised a brow and went on, "While the younger son is a great fool, the elder son is a warden to use John's expression. The dungeon of his mind is lined with corpses hanging in stocks that cry to be released."

"The younger son has no rules or fear while the elder son keeps a strict and meticulous score card; he lives by the code and is a favor killing collector. He remembers and files away every wrong. He has no joy, no smile, just continual judgment and criticism of the father's lavishly dispensed favors. The younger boy will gorge himself on chocolate cake and find no milk, while the elder son has access to both, but treats himself to neither one. The story of the elder son's life falls like a bombshell upon the playground of militant fundamentalism.

"Jesus, don't stop now, they pleaded, we want to hear the blast," while chair legs squealed on tile as two men across the way shifted positions.

"The two sons represent two types of people," Jesus summarized while underlining an important contrast: "Those who involve themselves in outwardly grotesque sin," chairs beneath his own table moved, "and those who involve themselves with inwardly grotesque sin. Something you have to understand men," Jesus offered an important editorial comment, "the son of man has come to search out and apprehend run-a-ways. When a man or woman loses something important to them, they search for it very carefully until it is recovered. When God loses a child, and all the children of Adam are lost, he seeks them until they are safely recovered."

"It's incredible, isn't it, Jesus?" said Simon's maturing side, "God gets excited about rescuing deadbeats while the hardheads down at the synagogue complain about the very thing that makes angels rejoice."

"Simon, you're beginning to see the character of God," Jesus said, while continuing the story. "The Law provides guidelines for the division of property. The first born receives two-thirds while the remainder in this case will fall to the younger son. When a father breaks up an estate like this before his death, he retains control and use of property earnings. Titles can be transferred but the heirs would never consider selling the homestead or anything of material value until the father is dead. In this story, the younger son liquidated his assets and made haste to the west coast."

"Wait a minute, Jesus," said Thad. "How did the boy sell the property if his father is still living?"

"Good question, Thad. You see, the son is insisting, without legal grounds or cultural precedent, that his dad give him full ownership so that he can dispose of it however he wishes. The demand is outrageous—he's saying in point of fact—Dad, you're standing in my way, I wish you were dead so that I can get on with my life! Surprisingly, the father grants the boy's wish. Can you imagine this—a father who raised the boy and provided for him, now being rejected out of hand for a fist full of dollars?"

"Cute, Jesus," Simon said, "I saw that one, too."

Jesus placed his foot on top of Simon's and continued, "It's the kindness and humility of God which often makes him turn his cheek to the ungrateful and hardhearted."

"Well, you might well imagine how someone inexperienced handles money. The boy left town, burned bridges behind him and began a lifestyle of the wildest extravagance, living recklessly and unrestrained. He visited cities far and wide. The lights and glitter pointed like a huge neon arrow: "PLAY HERE!" But the glow attracts the moth only to scorch and kill it."

"So is that it, Jesus?" asked John.

"No, but I won't be long. We've heard about the good, and we're almost done penciling in the bad," Jesus took a drink, then continued by saying, "Be careful of inexperience, dislike of discipline, self-will and flashy indulgences. Two bridges fell through on either side of this lad at once. He ran out of money and a severe economic depression hit the area. A fool counts on neither one but sometimes they come as mercies. The boy was reduced to a laborer's position on a farm tending feeder hogs."

"Cursed is the man who would breed swine," the remark carried over from the other table.

Jesus ignored the remark, "No one would offer him money and this is when a careful and fearless moral inventory began. Hardship has a way of helping us face reality. The boy begins to realize that he might fair better back home as a yard servant than face starvation surrounded by these so called freedoms from home. So the kid who was hitchhiking to the next manure pile asks the driver to stop. The boy does a 180 degree turn and heads east."

The men at the next table were growing sick with the syrupy tale and found the description of the father to be downright repugnant and foreign to any father figure they knew anything about or could possibly conceive. One who had been listening most carefully shouted across the floor, "They'll beat the tar out of that kid when he comes back to town. We wouldn't even allow him a foot in our neighborhood once a story like that began to circulate. What are you doing, Rabbi, just making this whole thing up as you go?"

"Never mind them, Simon," Jesus said. "Our time is short. Let me finish the story. While this son is still a long way off, his father sees him. He would know the boy's walk anywhere. He felt compassion for his son and ran out to meet him and held him and kissed him repeatedly.

Immediately, he walked him back to the house under his protection which silenced the hateful remarks that were being heaped upon him by laborers from adjoining farms."

"Bologna," the jeers erupted again, "Ben Siriach says that a man's walk tells you what he is. It is totally unacceptable for a man of this father's stature you've dreamed up to run in public. Certainly, he wouldn't do so for this worthless kid!"

"Tell them that's your whole point, Lord," said John.

"Jesus, it would take Thad and me just a minute or two to move them and their table outside on the sidewalk while you and little Johnny here take a potty break."

"Let it go, Simon," Jesus said.

"Yeah," said Thad, "let them keep nibbling. I want to see their faces when this bombshell you mentioned goes off in their faces."

"I'll be sure to leave that part off for David and Jonathan," said Simon. "They'd blow a wing off the house while Jill napped with the right formula."

"Be sure to record all the bombing remarks," one crone said to another.

"In this story," Jesus resumed his thought, "the returning son is not even allowed to give his father an apology. His father knows that words do not exist that would adequately atone or explain the boy's heart and the trouble he has brought upon his head. The father cuts off the boy's attempts and instead of scolding him, he shells out several brisk commands to the hired help. "Tim, bring him my jacket, the one with the family logo; Miller brothers, place shoes on your foreman's feet; and Russell, a hand who kept the farm records, 'see to it that he receives checks under my account name. And Ruppert, fire up the Bar- B- Que pit, we're going to roast the best calf on the place. All of you stop your labors, call the hands, we're going to throw the biggest party you've ever seen or heard tell of!"

"A huge party got underway and smoke from the green hickory thrown on top of hardwood that had burned down summoned people from even the most remote parts of the farm which would include the father's elder son who was the furthest away. He always found a fence or something of that kind on the perimeter to busy himself with. The location also gave him a view to the adjoining farms and he often wondered if the Fisher Brothers ran as tight a ship as he. His brother's action made him a laughing stock and the family's disrepute was hard for the elder son to countenance."

"The boy knew something big was happening because he could hear the sound system and smell the wood from way out where he stood. He jumped onto a four wheeler and drove cautiously back and up the long lane leading into the home place. The twin pinchers weren't there to meet him as usual, but he could see someone rolling in the lawn up ahead and as far as he could remember, there was only ever one person whom they allowed that privilege. He drew near the house and could have taken a picture of the place; the dogs broke from a boy who went back inside; there were more lights on than he thought Dad would normally allow; vehicles were strewn around the place like a used auto sales and people moved about eating, dancing and drinking while an old hit by Kenny Rogers and the First Edition played, "Tell it all Brother." He found the mood of celebration downright offensive.

The pizzeria was generally brisk, and it was no different today except a higher percentage than usual were choosing to stay and listen to an open air message coming from the mouth of a wonderful story teller. The only sad faces were those that usually hung in a museum run by a curator named Geiger who had sent them over to obtain more incriminating data. Allegretti and his brothers leaned from service windows or the bar to listen in on a guide share all his knowledge about things old and new with eager students.

"The younger son outwardly strayed from his father's house," Jesus continued, "while the older son inwardly strayed." John listened to pictures as Jesus continued with shades of lead that was working up a beautiful portrait of the heavenly Father and his love for sinners. Jesus paused his discussion long enough to upbraid the hardhearted and also to entice them to come into the house.

"Consider how great God's love is," he began, "and look for a moment at your own joyless lives. A lost son has returned, celebrate with us! Yes, they're incomplete," referring to his followers and spreading open palms to indicate his solidarity with them. "Come, join us at this table." But they would have no part of it. "The elder son," Jesus said, "will walk the same road just traversed by the younger son. From the lane, he calls a hired hand and asks him what the meaning of all the celebration is about. He didn't have the courage to just walk into the house and see for himself. He too had put up a wall to separate himself from his father. The father had been searching for his older son as well, and when he saw him, he called for him to come to the house where the refreshments were being lavishly engulfed. The father was met with stiffness and resistance that turned to an argument which cooled the guests. The flood gates opened in a moment of rare truth and the elder son began to reveal his heart.

"I've slaved for you all my life," he said, revealing the kind of relationship he had established with his father. The elder son didn't know his father as dad any more than the younger son did. He considered himself a slave and his father a taskmaster. He was enraged by the party that was under way and told his father in short order that he had never provided him with any special meats so that he could throw a party with his friends.

The more the boy vented the more he revealed about himself. He never stopped to consider that the meat was for everyone and not intended as a desert or something the youth had merited. The father was throwing a party because of his own personal overflow of joy. He had his boy back! The other thing that slipped out was the older son's commitment to his true family. The boy made it clear that he had his own personal friends that he would rather celebrate with, and it was clear that they were not presently on the farm. The people the elder son liked to associate with were men just like himself with similar complaints. So the elder son basically says, "I'm not part of this family. This son of yours….," he muttered with more contempt rather than identify him as a brother who had seriously blown it.

The father made an effort even in the face of another rejection to convince the older son that his property would remain his sole right and the younger boy's return would not effect anything. The father could not have been more generous, "All that I have is your property!"

"Yes," the elder son said, "but I can't sell it and do as I want. I can't even Bar-B-Que with my friends when I want without fear of your disapproval."

At this, the father was stunned to near silence. He breathed a deep sigh and said, "So you also want me out of the way. I just want my boys," said the father as he began to return to the house. "Come to the party," he implored.

Jesus lifted his eyes to two men who had not moved since they had all arrived and said to them, "Gentlemen, this all began with your criticism of my table company. I'm inviting you both again to join us at the banquet. Don't allow your religion to hold you in slavish bondage."

"The Good, the Bad and the Ugly," said Simon stretching while John looked pensively into Jesus' face.

"Jesus," said Thad, "that's an excellent story, but it sure is tough to walk into that house when you're feeling so crummy about yourself and all that you did. I mean, how did the kid know how to behave?"

"You keep working that, Thad," Jesus said. "I understand the problem but it's really your problem; just remember the climate out at the farm is outstanding so the doors are never shut."

Jesus rose up from the table and walked out of the building before a mixed company of onlookers. They gathered in his van and headed back over to the two bedroom on Cove in Mount Prospect. Everyone unloaded and joined friends who frequented Jesus' place that was always open for business and attracted a steady flow of folks—even some from out of town who had heard about the new teachings of The Way. Most everyone took a nap or found a place to lay low for a few hours. The mental drain listening to Jesus sapped out a lot of energy. Simon and Bart who had been on the premises most of the day had gone on earlier to spend the remainder of the day with their families while others fired up the grill and prepared the volleyball net for a game in the side lot under flood lights attached to the side of the building. Teams were selected and Jesus ended up as usual on a weak side with the inexperienced. He is the one who created an interest in the game, but it was quickly taken over by a ruthless crowd who lived, breathed and ate volleyball. And since the locals couldn't teach Jesus theology, they prided themselves in teaching him the finer points of volleyball. When Simon was available, he loved rotations that brought he and Jesus face to face at the net. Simon wasn't the most graceful, but he could put down a spike as well as any who had visited the court.

A group visiting from Nashville were especially competitive; they wouldn't even talk to the opposing team during a game—folks they had just been eating and praying with in group. And it all began as a game. John and Jesus faced the net with the help of Darlene, Barb and Gary. On the other side was a troop of point lusty hyenas, scratching around the lot with eyes like eagles, they battened the ball at will and laughed a Nashville gull they invented that sounded just like hyenas. They took points like scavengers that had torn flesh from a slain carcass. Holding their hands and arms forced down at their sides, they would turn down their heads like gooseneck faucets and spray out hilarity while stepping around the court just exactly like a bunch of hyenas. This continued to the other team's grief until a fresh serve was up. After three games of 14 to zip, Hoxley from Nashville, who was most intoxicated by the game, asked if Jesus had any board games inside. "This volleyball is getting too easy," he would taunt and the thought would begin them all cackling again.

"Jesus, it's no use," said Siva from the side. "You'll never get invited to the Olympics with this team."

"Yeah, I don't suppose." He said smiling back at a woman who had a heart of gold. "Look at the bright side," Jesus said to his team in jest, "these guys are all leaving tomorrow."

"You're loss," hollered, Baker with a laugh.

"Hey, Jesus, do you know if they make anything in an aerosol spray that repels this species of locust?" asked Carol in the hearing of all. "They sound like a bunch of cicadas swarming around the net."

"I'm not sure," Jesus admitted while playing her lead, "but to my knowledge, they don't last long. After they're done screeching for a few days they leave their dry crustations on the trunk's of trees, then go back into the earth and lay eggs before they die."

"Eggs!" Carol cried, "You mean to tell me that we have just escaped an infectious plague only to have it all return in a few short years." Mike and other losers started yapping with her but they were quickly cut off by an overwhelming howl from a pack who had endured after game jeers many times before. A neighbor stepped outside who thought a civil warning alarm had gone off and was invited over to enjoy hot sandwiches from the grill. Before leaving the party, Jesus reminded the thirty or so present that he wanted to see them on the lake near the fountain by 10:00 A.M.

Jesus left the party on Cove about 10:00 P.M. and drove downtown where he had access to an office on the top floor of the Fine Arts Building. He carried steps up the ten stories, entered a private drawing room and spent the entire night in prayer with God. Early the next morning, Jesus placed calls to Bart, Thomas, Simon, Matthew and several others inviting them to join him at the small studio. Siva excused herself from work where she trained new MBA's fresh from Kellogg and was met by Jean, Lazarus and other familiar volunteers who were answering questions and trying to escort a growing crowd away from Congress street and further into the park grass. After about 75 minutes, Jesus emerged from the front of the building with twelve men. They immediately crossed S. Michigan onto Congress and made passage between the great pylon statues that flanked either side of the broad concourse. Jesus' top hair lengthened in the lake breeze and the purple sports jacket flowed like a robe as it was picked up by customary winds.

One of the volunteers known to Jesus stood on the fringe of the crowd and quoted aloud from a book of wisdom as he watched his Lord approaching. "There are three things which are magnificent in the sea, yes four that are majestic when they move: the killer whale which is awesome among its kind and does not retreat before anything, the effortless floating ray, the cutting barracuda, and a Commander standing before his troops on the deck of an aircraft carrier."

Jesus had selected twelve men to be with him after careful consideration and prayer. These he personally commissioned and they followed him into Grant Park where a large crowd had gathered in the northwest quadrant to hear his words and seek a healing touch. On his way through the level area, many in the crowd broke human boundaries just to touch him and as many as did were healed of diseases and unclean spirits because power was coming out of him, and he demonstrated authority over them all.

An art exhibit featuring several life size sculptures created by the renowned Joyce Reynolds were on display in the confines of one of the large grass areas surrounded by trees. Joyce was presently removing chalk from a smaller work where she stood among crowds who were admiring her pieces. Jesus befriended Joyce days earlier while viewing her art. Today he approached one of the pieces, a thoroughbred with its head thrown high and held by reins that fell into the hands of a proud Sioux Chief who knelt below. Joyce took a seat on the limestone base along side the chief while Jesus climbed up on the horse and lifted his voice so that he could be heard by all those standing around.

"Drew, this will be remembered as the sermon on the mount," Simon said, as they listened with interest to one who taught with authority and not the same memorized rote they had been used to.

Jesus spoke for the better part of an hour about those God specially regards. Ancillary topics included principles of judgment between people, matters of worry for which he stepped down and drew attention to flowers that were clothed in splendor, seagulls which neither sow nor reap but nevertheless remained well fed and whatever else served as a graphic illustration of God's caring fraternal nature. He went on in time to correct prevailing views about personal piety as well as the misunderstandings many held regarding divorce, lawsuits, slander and several other important topics. The most memorable story for John and some of the others who had been with Jesus was his closing lesson which was a masterful vignette in the craft of composition using comparison and contrast. Jesus wrapped up his remarks talking about foundation materials used in the construction of houses which he likened to those who obey or disobey his words. The application was glaring for those who had been on hand in Hinsdale the day Milton pulled down the house. He spoke about one man who built his house upon sand and another man who built his house upon rock. When wind and storms assailed them both, the one built upon sand collapsed like someone had winched the inside walls out in an instant causing the roof to crash to the ground. Jesus told them that the fall of the house would be great and the picture was vividly remembered.

From a literary standpoint, John was always looking for biblical allusion, clues and insights one had to strain to sometimes get; but that's the way Jesus taught. He told his men privately that the crowd wasn't going to be privy to the same information they received.

"But be careful how you tune in," Jesus charged them. "Because those who have a great deal are going to get a great deal more—sagging under the load; but to the one who thinks he has arrived, yet fails to comprehend, even what he thinks he has will be stripped away. Ignorance is certainly not bliss. Excuses will not be tolerated when accounts are settled. But there are also some sobering responsibilities that accompany knowledge. Pay attention to that side of the ledger."

It was near the lunch hour when Jesus gathered the twelve whom he separated and excused for an afternoon of apprenticeship. Jesus walked south through Grant Park, stopped for Chicago dogs, which was an absolute must for his men who always threatened mutiny if he suggested anything else. Jesus cleared up a kosher issue weeks earlier when several Geigerites threw down a huge spade after catching Jesus and his men eating food that wasn't approved by Jewish Law. Unblessed food, they insisted among other things was prohibited by Moses and was absolutely off limits to anyone professing orthodoxy. But Jesus never claimed to play by their orthodox rules. He was the Law giver; but again, the circuitry wasn't there and so no connection was made. He taught his followers that food entering a person's body could not defile them; however, he was quick to add that evil thoughts and speech that proceed out of a persons mouth could indeed defile them. So he declared all foods kosher and to be gratefully enjoyed, giving God the thanks.

"Sanitation, circumcision, dates, periods and days," Simon said on that memorable, but infamous occasion, "is all those Geigerites can think about. I wish they would just castrate themselves, observe monthly feminine hygienic practices and stay out of a man's way!" Simon received a private lesson that day from one determined to temper a boiler that often leaked out unnecessary steam. Jesus actually found the mention of castration creative and insightful given their preoccupation with circumcision and the letter of law, but Simon was also a sexist and much of his speech received regular critique from Jesus who was working on installing a high efficiency unit in place of the old cast iron beast that creaked and fumed in Simon's chest.

After lunch, Jesus made up time walking the streets of the Loop before it got too late. His followers always felt like they were on some kind of force march when they were out in the open with him.

"Seems like panhandlers have taken over the news stands," Thomas observed. Shouts of *Streetwise* echoed around walls down deep in the man made caverns while others, who had no interest earning a few bucks pushing the news, just pushed out a paper cup and asked for a few dollars to get them a hot bowl of soup.

"Get back away from the man," Matthew shouted at a beggar who he perceived to be a little too greedy. Jesus stopped and offered the man a few singles and the exchange wasn't missed by a man wearing the same uniform less than a block away. When Jesus and his men crossed his perimeter, a barrage of verbiage exploded as he insisted on receiving the same treatment as the other beggar.

Jesus directed him to stand down the street with his fellow, "Perhaps it is a lucky spot," he said. The bag man spit at the joke, but Jesus was not joking and handed him no change.

Jude appreciated the lead and began, "Harry's got the unemployment rate so low in this City you couldn't scrape up what little is left with a spatula, and then you walk out on a fine street like this and find the low life's begging for a few bucks so they can buy another bottle of cheap wine. Then they vomit all over themselves and who gets to clean it up?"

"The taxpayers!" they all shouted.

"What do you think, Jude?" Jesus asked, and everyone in earshot knew that a school circle had just been dialed up. "Should the city banish these unsightly half-breeds and move them off these fine streets or maybe find a way to bring some of that smoked sausage Harry's so famous for grinding right down home and onto their breakfast tables? Poverty and wealth are two sides of the same idolatrous coin. There are people who live in abject poverty who are vicious enough to cut your throat for a nickel blaming it on their cynical conditioning or if they're real lazy, 'the devil made me do it.' Then there are people who live in king's palaces that are more frugal and philanthropic than you could even imagine. Many go on far, far less each week than people on welfare. You all know what's standard and so pay attention to the poor, but be aware; tables constantly turn in life. Stay on the right end of things men, for it sometimes means changing seats." Jesus concluded as he stepped up to yet another woman with her hand extended. The woman was docile and elderly and Jesus pitied her. He drew out a twenty dollar bill and asked the woman whose likeness and inscription it bore. The old woman could barely talk and was suffering from some obvious mental disturbance. Jesus placed the twenty into her ragged coat pocket while telling his followers to render to "Jackson" the things that were his and to God the things that belong to him. Jesus touched the woman in a way that went unnoticed by the others, and she immediately began speaking intelligibly and dropped some previous behaviors. Everyone but two or three knew Jesus had just been scammed.

It was getting late in the afternoon when Harry paged Marie and told her to send Brenda into his office to take several urgent letters that had to go out priority mail with the mornings first pick-up. Marie knew all about the Mayor's priority male habits; and after briefing the office on several important dates, she left Brenda with Harry and scooted out early to shop for groceries before going home. Geiger didn't like being ignored and because he was a familiar face around the Mayor's office and the crow's nest was empty, he casually unlocked the door, and stepped into Harry's private office unannounced only to find the Mayor and his secretary inflating numbers on a secret file.

"Good afternoon, Harry," the familiar greeting came from the entrance. "It's well past the lunch hour," Geiger said, taunting a man who was easily three times his size. "Thought I'd drop by and have a word with you before you expended yourself—I know you're a busy devil." He found the hat rack but held onto his umbrella which he almost always carried with him and took a seat with full view of the Mayor's private vertical file with the drawer still wide open. Brenda quickly rose to her feet without a word and grabbed some loose leaf from the floor on her way out. Geiger was a religious man and didn't find the exposure the least bit tasteful. It would be difficult to over exaggerate Geiger's cunning, wit and surgical like dissection of human beings: their environments, motivations, loves and fears. He enjoyed the critical analysis of others, but grew easily bored with garden variety demagogues that followed a basic pattern of lust for one individual thing or another.

While Harry earned most of his credits through the school of hard knocks, Geiger was carefully bred with choice stock and tutored throughout life by mentors who were fabulous at intrigue, lords of discipline, and carried letters written with the same black inky deceit that filled their own marrow. He was raised in a most affluent Skokie residence and schooled at the best universities that money could afford. But Geiger didn't like the profession of Rabbi any more than Harry liked being a politician. Geiger's first love was young boys and girls and the cloth was the best means he had found to facilitate his religious practice. Harry knew Geiger to be a pedophile but had no proof. Geiger loved the chess game he played with Harry; and if he ever became bored, he would return to his kids. Geiger was a small bald man with hollow eyes and a heart filled with insidious ploys he had personally developed over a lifetime of meditation that he waited patiently to test-fly with people like Harry. Geiger never smiled even when emptying rat traps form the previous night's kill. He was an inside trader exclusively and boasted a handsome portfolio which was the crowning effort of a life given to deceitful practices. Geiger's lamb like hypocrisy was so finely polished that it humiliated pharisaic wolves who tried to model cheap imitations of his strict methods. Men who loved him most often remarked that he could teach the devil himself a wile or two.

Brenda was already out of the office when Geiger dropped the point of his umbrella to the floor and began talking to Harry as though he had just hung up from a phone conversation. "Harry, so good to see you friend," said Geiger, and because he was having a relatively good day, he thought he meant it.

"Make it short, Geiger." Harry said and Geiger could see that the man was trembling in an office temperature that was moderate and comfortable.

"Look, Harry, I know how bad you'd like to just put me in my own private bath with plenty of the green gaseous stuff," Geiger said wincing and reeking of the same caricatures Harry reveled in, "but you and I both know what a huge mistake that would be. For the moment, my body surfaces without a pulse, the 98.6 and a good sound heartbeat, the switch will be thrown in your chair by colleagues that actually revere me and are more faithful than the Marines. They are convinced that I'm their Messiah. I can be yours, too. Imagine it, Harry, some 50,000 electrifying volts will pass into the publics ears in the form of documents, dates, names, places, pictures, no small amount of video, wire taps—shall I go on, Harry? I could basically make a full length motion picture just out of a few hours of your life and I've got years piled up, Harry, years of folly with your name on it." Harry was having an extremely difficult time breathing; and in fact, he and Geiger both thought for a moment that he might go into cardiac arrest right there in the office. Geiger didn't want that to happen because he needed Harry to do some work for him and so he backed off from his usual play.

"Geiger," Harry said with a sick catatonic look on his face that was frightening and required Geiger's attention. "I just saw a bright light," panting and stopping for breaths, "I'm not mixing meshugaas, you fool. My entire life passed before me in an instant, and it made me realize that you don't know the half of it. I thought I was going to die, Geiger. And do you know what?" Harry waited.

"No, what is it, Herod?" Geiger asked.

"I realized, Leonard, in that one precious moment, what eternal regret I would carry if I didn't risk what you know and fail to kill you with my bare hands before I die. Now I'm going to give you the thirty seconds you're dirt is worth and then you can walk out of here the way you came, or I'll have Brenda place a call and have you picked up with a coal shovel from the sidewalk below."

"Harry, Harry," Geiger soothed him, "we mustn't be so destructive with our tongues. I've merely come here in good will to enlist your support in the elimination of a mutual enemy—yours and mine."

"What are you afraid of?" asked Harry. "He's just a young boy with big ideas about the same God you pretend to serve."

Geiger rose from his seat (which he never did for anyone), and Harry understood he had finally stumbled onto something dear to Geiger. In Geiger's mind, God was not the ground of all being or whatever else theological systematitians taught, neither a deity to fear. He was no more committed to him than the book of code he chanted from on given Sabbaths. The Hebrew Bible was just a scroll filled with theological constructs and propositions that were antedated, spiritually impenetrable, but nevertheless served as an adhesive to hold together a social structure he believed to be the inevitable coming world order. And mockery or trite remarks about a young upstart he perceived to be eroding his base of power sent something deadly surging through his veins. Geiger held a prestigious chair of theology at the University of Chicago's Divinity School where he taught ancient and Semitic languages. He was a rationalist like many of his colleagues and was committed to a philosophy of historicism that ruled out any notion of the supernatural.

He sat back down and leaned forward, then said, "This Jesus from Buffalo Grove is walking in and out of our great City at will and the entire population is chasing after him. I'm concerned about the attention both papers are giving to reports that belong only in the picture packed trash morons are curious to read. Now, you've locked up one of them, but his greater accomplice is still at large, and I expect the job we agreed upon to be completed before any more arrangements can be made for the fund raiser you've been contemplating for early next year."

"Geiger, you're way over your time limit," Harry said. "I'll have my people get back with your flock of pedicured brains on sticks just as soon as I can nail down a time and place." Geiger knew he had lost something that day, but he was too engrossed in his own mission to worry over it. Almost mindlessly and staring in another direction, Geiger rose from his chair in his usual professional manner. He extended the tip of his umbrella pointing in the direction of his next step while excusing himself before an enemy who didn't know when he departed. Harry's fear of Geiger like other emotions was buried so completely beneath layers of hatred that it felt like a mild sickness in his gut whenever Geiger came near, but only to fade away and dissipate after his departure. Harry was equally resolved to achieve his own personal goals and wasn't about to allow a little nausea to make him buckle.

Chapter 9

On the second Sunday in June, Jesus was relaxing with a group of men and women following a Sabbath stay over at the home of Mary, Martha and Lazarus who were brother and sisters to one another and shared rent and household responsibilities at the same address on Quincy Court in Wheeling. Several who regularly spent time with Jesus picked up passes and walked down to the local outdoor pool while others read or enjoyed some personal time with Jesus which was rare outside of the usual three: Simon, James and John, whom Jesus was clearly working to develop as leaders.

Lunch preparations were underway and Martha had already dropped several heavy hints to her sister that it was their collective responsibility to serve the guests. Mary loved her sister and was generally out in front of things that needed attention, but today she sat with Jesus and was glowing with interest for the stories he told. Finally, in a moment of exasperation, Martha shouted at Jesus, interrupted the quiet serenity and insisted that he make Mary get off her soft side and into the kitchen to help with a fruit salad that would require some work. Jesus laughed aloud which got everyone else going because they all understood Martha's controlling personality and insistence on detail. "Martha, Martha," Jesus said, "slow down a little and enjoy the moment while I'm available. Life is filled with demands and some of them are necessary but one you can't afford to pass up is offering portions. And Mary's will not be taken from her."

A space of silence was interrupted by a rap on the storm door where some Jewish elders from Waukegan stood waiting to deliver a message to Jesus. Word about him and the signs and wonders that accompanied the proclamation of the special news he presented had begun to spread all over Illinois and even into adjoining states. A retired Army Colonel who remained in the area following the closing of Fort Sheridan had heard about Jesus through an old Navy acquaintance he thought had died years ago from cirrhosis of the liver. Captain Roger Reeves took early retirement due to health problems related to a heavy drinking habit. Roger and Lucy had such a promising and enjoyable retirement awaiting them at choice property in Brunswick, Georgia, that they had fallen heir to years previous. But Roger's courtship with alcohol, which he blamed on the death of countless dreams, and Lucy's emotional deadness led them slowly and almost imperceptibly back to the Great Lakes where his career began. The vacation home in Brunswick had to be sold in time; they couldn't afford additional taxes. And now, instead of experiencing the benefits of many years of work and a living environment comparable to the amenities of senior officer housing, they found themselves lords of a small square of maintenance hungry apartment units which barely generated enough income for them to survive. Nearly all of the Captain's monthly retirement income was leached away on accumulated debt. Lucy had begged him to file for bankruptcy, but he was born in a different era and wouldn't even consider it. They realized that if it were not for naval medical benefits, they would be facing even more serious straits; on the other hand, it was hard for them to imagine how anything but skid row could be appreciably worse. Thirty years of travel added to the double vise pressures of marital unhappiness and loss of personal vision for his life nearly drove the captain to an early grave.

There was a day when Lucy would have been glad for it but things were changing, not overnight, but the old salt was up more than usual due to the tidiness of the place. Fresh cut flowers and scented bowls of potpourri brought a new fragrance to their home; summer was upon them and the captain thought he might get a view of hope. Windows that hid behind blinds he honestly didn't even know were there brought in light almost as bright as that which ruled Lucy's new heart. And it was Lucy who showed her beggarly husband where to find bread. She rose in the morning with a song, put on make up and fixed her hair in a way that made her look younger. Lucy was now fitting into a size 14 that called for some additions in her wardrobe. And though she had little to spend, she shopped thrift stores and second hands only to be rewarded with what she considered a gold mine in clothing and shoes. Lucy looked absolutely stunning on her 57th and Roger made kind remarks that made her feel cherished and like his bride again. Lucy had been given a taste of life by Jesus, and she wanted to share it with the man she forgot how to love, but now desired more than ever as a confidant, companion and soul mate.

"Roger," she would fondly tease each new day, "you better get up from there and catch me before some boot recruit comes along," while she picked up empty quarts from the living room floor. Lucy was more playful than he had ever remembered. Her behavior reminded him of the time shortly after they first married when the two of them used to walk along the Pacific shores near San Clemente to watch the sunset before he chased her back to the weekend beach rental for wonderful love making that usually began in the hammock, then moved to the floor and then to the feather bed with a view to the night's natural lights. Little did he know but that Lucy fully intended to supplant those infatuated days of childish play with new and mature experiences of volcanic proportions. Her mind was made up and the timing scarcely controlled a potent mix of desires and hormones that awaited her troubadour's arrival.

"Lucy," he said sobbing, but then lost total control again that turned to a cry from the depths of his soul, a sound Lucy had heard before and knew there were no imitations. When a soul cries, it doesn't expend anything because it's generally completely deflated. It has fallen on its back on the interior base of a fleshly manifold where, when healthy, it sucked in volumous takes of air that would race down a tight vent and power a countenance. The sounds that emanate from a soul in Roger's condition doesn't enunciate at the tongue. Rather it resonates around the cavity cradling the soul and moans deep anguishing reverberating sounds unlike anything that can be created by instruments or electronic synthesizers. The moan of a crying soul sounds more like a cross between a V-8 engine when kids take the breather off dad's four barrel and cruise around pumping the accelerator for attention, and that of something higher pitched like a mother who cradles a slain son.

"I want to live" he said. "I don't mean getting another meal or a clean bill of health. I don't care how long I live," he wailed, "I just want to live! Do you understand me, baby?" Roger groaned with wrenching anguish. He was an emotional mess the rest of that day and much of the following week. Episodes of emotional breakdown didn't clear up over night. Roger didn't get on his feet immediately. But on one special night, he was awakened to what he thought was a vision but was too afraid to ever ask—the night his wife, Lucy, danced with the man in the moon and right before his eyes. It was glorious. An unforgettable experience he couldn't adequately put into words. One evening he lay alone in his living room on the couch like countless nights before while Lucy slept in the other room. The front drapes were pulled wide open there in the front room which provided him a view of the stars. Roger was not drunk; in fact, he hadn't been drinking, but he knew he lay paralyzed and strangely afraid when the moon came down and bumped his house the way a small boat rubs up against a dock and it moored there. It wasn't the fear one feels when an intruder has broken into a home, or that of combat, but a fear of change and the uncertainty of what being a man might mean. The entire flat grew quiet as though he had placed ear plugs deep into their canals. The only sound was the faint tones of love songs from days past and incredibly, he knew every word. He could hear himself breathe, and his heart keeping regular rhythm. He grew peacefully detached without the slightest care when another marvelous portent appeared. A gallant prince riding a white horse with a royal blue robe and a broad chest more highly decorated than anyone he had ever seen, and Roger had been through two wars. The man before him had hair thick and long enough to braid, his eyes flickered and leaped like tongues of fire. His feet were graceful and bare. But his voice—it was his voice that Roger would remember most vividly; like the sound of confidence when it leaps from great heights—barehanded, landing on its feet and daring the world to try and bind him.

The prince stepped right out of the silver ball through the front picture window on the second deck, called Lucy's name and took her by the hand when she entered the room. Lucy dazzled in the light of the ball and her silk gown hung like sheers as they waltzed until he wondered how they could stand any longer. The man was beautifully skinned and handsome and manly and powerful. Lucy was drugged by him as she laughed and played and opened herself and exposed a beauty beyond anything Roger could describe or knew resided inside of her.

Lucy was thoroughly ravished by the visitor's love—a love that didn't touch her in a concupiscent manner; nevertheless, when he left, she lay exhausted and womanish having spiraled down to the floor in a position that was almost prone; her body and gown looked like a fancy unfurled fan that had been set down during opera intermission while the symphony played on.

The vision grew in Roger and he knew he could dance if he could just get up, and he was beginning to during the days when he ran into Colonel Bryant down at the V.A. Hospital. Roger was there for blood work up and a physical when he walked right into Colonel Aiden Bryant whom he easily identified even after the many years. They greeted one another warmly and caught up on old times and dispelled some myths. As it turns out, the Colonel was looking in on his First Sergeant who served faithfully under his command for many years, but now lay seriously ill. Taylor had saved the Colonel's life during a boat ambush on an inland waterway in South Vietnam back in the late 60's. The Colonel was part of an intelligence operation and he and a few of his men were being transported up river by a Navy gun boat when they were hit by a powerful blow delivered by an enemy rocket and it sunk in minutes. Taylor placed his own life at serious risk and was hit by hot shrapnel that found him through light brush. In spite of serious injuries, he carried the Colonel who was unconscious several miles through swamp and jungle before they could be safely helo-lifted from inside a more honored strip of the DMZ. There really were no areas in Nam quite so propitious they would later joke when recounting the near fatal incident. Their friendship grew from that day forward. Now Dave Taylor was in serious trouble and Aiden wasn't hanging around for humanitarian payback; this was a man he had grown to love and he was obviously troubled about his possible loss.

After hugging one another goodbye, Roger and Aiden agreed that they should get together very soon for coffee and catch up on their individual lives. Only after Aiden departed did it dawn upon Roger who was beginning a new childhood, that Jesus, whom he had never personally met, might possibly help in this situation. He ran to the parking lot and chased down a late model Volvo that was about to exit the hospital.

"Aiden," Roger said catching his breath, "this may sound bizarre, but I think I know someone who can help your man, Taylor." Aiden listened carefully to his friend relate more exact detail of stories he had only heard bits and pieces about. Aiden hurried home the same day and asked some Jewish friends if they would be willing to contact Jesus on his behalf. Aiden was a man who lived by the chain of command and wanted to respect a protocol that was unfamiliar to him.

Jesus got up from his chair, joined the elders in their car and rode to Waukegan. On the drive up, the elders began explaining to Jesus what a wonderful man Aiden was and how he personally funded the entire construction of their modest synagogue. Aiden was a God fearer and read daily from the books of Moses. His entire career in the Army reflected personal values and choices drawn from a careful consideration of the volume he revered. As they passed Lake Forest, a cellular call rang into the cab of their car, but the reception was poor and the driver pulled onto the shoulder at a higher elevation and dialed Aiden—it sounded urgent. Another car loaded with Jesus' followers pulled in behind and joined the circle of men who waited on a phone message for information relay. Althaus nodded in acknowledgment as a man on the other end spoke on momentarily. He held the line open and turned to

Jesus and the others and said, "Aiden says for us not to trouble you any further Jesus. He recounted Aiden's words and related that he is a man entrusted with authority over men and women under his command and he orders them at will. He has changed his mind about you coming any closer. Says he feels totally unworthy to even call upon you, and certainly cannot have a man of your rank come under his roof. Said he called on us in a moment of fear and wanted to apologize for the inconvenience. Jesus, he asked if you would be willing to simply speak to his friend's condition. Aiden believes that is all that would be necessary because he understands authority structures; and although this is something way outside his control, he believes it to be an area in which you have absolute domain."

Jesus turned to all those present and said, "Not even among the Jews have I found such thorough going abandoned-control trust!" He turned to Mr. Goldsmith and the other elders and said, "Go back to Aiden and tell him that his friend Taylor will live." Jesus caught a ride back with his men; and when the elders returned, Aiden asked them at what time Jesus spoke of Dave's healing and when they told him he gave God praise for that was the moment Dave stirred and sat up in bed.

* * * *

The following day Jesus was standing in a parking lot on Northwest highway with his followers while they tried to make up their minds on whether to eat at a Mexican place Thad had in mind or at the Chinese buffet that was a new favorite with Jude. Jesus' lift of the food ban opened up all kinds of possibilities although Simon was reluctant to sample anything that wasn't kosher. Simon suggested they flip a coin before he made the decision for them. All the while Jesus had his eye on the activity across the street at a funeral home.

"There was a small piece in the Herald," John said as he looked on with Jesus. "The paper said she lost her husband two years ago and now her only son was hit by a drunk driver and killed on the anniversary date."

"Not today!" Jesus screamed while streaking away, "lo, lo, lo!" he continued yelling while crossing Northwest and approaching pallbearers who had already stepped outside with the casket and were moving to the rear of the hearse. An assistant quietly produced a hand held radio as nondescreet as possible and reported to the funeral director that they had a very serious nut case out front and that he needed to get out here as fast as his legs would carry him.

Jesus was already across the street and looking into the eyes of the mother before the initial shock faded from his followers and they decided to join him. Even John was caught off guard and thought Jesus had misunderstood his words. The pallbearers, all grown men, were incensed that anyone would create a disturbance or attempt to use a tragedy like this to draw attention to himself. Jesus looked to heaven momentarily and laid both of his hands upon the casket. One of the bigger men, an uncle of the deceased, was already trying to leave the casket without letting it fall. He wanted to step aside and have more than words with Jesus when Jesus himself insisted that they set the casket down.

"Stop and let the boy out," Jesus ordered. As soon as Hank released his grip, he stepped up to Jesus screaming abusive language that he was hardly trying to muffle, any sense of honor or propriety had already been lost. But the boy's mother stepped between the two men who were equally enraged for different reasons and begged Jesus to help. The very hint that her son could be brought back rekindled hope in the mother's breast. The woman was physically exhausted and neurotic after three days of unspeakable pain and had no idea who Jesus was, but a mother's love, especially under these conditions believes all things.

Mike Hancock, the funeral director, arrived in a moment, stood in the middle of a large crowd and wasted no time reprimanding Jesus and his magicians in the most solemn terms that he himself could conjure. He ordered them to leave the premises immediately. Mike had already called the police whom he knew would arrive at any moment. He and his brother Joe had seen fist fights at grave sides, prayers interrupted with profanity, estates settled with blows at the bottom of a hole where the casket would soon be placed and about every other outbreak one could dream up. There wasn't too much left to their imagination that they themselves had not experienced first hand or heard described. But Jesus was telling them in no uncertain terms that the boy would soon run out of oxygen if they didn't release the lid and let him out. Mike did all the preparations himself and knew that the corpse was full of formaldehyde, but the mother also insisted on raising the lid and it wasn't until her bawling took pause between breaths that those standing by heard very definite and audible sounds coming from inside the casket. Local police from Arlington Heights pulled to the curb and removed sticks when an assistant called them off, while the funeral director produced a key and directed his men to crank open the lid so they could view the one who lay asleep.

As the lid raised, invisible pressures whistled release, and began shooting out and furiously pinching at people's faces!

"Unbelievable!" Hank shouted while slapping his face simultaneously with open palms of both hands.

Astonishment, pandemonium and heart stopping hysteria filled the air when the lad of eighteen years rolled out of the casket and received a new lease on life. People didn't know whether to run up a flag pole or go crazy. Not a few were vertical, rolling on the ground pulling their garments and doing something very close to calisthenics while traffic was stopped in both directions. North Carolina State just scored a desperation basket with precious seconds remaining in overtime during the NCAA final, and it brought down the house. People poured onto the streets for fear had fastened onto them like bees, and they all yelled and brushed their hair screaming that a prophet had arisen. It was later reported that a prophet had in fact been raised from the dead while other versions stated that the boy had never really died. National picture magazines that recently carried stories of elephant size beavers eating the roofs from people's homes in Montana and computer viruses that were actually inoculating people's blood and killing them in mass, reported the present incident as an escape by the great Houdini who had come back to life. But for everyone who stood over the empty casket, there was no question about what had happened and especially in the minds of those who embalmed the boy who was presently being held in a death grip by his mother who was grinning from ear to ear and sobbing with inexpressible joy.

Jesus walked back across the street unnoticed by even his followers when Joe asked his brother how he thought they should bill this one. Police officers took a detailed report as part of their routine, but basically laughed most of the way through it, going on skeptically with the delusion of the moment. Back in their cruiser, they later remarked that Jews were worse than Blacks in New Orleans ever thought about being.

"This will probably become a new trend—faking deaths and staging absurd religious outbreaks; they flat quacking sure don't have any sense of what's sacred," said Ernie. No arrests were made but John was taking names, locations and times with a shaky hand that rendered most of it illegible even to him.

Jesus' followers joined him for lunch as Jude won the coin toss. While they sipped won ton, Simon cautiously asked, "What was the meaning of all that?" Everyone knew by now that everything Jesus did, he did on purpose and usually had some greater significance. "I mean, you just don't like death, Jesus." he said while thoughtlessly tamping an egg roll on the surface of the table.

"It's the one last enemy," Jesus said, "but it too will be dealt with very soon." The remark wasn't understood and most of the men just wanted to know why their Rabbi let a couple of choice superlatives fly in the face of the incident.

Jesus' only reply was, "Never vent around a fool, they don't understand it." Jesus was incredibly passionate about pursuing his primary task—to please the Father. One day he could be found rolling in play at local parks with small children, running the slides and chasing them on playground equipment, but he could also be found clearing out synagogues, letting his belt lick the backs of those who had a disregard for its true purpose. Jesus called for a solemn meditation and personal examination as he began his meal. "Be sure of this," he told them to ponder privately, "God doesn't get excited about the death of the wicked; he prefers that the wicked turn from their evil habits and live."

None of Jesus' followers really quite got a grip on what occurred that day; and when they shared it with others, the story was modified and tweaked a little so as to be palatable to even the larger number of Jesus' extended company. Jesus called Siva before leaving town and directed her to spread word among the larger group that had been forming that he was making a spiritual retreat for a few days. Jesus drove out to Prophetstown that afternoon and learned from a neighbor who recognized him that the Strassfelds had driven to Carbondale to attend a wedding and take a week of vacation.

"They left yesterday for a trip," Lester said. "They are traveling on to Kentucky Lake and Barkley Dam from Carbondale. I'm sorry you missed them, they would have been pleased to have you sit down and visit. Jesus related that Al had given him verbal permission to visit the farm when he cared to and after a word or two more, Jesus walked down a path familiar to Jack. Jesus could tell that the little private enclave hadn't been disturbed in some time. Jack had been in lock up without a visit by Jesus for over a year now. A small pile of rocks caught Jesus' attention and he walked over and stooped down for a closer look. The name 'Wes' was scratched into the sandstone by Amy's hand, and Jesus knew the frail animal had died of a broken heart. He was not a cat that could take up with another. Only Jack would do and Jack hadn't been around for a long time.

Jesus stepped inside a lean-to that smelled of sweat and man. He knelt by Jack's cot and wondered how it ever supported the big man's weight. Jesus began to pray which turned to loud cries of lament for Jack and man and creatures and death. Jesus spent three days mostly hiking the backside of the farm, eating tough hybrid corn and dozens of other nutritious finds including blackberries as big as your thumb from secret briars known only to Al and his family. Jesus smiled as he savored sweetness strained from the berries and thought to leave Al evidence that his reserve had been found out but chose against it and followed a dry creek bed beneath a canopy of maples, sycamores and smaller birch until it butted into a live one.

In the meantime, a neighbor who resided next to the Strassfelds began to wonder about a recent visit by some plain clothes detective looking types that had recently stopped to ask questions of the locals. They were sure full of business; he remembered their riveting speech and expressionless faces. They drove a dark blue sedan with federal tags and had been inquiring around town asking questions related to the Chicago bombings last year. Men were in custody, but everyone was sure that many more accomplices were still at large. A.T.F. agents were following a faint trail almost completely swept away involving a light blue van, with Illinois tags that may have originated out around Dixon. Madding knew of a vehicle that fit the general description but couldn't put it all together in his mind, or conceive of Jesus being involved with such a plot. The last afternoon Jesus was around, Madding thought it unusual that Jesus would dismantle the lean-to and stack all of its contents away from the trees in a pile to burn.

"They would not find me changed," Jesus recited words from Frost as the flames grew, "from him they knew—only more sure of all I thought was true." He raked up the ash and reseeded both bare spots before returning back to Chicago the same evening.

Talk show hosts who regularly performed moral lobotomies before large viewing audiences were working their scalpels overtime in the wake of recent news that an area youth had been raised from the dead. The Ritchie Raves program had done some earlier coverage of Jesus' ministry activity, but this was the best to date. Matthew, Bart, Thad and others watched at home the reenactment of last week's episode on Northwest highway which someone had caught on amateur video. Cecilia was paid big bucks to bring her son down and sit for the live interview along with two morticians who sat quietly flicking their nails, so as to say, 'it all happened at our place.' Mike and Joe waited patiently for their turn to testify. The live in-studio audience started the 'Ritchie Raves' chant that just couldn't be squelched. Mention by his mother and even his own testimony that Jesus from Buffalo Grove had raised him up from the dead was just more than these small minds could contain. Ritchie, the host, stood back from the guests so that the entire panoramic view could be enjoyed by those at home. After asking whatever inappropriate lead that came to his mind, Ritchie always cocked one hip lower than the other, pulled the mike up beneath his arm, put on the same pasted half grin of disbelief, that says, 'say it ain't so.'

"The expression I like is when he gets a jolt from the audience following really believable news," Thad said. "Like the time someone reported that Godzilla had just stepped into downtown Tokyo—now that they believed with no problem!"

"Yeah," said Simon, "Foreign stock was sold only ahead of weak minds who turned in to CNN for the latest."

"Where does Ritchie get an audience like this? Do you think they are just put up to it?" asked John.

"No way," said Simon, "these are the skeptics, let me surf over to Pandora's Palace and turn you on to the real believers. Well, what do you say happened, John?" asked Simon in a rare moment of teachable sincerity.

"He raised the kid from the dead, Simon. You and I both know the boy was dead. Jesus has been demonstrating his authority over all kinds of things and while I was no more ready for what happened last week than the rest of you, the kid got up from a casket and went home with his mom. Jesus is up to something for those of us right here." Simon, James, Thad, and others looked into one another's eyes. "I think he's revealing to us who he is and rather than take it to network T.V. where only the most bazaar is paraded about, mocked and forgotten with each day's news cast—he's laying the foundation he spoke of on a track record of integrity and truth authenticated by power."

Simon offered John no wise cracks. "You're right about all of that, John. I'm going for a walk before I pick up Jill and the boys for dinner." John went back to a room he shared with two others and began to write again. John found that journaling helped him debrief and sort data, but it also opened his soul as he often pondered direct quotes he heard from

Jesus and wrote out prayers in a new way he was learning to express by Jesus' example.

Today's entry began as a prayer, "Father, you've been good to reveal your will to us in such a personal way. I know you are real and personal and that you are a God who seeks men and women who have gone astray. I worship you for the power and authority you've given to your servant, Jesus, and for all the lessons that he has brought to us including grand stories about your character and nature. Help me and Simon, James and the others to grow stronger in abandoned-control trust because our own reaction to what we see is too much to take in at times. God, because Jesus describes you as a father, I've come to believe that he is your unique, son. Somehow you two are inseparable and surprisingly you are offering a relationship of this quality to me and the others." John pulled out a different spiral that he kept for letters he wanted to one day publish and entered a fresh paragraph: 'The One from the beginning, whom we have listened to for hours, we've seen with our own eyes and our hands have gripped—the word of life. For, the life was presented to us and we have seen it and affirm and place before you the eternal life who was with the Father and has been made known to us. Him who we have seen and heard, we pass right on to you so that you can experience what it means to be tight knit with the Father and with his son, Jesus Christ.'

John had already determined in a provisional kind of way that Jesus was more than a man and that he was everything the prophets promised the Messiah would be. "Help us," John concluded his prayer, "to clear our minds of confusion and especially the contrasting and competing views of the kingdom Jesus is presenting as compared to the kind that has ruled men since he first began to govern himself—amen."

CHAPTER 10

Shortly after Jack was placed on deposit downtown at the county jail, he left the Criminal Courts building and was transported to the Stateville prison farm at Joliet for matriculation as a permanent inmate based upon notorious charges that had been trumped up by Geiger's associates and collaborated with police reports. Jack's chief offense was the alleged and repeated beatings of police officers who sought to cuff a brute who was bent upon breaking city and county ordinances and making a mockery of the law. But Jack respected authorities, the law, was a model prisoner while incarcerated and did the work of three men without any special effort. He just did what came natural to him and viewed work as God's invitation to participate in something important to him no matter how menial the task. Jack's parents lost touch with their son years ago, and their hearts lived mostly on hearsay about a man whose whole life seemed to have been given for one important purpose.

Jack's disciples continued to see him regularly and it was never disclosed to them if Jack's parents were even alive. The men generally came to Stateville on Sunday afternoons, a day after Sabbath and remained for as long as the guards would allow them to visit. On this occasion, Jack sent his men back to Jesus with specific questions for which he wanted answers. Moments after their departure on this pivotal date, Jack was placed in solitary confinement pending the investigation in which it was alleged he murdered a prison guard.

Jack was in the back of a tool shop with two other inmates following breakfast just two days previous; the three had been given the responsibility of washing down a prison block with steam cleaning equipment in order to prepare it for a fresh coat of paint. Earlier in the week someone ignited a mattress and other flammables which covered the ceiling and walls with a greasy black residue. Jack had been handling the air compressor and high pressure nozzle the previous day and finished with it about an hour after the new day's work began. He lined out work for the two painter's under his charge and rolled the compressor and equipment back to the shop which was vacant as usual. Just as Jack was turning to rejoin the paint team faint cries from an adjoining office that contained mostly maintenance records grabbed his attention. Truman, a familiar guard lay nearly unconscious asking for his wife and kids. His trousers were wet beneath the belt and reeked of odor. Jack carried Truman to the front of the compound and was conveniently ignored until the guard he cradled lapsed into unconsciousness. Jack shouted for help until he was nearly hoarse in the direction of a prominent post that was never vacant. Only after the body lay limp did the guards come and assist Jack. He learned later that fellow guards had forced a high pressure nozzle up Truman's rectum and blew out intestines that rendered him septic before he could be given medical attention. Truman died late that evening, a well respected guard, and Jack was accused of the murder since he was the only inmate who was ever entrusted with the power sprayer. The incident made Jack odious to other prison guards as well as many inmates who liked Truman. Jack knew immediately that some new oil had just been laid down on a deep and mysterious canvas called 'Providence.'

Upon his arrival back in the Chicago area, Jesus was invited to teach a large gathering of students at Northwestern University. He arrived early for a game of soccer near the lake, then showered and was led by Professor Nathan Grishaver to the back side of the historic University Hall, where he delivered a message in the courtyard, pacing along the sidewalks that cress-crossed the lawn. Students at Northwestern were anxious to hear Jesus but not nearly so baited as Professor Nate. He had followed the teachings of Jack and had waited for the hope and fresh baptism he said would be brought by Jesus. Nate believed that the personification of promise now stood right before him and pacing paths that he himself walked everyday. Nate taught courses in philosophy and his first love was phenomenology, though he sprung into readings of history and anthropology almost as vivaciously.

Following a word or two about the humiliating defeat his team just handed the Michigan Squirrel Thumpers, students at the University built a quick human totem and poured out a war cry that mimicked barking squirrels. Professor Nate was embarrassed as he looked over to Jesus who was shaking his head in wonder.

"Professor Nate," Jesus yelled above the post game hoots, "you're an anthropologist; do all humans who involve themselves in contact sports behave with animal like behavior?" The observation brought more laughter and after Nate related that even a chess player or two he knew did hyena dances after a win; Jesus wondered out loud if in fact some DNA didn't get spilled on a work bench somewhere and folded into the wrong species.

In time the Thumpers cooled their jets and Jesus began talking about the spiritual nature of God's kingdom, when three middle aged men he had previously seen outside a party approached him on the lawn without any regard for a lecture that was clearly underway. Two of the men held a young girl by her arms while the third began an insulting and shaming diction of onslaught that destroyed her dignity.

"We pulled her right out of bed butt naked with her boy friend from a cat house just a street over," referring to an otherwise respected sorority house. Hissing and abusive speech erupted from those seated who fully understood the gross hypocrisy being teased out before them. Nate started to address the intruders, but somehow knew the situation was in better hands when Jesus motioned for him to stand by. Jesus was always looking for teaching moments and this was one he really didn't want to slip through his hands. Looking at her, Jesus felt compassion for a young girl who had been seeking water from inappropriate springs while this caste of males whose egos were dominated by threats of inferiority stood guard over broken cisterns they claimed were full.

"The Law of Moses commands us to stone such a person; the whore was in bed with a married man!" they insisted. "We caught her in the very act!" These Jews, were always scouting opportunities to test and discredit Jesus. The grand prize was offered to the man who could catch him in a contradiction in which he couldn't extricate himself. Jesus looked at them wondering at the indictment they just leveled at a man who was mysteriously missing.

"You say you caught her in the very act?" asked Jesus.

"You heard that loud and clear Rabbi," one of them disrespectfully mouthed back while scouting for bricks.

Jesus knelt down and began doodling with his finger on a soft tablet created by hundreds of missed steps off a stone walk. In that moment, even as the drama was unfolding, Nate pondered a hand he had often read about that wrote upon tables of stone from a mountain top. He wondered in his wildest dreams if he might now have considered stooping so low as to draw the international symbol for love on clay. Nate's eyes were opened to a grand horizon where scholars who theorize about hermeneutics cannot survive because there is no oxygen, only open space—where the human and divine finally meet.

"How can I describe this to my students," Nate whispered it to himself, "and how can these possibly be so blind," he thought, referring to the men who were serious about stoning the woman with little regard or fear of the authorities. These Reconstructionists were firmly committed to establishing the Torah as the only law of the land through efforts of zealotry that touted promise of a renewed earth where their brand of Judaism would flourish and cover the entire globe.

Jesus rose and straightened himself, then said, "Alright, we're now ready—go on and crush her—bury her beneath a rock pile. Achan, you have nothing to hide—since you are without sin, you can go first. Go ahead—throw the first brick!" They looked at one another while wondering who Jesus addressed.

When Nate could stand it no longer and fearing the worst, he shouted, "None of you can keep the law perfectly and the harder you try the further you distance yourselves from God and harm your fellow man. Has it never entered your myopic minds that perhaps a rigorous unattainable law has been effected in order to place the participants in a covenantal contract that promises life only to him who can keep it and to him alone. Look at him—he's the one—all he wants to hear you say is, 'Uncle! I give up! Save me from this impossible taskmaster!'"

Jesus marveled at Nate's insights which surprised him, but his kind words and compassionate tone could not penetrate the hearts of the woman's adversaries. These men like so many others Jesus encountered had been inculcated with an infectious disease that was hardening their very hearts. One by one each of the men left Jesus' presence as he squatted again with the woman in his presence. "Have they all cut out?" Jesus asked after a moment, "Did anyone convict you?"

The woman replied, "None—not today, Sir."

"Looking at his slate and etching in one last detail, he stood up, drew near to the woman and whispered, "I don't condemn you either. Hike out of this troublesome valley and pass through the door of hope." Although bewildered, the woman somehow found the knob. Releasing Jesus' hand, she passed through the audience bawling, while some understood that had firmly scolded her.

Jesus took the opportunity to describe several important values that were characteristic of the kingdom, not the least of which was the forgiveness just demonstrated which was the very rite of initiation. It was difficult even for the learned who were present to fully grasp the notion of kingdom that Jesus presented. "I'm bringing you something new," Jesus said, as he described the kingdom to Nate and others. "Think of it as a multifaceted diamond that glows before men—a galaxy infused with light, come to earth."

Nate later wrote in an academic journal he kept for personal notes, "The kingdom Jesus described is already here, but interestingly is still coming; it has been inaugurated but awaits its ultimate fulfillment. Jesus said it would grow like leaven, which he further explained and like a tiny seed which although extremely small would grow to support nests for birds." Students were fascinated by Jesus' teaching style that used countless pictures, stories and meaningful figures of speech to communicate the new concepts that were reaching their ears. He summarized the kingdom with words about responsibilities given to laborers until their employer returns from an overseas business trip. The graduated responsibilities he left them with would be reviewed when he returned, and accounts would be settled. He also mentioned the grim consequences one would suffer if they rejected such a kingdom and this word of summary was memorized by everyone.

After Jesus concluded his stirring address, one that was accented by a provocative visit, he joined others inside where several of the student body who sponsored the event along with Professor Nate's support were serving refreshments. Herzl Holdheim, Geiger's closest and most trusted colleague, in a Kantian sense, thanked a man of purer intentions for the invitation to hear the young Rabbi before he and his associate, Simon Neusner, spoke to Jesus on their way out.

"Jesus," Simon said with deceitful admiration and flattery that was as much a part of the fabric of his life as warp is to woof. "I would like to invite you to a banquet at our Yacht Club being offered in your honor tomorrow night," while handing him an address printed on elaborate card stock. Nate was standing by and told Jesus that he would be honored for him to stay with him and his family until the next night. Jesus accepted the invitation, then Simon and Holdheim departed.

The reception was still going strong an hour later when an additional 20 -30 men and women came through the front of the building to join the reception. The larger crowd had pooled over behind four of Jack's disciples who had remained faithful to him during his stay in prison. Jack could deal with solitude, in fact he preferred it, but the jail sentence and apparent mid air free fall everything seemed to be taking just didn't add up even in Jack's mind. Doubts were mounting in the big man's head as he lay against a cold concrete wall two stories below campus level at Stateville where it was dim and smelled of human excrement.

"Rabbi," one of those deputed by Jack called for Jesus' attention, "are you the one we are to expect? Jack sent us to ask you specifically, or should we be looking for someone else?" Jesus didn't answer their question with a verbal response, instead he turned to two men who were completely blind holding walking sticks there in the front row and healed them of their blindness. Others present who were suffering from cancer, diabetes, a man lame sitting in a wheel chair, another woman dependent on sign language, all of them were healed right before their eyes. The room was stirred by a presence no one could identify but they all felt its powerful influence. Jesus moved briskly about the room; power was coming out of him to the extent that evil spirits were identifying him as the son of God. Hair stood on the backs of people's necks and fear filled their stomachs as though they were standing before a terrorist who was committed to blowing their brains out after a few nationalistic remarks. But the only one's who dare fear destruction from this man were the demons who fled with a screech from something more than a 180 grain hollow point in hot pursuit.

Jesus lowered the tempo by turning to all those emotionally paralyzed, for fear had gripped them. Everyone realized that this was no floating casino with a single act. This man read people's hearts like cards out of an infinite deck and he always turned up the required count. He pulled levers and emptied people's life savings onto the floor. Craps were no risk while he held the die and no one could snatch them out of his hands. And there were no hat tricks on this voyage. "Go and tell Jack," said the gentle shepherd, "that the most extraordinary things are taking place wherever I go. The lame walk, the deaf hear, the blind see, the dead are raised and the poor have the special and wonderful news proclaimed in their hearing." As the men backed away from Jesus like hostages freed from gunpoint, Jesus added, "be sure that you relate to Jack that those are singled out and specially regarded indeed who keep from getting all tripped up on account of me." Only after the messengers left did Jesus begin to talk to the audience about Jack. Jesus was aware that Northwestern housed a small contingent of Jack's followers rallied primarily by Nate and that Jack had spoken there once or twice in his early years. "What kind of spectacle did you think you'd find when you heard about Jack and ran over to the DesPlaines River to see him? A flimsy stalk of timothy grass whipped by the wind? Well how about it anyone, an executive with suspenders and matching tie? All those folks reside on the north shore and work downtown on the top floors of prestigious buildings named after their fortunes. No, you went to have a look at an honest to goodness prophet, but Jack carried a lot more clout than that beneath his burly chest. You see, Jack is the one about whom it is written, 'Look, I'm sending my herald ahead of me. He will make preparations.' Friends, I'm telling you the truth; of all the people who have passed through the womb of woman, there has been no one who has shone like Jack, but whoever is smallest in the kingdom of God that I've described tonight is brighter than he." Many crooks and people of questionable character followed Jack's recommendation for baptism to fulfill God's just requirements, but the religious elite and professionals in both Jewish and secular law rejected the nonsense and said it was only fit for the dregs who needed it.

Jesus spoke to a mixed audience who realized he had begun a fresh lecture for those staying over for second hour—'Rudiments of Theology 401.' "How can I describe the men of this time?" Jesus asked in his rhetorical style. "Ah, here's what they are like," and he bent down again, this time on tile and said, "they are like young kids running around the Woodfield fountain playing their familiar games while dad and mom shop. They are all selfishly caught up in themselves and couldn't think of agreeing on teams or participating in the other's game. 'We ran tag around the ramps,' Jesus filled in for them, 'but you wouldn't join us.' 'Yeah,' said their friends, 'but we sat down to guess pantomime, and you couldn't get interested in that either.' In the same way, Jack appeared in his ascetic dress and ways and, he is charged with having a demon; the son of man on the other hand shows up eating and drinking, and the cascades begin—a drunk and party animal who befriends crooks and lawless people. You take that home and study it awhile," Jesus said looking at those for whom it was directed, "and know this," he concluded before departing, "wisdom is exonerated by her fruit."

Simon rose from his chair and spoke with James and John while the Chancellor made passage out of the building after issuing a final exam worth the entire grade. "Everywhere we go, he turns a perfectly calm and relaxing evening into a vortex that threatens to sweep away everything standing."

"Yeah," John said grinning, "if it's not a flood, it's a tornado."

On their way out, Simon who often had the last word said, "I guess one redeeming thing about a tornado over a flood is that you get a clean foundation to work from."

The next evening Jesus showed up in the front lobby promptly at 7:00 P.M. to join his host who had invited him to the Yacht Club. Jesus' read of Simon was crystal clear, but he cared for the man's soul and wished to offer him the same medical treatment he did for others. Those outside of community circles like Geiger's keenly felt the ostracization, but they would never be able to guess just how deep the feelings of hatred and disgust really flowed. They utterly abhorred Jesus and his rift raft band of followers. As a result they constantly contradicted the message he presented and insisted that personal righteousness could only be achieved through strict observance of the Law. But Jesus was culling out a new community of believers from the general populous, one based not upon religion, something he didn't promote, but on relationship; and the only persons admitted were sinners who confessed their need of criminal amnesty.

Jesus looked at his watch and waited for his host who already told him that the entire dinner was being offered in his honor. Twisted smiles and soft whispers told Jesus that the game had begun and that Simon was in the kitchen with a candle stick. Greeters met Jesus at the entrance to the luxurious banquet area and hassled him in a polite, but professional manner regarding his attire and identity. Simon finally showed up in the lobby and totally ignored Jesus while directing valet drivers and waiters to help his special guests with parking and rain gear since it was pouring down outside. Everyone knew Jesus was a rabbi but the whole evening had been launched in an effort to get a closer inspection of him amidst a room of talented and savvy clones away from the quasi—miracles and usual antics raised by Jesus among less discriminating company. Servers filled glasses with water and offered wine and hors d' ouevres to everyone except Jesus. He continued mixing casually with men of high degree and importance, invited exclusively from the surrounding Jewish communities. There were no women invited to this frolic that was billed as a dinner. The finest exhibitions in male intellectual testosterone was promised those in attendance. Simon's omissions as a host were deliberate and noticeably profiled. Men all over the room congratulated him with their eyes. Jesus felt deeply touched by their cruelty, but his mission involved seeking lost sheep even if it meant wading through a swampy morass that laid before the entrance of hell itself. There were not the same vehicles as one would find in a gravel lot in west Hammond nor was anyone raving aloud at brick walls and slicing their look alikes with razors; no this company was far more insidious and virulent a breed than those who drove two wheelers. These men rode upon softer hides that were quieter and boasted the names of their gods—Mercedes, BMW, Porsche and a few others they had called upon during times of emptiness.

Seats were taken and Jesus still had not heard from his host. After a moment, Simon reentered the room and took a seat at the head of the table without even acknowledging or introducing Jesus. He asked a subordinate to offer a word of thanks for the wine.

"Baruch atah Adonai elohaynu melech ha'olam boray pri ha'gafen, Praised are You, Adonai our God, Sovereign of the Universe, who creates the fruit of the vine." No sooner than the elder concluded the blessing, weeping was heard beneath the table. Faces all around felt a little control slipping from their hands as the cries were desperate and heartfelt and grew louder. A woman had slipped in through the waiter's entrance and found her way over and hid beneath the head table near the windows and facing the lake. Simon and his company were startled beyond words and reeling from the realization that a woman had invaded their private sanctuary. But the woman was lost in her quest and cared nothing for what their expulsion would mean before this hardened company. She had been rudely kicked out of several of their beds before when the wife was away or traveling abroad. She was aware how rudely they had treated Jesus and the way they ignored him. Her devotion and gratitude from the earlier encounter at Northwestern catapulted her forward to perform some extraordinary honors. She removed Jesus shoes and began kissing his feet, which many could observe for Jesus had backed away from the table and brought her into clear view. The men at the table were absolutely repulsed that anyone would kiss another person's feet. Since earliest times in their tradition, feet have been abhorred and considered offensive, something that only servant's cared for in an earlier culture when a host was entertaining a guest of honor. Jesus was utterly silent as was everyone else, but his eyes said, "Look at this woman, Simon."

Then Jesus broke the ice, as thick as the distance from the table top to the floor, with gentle words and hand gestures targeted at concrete in need of a jack hammer, "Don't repent over what you've done," and they all assumed he was speaking to the woman, "that's symptomatic. Rather, come to grips and agree with what you are!" Jesus quoted the prophet Isaiah, "From the bottom of the foot to the tip of the crown, there is no ground in man, only swollen limps and pus filled sores, not pressed out, wrapped nor covered with any balm. Yes, a desperate kind of sickness fills the human heart" he continued while the cries grew stronger, the way a child bawls and simultaneously gasps for air, when fellowship with a parent has been broken.. "God is weary with your laundry list of symptomatics, so laden with antiseptic phrases, it would cleanse bacteria from mouthwash. Look at my feet," and now they understood that his eyes and voice inflection pointed to the real audience. "Here is a picture of repentance that leads not to regret over what you've done, but true repentance that is heartfelt because a load has been lifted." No one dared obey Jesus and look down. Simon couldn't speak. Words could not be formed by his tongue. Never in his life had he been so absolutely stupefied.

Finally two of the men looked below and realized that the woman had loosened her hair, which they found provocative and worthy of fierce defamation; for no woman looses her hair except before her husband in the privacy of her own home. The men failed to realize that Jesus was the husbandman of every follower who entered his community. She was in good company. Besides wetting Jesus feet with her tears, and kissing them profusely, she also opened a bottle of perfume and spilled the entire contents over his feet before toweling them dry with her hair. She was treating Jesus as a guest of honor in spite of Simon's evaluation of him. The entire dinner that had been temporarily postponed was being crashed by the most silent of lips as they traced the contours of Jesus feet.

Simon broke the silence of his company by leaning over and relating to other Jewish experts of the Law, that Jesus couldn't possibly be a prophet because he didn't have a clue who it was who was touching him—the kind of person she was, that she was an unclean sinner and that the Rabbi was defiling himself by permitting her sinful caresses. Simon concluded, along with his guests who had already made up their minds, that Jesus was not a prophet at all but a charlatan of some kind interested only in a mass movement that would gain him fame, something that made them very jealous. Simon was wrong on two points at the early stages of the dinner which now featured his own ribs. He underestimated Jesus' ability to read the woman's heart and he also didn't consider how Jesus might be reading his heart. Simon had not even a remote idea who it was he invited to grill. But he had collected the information he desired even though the intended snub had missed the mark. All that was left to do was figure out a way to purge the place of this rift raft and turn to the meal that awaited his guests.

But Jesus asked a polite question of his host and one could no longer hear service trays approaching the table but the rumble of a locomotive in the distance.

"Simon," Jesus said, "I have a question I'd like to ask you." Everyone at the table understood the teaching methods for which this man was known.

"Go ahead, Jesus," said Simon maintaining his confidence before his peers.

"A certain Tycoon had lent money to two of his friends. One owed five hundred dollars and the other fifty- thousand. When he graciously forgave them both because of their inability to pay, who do you think will love him more?"

"I suppose the one who was forgiven the greater debt," Simon said quickly, having waited a long time for an opportunity to set up the kill.

Jesus said, "You have made the correct choice, Simon." And if you throw a rock into a pack of dogs, how do you know which one got hit?" Jesus said drawing on a childhood experience.

"I suppose the one that yelps," said Simon.

"You have answered correctly," Jesus said and everyone knew that Simon had inadvertently incriminated himself. Simon wasn't yelping on the outside, but he was on the inside as a train came racing through the middle of the banquet hall chasing him down a track he couldn't exit. It wasn't Jesus' intention to issue Simon a ticket summarizing all his offensive outward behaviors, rather he prepared him a packing list for everything inside. Most of Simon's sins could not be felt by him—the hypocrisy into which he was ordained nor the judgmental spirit and blind arrogance he never recognized in himself. Jesus thought to query Simon and his guests to judge something of eternal significance—the distance between heaven and hell, for they loved to occupy themselves with such questions. Jesus knew it was about eighteen inches that separated the mind and the heart, but it would be like setting these gentlemen in a circle and asking them to sit in the corner and so he set the thought aside.

Jesus pushed back his chair further and helped the woman to her feet. To their amazement she was recognized not only as a prostitute, some of those present had often used through a professional escort service, but also the woman who had recently appeared at Northwestern having been escorted for different purposes. Simon and his cronies still rejected the woman as a sinner in spite of her moving display of repentance and change in life orientation. The room was filled with a costly perfume that she had poured out upon Jesus' feet and now she began to pull up her hair, her crown and her best, that she had just used as a filthy rag. The good woman had no idea what she had just alluded to by her actions.

Simon was suspicious and totally misunderstood the drama before him. Jesus then said, "Simon, when I came in this evening you greeted me without a kiss or handshake. In fact you ignored me, while this woman has not ceased kissing my feet and anointing them with perfume since I arrived." Simon had misinterpreted the center piece of the entire story. Jesus directed Simon to look at the woman so that what he had to say might stick in his mind as a picture. Simon knew that Jesus had just cast he and the wench as the two debtors in his story. Simon failed as a host while the woman picked up the towel and exceeded in every category expected of him as a host. Among them stood one they did not know, the laces of whose shoes they were not worthy to untie. They may have felt that their time with Jesus was spent for they surely thought that he would now excuse himself. But they had not counted on his nature as a shepherd, and there would be no thought in his mind to leave a small lamb in the presence of these wolves. Before departing he excused the woman ahead of himself, "Gentlemen, this woman's sins which are without number have been forgiven and that's why she has loved in such a dramatic manner, but he who has been forgiven little—well, that's really not a film worth watching." He turned to the woman like a king before angry subjects and said for emphasis, "Your sins have been forgiven." For the first time since the dinner began, murmuring could be heard all around the table. Simon felt a surge of strength for they all knew that no one could forgive sins but God alone.

Before they could launch a counter-strike, Jesus said to the woman, "be going now in peace; your abandoned-control trust has saved you." Jesus then excused her and he departed behind her. Simon's failures as a host were but the tip of an iceberg. Below the water level was where the real dangers lurked in ice cold depths. From the outside, Simon and his friends were beautiful to look at—much like the icebergs one admires from the deck of holiday cruise ships that enter the waters of Alaska. Beneath the white protrusions lay deep levels of pride, rage, control, hardness of heart, rejection of sinners, sexism, insensitivity, and a vague understanding of what really defiles.

"Simon," Herzl said by word of encouragement, "you are obviously the man of few debts, what does this odd nomadic celibate know about love. Let's eat I'm starved."

"Thank you, Herzl," said Simon, "and believe me there will be other opportunities to skin this cat." Simon was completely untouched by what had transpired and viewed himself as a man with few debts. "The low life wench," said Simon to three men standing by, "How do you expect she got in here? She has defiled our dinner!"

Jesus opened the door to his van and found John reading by the light of a flashlight in the passenger side seat. "John, how did you know where to find me?" Jesus asked.

"I sat in on a lecture by Professor Nate today and afterwards he told me you had a dinner invitation to this place. So, how did the dinner go anyway?"

"The whole thing was utterly defiled by a sinner," said Jesus. "Hey, I'm starved and they both gave one another a look that said "pizza." While pulling away in the van, Jesus said, "John, you know all about irony. That's the one word that I would use right now to summarize the escapade I just experienced." John could tell that Jesus was emotionally weary of playing games that involved real lives, the stakes were just too high. "The meal began as you might expect. I was under their magnifying glass, but the woman that was brought before us last night during the outdoor lecture showed up beneath the table."

"What did you do? How did she get there? What was she doing?" John asked with surprise, "Did she turn the table over on top of them?"

"No," said Jesus, "but the table did turn. Simon ended up under magnification and it wasn't pretty."

Jesus and John pulled into a pizza carry out as they neared Mount Prospect and called over to the Cove to get a head count for anyone hungry before driving home. There were 15 men and women which told Jesus he'd probably be sleeping on the table top again tonight. "O.K.," he told the man at the register, "We need four large with your surprise mix but spare us the anchovies."

John was never guilty of squandering time and especially if it meant one on one with Jesus tutoring him in an area of interest. "Jesus, what do think about the problem of evil the way it's normally presented?" asked John.

"That's a most serious question, John. What do you happen to think about it?" Jesus asked, realizing John was looking for some room to test fly something beginning to take wings and was no longer mere conjecture to be trifled away on debate teams.

"Well," John began, "I've been reading several Greek and Roman classics that have made me think about the greatness of God, the world in which we live and the evil that you've been teaching about. I mean there seems to be plenty of it around, and it doesn't seem to discriminate—everyone seems to have been snake bitten. But how did it get here? This is what I think; I believe God created the best possible world..."

Jesus listened to John talk, and though they were not too far apart in age, Jesus tilted his head and listened like a much wiser sage, old of days or perhaps a parent who prides himself in the discoveries of a child who has taken up a new book and wants to tell them all about that which they already know.

"And when God created man and placed him in the garden," John continued, "he must have felt like he gave him something dangerous, I mean Adam and Eve had a will. And that's about as far as I've gotten right now; God gave them a will so that they could choose to love him without being forced. I'm glad he created us the way he did in spite of all the evil choices it's presented; it's still better than living out an existence as a chatty doll with a pull string." John paused for a moment and without any introductory clauses or apologies said, "I love you, Jesus." John was a man in a serious relationship with Lynn which was well known, but because of some controversial social morales, he added with childlike prudence, "I love you like a son loves his father, do you know how I mean?"

"Yes, John," Jesus said. "I love you, too." and he couldn't think of a reason to qualify his affection.

When they arrived back in Mount Prospect, Jesus though tired wanted to take the opportunity to teach the larger crowd about some issues of treatment for the poor that others felt Jude had misrepresented. Jesus would rather teach than eat and it was his habit to carry on a teaching dialogue with groups of 15-20 most any evening he was available. People enjoyed Jesus teaching style because he had a wonderful way of lacing stories with events of everyday life to which everyone could easily relate. His messages differed from the standard stock in trade at local hubs and synagogues because he taught with authority and didn't mince words in an effort to build membership. He had a reputation for 'telling it straight' and undiluted.

"Rabbi," Jude said, "I was just relating to these men and women the other night, after our experience with the panhandlers downtown, that you were committed to abolishing welfare and really didn't have a lot of tolerance for beggars, scam artists and those who look to the State to provide for their material needs." The room was strangely still as everyone wondered how Jesus would correct a man who had a reputation for being so incredibly intense and outspoken about his militant political views.

"My sheep know the sound of my voice and I know them and they follow right after me," Jesus began, "and I provide them with eternal life. They will never die and no one will ever break in and take them from my fold." Tension in the room melted as Jesus ignored Jude's preoccupation with his own personal agenda that he was never willing to sublimate. "Poverty is a great evil," Jesus said, "and it comes in many forms. The one we recently discussed involved the abundance of personal riches held by individuals on the upper side of the tracks." Jesus had already been telling his followers that a person's heart could be found piled somewhere beneath their treasures and this was a poverty they had never considered.

"There once lived a wealthy man named Dives, nicknamed because of the Olympic size indoor pool that was attached to his house; he lived on the near north side. His wardrobe alone was worth more than the combined net worth of a dozen families over in a certain part of South Chicago. This gentleman smoked fine tobaccos and had an extremely discriminating taste in wines and choice meats that were delivered to his door weekly. Up from South Chicago a poor man named Larry drove his pickup truck through Dive's neighborhood the evening before trash day and he would rummage through articles at the curb in hopes of finding some things to resell at a booth he maintained at a flea market. Larry was barely able to support his family on such a low income. It wasn't uncommon for dogs who also visited the receptacles to lick open wounds on Larry's hands that had been cut by sharp objects hidden in the containers and made infectious. Dives observed Larry pilfering garbage tubs one evening and ran out with a golf iron and threatened him never to come back. Dives retrieved some day old pastries that had been pitched by him—still unopened as well as some miscellaneous garden equipment from a recent garage cleaning discarded by the hired help. The hoses and hand tools would have fetched a fair price Larry thought, and his children hadn't seen fruit pastries in the past year; but he laid it all where he found it and returned to his truck under the threat of eviction.

Ironically, the papers marked the death of both men in the same obituary column on the same day just one month after the confrontation out front of Dive's mansion. Their bodies were clothed in different wraps for internment, and the ashes would be all the same, but the procession home and destination of their respective spirits would differ radically. Larry followed a step or two behind Dives as they walked together until they reached a great fork just out beyond the planet's atmosphere. Here they parted company and said goodbye to one another for they wouldn't meet again. Moments later in a different life, Dives was suffering from some of the same discomforts that used to plague Larry and from his place of anguish he could see father Abraham and Larry seated in his lap like a small child. He yelled over and asked Abraham to send Larry off to get him a soda pop, for he was experiencing torment. But Abraham shared with him that, that would not be possible because of boundaries that prevented their transport. In desperation he asked if Larry could be sent back to warn his brothers of this place, but Abraham told him that his brothers have the Torah and messengers from God. If they won't listen to them, neither will they listen to someone who has returned from the dead was his reply.

It was nearly 2:00 A.M. when Jesus concluded the time with a prayer. He encouraged those present to ponder his words and not allow them to slip away like the five o'clock news. And everyone agreed, his messages were worthy of memorization. Jude was not terribly pleased with Jesus' topical lessons and it was clear that he was becoming more restless by the day, but Jesus confronted him privately and warned him not to ever controvert the details of his messages again.

Chapter 11

The last several weeks had been exhausting for Jesus' followers. Some were at their wits end because of the hectic pace created largely by a multitude of unexpected people demands. Andrew and John had felt that the clip Jesus ran was even beginning to wear on him. Although Jesus was disciplined to eat a nutritional diet and his devotional practices kept his mind and emotions sharp, physical stamina was waning because of a lack of rest; and the marathon he had embarked upon wasn't half finished. On one occasion, his family came by and demanded that he come home with them so that he could get some needed rest and refreshment, but Jesus rebuffed them in the middle of the living room on Cove by asking in the presence of all, "Where is my home and who is my mother and brothers and sisters? I'll tell you who they are—they are only those who hear the word of God and obey it." For Jesus was aware that even some of his own family didn't believe in him.

Simon realized that Jesus was being consumed by his mission and the needs of people; and though it wasn't uncharacteristic for Jesus to initiate mini-breakaways and retreats, some of his men jumped ahead on this occasion and carried him down to Belmont Harbor where Simon and Andrew kept a sloop they jointly owned. The vessel was rigged fore and aft and could carry six or eight men safely. It was a brilliant July morning; Jill had packaged enough food and drink for the crew and kissed her husband goodbye just after 7:00 A.M. The men sped in route to Mount Prospect where they pick up Jesus and several of the core leadership who kept him unaware the trip had been planned. Jesus went along with their play as four men removed a coffee and bagel from his hands, hoisted him from the floor and carted him to Simon's vehicle that waited outside.

"Here, Jesus, have some real food," Simon squinted as though he had just encountered something putrid while handing him a jelly filled doughnut and piping hot coffee. "How can you possibly drink that instant crap?" he asked seriously. Simon was a true connoisseur of fine coffee and detested those who drank anything substandard. Jesus caught raspberry filling with his fingers and poured Simon another cup as they drove downtown. Simon had a habit of popping his favorite mug, the only one he could drink from, against the steering column when he meant for Jill to offer him a refill. Jesus played along with Simon's game which made him feel good, but Jesus marked the behavior.

"Simon, what do you do when no one's around to fill this cup for you?"

"Oh," Simon said matter of factly, "I just pull up to the curb and motion for some walker to do the honors. I've found that if I offer a cold stare, keep one hand out of sight which gives them the impression I'm holding a weapon, and don't break a smile, I get refills 95 per cent of the time."

"What happens on the other occasions?" asked Thad.

"Those other occasions are lying on their backs down at Cook County hospital only wishing they'd complied," said Simon, beginning to grin. "You ever seen anybody that's been run over by one of these things? Once you've had your back massaged with mud grips under the weight of a rolling ton you simply need no further adjustments—you're just kind of fixed forever. Right, Jesus?"

"Thad," Jesus said, "We both know better than to go there."

"Yeah, you're right, Jesus, because there is no bottom to the man's skull casing. All his brains dripped down into his stomach and got flushed down the toilet one day when he was thinking real hard."

"Thad, you remind me of my first wife," said Simon in reply. "You see up ahead? I threw her from that overpass in front of the 'L' one night for a similar remark."

"You guys are scaring me," Jesus said and he tuned to an A.M. channel for news. The weather report preceded an abstract of the regional updates.

"Quiet everyone," said Andrew, "Let me hear what he says about the wind direction. Six to eight miles an hour and from the west," he said copying the report. "Should be a great day to sail, Jesus!"

The men pulled into Belmont and parked the truck. Simon drove his Pathfinder which carried five and was met by Jude, Matthew and James who came together and arrived before them.

"Anytime gentlemen," said Jude who was finishing up with the sun screen.

"Yeah, yeah, we're with you," said Simon, "we got delayed cleaning up a fatality on the Kennedy. All of the dead walked away, thanks to Jesus." Jesus turned smartly to Simon and told him that the two of them would carry the cooler down to the boat.

"O.K. Jesus," Simon said as they walked to the slip. "I went over board and before you get started I want to apologize for the levity about the dead. I guess I'm a little overly tired and getting this break to do something different has brought out a little too much play in me."

"Thanks for coming clean, Simon. It's getting late," Jesus continued, "the stakes are higher than you can imagine, and I'm cutting you some slack because I believe something bold and mature wants out, but just isn't sure if it's O.K. to show itself. Try him out sometime, Simon, but brace yourself, it might scare off your sails."

"Is this the boat?" asked Matthew. "It's a beauty!"

"Yeah, Simon and I went in on this some years ago and it works out pretty well between us," said Andrew.

"Are we going to all fit in this tub?" asked Jude with a mild snarl.

"Yeah, we'll make us fit," said Simon who ignored the remark about a vessel he prized. "Take us out, Drew," and they cast ropes and idled out of the harbor and onto the wide water. After motoring out a few hundred yards, Simon ran up the main sail which carried them along at a moderate clip while the men enjoyed fruit, the warm breeze, and discussions about some of the wonderful people being attracted to the work of the kingdom Jesus had been teaching them about. The sailing excursion wasn't intended as another time of intensive teaching; something they were seeking a little reprieve from for Jesus' sake; but after Jude climbed back aboard following a dip, he asked a question that got everyone's attention.

"So, Jesus," Jude began, "when are you going to make your move and start kicking some butt. Friends ask me almost every day about the status of the kingdom you've been teasing before us." Jude was starchly impressed with the special mental tenacity he observed in Jesus not to mention the miracles he himself went to extra lengths to authenticate. But Jude was becoming impatient with Jesus' protracted wait with a godless heathen government that sported stars and stripes. He wanted to see Jesus begin confronting powers in the City as well as Washington. Jude was a Zionist of the most rigorous stamp. He attended clandestine meetings with three different groups who were seeking to create a ground swell of resistance aimed at the United States Government, even if it meant terroristic acts to make their voices heard. Jude and many like him wanted the State of Israel to reign unmolested and out from under the pathetic wing of the detestable eagle which overshadowed their sovereignty. Jude lived in Chicago, but his heart was in the old country and he would die for her. Any talk of negotiations with the PLO or efforts at peace agreements enraged a man who believed the only path to permanent peace was the expulsion of Arabs from his holy nation and the destruction of the abominable dome that rested ironically upon their most sacred mount.

Jude had no categories for understanding that the kingdom Jesus spoke of had little to do with monuments and man made governments. The only effective means of change Jude knew anything about involved weaponry and relentless pursuit of purging inferior blood. The kingdom Jesus had been describing to them was spiritual and one that would require him to preside over human hearts of all blood types. If Jesus were prescribing a new religion, a term he didn't like, it was a religion of the heart. Jesus took a quick dip in the lake and after dabbing off some excess water began to relate again, in different terms, a new facet about the kingdom.

He looked at Jude and related that it was like a man who went to a monarch in order to receive a right to rule. The kingdom Jesus was referring to was the rulership imposed, and not primarily the domain and subjects of the kingdom—a concept that never really penetrated Jude, who only thought in terms of nationality, geography, annexation and bulwarks of protection. Jesus concluded a semi-private discussion by telling Jude that unless he became as a child he could not enter God's kingdom at all. This last phrase stung him because such things as humility and nesting with the mother of all prostitutes was just more than he could stomach. Jude was a revolutionary and if he had to ignite it himself, he was prepared to force it to happen.

Early afternoon was spent diving and playing a round or two of water volleyball. James laid out some floating markers for a net and two sides of four men each went for the gold in the middle of Lake Michigan. It was just after 3:00 P.M. when Jesus climbed below for a nap while others gleaned fruit and leftover sandwiches from the bottom of the cooler. Simon nearly devoured a crisp Granny Smith in two bites and made mention mostly with head movements that they should think about heading back to shore. They were about three miles out and he didn't like the looks of the dark sky hovering back over the city. Summer thunderstorms were not unusual, in fact they had to be counted on; and although this one looked long in coming, wisdom said they should take their time but head on back. Simon and Andrew moved with the wind that had been at their backs and swung the boat around 180 degrees, laying *Esther* on her side to the delight of the new hands. Waters that had glistened in the sun like a plethora of small eyes had now darkened and were drawn below like trillions of periscopes. Following the dramatic change in course, Simon took his time tacking back and forth against a stronger wind than that which escorted them out.

"Simon," Andrew alerted everyone, "those are streaks of lightning, flashing around the city, and this wind is picking up speed pretty fast, I'd say 20—30 knots." Gusts increased even as he spoke. While Jesus lay asleep on a cushion below, the others thought about how to get to shore as quickly as possible. The five horse gas engine was little better than a trolling motor with the weight and wind velocity. In fact that was all it was used for, to idle in and out of the harbor.

Simon shouted, "All of you begin putting stuff away and get on preservers just to be safe."

Simon and Andrew had been on expansive, open bodies of water during a storm and realized there was nothing any more terrifying than being 'caught out in the middle' without power during an angry thunderstorm. The feeling is one of utter helplessness. Eight men aboard a small sloop that was really a bit beyond capacity were getting in touch with that feeling as thunder shouted from the city and rumbled out over the lake. Barking could be heard in the clouds. The defensive line of the '86 Bears are fourth and goal. When the lightning snapped, hail charged down all around them like somebody had ripped open the bottom of a blimp full of marbles from overhead.

"This boat's going to be wrecked," screamed Simon with water coursing down his bare back. "You guys lift those jackets over your heads before this stuff slaps out your brains!" The hail stung on their hands and faces while Andrew worked furiously reefing sail to the boom, but that's not what troubled him most. The waves had grown to over eight feet and the keel seemed little help as the small Styrofoam cup kept jibing wildly, being tossed about by violent winds.

Simon and Andrew didn't want to over excite the others especially on their own vessel, but he was sure the little craft was going down because of the distance from shore and the looks of a gusty storm that didn't want to be tempered. A sizeable water spout that originated off shore dissipated nearby but not before creating enough havoc to send several tubs of water over the bow. Andrew was scared earlier when his guests were too naive to know better. Now, he was terrified and realized that they were all in serious danger of drowning. Matthew smelled the adrenaline as it filled the base of his ears and throat; he could taste it. Hair from his crown swept around either side of his head and clapped furiously against his face.

"Simon!" he shouted while turning to a life preserver coiled in the bow that everyone had forgotten. "Get him up before we all drown!" Everyone was crawling on the deck of the small boat and bracing themselves for the final swell when Jesus awoke, stepped top side and grasped the boom. The powerful Kodiak had been disturbed by an enemy. He saw fear in the eyes of his men and he felt compassion for the untrained.

Jesus faced the wind that was pushing his clothing the way a stout March gale whips clothes on a line. His voice had a very definite growl as he shouted, "Be calm and lay down!" The waves immediately crawled under the bow the way small children quickly shoot under covers after staying up too late and testing mom's command to turn off the lights and go to bed. Dark clouds retreated and thunder was not heard from again that day. The men in the boat were speechless and some of them cried aloud, having no ability to hold the terror in any longer.

"Who are you? What are you?" James burped, "I'm not a drunken man," he continued jabbering while trying to find his footing, "I may have just crawled out of a gutter, but I know I just saw a ghost!" He was utterly stunned to silence as were all the rest.

Simon and the First Mate knew they were more than two miles out and probably further by the time the storm had pushed back their weak defensive line. Jesus picked up the ball at the one yard line and led a drive that placed them on a beach near Oakton at the foot of a cemetery in time miraculous enough to compare with the experience of stilling the storm.

"Thanks, Jesus," said James as the men waded ashore. "You saved our lives today." Everyone would have preferred to have just gone back to harbor, but Jesus anchored above Juneway Park for his own purposes. Andrew stayed on board and tried to tidy a ship wreck that never submerged while the others took opportunity to scratch around on solid ground and let their stomachs settle. John tried very hard to be a good sailor; but when he could stand it no longer, he made haste to some nearby cover and vomited until his heaving threatened to suck out his intestines. Surprisingly, no one found the picture especially humorous and the men were basically trying to make sense of what felt like a dream.

Matthew would describe the feeling later to everyone's satisfaction like leaving a motion picture with 3D and surround sound. "You get so caught up in the story, events, locations and actors only to exit the dark theater on a sunny afternoon, jump in your car and go home."

"Simon," Jesus asked, "Why all the control out there on the waves? Will you ever abandon yourself and trust?" Before he could answer, a new episode began, the lights all dimmed, credits on the tail end of the first flick scrolled out of the way and an honest to goodness, flesh and blood, raging maniac, of enormous size came crawling down the bank from the cemetery nearly naked, and threatening with broken speech to kill eight sons of intruders that dared to approach his home. The blasphemer was unaware that these were not troops launched from an LST making a beach assault. Something far more lethal stood before him. But Jesus studied his enemy as though he were accompanied by a battalion.

"What is your name?" Jesus shouted, while three of his followers who had heard that somewhere before took up defensive positions along the bank. The huge man poured out blasphemies and filth that would have excited Maggie in another life. The hulk was approaching John when Jesus concluded a demand which sounded like name, rank and serial number. John was still too green to really care if the thing broke him in two. He had just survived a ship wreck, was sicker than he could ever remember, and if he had a fire arm would have cut the beast down in his tracks, and John was not a violent man by anyone's estimate. John was sure he was having a nightmare because all of this couldn't possibly happen in one day except perhaps in the case of Indiana Jones.

Word about the existence of Luther was doubted by most people who read ordinary papers with thoughtful editors, but it couldn't be denied by folks in lower Evanston, no matter what reporting you listened to. Luther had been carried out of the cemetery more than once after tranquilization and wrapped in a straight jacket. He walked out of asylums and local mental wards with such frequency that authorities tried to leave him alone so long as he stayed out of sight and away from citizens.

Luther was actually employed. He was a grave digger who had a fetish for the dead and even had been accused of some strange relations with many deceased, but it was difficult to find anyone who would testify to the outrageous notion. A handful of people knew these were no notions and that Luther actually made his home somewhere in the 100 acre cemetery. Luther did not come from the same blood thirsty stock that berthed Maggie. He didn't especially like blood, but sometimes it was necessary to draw some when his enemies invaded his private beach. And because he dwelt by the lake, he often swam nude followed by leisurely walks through gardens in the back yards of local neighborhoods an hour or two before day break. Because Luther's animal like instincts told him that it was most propitious to work at night most rumors about his private life were ignored as too weird to be true. On occasion, he would lift fresh flowers from graves and visit some of the elderly neighbor ladies. They always made over his fine and varied articles of clothing.

"You are such a clothes horse," they would flatter him with flirtatious smiles. Of course Luther had a store of keys and cranks fitted for caskets that passed through his care. As a result he helped himself following funerals to dozens of select suits drawn from corpse his size.

Before Luther could seize John's leg which he would have easily snapped like a toothpick, Jesus' words finished resonating in his hollow head. He spun around out of bodily control, if he had any to mention, and bent over and began gagging on vomit while hoards of snake like scorpions with wings not seen by human eyes flew from his mouth and entered a sausage delivery truck parked on South Road near Sheridan. The truck was presently unmanned because the driver had taken frozen patties to a nearby door. Suddenly, the truck was thrust onto the beach and drove furiously into the water without being powered by its diesel. Luther raised his head after purging himself; he was transformed into a beautiful man who resembled Michelangelo's David. Jesus' followers were reeling with shock. Matthew who had not been exposed to so much excitement in his entire office career remained sitting where he expected to die, chewing recklessly on a thong and was sure he was having a nervous breakdown. The riotous atmosphere concerned Jesus and he wasted no time comforting his men and drawing them close to Luther who was coming around to a brand new view of the lake.

The driver of the sausage truck knew he had parked on an incline; but he never, ever left his truck without pulling the emergency brake. A neighbor called 911 and it wasn't long before a wrecker, ambulance and local police arrived with straight jacket in hand to try and lasso Luther again. To the astonishment of the locals, Luther sat peacefully among Jesus and his men clothed and in his right mind. Jesus directed his men to take the boat back while he remained behind with Luther, James and John. He and Jesus sat on the beach for the better part of two hours while Jesus related to him what had happened to him. As it turns out, Luther grew up in Highland Park and taught at an elementary school. A fellow faculty member introduced Luther to satanic occult rituals after bathing him with a lighter side of black magic that raised his curiosity and he thought was basically harmless. Over the years, Luther's interest grew beyond a fascination into a leading practitioner. He began inducting young children into a local cult that mostly just sacrificed small animals around the school lots and local parks at night. In time, Luther grew bored with the practice, quit the school and began working for a mortuary company located on the north side of town.

Jesus listened to Luther and counseled him in ways that convinced him that Jesus knew far more about witchcraft and virulent strains of evil than he had any capacity to comprehend. Simon showed up a couple hours later and found Jesus still talking with the man.

"You think Siva has got a place for him?" Simon asked.

"No, I've asked Luther to find employment and settle down right here," Jesus said while scarcely preventing him from joining them.

"Luther," Jesus said, "stay in the area and tell everyone about all the great things that God has done for you." Simon and the others pulled away from the lake after hugging a man that wished to crush them just hours ago.

"Jesus," Simon asked wearily, "just tell me right up front, will it always be this way with you—are the Cubs going to take it all this year? I mean every time we go outdoors, the sky falls, or the boat sinks, or hell is raised, or heads roll, or tables turn, or somebody dies while another is brought to life."

"I can't make any promises, Simon. Are there not a dozen hours in the day? If anyone walks in the day, he doesn't get tripped up because the sun is shining; but if anyone gets tripped up at night, he falls because there is no light in him." Simon began to turn west and intended to drive through Skokie in order to drop Jesus and John off over in Mount Prospect, but a call came into the cab from Jill who received word that a synagogue official in Glencoe feared losing their twelve-year-old daughter whose life was slipping from them. They pleaded with her to locate Jesus and send him to them. Simon relayed the message to Jesus and picked up Green Bay north.

* * * *

The truth would never surface, but last night while Simon and the men made preparations to steal Jesus away for an all day sail boating excursion, preparations were being completed at the Harrison, where Harry had invited a number of family members and local officials to his birthday party which promised to be a fine dining and entertaining experience that would not be soon forgotten. The Harrison was a full story-and-a-half stone structure placed atop an existing high rise which was an engineering feet admired by many. The Mayor's Palace, as he called it, was a loft elevated above the grand ballroom and closest to the stars. Harry had built the costly addition in order to show off his creative genius and elevate his night activities up above the University Club which was blocking his view of the lake.

Guests began arriving around 7:00 P.M. and the register read like Who's Who in Chicago and included several from New York City. Over five-hundred guests mingled on the ballroom floor where drinks, fruit and expensive hors d'ouevres were being sumptuously enjoyed. Harry's favorite eight piece Jazz band who always dropped everything to accommodate his schedule had been playing for a full hour when they took a break, and guests were encouraged to begin taking their seats. The Master of Ceremonies was none other than the Governor of Illinois who smiled broadly. He looked to be standing barefoot upon a bed of hot coals and pretending not to feel a thing. He then raised his wine glass for a toast that would coronate the evening. His words were followed by another address by the Mayor of New York who lavishly portrayed Harry as the greatest philanthropist of the Century, a man of extraordinary benevolence which was rivaled only by his predecessor and protégé—Harry's father.

"Have you heard all this poppycock before?" Treep asked her husband, the Governor.

"Go easy," he said, "just a couple of more hours in this sweltering cotton patch and we can fly back to Springfield. I just hope that's not ham hocks and greens being pushed through those doors right now." Just before the meal Harry offered some humble words of appreciation and spied an uninvited guest right out in front of the head table filled with dignitaries. Harry who was in a slight stupor with alcohol felt a strange compulsion to ask Geiger to bless the wine and call upon deities to avenge their political enemies.

Geiger drank wine sparingly but was thoroughly intoxicated by the pomp of ceremony that called upon his religious expertise. He recited the Jewish blessing over the wine in fluent Hebrew and lids were raised revealing beef tenderloin and a variety of steamed vegetables prepared by a French culinary team who often served up fine dinners at Harry's request and at a price that would roast taxpayers. The dinner and laughter progressed to softer lit moods out on the dance floor where Harry led his wife, Harriet, in the opener. Harriet was previously married to Harry's brother, Philip, who was Mayor of Peoria. The two men hated one another and it was Jack now laying in prison who drew the public's attention to the blatant adultery. Harriet would have had Jack killed, but Harry feared him in the same way the Jews feared a prophet. Therefore, he kept him alive but safely behind bars where his mouth could be harnessed. He enjoyed listening to Jack and even placed private calls to Stateville on occasion to speak with him. Somehow he thought he appeased the deities just by doing so, the way folks at the hub attended weekly services and then return to whatever lifestyle they please.

Around 11:00 P.M. when Harry was just beginning to roll, he ascended steps to the loft where security officers were always stationed and only admitted a select few. While up above, Harry presented his men with Cuban cigars the length of a baby's arm, and ventilators carried the rich smoke outside and above Chicago. It was clear to his close friends that Harry had gone over the legal limit about two hours ago, but he was still belting down drinks when his birthday present sent up by Harriet arrived in the room. Sabrina was Harriet's daughter by Philip, a gorgeous woman, perfectly formed and an accomplished dancer. She danced to a rhythm set by the band below and seductively entranced her male harem with a bewitching style developed over years of experience. Sabrina was nude by the end of the dance and brought all the men to their feet in a standing ovation, which applause was carried through the entire hall. Sabrina caught her gown and joined Harry on his lap. She was the only woman on the upper loft and could feel dozens of eyes massage her body, and she relished the moment. Sabrina was a richly colored woman of dark olive skin due to her immediate Latin and Afro-American lineage.

She was gorgeous to look upon and Harry was so impressed with her gift to him that he announced in the hearing of all, "Sabrina, ask me for a great gift, you name it and it will be yours." Everyone at the table was caught up in the moment and were happy for Sabrina the way a best friend cheers when hearing good fortune. And there was no doubt that Harry meant what he said. Harry kept his word in cases like this even to his own personal hurt; however, the one thin sliver of integrity was about all that Harry could boast. Sabrina got up from his lap, feeling lusty and free, threw her hands over her head and declared that she would be right back with an answer.

"And don't be long," Harry shouted playfully behind her. Sabrina went directly to her mother who had habitually hired her out throughout adolescence and beyond to a prestigious escort service. Sabrina wouldn't dream of making a decision of this magnitude without consulting her mother. Harriet was visiting with a Senator's wife whose husband was out of the country when she excused herself to speak with Sabrina who was now standing aside and waiting for her.

"Yes, Sabrina, what is it darling?" asked Harriet.

"I delivered the present like you asked and I've been offered one of my own. Harry told me to ask him for anything I want and he will give it to me. He promised me right in front of his guests."

"Sabrina," Harriet said in a tone that was familiar and would require absolute obedience, "you go back and ask for the head of Jack, he'll know what you mean; tell him you want it delivered to you tonight in the loft on a silver platter. Sabrina, whatever you want, I'll get for you after tonight," and she meant it.

Sabrina twirled back into the lounge, sat back down on Harry's lap and without flinching said, "I want the head of Jack given to me on a platter tonight before I leave." Harry could not move his lips and played back to himself what he thought he had heard. Harry understood the history of this old route and so without argument; but to everyone's surprise, he ordered a special aid to see to it. Geiger caught a security officer leaving the rotunda and offered him precise instructions and a list of names that would be needed for decapitation, then greeted Harriet and excused himself for the night. Most of the men seated there were confused by the transaction, but not all of them. A phone call was placed to Stateville, then around 2:00 A.M. with several prominent guests still lounging with Harry, a courier arrived and placed the head of Jack in the hands of Sabrina on a silver platter. Sabrina was delighted by the ghastly sight because she knew it would buy her a new condominium in New York City. She immediately covered the prize and took it to her mother who promptly disposed of a voice that had caused her much humiliation and distress.

A paper trail left Stateville over to a corrections facility downstate on 51, then turned and traveled south to a penitentiary in Texas where it mysteriously ended without further trace. Jack's disciples later discovered the truth and recovered his body at the Stateville morgue under a different name. The deception laid down by Geiger and Harry together with the heavily protected and skewed evidence prohibited them from even considering judicial options. There wasn't an attorney in the State that would touch this case because one could not even remotely be established. Jack's finger tips had been sufficiently charred and dental records were useless without a head. That bust had been carefully put away forever. A long and glorious era ended that night at Stateville. An oil on canvas that had been patiently and masterfully worked up over several millennia by invisible hands was hung upon the north on that eventful night in a gallery few tour and it shown as brilliantly as all the rest.

* * * *

Simon along with Jesus and the others pulled into Glencoe just below the Temple of North Shore Congregation Israel synagogue where a small crowd had assembled outside a residence that held a young twelve-year-old girl they were seeking to keep comfortable as her last signs of life slowly ebbed away. Simon was becoming accustomed to rolling with the flow, paying attention to the gravity of a situation and basically watching and only assisting when asked. It was after 6:00 P.M. and Jesus was recognized by several of those huddled in the front lawn who were secret followers but were not confessing him openly for fear of being thrown out of the synagogue. They were trying to quietly console a couple who were full of fear and anxiety. The father shouted repeatedly from the steps to let Jesus through before his daughter died. The girl had suffered a long bout with cancer and physicians had given up hope after the usual chemotherapy treatment. Her breathing was terribly erratic and faint and they were sure she would die in the next several minutes, but their confidence was renewed when they learned that Jesus had arrived.

Jesus began walking to the house when the crowd enveloped him and walked on with him. After a moment, Jesus stopped and asked those surrounding him who it was that just pulled on his shirt. Even among such solemn faces it was difficult not to laugh at such a question.

"For crying out loud, sir," Simon said, "These people are all over us! Who knows who pulled your shirt; does it matter?"

All of the crowd was denying it, but Jesus said, "I'm aware that power has gone out from me." Jairus the synagogue official made his way to Jesus, but could hardly contain himself for the delay this presented.

"Please sir," he implored, "my daughter is about to die any moment!" After another minute, a woman in the crowd raised her hand and told everyone listening that she had been suffering an abdominal hemorrhage for twelve years, one that doctors could not successfully treat and so it caused a constant flow of blood.

"When I touched the Rabbi's shirt I felt the healing of my body."

Jesus turned to a woman who was trembling and said, "Your abandoned-control trust has made you well, daughter. Go on without worry."

At that moment, men and women close to the family entered the lawn and told Jarius not to bother Jesus any further for his daughter had died.

Jarius nearly collapsed with anguish, but Jesus held his arm and said, "Do not allow fear to rule your heart right now. Believe that I'm able and she will be healed." Jesus led he and his wife, as well as Simon, James and John into the bedroom alone while asking the others to stand outside. When Jesus looked upon the body he said, "The little girl has not died but has just nodded off for a nap." At this, many who heard the remark from the door began smirking. But Jesus took her hand and said, "Little girl, get up." Her spirit returned to her and she rose up in bed. Jesus asked that she be fed, while his three interns took copious mental notes. Before departing, Jesus said to the parents, "Make sure that you tell no one about what happened."

Simon led others to the truck before the streets were cordoned off with people. Jesus didn't promote himself and asked others not to, but news of this kind could not be contained. As a result it spread all over the region so that his name and the core of followers known only by 'The Way' were beginning to be esteemed and revered by all, even their enemies.

The drive over to Mount Prospect was a lively and giddy one because of the day's events and lack of sound sleep. Everyone was feeling intense jet lag, but the flight wouldn't stop long enough at any one place for those caught up to regain their bearings and sense of time. It wasn't that the signs and wonders were unimportant or that they could be explained as some other natural phenomenon, but they were occurring everyday, and there wasn't much sense of surprise left for the three who thought they were about ready to handle some fire as well.

"Jesus," James asked for the three, "when will we be able to perform the kind of miracles you've been doing?" Everyone braced themselves because they had no idea how he might answer that question. They thought, at worse, he might drop the three where he found them.

"Very soon," Jesus said to their pleasant surprise. Jesus knew what plans lay ahead of him in coming months and he fully intended to invest the twelve with authority like his own and allow them a taste of the powers to come. When they pulled in on Cove, Jesus told Simon,

James and John to gather the other nine and meet him for lunch at The Chicago Chop House the following Monday. He was buying everyone a steak and had a specific mission for the twelve that would involve each one of them.

CHAPTER 12

The Chicago Chop House came highly recommended by Siva and Darlene who often treated graduates of their recovery program to a thick juicy porterhouse after six months of sobriety. Bob was one of the photographers for Quest, and he made it his volunteer duty to ensure that everyone who passed through Siva's caring hands got their picture shot and added to a growing collage that nearly filled a wall. It was easy to tell where it all started, right up there in the upper left with some old Polaroid photos that were yellowing and trying to roll up. Terry, Warren, Barb, Allegretti, Gary, Jean, and nearly a dozen others were among the first to enter the program the year it opened. In the early years, Siva ran a halfway house from the back wing of her home that accommodated four adults who were only admitted by same gender per group. A few years later, she found an old elementary school that had been abandoned near McHenry and put in place a fully operational recovery program for folks dealing with substance abuse, battered men and women and a few homeless—people from all walks of life: singles, divorcees, widows, professionals, blue collar, you name it, because problems she treated showed no preference and crossed all socio-economic lines. Those who experienced community through Quest often bonded with one another and created lasting relationships they valued like family.

Simon, James and John parked on a deck off west Ontario and strolled into the Chop House looking like hired guns as they took up seats opposite Jesus. While they made drink orders and searched for appetizers, the others found their way to a table Jesus had requested that would accommodate all twelve.

"What do you think of this beef gumbo and homemade fries as an appetizer, Simon?" asked John while nudging Jesus' foot beneath the table. "Jesus is picking up the tab."

"No way," Simon answered without looking up from the menu, "you young 'en's go ahead with the kid's meals, I'm taking a look at these marinated beef tips as a warm-up. I have to prepare my delicate palate for the steak these people brag about. Jesus has put me through the harrows of hell the last few days and its time for him to pay up," and everyone broke into laughter while a few applauded the idea. Jesus accepted the remark and Simon got his beef tips; but when Jesus prayed over the wine and meal, it was understood with just the right tone and choice of words, which was one of his hallmarks, that they hadn't come near the precincts of hell to date.

Baskets of yeast rolls were scarped up almost as fast as they made it to the table; and a relaxed time of fellowship was being enjoyed by men, many of which were perfect strangers not more than a year ago. Jesus smiled upon the liveliness and chatter he knew was a welcomed experience to a small platoon that had needed a little R&R away from snipers and surprising sets of ambush that had begun to take a toll on them. To date there were no casualties, but Jesus was suspicious of one in the making. While desserts arrived, Matthew asked what armored carrier Jesus used to pick up tabs after this kind of event.

"You know Jesus," he said, "I wouldn't carry that kind of money on my person in the areas you are accustomed to frequent."

"Not to worry," said James, "when push comes to shove and fat meat comes to grease, Jesus can flat get butter from a duck."

Jesus asked, "Can you say that again?" while everyone laughed at the comical truism.

"Everyone go on with your pie and ice cream while I relate some important information." He paused while everybody stared at Simon who was beginning a second soufflé.

"Go ahead," Simon said, "never mind me, I eat like this at home, too."

"Jill, the dear woman," Jesus said, not under his breath. "Look everyone," Jesus launched into an explanation for the special meeting, "the twelve of you have been with me day and night for over a year now and have been exposed to some lessons and experiences that others have not. I've placed a great deal of confidence in what God is going to do through you and I myself have been praying that each one of you would abandon yourselves to trust. Following this meal, I'm sending you out from here in pairs of two. You have until Sunday morning to care for personal needs and I recommend that those of you who have families; go home and be with them for the next few days. After that I want you all to follow the instructions contained in these envelopes and visit only the communities that I've outlined for you. Don't worry about money and how you will finance the two week venture. You will stay where you find room for there are many who are worthy in and around the city. Listen carefully, I'm sending you out like innocent children in the midst of an adult world."

"What do you want us to do?" asked Thad. "I mean aren't you coming along?"

"Not on this trip, Thad," Jesus said. "But I assure you, you will not be alone. I'm sending you out for the purpose of spreading the special news that I've been telling you about. As you go, restore the sick, lift up the dead, rule out demons, and give to others as freely as the gift has been given to you."

Several at the table were a little unsure of themselves, while Simon, James and John were much more anxious to embark on the adventure. Jesus divided the twelve into six groups of two and provided each team with a city map that had already been partitioned into six sectors. Each map also indicated where the other teams were working.

Friday morning rushed around before they knew it and twelve men met up in pairs as Jesus directed and began pursuit of a mission that would grow them up in ways they hadn't expected. Jesus concentrated efforts along the lake by stacking three pairs of two with boundaries separated primarily by major interstate arteries. The other three pairs were likewise stacked and further distanced from the city. Bart and Matthew worked between Northbrook and Lincolnwood, while Simon and Jude worked the interior of the major arteries surrounding Oak Park, Cicero and Berwyn. Thad and Andrew picked up everything south of the Stevenson over to the Illinois—Indiana State line. Similarly the others beginning north and outside 294 worked large sectors mapped out by Jesus, with James and John topping their partite in suburbs that lay above the North-West toll way. Jesus gave his men specific instructions to enter only communities and synagogues of the Jews. Any ministry directed at converting Gentiles either wasn't on his mind or he chose not to reveal it at this time.

Jesus and his closest followers already had a reputation for working right out in the streets among people and so it wasn't unusual to find them close to neighborhoods or to hear a report that they had been in the area of one's business or workplace. Efforts to spread the special news had been multiplied six-fold due to the new canvassing arrangement. Many who had not yet heard of The Way or just ignored the half baked reports as they understood them, thought that small crowds being stirred by the new push were only political volunteers peddling literature or pesky solicitors who broke off from the World Wide Hub, which was the flag ship of many national and foreign religious groups. Several smaller splinter groups had formed over the centuries based upon a different twist of mainline Hub doctrine.

Jesus had no intention of creating a world wide religion that people could easily adopt and pacify themselves with on a few "holy days" each year. Conventions of that kind he sought to abolish. His stated purpose was to seek out and rescue run-a-ways and throw-a-ways. When they were found, they were introduced to a relationship with God, whom Jesus taught to be personal, caring and intensely interested in individual lives. Because most of the people who confessed Jesus as the Messiah were ostracized from the synagogue, many home groups had begun to sprout, and Jesus was already warming them up to a new concept he described as his select community—the Church. He described this loose fellowship as men and women who had been called out of the world, which meaning had to be learned since he also encouraged them to remain vitally involved with people in the world and to participate as model citizens. Most of Jesus' teaching couldn't be digested shortly, but day by day, and one part at a time, men and women were beginning to learn the wonderful trade. Jesus would describe spiritual growth as, "First the crank, then the cam then the full combustion in the head." His followers often joked about who had the most combustion in the head and of course Simon got labeled in short order with a lack of compression due to blown gaskets.

Simon and Jude were walking the streets of Berwyn when they entered a music store that sold instruments, speakers and had a large rental selection. Jude had given Simon the idea that the special news needed to be broadcast and he had already concocted a plan that would place Simon in the parking lots of three major business centers during their first week.

Jude was not much of a spokesperson, but he had great ideas about communications. Simon was shut down at their first attempt near 34th and Ogden by police who warned them that any more violation of City ordinance would win them a fine and possibly a night in jail. Simon was not one to give up easily and he himself was motivated to share a message Jesus had been offering, for his own life had been changed and he wanted others to hear all about it. He and Jude muscled equipment back into the truck and thought to return it to Paul & Rudy's, but the store manager learned what they were doing when he eavesdropped on a conversation between the two men over his counter.

"Hey," Rudy asked, "You guys are with the Jesus guy aren't you?"

"Yes," Simon said, "and we're back to return the rental equipment." Rudy had a more than passing interest in what Simon and Jude were up to and offered to buy them sandwiches down the street for it was nearly lunch time. Simon and Jude took him up on the offer and remembered Jesus' words, "a laborer is worthy of his hire." Rudy finished his sandwich way ahead of Simon because he asked one question when he sat down that led to a lengthy answer by the two men.

"So, you two are just out on the streets for a few days?" Rudy asked. "Listen, I've got a pretty nice place up above the store with a bath and private entrance. It's all yours for the rest of the month if you want it." Simon and Jude set up makeshift housekeeping and were back on the streets, this time at a local high school near the end of the week for a fresh attempt at spreading the news. The two or three days previous were spent walking door to door with flyers announcing their intentions and inviting people to join them for a short presentation of a message they were seeking to distribute in mass.

The two men received mostly polite 'no thank-you' looks, but a few were interested and they agreed to call other family and friends by Jude's request.

"Let's make one last stop," Jude said, "before we call it a day," and they stepped up to a residence off Central Avenue and were surprised to be invited in for refreshments. Their host was an elderly woman who made half steps along with a walker, was seriously overweight, spoke faintly and was the epitome of kindness. They were sure she was Haitian because of her accent and color. The house smelled of must and the men could tell that a window or door had not been cracked for ventilation in years. The old woman related that she had lived alone following her husband's death more than twenty years back and that a neighbor cashed her social security checks and brought her groceries but had never been in even once for a visit. The old lady couldn't hold her head steady and it bobbed along as she spoke rather deliberately but slowly while brushing slobber from her chin.

Simon and Jude were grateful for the oversized oatmeal cookies and pop, but neither one of them had any real experience with elderly folks and were finding the visit down right uncomfortable since they didn't know how to carry on a conversation with a person who had little idea that there was a world outside. Though they didn't say it, they were anxious to get moving and back among the masses who awaited their salvific message of redemption. The sooner they could ease out of Eva's presence the better. Simon had secretly tucked away in the back of his mind a little score card with his name on it. He knew Jesus well enough that they were all going to sit down again upon their return and go over the results. Simon was dead set upon winning his Boss' top marks for the little mission. "Who knows," he thought to himself, "there might even be a little cruise awarded the winner."

The men wanted to excuse themselves when Eva asked them if they could explain to her what they were doing around the neighborhood if they weren't trying to sell anything. The men had passed over their usual introduction when they saw that she was just an old woman without any real capacity to understand the momentous nature of their crusade. She would have happily purchased most anything they had to offer, just to conduct business and try to be useful.

"Well, Eva," Simon began, "Jude and I don't work for companies and employers the way you might be used to thinking about them. We are followers of Jesus whom you maybe have heard reports about." Jude and Simon both were sure they were wasting their time, but there was some noticeable changes going on within Eva as they talked and she had a very definite reaction to the name Jesus. To this day, Simon was not sure if what he saw was real, but the woman's head began to elongate before their eyes and a stench filled the room that made both of the men nauseous. In just a minute, Eva began throwing her head back and forth and making screams that sounded like an elephant. She rose from her chair and began pounding the floor with her walker and jumping about the way a young person might throw a tantrum. She began screaming at the men and identifying them as servants of God. Her size and widening mouth looked formidable and Simon realized in a very serious manner that he had no handbook instructions for this kind of encounter. He and Jude were thrown from the woman's front porch and Jude seriously bruised his shoulder upon impact with tree roots that lay exposed on top of the grass out front. Both men scrambled to their feet and limped away from her door to seek refuge on another street. Simon sat down and tried to assess Jude's wounds when he himself lost emotional control momentarily.

"What in the scratch was that!" he asked Jude.

"Some kind of crazy woman who hates the name of Jesus would be my first guess," answered Jude. "I'm O.K. nothing is broken, but I'll need to get some ice on this. I should have mopped the floor with the old hag," he said with hatred as great as hers.

"Yeah, well I don't know if you were looking, but she picked up your 180 pound carcass and threw it to the front lawn," said Simon.

"No way," said Jude who thought he had fallen over the wrought iron rail in all the confusion. "I was just running to get out of her way and dove over your back on the way out." Jude would not believe that the woman had lifted him from the floor and tossed him to the front lawn.

The incident made Jude angry and he marked the address for possible retaliation at a time when he was better armed. Simon, on the other hand, was sobered up by the experience and lay awake that night on a bunk above Rudy's looking again at every piece of the scenario and wondering what Jesus would have advised in the situation.

"One thing is for sure," Simon said to himself, "we will go with Jude's version of the story since he wasn't going to become the laughing stock of Jesus' band. Jude could embellish anything and had little conscience, so lying or rewriting the episode was no problem. Like Jude, there was no way an 85 year old woman was going to throw two grown men off the front porch of her house.

Saturday night rolled around and Jude put the final touches on the public address system he assembled including speakers mounted on stands near the front of the cafeteria. People who had an interest in the advertised meeting were afraid to venture out of the foyer and come into the school. They had heard a great deal about the men who followed Jesus, mostly rumor, but that signs and wonders accompanied their work. The few who dared come out were a scant handful and while Jude tried to encourage them to take seats, he was joined by Simon who was recognized by a lady in the foyer as one who had often been with Jesus. She approached Simon to speak with him, when power went forth from Simon and healed her of a migraine she was presently experiencing as well as a bad case of vitiligo which she didn't notice until later. Simon was a novice at this kind of 'hands on' involvement with people, but he could sense power emanating from his hands as he touched those who were suffering from one sickness, disease or another. One man recently diagnosed with Crohn's disease was instantly healed as well as a gaunt bulimic daughter who accompanied him. Simon and Jude never made it back in doors to the cafeteria but stayed plenty busy visiting with people in the lobby which after several minutes spread to the outside of the building where the sick and dying were being brought to them for healing. Jude found his way back in doors away from the crowd but pretended to stay occupied at some level. The hysteria sometimes associated with similar moments of healing under Jesus' direction was not being evidenced, just people marvelously grateful for all that was happening to them and their loved ones. The few who showed up stood aside the way corralled sheep wait their turn at the shears. Some would whisper a diagnosis to Simon that he didn't have training to understand, while others just extended their hand and pointed with the other. The expectation was so great that those being healed just accepted it as that which they had heard about and came to expect. Not long into the event, a woman told Simon that she knew a friend on her street that she felt was suffering from some sort of delusional episodes. She described an elderly woman who often had seizures and was seriously ill.

"Can you help a person in this condition?" Wilma asked.

"Yes, I think so," Simon said, "Bring her along, we intend to be here for awhile," as he looked for Jude who was visiting with an old timer inside about political theory. Minutes later, Wilma showed up with Eva, whom she helped along the sidewalk in procession to Simon.

"Here is my friend, Simon," Wilma said, and the woman broke into a tirade when their eyes met. It appeared that he had thrown acid or something volatile on her. Simon didn't know what else to do but shout at her and that is what he did.

"Come out of her!" Simon demanded, and to his surprise, the old woman heaved backwards on her heels almost doubling her body. She struggled as though someone was choking her and wrenching something valuable from her arms. In just a moment, she rebounded slowly without moving her feet that remained stationary. Her movements resembled a circus dummy that is spring-hinged at the base that had just been hit and knocked back with a softball for the stuffed prize.

Forgetting about the previous incident at Eva's home, Simon stepped forward to stabilize her, but she kindly said, "No, I'm fine young man, it's over." She folded the walker before Simon's eyes and thanked him for a mercy she would never be able to repay. She related to Simon and her friend that she had been ceremonially sacrificed as a child to protect her father's land right that was being disputed back in Haiti when she was a small child. She migrated to the United States some years ago and couldn't remember when she didn't have bouts of suicide, such that claimed her husband's life, and other self destructive thoughts. Simon grew some more that night and experienced something about life and serving others that brought an exhilaration to his heart that far outstripped the praise he thought he was after.

"Simon," Jude said, stepping outside to have a look, "Wasn't that Evil Eva?"

"No," Simon said, "it is someone else. Let's pull things together, Jude. We've seen enough action for one day." Simon pulled down the equipment and loaded it alone since Jude's shoulder had swollen to the point of needing medical attention; however, he never asked for assistance.

The day's that followed were filled with experiences not unlike what happened out in front of Morton High West. Simon approached his involvement with people more and more like a physician than the man he used to be—one interested only in handling fire. Others of the twelve who were situated in other sectors about the City and suburbs were finding similar provision for their daily needs as well as the demonstrations of power that were new and fascinating to them. The twelve were not much different than new hands brought in to make steers of young bull calves. About the only way to learn is to lace up your boots, step into the lot and wrestle the animal to the ground. I guess that's why Jesus sent them out in pairs so that one could hold the calf while the other attached the band.

On one occasion, James and John were passing through Palatine on Plum Grove Road and felt compelled to follow a fire truck into a nearby subdivision. They parked several feet behind a paramedic unit that apparently had already been on location for some time. Scuba gear and trays of medical supplies lay open upon the bank of a water retention pond that was nearly an acre in size. Earlier that morning a neighbor lady witnessed a little boy playing at the bank's edge with a puppy. She turned her head from the window to fill a vase with water, according to the report, and when she looked back observed the dog yapping at the water that was still rippling from the spot she last saw the boy.

Mitchell was a skinny little four year old, and the older brother of two other children; actually the third was still being carried by mom. An ultrasound revealed that it would be a little sister for he and two-year-old Jeremy. The Fackenheims lived just a block away. Mitchell had wandered away from his mother's close supervision when Buddy, the family's sheltie, left the yard with his nose to the ground. There was really little question that Mitchell lay covered in a watery grave somewhere out front of where the men had been working to recover his body for over thirty minutes. Footprints at the banks edge showed definite marks of slippage and indications of small fingers that had clawed the moist clay in a desperate effort to crawl onto a steep, slippery bank. The hungry waters that were always dark and murky made slit and transported the little body heavy with wet clothing and tennis shoes to grounds never intended for Mitchells, and T-ball, and pups, and carnivals, and all good things lost. Lois would not be comforted. Her husband, Isaac had been contacted and was presently being driven by his employer to join them for the awful vigil. Lois never took her eyes off of the water, hoping perhaps it had all been a dream and that Mitchell would surface soon, having made his usual dive from dad's shoulders at the local pool. Then at the shout of a fireman, reality would return like a breeze that had momentarily laid down bringing back the horror of a parent's worst possible nightmare.

James and John stood on the bank with the others and were both deeply touched when the father arrived and wailed aloud. Seasoned paramedics who were used to arriving at crash sites or assisting their comrades with victims of fire were emotionally torn by the continual, ongoing cries by the boy's mother. Her cries would begin low and quickly follow fierce emotions that climbed untiringly to a high pitch before being extinguished and made to begin again. As the clock continued ticking and hope of recovering the body in time for resuscitation had long slipped away, emergency personnel could be observed shifting almost unnoticeably into the second stage of recovery. One rescue worker sat down on the bank and placed his face in his hands while his fellow workers continued sifting mud through their fingers in hopes of finding a small limb or shoe that marked the location of Mitchell's body.

"John, we know that the powerful acts that God has been working through us are not to be used without discretion. Something is moving in me," James started again after his voice broke momentarily, "Jesus taught us not to abuse a gift but to use it to glorify God," James continued talking to his brother in a consoling manner, like the time the two of them stood over their mother's grave and he summarized a grand and colorful life in just a sentence or two.

"James, I can see the body of the boy," John ignited.

"Where is he?" asked James with a squint and one hand resting on his brother's shoulder as if they were bird watching at the forest preserve.

"He is well out of their reach, maybe 20-30 feet further out. He is face down on the bottom, holding a stick and his striped shirt is floating back and forth in the weak current. James, it looks like the little boy has just laid down for a nap, after exhausting himself with play; he looks so restful," John said. James burst into tears at the description by John and called out to two frog men who were considering dredging with a weighted seine.

"Men, the boy is beyond you another twenty feet," James said while John motioned with his hand. "A little further," James shouted with one eye on his brother. The Fackenheims lifted their heads because of the new stir around the deep end of the pond and limped along slowly, with no desire to identify their little fallen love. The frog men surfaced near the middle and there was little question, but they had secured the body as they paddled reverently together with a small corpse that either one of them could have easily handled with one hand. Mitchell was covered with mud and John could see that his lungs were full of the dark gook from the bottom. The coroner was already on hand and the matters that remained were more or less formality with all due respect given to the family who were emotionally spent and cradling little Mitchell. John bent low to look at Mitchell while James dropped down on one knee behind him and returned his hand to his brother's shoulder. The parents were oblivious to everything around them. James and John might as well have been paramedics or locals on hand to watch and wait. But they were neither one.

"Mitchell," John said in a voice as tender and caring as his mentor, "wake up Mitchell. Mommy and daddy are here to take you home with them." Before anyone could react to John, or really digest what he said, Mitchell sneezed three times and began vomiting the foreign drink that filled his stomach. Mitchell stood up on his own strength. The little boy resembled a wet raccoon that had just come up from a water hole where he had been noodling for crawfish. Mitchell's eyes had circles of mud around them and his hair lay flat and swept back by water that was the consistency of brine. James and John laughed at the sight, then audibly cried out at the powerful realization that life had been stripped from the grip of death. The two men walked away from a group that was too bewildered on the one hand and filled with unspeakable joy on the other to even remember what they looked like.

News about the marvelous works accomplished by Jesus and his followers continued attracting attention. Even some of the most unbelieving skeptics were developing an interest in the news that was circulating. These men were different than others who had arisen in recent years. Unlike those who claimed to be someone great regularly filling auditoriums and stadiums with promises of healing that were little more than positive thinking, conversion disorders, but all targeted to empty the pocket books of the naive. Even Harry, the Mayor, declared that Jesus or one of his associates was Jack risen from the dead. This is how he accounted for all the miraculous reports that were brought to him.

While Jesus' followers were wrapping up their individual missions, Jesus himself stood in the open plaza at the Richard Daley Center and began to upbraid the hardheartedness and unbelief that he had encountered in communities where some of his greatest miracles had occurred.

"Be warned!" he cried aloud, "All of you—Chicago! For if the miracles that occurred in you had been performed in Milwaukee or Detroit, they would have repented long ago in a very heartrending and observable manner. I tell you most solemnly that it will be easier for Sodom and Gomorrah on the day of judgment than for you. And you, Waukegan—you won't be exalted to heaven! No, you will instead be brought down to hell." Jesus had already told his men to rendezvous with him at the Daley Center on the day's date; and as he concluded his address, two by two, they joined him there. "Whoever listens to these men, listens to me," Jesus said, gesturing to the twelve, "And whoever rejects them, rejects not only me, but the one who sent me."

James and John waited for Jesus to step away from two men who had listened to his message, then they both embraced him and shared with him all that God had done through them in the last two weeks. Others of Jesus' followers crowded around and couldn't contain the stories they shared with one another. Jesus held both his hands above his head hoping to gain the floor and after the talking had mellowed out, he related, "Yes, I know all about your stories and I want to hear each one. Men, I saw Satan fall from heaven like bolts of lightening. But, don't bounce off the walls that spirits are subject to you, rather be glad that your names are written in heaven." Jesus went on to express his gratitude to God, which turned to a prayer, thanking him that these truths were hidden from the wise and the intellectuals of the world; they were being revealed by God's good pleasure to mere babies. "Friends, many righteous people and prophets wished to just have a glimpse at what you see and it was not granted, and to just hear a little of what you hear and it never happened."

* * * *

Great smells filled the air when the twelve returned from their two week mission. The annual 'Taste of Chicago' was in full swing and Grant Park was carpeted with crowds numbering more than one million people who were hungry to sample the rich diversity of food. The harbors were filled to capacity and if you weren't under a tent or beneath one of the groves of trees, you were soaking up all 95 sweltering degrees of a late July sun. Jesus and his followers were not downtown on this day, but they were in need of a quantity of food that would have made many of the vendors happy. A crowd of well over 5,000 had gathered the previous day to hear his messages and spend time with he and his followers several miles northwest of Chicago at the Kane County fair grounds. Almost all of the Jews who joined Jesus in this remote area were from poor economic backgrounds. The condition of their clothing and mostly early automobile stampings gave indication that the crowd was of middle to lower income brackets.

Most of the people had stayed over on the fair grounds for each day of Jesus' lectureship, that was scheduled to end today, while only a few made daily trips back into the City by late evening. Jesus was as skilled a communicator among crowds with simple understandings like these as he was walking among intellectual giants that held impressive chairs of learning at universities in and around Chicago. Jesus' followers found that he often reiterated lessons they had heard from him before or he might expand upon certain portions and leave out others equally familiar altogether. Before Jesus concluded his three day itinerant, he turned to his followers and told them to feed the crowd before sending them away. "Many of these people are famished," Jesus said, "and they've come from many miles around to be with us. If we let them go in this condition, some will collapse on the way home for they have no money to buy food." Jesus felt compassion for the crowd because they reminded him of sheep without a shepherd.

"Speaking of money," said Andrew, "where are we going to find enough to feed a crowd this size? I'll bet there are at least 5,000 men without counting all the women and children!"

"He's right, Jesus," said Simon motioning with his finger. "All we've got left from yesterday is five loaves of sliced bread and a couple fish sandwiches Matthew was too finicky to eat. There right over there in the top of that cooler."

"Tell them all to sit down," Jesus said. "The twelve of you move among them and seat them in groups of fifty. Round up some more volunteers and help distribute this food." Simon and Andrew knew of no other food on the premises, but did as Jesus directed, understanding that he had made previous provision with a catering service. While the crowd seated themselves, Jesus directed others to pull stacks of peck baskets from one of the barns that stood on the property and line them with paper. Volunteers stood in front of a table facing Jesus, who kept filling baskets stacked on the ground directly from his hands with fresh fish and bread that smelled like it had come from an oven. Upon filling each basket, he lifted it to the table top and stooped down to begin another. Laughter and talk filled the grounds as hungry men, women and children filled their aching stomachs with tasty food that was being served by their kind host. No one in the crowd knew any better than that Jesus had set up the meal and plans for distribution well ahead of time; but his twelve men, fresh back from some harried exploits of their own were awestruck when Jesus directed them to collect fragments and they each filled a basket apiece. It was quite a sight for Jesus and he didn't say a word, as they stood before him, each one holding his own letter of indictment. The sinful grip of unbelief had worked its hands around the hearts of each of his men over a lifetime of experiences with a world that was governed by a code of dog eat dog, take no hostages and trust no one. Jesus had precious little time to teach them to be children in terms of their belief in him and his promises.

While they were loading their vehicles and preparing to leave the fair grounds, Jesus related that he would spend the evening on the fair grounds alone but wanted to see all of them at Illinois Beach State Park, north of Waukegan the coming Thursday by lunch time.

Jesus was found sitting at a picnic table facing the lake when the first of his men pulled up at the time and date Jesus had indicated. By 12:30 P.M. everyone had arrived and spread out on picnic tables as Jesus began outlining a plan to visit three or four communities in the northeast corner of the State before working their way back to the area of Mount Prospect. A blind man had been brought to Jesus earlier that same morning shortly after he himself arrived at the State Park. Jesus was seeking some solitude and sent the blind man and his friends away until he should call for them. The small group led Samuel down to the water's edge where they awaited word. After a few more sentences of instruction, Jesus directed his followers to divide up for the ride into Zion. In that same moment, Jesus called for Samuel who stood gazing in the direction of Jesus' voice. Samuel had often confessed, that he was ready to die. "I just want to wake up one day and see God," he would admit. His devotion was tremendous in spite of his terrible handicap. Jesus led him alone a few paces away from the others and spit into his eyes. Several in the small crowd audibly reacted. Ignoring them, Jesus laid his hand over Samuel's eyes. After a moment he removed his palm and asked, "do you see anything, man?"

Samuel didn't even hesitate. He spoke right over Jesus saying, "Yes, I see some people, but they are cloudy. They look like trees with legs walking around." Jesus laid his hands on him a second time. Samuel strained to look and was completely restored. "Go home," Jesus said, "and don't even think about passing through town!" Samuel just kept raising and lowering his open palms wide open. He was so swollen with joy that he could neither move nor speak.

In the mean time Jesus and his followers loaded up and drove the short distance to Zion. On the way over, Jesus was unusually quiet and suddenly asked those in his van, “So who do people say that I am?” Simon, Jude, James and John looked at one another as to ask who wanted to go first because it seemed to be an odd question in their ears.

“Some that I’ve talked to think you’re a baptizer like Jack,” said Jude.

“Others around say that you’re one of the great prophets,” said James.

“But who do you men say that I am?” asked Jesus.

Simon, who sat in the front, turned in his seat and said directly to Jesus, “Jesus, you are of course the Messiah.”

The three vehicles pulled off the road at 29th and Lewis where Jesus gathered his men and said to Simon, “You will no longer be referred to as Simon, but Peter. And right on top of this rock I’m going to build my select community—the Church.” All of the others were also confessing that Jesus was the Messiah. Simon usually beat everyone to the punch on some of the more memorable occasions, but this time it was rewarded with words of approval.

Immediately following this important road side talk, the men grabbed lunch at a fast food outlet where Jesus took a pass and began to teach them that he would suffer many things, be rejected by the Jewish authorities, be executed, and after three days rise again from the grave. Peter about choked on his lunch at the mention of such outrageous remarks. He had listened to Jude enough to know that it was utterly absurd for Jesus to think in those terms and infect his men with such ravings fit only for rabid animals.

Peter took Jesus aside as a political advisor and began to shout at him with sharp words, “Jesus, we’ve come too far and have too much invested to allow things to just unravel and self destruct. No one is going to harm you; in fact, we will have a political party of our own very soon, and you will be our president just as we agreed." Simon was not prepared to hear from his king—a real king with authority.

"Get to the rear Satan!" Jesus shouted at Peter while snatching his sandwich from his hand and throwing it to the ground. Jesus stared at Peter in a manner that shook him and concluded by saying, "You are not seeing this from God's viewpoint, but only your own." Some of the men moved quietly back into the vehicles, while Peter literally stumbled while shifting his feet to move in a direction opposite, Jesus.

"That's it," Peter said in a voice without wind as he kept stepping away. Right when the men thought they were making some headway and about due for promotions, they all seemed queerly blind and in need of yet another touch.

"Look intently!" Jesus shouted into the air with his back doubled back, "And for crying out loud, get grounded!" He left his mark before climbing back into the van where he awaited the rest of his walking sticks. Simon was the last to board. He was in no mood to ride with Jesus.

Having found no faith in Zion, Jesus traveled to Gurnee and stopped at a number of the smaller 'Lake' communities on his way to Fox Lake where a friend gave him a furnished home for a week. Upon their arrival, they were met by a number of new faces as well as many they had not seen in a good while. Jesus never made apology for his words and before they could even unload the vehicles and take advantage of a shower and laundry, he began teaching everyone present what it meant to be one of his close followers.

"If you decide to follow me, you must deny yourself. You will feel the death hanging on your shoulders as a weight." Jesus had taught on the topic of self-centeredness before and many already agreed that it was a dreaded disease that infected the entire human race. Indeed no other craving seemed more central to a human being according to Jesus' diagnosis. His only prescription was: machine gun it down, blast it with ordinance, shoot it again, and if it tried to get up—nuke it. Jesus treated the sin of self-centeredness the same way poison control officials in Atlanta deal with things like bubonic plague. Some of John's favorite messages were delivered from the bed of Mrozinski's pickup truck on that evening in Fox Lake.

"The one who wants to secure his life will find it looted." Jesus promised, "And the one who leads an insecure life on account of me and the special news will have it locked up tight for all eternity. Look, what good will it be if you get the whole world while someone steals your soul in the process? What will a person barter or trade for their soul? And whoever is embarrassed of me in the middle of this hedonistic generation, of him the son of man will also be ashamed when he returns in exploding light with his fiery spirits. Jesus wrapped up his messages by telling those present the astonishing fact that there were some standing around present who would not taste death until the kingdom of God had come with power.

John took notes on a tablet he was seldom without while Peter and James sat along side on the same porch wondering at all that Jesus taught. The mood throughout the evening was a little subdued even though there were many friends to catch up with and exciting news to pass along. Peter and Andrew excused themselves to go home and Jesus walked them to their vehicle.

"Peter," Jesus said, "hold steady like a rock. I didn't teach you about foundations and houses torn by storms for no reason. Sin wants to get a foot hold, but you're going to have to out-pull it. Live up to your new name," Jesus said as he waved them goodbye. Simon had been stung by Jesus' words before, but the outbreak today cut him deeply and right before all the others.

"I'm going back to work with Zeb," Simon said while driving south along route 12. "He said I could have my desk back anytime I wanted when I was in to see him last month."

"Simon, I mean Peter. I'll have to get used to that one," said Drew. "I know how you are feeling, and I know Zeb would be glad to have us back at the firm, but you're not going back." Drew spoke to Simon in a way that made him know that he wasn't stating the matter subjunctively but more like an enemy that would stand in his way. Simon looked over at Drew and he got a glimpse of a veteran who had been through perhaps more battle scars than himself, and while no less exhausted knew when a companion needed encouragement and when they needed to be reminded why they signed up in the first place. "I've made a lot of mistakes in life, Peter, and you probably know all about the big ones. But ever since I met Jesus through Jack, I've been given a reason to live. I don't care if I ever achieve anything great in life. If I can just be my brother's keeper, I will feel satisfied—like I accomplished something important in life—something that really mattered. Simon," Drew paused, " I'm praying for you, Peter." Drew's elbow touched the arm rest at the moment his chin fell in his open palm. He turned his head to the window and began lines of silent intercession. In the same instance, Peter pushed the pedal to grab a passing gear and as he went around a semi he brushed tears from his cheek as he read the road sign that reminded him that they were still on Route 12 and that Jesus was counting on each one of them.

All of the inner core would agree that the relationship with Jesus had been a sailing adventure that included riding the crests of waves unimaginable which were exhilarating experiences to slamming the bottom of troughs with magnum force that nearly knocked one unconscious. Six days later, Jesus called Peter, James and John and drove them downtown to the 333 West Wacker Building where they parked the van and took elevators and stairs to the top. The men found the hatch to the roof unlocked and Jesus stepped ahead of the three and motioned for them to follow his lead. Once on top the building, they clung to HVAC equipment and peered over to have a look at the Chicago River and top side of the Merchandise Mart. Jesus hadn't told them his purpose in bringing them to the top of what felt like a high mountain, but a cloud soon drew near on an otherwise gorgeous and perfectly clear day. The atmosphere felt a bit eerie and the cloud smelled of something rich and exquisite that none of them could identify, label or compare. The cloud created no precipitation, but as soon as it rested over them, Jesus was transfigured before their eyes. His slacks and shirt became brilliantly white unlike anything bleaching solutions could produce, and Elijah appeared to them along with Moses, and they were having a conversation with Jesus. Peter felt so invigorated by the surprise that he insisted that they camp there on the roof.

"Rabbi," Peter said, allow us to create space to visit for the three of you. Jesus' followers were terrified and didn't know how else to respond to the happening.

Suddenly the cloud overshadowed them and a voice came from the cloud which said, "This is my son whom I deeply love; give him your focused attention!" The voice made them shut their eyes and brace themselves; for though it was intelligible, it also sounded like thunder. When they opened their eyes they saw no one except Jesus alone. Calls were placed from adjoining skyscrapers who thought an unexplainable bolt of lightning had struck the building and created a fire on the roof. As the men descended the steps, Jesus gave them strict orders not to tell anyone what they had just seen until the Son of Man rises from the dead. Peter and James reasoned among themselves as to what rising from the dead might mean for they had no mental or spiritual categories for such a bodily event. John also pondered the remark. The strange episode and appearance by Elijah spawned new questions, and Jesus was eager to improve their interpretation and understanding of scripture.

"Why do the teachers at the synagogue tell us that Elijah must first come?" asked James.

"Elijah has come," Jesus said while reminding them of Jack's role as a forerunner, "but they did to him as they pleased just as it is written. Jesus then took the opportunity to expose a thread of teaching that had been given less attention. "And what is said of the Son of Man, that he should suffer and be treated contemptuously?" He offered no further explanation but rather let them consider the apparent void. Jesus and the three men rejoined the others who were waiting at the far north end of Grant Park near Randolph. As Jesus approached his other followers, he noticed several Hasidic Jews who were arguing with them. Some in the crowd recognized Jesus and ran to greet him.

"What is all the commotion?" asked Jesus. At that moment a man approached Jesus and explained that he had brought his son to him in order to cast out a demon, but his men were not successful.

The father described the boy's convulsive behavior and said, "The demon often makes him mute and casts him to the ground until he stiffens out and foams at the mouth." Jesus asked the man how long this had been going on in what seemed to be an effort to help the father get in touch with the duration. "Since childhood," the father cried, "and it often throws him into camp fires and even Lake Michigan seeking to kill him. Please help me if you're able," he pleaded.

"If I can?" Jesus took exception to the doubt inherent in the expression. "All things are in the realm of possibility to the one who believes," Jesus said. Turning to his followers, Jesus had one eye on the top floor of the Harrison and could smell the lake when he said to them, "I assure you, whoever says to that skyscraper be lifted up and thrown into the lake, and does not doubt in his heart, but believes it will happen, it will be awarded him."

The young boy's father cried out, "I believe, please help my shaky belief!"

Jesus sighed deeply while he waited for one of his men to move, then said, "What a perverted and unbelieving lot. How long must I put up with this, bring the boy to me!" When the boy saw Jesus, the demon threw him to the ground and he began grinding his teeth as before. Jesus cast out the unclean spirit and gave him back to his father who started praising God for the miraculous deed. While many of the others were still reeling from the demonstration of power, Jesus said to them, "Listen loud and clear. The Son of Man is going to be betrayed into the custody of evil men." The statement went over their heads because its meaning had been kept hidden from them.

The Hasidic Jews marked the event and went away to report their finding, while the father and son sat down to begin catching up on many lost years. The crowd followed Jesus south into Grant Park when an argument erupted which almost turned to blows between James and Thad who had been comparing notes and insisting that their own achievements over the last month far outstripped the insignificant performance of the other. Others pulled the two apart, but the general sentiments were tightly held by each one of them. Jesus stopped the movement of the crowd and singled out a small eight-year-old boy who had come along with his mother. Jesus stood the boy along side of him and used the lad as an example of kingdom rank. "He who is least among you will be the greatest," Jesus said, "and again whoever wants to attain the highest rank must be the lowest rank. The path to greatness is down." Jesus repeated himself. "Unless you become like a child, you cannot step into the kingdom of God at all."

While Jesus had everyone's attention, he went on to speak to the crowd about some of the same stringent marching orders he had previously issued to his closest associates. Because Yom Kippur was the following day, Jesus chose to leave the city and observe the fast in a remote area.

* * * *

A few days later, Jesus moved what few personal items he owned out of the rental on Cove and turned the lease over to John and some other singles. He then led the twelve back downtown for the Feast of Tabernacles where they celebrated the occasion with the Noonans who owned a place just west of Douglas Park off Kedzie. Jesus' followers had brought back enough corn stalks to build a skyscraper of a Sukkot and they ended up building three which rested against the Noonan's house. Willow branches, citrons, gourds and pumpkins decorated the small huts as well as greeting cards sent by friends and folded on a string overhead that spanned the outside walls. The air was cooler now and everyone donned jackets and scarf's to sit outside and visit with warm fill ups of cider from Kelsey's special blend. The decoration party had been a wonderful time to visit with old friends who were always bringing around new ones to be freshly introduced. In the middle of the festival, Jesus left the Noonan's and traveled downtown to the Plaza at the Daley Center where he lectured a sizeable audience of Jews who had gathered for a city wide address by Rabbi Leonard Geiger.

Geiger had already concluded his address several minutes prior but was still in the Plaza along with the throng who were visiting and exchanging well wishes with one another. Without introduction, Jesus ascended the portable risers and began teaching them about the kingdom of God, issues of spiritual epistemology and judgment. Geiger was incensed to find Jesus within arms reach and seeking to overthrow his authority and title by winning over the masses. He quickly summoned two of his men and ordered them to physically remove him from the Plaza. Geiger's appointees found the audience impenetrable for everyone there had only heard about Jesus but was now seeing him live for the first time. There was really nothing Geiger or anyone else could do short of shooting Jesus where he stood, and Geiger may have done just that if he owned a firearm.

Jesus taught from familiar portions of the Torah and applied it to the audience in ways that made them look ridiculous and grossly out of step with its true meaning and import. For instance, at one time he reprimanded the crowd for their partiality in circumcising a baby on the Sabbath in order to keep the Law while criticizing Jesus for making a man or woman entirely whole on the same sacred day. The irony was so great that many began grumbling among themselves and so the crowd was divided. Jesus concluded an address that would highlight one of the most central tenants of his teachings. Jesus described himself as a well of water, thus harking back to dry cisterns the prophets used to caution their generation about. He encouraged the crowd in front of him to come to him if they were thirsty and experience the living water that he promised would flow out of their innermost selves.

When Geiger could stand it no longer, he forced his way through the audience and had already made up his mind to pull Jesus down by the hair of his head. During all the ruckus and parting of human flesh, Jesus quietly stepped off stage and walked to the edge of the building away from Geiger's grasp. When he reached the risers, Geiger was out of breath and lunged with his eyes in each direction seeking to get a glimpse of his enemy. Others joined Geiger.

"These fools know nothing of the Law," they grumbled among themselves.

Geiger lost the skirmish at Daley Plaza but was pleased to learn upon his arrival back at campus that A.T.F. agents had been by to see him and brought attorneys who wanted depositions regarding information he had of threats of sedition and terrorism. Geiger had already begun to court Jude and quickly found a man who he thought would make a wonderful mole. Geiger convinced the A.T.F. and F.B.I. to be patient and he would soon place a man in their hands, a man he alleged was the ring leader and mastermind behind the V.A. and Cripple Children's Hospital bombings that nearly leveled both facilities and claimed the lives of hundreds of people including several small children who were sleeping and recovering from surgeries when the heat and concussion ripped through brick and steel. Geiger was a mastermind of his own and kept in close touch through a newsletter to each family who lost loved ones in the blast. He had a sadistic way with words and could invite himself into the most private areas of one's mind, more sacred than the holocaust museum only to silently break glass, loose foundations, rumble memorabilia until it fell from shelves and shattered. Geiger led the families to relive the horror on a monthly basis while promising them that he had made it his personal vendetta to chase down the murderer, for he singled out only one, and bring him to the people's bar of justice. Geiger never dropped the name Jesus nor hinted at the growing Jewish sect. He simply wanted to construct another bomb that would detonate on his command and send shrapnel through Jesus that would pin him to a post. The Jewish historian, Josephus, who Geiger was fond to read, had already planted in his mind the means of execution he would employ. He turned a hewn model in his hands and pacified himself with monstrous thoughts and awaited his day with the patience of a scavenging bird.

Jesus left the city that afternoon and retired himself for several months from public ministry around Chicago. He spent the day at Peter's house with Jill and the boys who had not seen Jesus in more than eight months. Andrew and Rebecca joined them for dinner and Jesus got quite a work out giving trolley rides to four small children that extended from one end of the house to the other. After dinner, while the men cleaned dishes and tidied the kitchen, the ladies put sleepy heads to bed and regrouped in the living room for some wonderful wine and conversation. Jill quietly looked at Jesus and reflected on a man's face that looked to have aged twenty years since they last met. The five talked on in the living room like folks who had mortgaged everything they owned to begin a business. They had watched it take off—only to crash and burn. Jesus was sounding an ultimate death nil, but the others just couldn't comprehend how death, which he wasn't terribly clear about could result in life. Jesus thanked his hosts for their hospitality and asked them to hold their seats while he grabbed a coat and scarf from the closet. Jesus knew that there was confusion in their hearts and one of the toughest challenges he faced was holding their questions until the appropriate time.

"Jill," Jesus said as he turned from the foyer and looked into her worried face, for she was having the more difficult emotional time with everything, "unless a grain of wheat finds its way to the soil and dies, it's all alone by itself. But if it dies, its yield is huge. Consider the harvest. Let your faith lean into the future. Goodnight everyone. Peter and Andrew, I'll need you the first of next week and we will be out again for a pretty good stint. I'll give you a call."

Back on Cove, John pulled out his journal before dozing off to sleep and began recording the events of recent weeks including the trip to the top of 333 Wacker Building. "The law and the prophets were until Jack," he wrote, remembering Jesus' words from a different conversation. Putting down his pen, he wondered about the voice from the cloud, the timing and how he had spoken only after Moses and Elijah disappeared. John understood that those two names were highly revered and represented the law and prophets unlike any others possibly could. John made a note or two which would underline the importance of obeying the voice of God and paying close attention to the instruction Jesus was offering.

"Father, thank you for your kind manner," John prayed before hitting the pillow, "and patience even with the hard hearted. Forgive us for periods of unbelief, when we stop walking with you and insist that our ways are the best ways. Continue to root out areas of self-centeredness from our lives so that the world will know that we are different because of your presence in our lives. I pray that you will continue to strengthen us and give us resolve like Jesus to follow you in everything. Continue to show yourself off through your servant, Jesus, and may our confidence in him bring a smile to your face. Amen."

CHAPTER 13

Ann Geiger placed Leonard's half onion bagel, cup of decaf and the Wall Street at his place in the Florida room before leaving for work. She needed to be at the Criminal Courts building by 10:00 A.M. to meet with the District Attorney prior to an arraignment that was scheduled for one of her clients. A small red light flashed in the fully finished and furnished lower level indicating that Ann was on her way out and Leonard was cleared to come upstairs. This is where he made his home away from his wife for 32 years. Both of them made it clear to one another from the beginning that they neither wanted to see or speak to the other inside the confines of their house so long as they both should live. Enlivened conversations carried over from evenings out with friends or dinner parties were cut off at the threshold when they entered their house. Strict and meticulous schedules were maintained in order to ensure that their paths should not cross in the same room of their immaculate 6,000 square foot ranch dwelling. Their marriage had never been sexually consummated after all their years, but strangely they cared for one another in a business kind of manner that benefited both of them. Leonard was fed regularly and Ann was accompanied by her prestigious husband to dinners and other occasions when it was socially more advantageous for him to be along. Otherwise, Ann spent a great deal of time at her mother's place. She hated her mother.

While Geiger climbed steps from the lower level cradling a small arm load of files and taped documentary, Jude excused himself from a prayer and planning session being conducted at Matthew's place and drove instead to Hyde Park where he would meet Leonard Geiger at Smart Museum on Greenwood Avenue. The two men had never met, but Jude had heard stories about Geiger and read articles he had published in scholarly journals of which they both shared an interest. Geiger, on the other hand, knew a great deal about Jude; his origins, fiscal state, education, preferences of every type, loves, fears and most importantly for his purposes, Jude's unwavering commitment to Zionism.

Fire proof files stood behind a false wall in the basement of Geiger's home that contained stacks of highly confidential and incriminating data on dozens and dozens of prominent names around Chicago and the entire country for that matter. The list of names was an elite Hall of Fame enshrined by Geiger, but only after satisfying his most rigorous investigative demands. Besides Mayor Harry, other inductees and Heisman winners included select Board Members of the University of Chicago, key editors for both of the Chicago newspapers, the Illinois Governor, New York City Mayor, both U.S. Senators from Illinois, as well as the current President of the United States to name a few. Entire walls in the secret stow were lined with video and audio taped meetings including secret and illegal banking transactions, deviant sexual acts, and impeaching conversations between partners about fellow partners and business associates.

Geiger treasured a few rare escapades that were obtained in remote, hard to reach areas with the help of a camera from a military spy satellite that could read a license plate tag from outer space and deliver the same quality resolution as a high priced 35mm at a distance of five feet. Leonard had contacts on the inside of the headquarters building at NSA who worked in a Blue Room that handled highly classified collections of data. In fact, Geiger had been on the second floor of NSA on several occasions and had his own permanent metal badge that was created by a woman he owned on the inside. She was paid a salary through M5, NSA's personnel and in house security division, but she was Geiger's exclusively. Geiger's fetish with intelligence ran deep and he pursued his biographical craft as though it was his primary employment. Unquestionably, he was as organized as the most fastidious librarian. In a moment he could retrieve computer tapes from archives that were current and backed up as well as full length licentious video featuring top ranking public officials. These were his prize possessions. He enjoyed occasional visits to his collection in the same way a safari hunter admires his mounts, pausing along the passage in order to relive the adventure and savor the kill.

On occasion, Geiger felt an overwhelming sense of something so incredibly evil while walking that narrow corridor that he would stop and breathe in its presence. But he no longer knew it was evil. Only once did Geiger see him and the sight was sensually arousing. A man stood at the top of the corridor in banker's shoe, impeccably dressed from head to toe, including a top coat, hat and holding an umbrella. He was a small man of medium weight with a face that looked to be chiseled from flint. His color was a dead, ashen looking gray with a wicked tint. His lips were thin, toxic and expressionless like Geiger's, but he knew the man was offering a pleasing smile at his malignant work. Geiger wasn't a spiritist nor did he dabble in satanic occult for he found the practice childish not to mention iniquitous and morally deplorable. Geiger was more interested in deeper discovery about Geiger. He didn't wake up one day with a resolve to pursue the paths he'd grow to love, but little by little, day by day he laid up deceit in his heart until it grew so dark that he could no longer discern the difference between right and wrong. The path to innocence had been lost and he didn't want to find his way back.

Jude's life story could be found in chronological order in the form of video, still frame, telephone—wire taps as well as signed confessions in his own hand that Geiger obtained from secret FBI files who investigated Jude on the occasion when he burned a synagogue to the ground in Park Ridge. It was never proven that Jude ignited the accelerant and his attorney was able to persuade authorities to place the deed at the feet of a hate group notorious for defamation and other arsonist type violence. During their investigation, the FBI uncovered evidence that linked Jude to intimate ties with militant pro-Israeli groups in the Country and abroad. Jude didn't appreciate the cool reception he received after laying out his carefully argued philosophy before synagogue officials he sought to recruit for an upcoming rally. Later that same week, he lathered their place of worship with a napalm jelly of his own recipe and detonated it from a block away. Geiger had record of the entire incineration from inception of plan to aftermath, including a few pieces of confidential correspondence lifted during a break in at Jude's highly secured residence that he thought he had somehow lost or misplaced.

Geiger was aware the moment Jude arrived in the parking lot, but waited inside, walking the corridor with umbrella in hand and feigning interest in several pieces of contemporary art that were on display. Geiger's game, though technologically intricate to the novice who had no experience with his play, was in reality the old and simple game of espionage, blackmail, capitulation, cooperation or death, or both, followed by the next file.

"Hello, Judas," Geiger greeted a man who didn't know exactly whom to seek.

"Yes, Rabbi Geiger, it's a pleasure to finally meet you," said Jude.

"Why don't we walk over to the campus and enjoy the crisp air God has given to gladden our hearts and remind us of his covenant promise to continue the seasons unabated," Leonard suggested. Geiger had nothing more in mind than taking Jude on a stroll around the Oxford style gray stone buildings as part of his initiatory rites of passage to submissions prescribed by his new mentor. Geiger was greeted on campus by faculty as Doctor or Rabbi, and he seldom returned the greeting whether he shared the company of another person or not. Jude was eager to learn about Dr. Geiger's long range objectives and how he and his organization had proceeded to date. Geiger allowed Jude to invent his own understandings of how he thought a cultural magnate would occupy himself. He only gave Jude enough false assurances to appease his growing appetite the same way a sage wraps his chin with the palm of his hand and nods at astute perceptions of a student.

"Rabbi Geiger," Jude began, "I mean may I call you, Leonard?" he asked. Geiger paused on the sidewalk and Jude realized immediately that the comment had splattered against a wall.

Geiger read his nonverbal reaction loud and clear, then responded in a firm unfatherly manner, "Judas, it is the quality of a noble man to excuse and forgive imprudence in a subordinate." Then he lifted his voice for he couldn't control his rage, "And you must understand that I have absolutely no tolerance for poor judgment and no capacity to excuse and forgive those who do! Do you understand my words, Judas?" Students walking a sidewalk fifty feet away could hear Geiger scolding a grown man while he wrenched his umbrella with both hands.

"Yes Rabbi Geiger, I'm terribly sorry for slighting you in that manner. It will not happen again, I assure you," Jude said while wrenching hands of his own.

"Let yourself not be drug down excessively by it but resolve in your mind to refrain and reform," Geiger concluded while wiping saliva from his lips.

"Refrain and reform," Jude replied, "I intend to commit it to memory." Jude had no problem whatsoever with Geiger's apparent mistreatment and very definite overreaction. Jude liked his ruthless style and would have delivered the same reprimand to others who failed him.

After the uncomfortableness washed over Jude, Geiger walked him to his car and the two of them drove to the Museum of Science and Industry, a place of mechanisms and mathematics where Geiger felt more at home, and they could continue their conversations.

"Judas, I would be very interested to learn about the methods and teachings of the young rabbi who has been recently featured in the papers." Jesus himself had seldom been caught on camera, but those he helped as well as other spokespersons for The Way were sometimes carried along with short articles dealing with local occurrences. Geiger couldn't bring himself to utter the name Jesus and found it convenient to delete the name from his vocabulary except for an occasional outburst wrapped with derisive jeers.

"Well," Jude began, "Jesus isn't a typical rabbi. He doesn't insist upon all the regulations a man of your imminence would be careful to observe." Geiger stopped to correct Jude.

"These disciplines, Judas," Geiger related in a kinder tone, "are not something we participate in—they are who and what we are. The Law requires not our best efforts but perfection. But please speak on, your inside observations are of great interest to me." Geiger flattered Jude one moment and scolded him the next. All the while Jude accepted the throws as part of his new stringents of training.

Jude never really bought into Jesus' way of thinking simply because he never understood it. The way Jesus taught, the concepts he used as well as the issues that topped his agenda were so far removed from the area Jude wanted to explore that he slowly drifted away and lost interest in what Jesus was doing. On the other hand, Jude had learned not to burn bridges behind him and he was still impressed with many of the miracles performed by Jesus. Jude was standing right next to Jesus that day on the Kane County Fairgrounds and watched sliced bread and oven temperature fish fillets extrude from his palms which were turned down to fill baskets. While John, one of the inner three was recording spiritual insights, Jude was reckoning with the multiplication of machine guns. He couldn't put away the thought that Jesus was someone great, but his political outlook and what little foreign policy he could ever distill from Jesus was so weak it placed him outside the possibility of qualifying as Messiah. This bit of information pleased Geiger who had a following of his own and many Hasidic Jews secretly believed him to be the Messiah.

"Judas," Geiger inquired, and he was one of only a few people who ever called Jude by his fuller name, "this young rabbi you previously named, you've already related how he teaches his followers to disregard the holy Law and that he has even testified to being equal with the Lord God himself." Geiger uttered a prayer of blessing in Hebrew at the mere mention of the deity; no rabbi would think of using his personal name by which he revealed himself for fear of mispronunciation. And while Geiger paid little attention to things unseen, the practice had been learned early on and eventually became an habitual routine. Of course, the practice was useful to Geiger since it provided reassurances to strict Jewish sects who sometimes wondered about his hellenizing with the world.

"Yes, that's right," said Jude, "on one occasion while just the twelve of us were with him, he said that he and the great I Am were one and that Abraham and the patriarchs had worshipped at his feet during times…" Geiger cut Jude's sentence off and dropped the point of his umbrella onto the top of his foot which caused him to cry out.

"Son, you be sure of this," Geiger said inflexibly, "any other mention that he or anyone else should rival the Most Holy will be met with penalties that I cannot presently discuss. Judas, you must realize more than others that there will be no clemency or mercy for talk fit only for fools. And no one can back away my hand or say to me, what are you doing?" Geiger often didn't know when he was quoting from the Scroll. And many of the statements attributed only to God, he adopted for himself. Geiger raised his umbrella from the freshman's foot and pulled his slight body weight from a man he had pinned to the rails overlooking the first floor. Jude wasn't about to lift it himself and invite further wrath but was relieved to have the rabbi out of his face.

The two men spent another hour in the museum while Geiger carefully sifted Jude's memory for more exact detail of specific events. Geiger of course was wired as usual and led Jude into a conversation regarding trips by Jesus west of the City in which he was curious to learn more about. Geiger knew that Jesus had made a major trip to Arizona nearly two years ago and that the day of his departure coincided with the bombings of two hospitals in near Chicago suburbs. Authorities were still searching for suspects while Geiger was working overtime to produce evidence that would expose the kingpin of the entire operation. Jesus' disappearance into the desert for forty days right on the heels of the blast was incriminating enough for Geiger to begin building a case. He had purchased embellished affidavits from an Indian woman near Tulsa, Oklahoma, that were dictated to her by his cohorts. She remembered speaking to him about a big blast and he mentioned that it was but the birth pangs, as well as conversations out in the open back in the Chicago area where he boasted about bomb shells and disrupting fundamentalist and time honored Hasidic beliefs. Geiger wanted Jesus executed and knew he had to reach the most tender sentiments of the American public in order to spring a trap he was carefully constructing. Only Satan himself would dare touch and manipulate the heart strings of those who lost loved ones in such a cruel and cowardice act, such that took the lives of so many on that terrible night, but Geiger could see his way through to an advantage. The Veteran's Hospital, Hines and the Shriner's Hospital for Crippled Children on Oak Park became Geiger's targets. Several sealed 55 gallon drums of ammonia nitrate saturated with high test aviation fuel and marked as floor stripper were transferred from trucks to loading docks two days before the fateful blast at each institution. Geiger had already combed Jesus' van on an earlier occasion and his private forensic team found traces of ammonia nitrate and diesel fuel in the cargo compartment around rear door weather stripping as well as a receipt from the glove box indicating a purchase from a local seed and fertilizer company. These discoveries led Geiger in his selection of the preferred method to bring Jesus down. His goal was to pin on Jesus—an innocent lamb—one of the most offensive raps of the Century. The American public was already growing angry and impatient with lengthy court proceedings that sometimes ended up exonerating criminals others knew to be worthy of imprisonment. When American militias are stirred and tolerances spent, it is not safe for the accused to be caught on the streets even when guarded by well armed escorts of U.S. Marshals.

"Judas, would you characterize the young rabbi as a violent man or one hungry for power?" asked Geiger.

"Oh, without question," said Jude who was overlaying much of his own private interpretation onto Jesus' teaching and actions. "I was with him one day when he drove several people from a synagogue with his belt."

"Was he verbally abusive, Judas, did you have the sense that he could kill for lesser evils?"

"Sure," said Jude, "he even taught us as much. He said a day was coming soon in which there would be a great blood bath and he cited some portions from the prophets to that effect."

"So does he actually think that he will take over the world?" asked Geiger.

"Yes, he intends to rule them with a rod of iron. But this is where I find him awfully fuzzy," Geiger paused his recorder, "he always speaks in terms of a kingdom that is not of this world—one people can't enter without some sort of a new genesis that involves spiritual regeneration. Even the judgments he speaks of seem terribly futuristic."

"That's enough today, Judas. I have a board meeting in less than an hour. Whatever you do, don't fall prey to the foolish ramblings of this dreamer. Centuries of experience and scholarship has proven but one path to life—the perfection of one's soul by the Torah. Judas, before I see you again, you will immerse yourself in these rabbinic readings," handing him a list, "and begin cleansing yourself of the defilement this association has brought to your soul. I want you to stay involved and keep me informed of everything you know including his weekly schedules. You are doing a great service to God, bless his name forever, and he is not slack to forget your faithfulness." Geiger extended his hand and said, "For God and his holy hill."

"Yes, Rabbi Geiger," said Jude who could not believe the doctor would actually shake the hand of someone common, "for Zion." And they departed.

*   *   *   *

Snow flurries were predicted by 'Dan the Weather Man,' who was a much enjoyed weather forecaster for Green Bay. For a community that relied heavily on Doppler and accurate weather vanes, Dan was indispensable and considered a celebrity. More than once the locals were sure he conjured snow and sub-zero temperatures on game days when southern teams with better football records were scheduled to play. Three car loads of men left Green Bay on 57 and made their way north to Door County, Wisconsin, for a winter retreat that would last over three months; however, several overnight trips would be made to Milwaukee during the period in order to pursue work in that City as well.

Jesus had not been back to Door County since he was a kid. The family would often bring Jack along and spend a week in cabins while fishing, swimming and enjoying late night talks around a charcoal fire that had burned down from a large heap. Joey never started a fire with less than 15—20 good hardwood sections. He would always dowse it with camp stove fuel, have everybody stand back, then throw a match onto the pile which would flash and make a gulping noise as Joey would describe it, sucking up all the available oxygen. Mary never thought it was a particularly good idea to teach the boys risky fire lighting techniques.

"Can't you just begin with some kindling like a good scout and keep adding wood until you create a nice cozy fire," he remembered his mom's question.

"Mary, I've got a dozen things to do if I'm to put this camp in shape, and I don't have time to piddle around rubbing sticks together. When a man wants a fire you stack combustibles, add accelerant, stand back out of the impact area and throw on a match." All the boys loved Joey's method, but flames did claim a cooler of food on one occasion and melted it down before anyone could get near the inferno and retrieve it. The steaks Mary had carefully trimmed and savored might have survived the fire ready to eat, but they were encased in polymer, which jaws now claimed the choice meats. Those were some great memories as Jesus recounted them, not to mention the fish and potato boils and cherry wine for which the County was equally famous.

Their destination was Egg Harbor where a lovely Jewish couple, Nick and Beulah, owned an oversize cottage right on the bay and lent it out freely to friends. Nick did not easily embrace the teachings of Jesus when he first encountered him, but he was a prayerful man, and a God-fearing rabbi who was a spiritual seeker for truth. One Summer night as Jesus walked alone on Navy Pier, Nick approached him, having followed him there and engaged him in a long spiritual discussion that changed Nick's life. He came with many important questions and because he was sincere he left with answers, although perplexing, answers that became life milk to a newborn. Nick wasn't confessing Jesus publicly because he was still dealing with some fear of being ostracized from the synagogue and stripped of his religious credentials. Nevertheless, he carefully considered every report he heard of Jesus and highly anticipated more private conversations with him.

Peter, Jude, James and John were the first to arrive and claim bunks. James noticed what looked to be a sophisticated recording device in Jude's back pack, and when questioned about it he remarked that it was an expensive CD player for playback only. James enjoyed electronics and while he was well read and current on many new models, he passed off the unfamiliar piece but was disappointed that Jude wouldn't allow him to handle it. Jesus rolled in shortly with groceries and because it was lunch time everyone broke for something to eat. Peter fired up a gas grill on the back deck standing in six inches of snow while a couple of others who enjoyed an occasional cigar walked around on the ice covered bay and caught up on some small talk. "Thomas, how long are you going to be around?" asked John while stamping the thick ice with his boot and wondering at its depth.

"I intend to be here two weeks, then I've got to be in DesMoines to host a workshop for the company. I'll be back around just as soon as I can wrap things up. The trip was on my calendar before Jesus moved to schedule our time in Wisconsin."

"Well, it's good to have you on hand," John said. "I've hardly had time to say hello."

Thomas continued shuffling snow between his feet, then asked, "So, what do you think, John, is this all as credible as we've been led to believe?" The question offended John who had made up his mind about Jesus and his self-authenticating miracles long ago.

"Thomas, I'm surprised by the question," John said. "What would make his claims credible in your view?" Thomas wasn't ready to answer the question, and John knew he wasn't so skeptic as to quit the team, but the inherent doubt didn't set well with John, and he let him know how he felt.

"C'mon, John, ease up," Thomas said. "I've just got some honest questions that need a little more time." Peter rang a large brass bell that hung from a post. Nick salvaged it years ago from a ship that had been scrapped out for steel. Heads lifted and several men out stretching their legs from the long ride up from Chicago, turned and headed to the house for a bite to eat.

During lunch, Jesus informed his followers that it was his intention to remain within the Green Bay, Madison, Milwaukee triangle for the winter and return to Chicago after Passover. Winters were often cold and hard in these parts, but Peter would often comfort the others by reminding them Jesus might have chosen Fargo, North Dakota, where today's temperature was a brittle 60 degrees below zero with wind chill.

"I don't suppose a strand or two of barbed wire is much buffer against those winds," said Thad.

Jesus enjoyed the cold weather having been raised right in the middle of one of the finest deep freezers the Midwest has to offer. Besides this, the season afforded him concentrated time to continue modeling the exact representation of the Father's nature before their eyes. There would be plenty of time for verbal instruction, but one thing these men would not have long was a flesh and blood example of one who was utterly characterized by limitless favor dispensing habits and truth, a balance very few would ever be able to maintain.

"There are those," Jesus was famous for teaching, "who freely dispense favor and forfeit the truth. On the other hand, there are those who are galvanized with truth and demonstrate very little ability to dispense favor. Avoid both extremes," he would caution.

Following clean up from lunch, Peter popped in an expensive cheroot, opened the damper over the fire box and with head on a pillow blew smoke up the chimney while listening to Jesus teach. As was often the case, Jesus taught according to need which usually meant he was led by a question he felt was important enough to spend time entertaining.

Earlier that morning before leaving the Chicago area, a smartly dressed Jewish attorney recognized Jesus at a filling station with his entourage and yelled over while they were attempting to load up for their trip. "Rabbi, what shall I do to inherit eternal life?" Jesus' followers couldn't discern if it were an honest question or wiped with sarcasm. Jesus often pointed out ironies and was quick to call a spade a spade but never responded with sarcasm of his own, especially to such an important question regardless of the inquirer's intent.

"You know the Law," Jesus said. "What does it say—how do you interpret it?"

"The man pulled a fuel nozzle from his late model Cadillac and said, "Of course, one should love the Lord God with all his mind, soul, heart and strength and one's neighbor just the way he would love himself."

Jesus told the man in the hearing of his followers, "That's the right answer. Do all those things and you will live eternally." The attorney realized how far short he and everyone else fell from attaining the righteousness of the law and so in an attempt to justify himself asked, "Yeah, but define 'neighbor' for me."

Racial prejudices were no less masked among Jesus' band than would be found among any other subculture on the continent.

"Jesus," Philip asked, "how could you let that slickster back at the service station get away with all that double talk?" Jude's car load wasn't around for the full answer he offered the man, and for the benefit of the twelve, Jesus gave them another version which taught the same truth.

"There was a certain man," Jesus began, Peter extinguished his smoke and lifted up to get all the facial expressions as Jesus began what he knew would be a great story, "who was traveling down to Peoria from Chicago. It was late at night when he pulled into a truck stop for fuel and after filling up and paying the attendant, he was accosted by two worthless men who were in need of some cash and transportation. The wicked louts forced him to the rear of the building, raped him, beat him unconscious, stole his car and left him for dead."

"Were the thuds niggers?" Jude asked, "It sounds like niggers."

"No." Jesus said abruptly. He then waited over the word in a manner that was decisive and intolerant. Everyone felt something brewing while Jesus continued by saying, "The man lay on the ground until morning with a torn rectum, broken jaw, other fractures and collapsed lung that had been pierced by a broken rib.

"During the night a certain synagogue official made a wide swing near the rear of the building and his headlights caught glimpse of the man. When he rolled down his glass and heard the moans not of a drunk, but a dying man, he pulled away quietly and without report. He had important business in Peoria and couldn't be detained. Hours later a rabbi making the same trip stopped for gas, noticed the fellow Jew half dead who had managed to crawl a few feet into the open. The man was so severely maimed, that the rabbi couldn't risk soiling the interior of his new luxury sedan. Besides, it was Sabbath and though he could justify resting comfortably while traveling a couple hundred miles in a car, personal involvement and the extraneous effort required to assist the man would render the rabbi ceremonially defiled. After brief contemplation, he too left the dying man without getting his hands dirty. Then, just awhile before day, a hated nigger was traveling the same artery," Jesus' eyes surveyed his men, " saw the awful sight, felt compassion for the man," Jesus voice broke with emotion as he told the stirring version and considered the hardness of some of his own. "The black man felt compassion and wondered if in a different world at a different time they could not have been friends. He made haste to break out a first aid kit and treat some superficial wounds, then loaded him in the car and drove to the emergency room for intensive care. Martin wasn't done yet. After waiting around and ensuring he got a room, all of which he paid in cash out of his own pocket, he also stopped by after the man regained consciousness to check up on him and even continued months later to pay for some psychological treatment. Which one," Jesus concluded, "proved to be the man's neighbor?" There was plenty of stirring in the room but also a lot of blank stares; and since an answer was slow in coming, Jesus shouted at the men in a voice that startled them, because he was incensed by their indifference, "I asked who proved to be the man's neighbor!"

"Easy, Jesus," Peter finally responded for everyone was looking to him; but before he could raise the bet, Jesus called his hand and turned the table over in their laps and walked outside to cool off." There was no bluffing at this moment about a man who was zealous for God and carried a short fuse for those insensitive to sin. The men were not upset with Jesus, just surprised at how deeply rooted their own prejudices ran, and most of them were extremely remorseful following the revelation.

One by one several of the Twelve walked outdoors only to watch the diminishing silhouette of their leader fade as he walked briskly across the frozen lake away from them. Jesus often sought solitude following episodes like that which just occurred; he constantly prayed for all of his followers but especially the core group who would one day be handed the baton. Prayer was the indispensable key to victory and he would leave that conviction deeply imbedded in the hearts of all those who followed him.

Upon reentering the house, a billiards tournament was organized while others played old pinball machines, read or took advantage of a space of time in which they could get some shut eye. Nick and Beulah had outfitted a large game room in the rear of the house for the very purpose of providing entertainment during the long cold winter months and were always happy to find the calendar full of reservations by friends. Jesus carried an ice auger in his hand that was mistaken by those on shore as a stick. Between long intervals of prayer, he would bait a light jig with dual sets of hooks using meal worms that Nick raised in quantity, then lower it to a depth of about ten feet and after a moment retrieve two hand size perch. It was not unusual to catch fifty perch and white fish in less than an hour. Jesus returned to the house in time to clean the mess and prepare them for dinner which was often his treat.

War cries ascended when Jesus arrived at the back deck dragging two stringers of some of the best tasting fish available to man.

"Hey everybody," shouted Philip, "Bill Dance is fresh back with supper!" Most of the men had never handled fishing tackle in their lives and could hardly believe that Jesus had caught so many with just a slight stick and thread thin filament. Everyone wanted to try their hand at the new enterprise, and several larger ocean reels were removed from the garage wall; their captains reasoning that bigger is definitely better. While Jesus began lessons in the fine art of fillet, Jude, Matthew and Thomas departed in the first wave in trek of the giant, Coho. Before the next raft of expedition departed, Jesus recommended that someone take along an ice auger and he briefly demonstrated how to use one. Because Matthew's crew failed to take a tool to break ice, they spent most of their time stomping the thick plate in hopes of forcing a hole. Arguments erupted in the galley kitchen over what food products might be sacrificed for bait. Peter wanted to cut up hot dogs while others insisted that it was a waste and would only attract catfish or something worse. Jesus was drawn away from his work again to direct the men to Nick's worm beds. The garage that was previously so well organized now resembled a federal disaster area as rods and equipment were drawn in haste by children in too great a hurry to look after one another. James picked up a hand saw on the way out with plans of his own.

"We're in deep!" shouted Peter. He and James cut holes with an auger in what would become four corners of about a 36 in. square. They didn't have the means to leverage the block of ice to the surface so Peter sent James back for his truck. "Here, James," Peter said, handing him keys to his Pathfinder, "go get the truck and drive it out here on the ice, we're going to need some tools and plenty of power to cart these fish back." Peter took advantage of his absence and tried to get a jump on his count. Everything he did was with a view to winning. His competitive side could be found amusing or irritating depending which side you were on. In this case, Peter wanted to be the provider and bring home the bread. Jesus and John shook their heads along with the others when

James pulled onto the lake with Peter's truck. The ice was plenty thick; it was just the way those two threw themselves into their work.

"If we're going to fish," Peter talked on with himself, "then let's fish. If you're coming with us, you're going to have to string 'em or cut bait; and if you can't swim with Barracudas, just stay in the school circle." Peter laughed aloud out on the ice by himself. When James arrived back with the truck, Peter had already pulled three nice northerns through the holes provided by the auger and he was a little reluctant to allow James to fish in the same hole. "Our lines will get tangled," Peter said to James who had approached the hole with an ocean rig big enough to land a marlin.

"You better be making room, son," said James who had patiently waited and run errands up until now. While Peter drew in his line, James began sawing between circles in order to completely cut out the square. Together the two men used tire tools and bars to pry the enormous block up out of it's place. The cold square was saddled with a folded tarp and became a seat for Peter. James dropped a freshly baited hook into the hole. After just a minute, something snatched James' lure, for he had decided to just jig with a spoon equipped with large barbs similar to those he once saw on a field and stream program. James had nearly a whole hot dog diced up and hiding the sharp hooks, and the hungry fish nearly yanked the rod from his hands. The fish fought furiously from below while James walked the surface back and forth wondering at the strength of the great fish. "I've got a horse," James yelled, and others several meters away ignored him as trying to be comical and exaggerating the size of the pan fish everyone else was catching. "Peter, find something to snag this Chinook," for he knew he had hung a huge one. Peter was disappointed that James would draw in the first Salmon, but he was anxious to see it since it was obviously an oversize one the way the heavy reinforced rod was dipping. The two men continued working the top side looking carefully for a fish that would surface soon since James had not dropped the line over 15–20 feet. A great pull brought James to his knees and he flipped over on his back to keep the rod in his hands which soon found its way up across his throat and pinned him there gasping for air and trying to call Peter's name, who had turned aside to begin rigging a larger outfit in hopes of topping James' catch.

"Boy, haven't you got that minnow out of the water yet?" Peter asked. He didn't expect an answer from a man who was as determined as the fish to win the bout; but when Peter turned from his tackle, he witnessed James, blue faced, but with no consideration of letting go of the rod. The big fish had him on the ropes and was pounding him with its weight while James gasped for air and tried without success to utter a distress syllable or two. Peter quickly grabbed the rod from James' hands who reluctantly loosed it to a fellow angler. Peter fought the fish for several more minutes without feeling that he had moved the monster a single foot. James caught his breath and a verbal fight ensued regarding who's fish it was since it had nearly suffocated James. The great fish tried several directional maneuvers to dislodge itself from the sharp barbs and high test line. Peter finally gave the rod up to James, but he doubled a glove and grabbed line ahead of the rod tip and pulled strenuously until he looped it around a towing hook on the front of the truck. The fish continued into the fifteenth, way ahead on points; but when Peter released the brake and began edging backward away from the hole, they all knew that the line would either break or the mystery fish would have to surface. Peter was probably 12 feet away when its nose broke the surface and James reached in to find a gill. Peter would remark later that he had never seen a man lunge back with greater velocity and determination in all his life!

"You would have thought the boy had been struck at by a rattler when the ugly Sturgeon showed its head!" James had never heard of nor seen a Sturgeon in his life and fully believed he had hooked a monster, come all the way over from Scotland. Peter continued pulling the fish back into James' lap who had slipped and fallen on the ice. He didn't care if the line broke because he wasn't interested in eating the 125 pound scavenger that was over six feet in length. Peter laughed so hard from the cab of the truck that he wet his pants, but just kept reeling until the weight of the thing had rolled up on James who was fit to be tied beneath its slimy under belly. James found himself staring up at the mouth of the rodent and said later, "I didn't know ugly came in such large denominations." Peter pulled out a pocket camera and captured the memory close up and in color. "This will be absolutely fabulous," he said to himself while the shutter snapped shut, "Jill can place this in her memories album along side the snapshots that feature James barfing all over the living room during an allergic reaction to some scallops he'd eaten last summer." James was beyond mad and would have tackled Peter and sought to inflict some real pain, but Peter remained in the locked cab and continued idling along, bringing the fish right over James body and towed it back to the house where he showed off the prize to the rest of the men. Peter had raised one foot and placed it on the back of the fish and was lecturing the others on the finer points of angling when James arrived and pounced on his back from behind driving him to the ground. James was determined to shove Peter's face up to the front of the Sturgeon's and have the two kiss, but Peter was much stronger and staved off the attack with a scissor lock around James' waist until he cooled down.

It was into the night when the men finally dressed the keepers, cleaned themselves up and sat down at the long homemade dinner table that was designed to accommodate 16 adults. The extra room was needed for hush puppies, cold slaw, drinks and hot ears of corn Jesus thought to bring along in the event of a mess. Together, the men had caught enough perch to satisfy even the most heroic appetites and there was still plenty left over for sandwiches the next day. Jesus and John placed the fresh fillets in a milk and egg dip, then rolled them in cracker crumbs before frying them in cast iron skillets a half inch deep with vegetable oil. As the meal was winding down and some of the men had a little more wine than recommended, Peter began leading a chorus to the tune of Mary Had a Little Lamb that would become James' memory song.

> Jimmy hung a great big fish, great big fish, great big fish
> Jimmy hung a great big fish, its scales were inches long.
> And everywhere that James would pull, James would pull, James would pull
> Everywhere that James would pull, the fish was sure to tow.
> It followed him to bay one day which was against the rules,
> But it made the real men laugh and play to see a Sturgeon rule!

Laughter raised the roof, and James was beginning to go along with the levity and creating a little of his own by reminding them that it took a man to wrestle the creature from the water, for James would have his own interpretation of what really happened at the mouth of the ice on that memorable day. Lights began to dim in the cottage around 11:00 P.M., some were grabbing showers while others retired from the pool table for a snack or went on to bed.

Jesus and John sat at the kitchen bar with fresh coffee and resumed a discussion they had begun while cleaning fish earlier in the evening.

"Jesus," John began, "we lost several followers late this fall when you were teaching about how we are to be salt and light to the world in which we live. I understand the seasoning and preserving aspects of salt, and of course the light you provide guides us in a world that has grown dim, but I'm still as puzzled as some of those who left about the remark: 'unless one eats your flesh and drinks your blood, they have no life in themselves.'" John knew Jesus was not speaking in literal terms, for the drinking of blood was absolutely forbidden by the Law.

Peter had pulled up a stool and began to eavesdrop when Jesus asked the two, "Do you men also want to go away as the rest?"

Before John could remark, Peter said, "Where are we going to go, Lord? You have the words of life eternal and we believe that you are the holy one of God. We've left everything to come along with you."

"You're right, Simon Peter, and because you all have stayed with me, the twelve will sit upon thrones judging the twelve tribes of Israel while I sit upon my glorious throne. And everyone who has walked away from houses, businesses, brothers, sisters, fathers, mothers and children for my sake and that of the special news, will receive many more times in this life, along with bitter harrassment, and in the life to come they will inherit eternal life. But many who are presently up front will be found in the rear while those in the rear will be brought up front."

"Boy, that's certainly a different philosophy than that which governs the world. We've been taught all along that he who dies with the most toys wins," said Peter.

"On the contrary," said Jesus, "for he who dies with the most toys still dies, and after that we settle accounts."

Men, listen to a vignette. Over in western Kentucky the locals still cut their tobacco crop one plant at a time and place it on a stick before hauling it to the barn to cure. The kingdom of God is like that farmer who drove to town during harvest to seek laborers who would help put up his ripe crop of burley tobacco. He found several men milling around the town cafe just after 6:00 A.M. and they agreed for a wage that was customary, and he sent them over to a twenty acre patch in the Ohio River bottoms to begin cutting and dropping sticks. About 9:00 A.M. he drove back to town for additional water and found others at the local filling station where he purchased ice, still loitering with nothing to do. They were willing to work, so he sent them along to work in the same fields as the others. Later in the afternoon when the leaf was wilted and some of the earlier help began spiking the crop, the owner went out and hired even more help. He now had enough men to work each end of the field. Just before quitting time, the farmer made a final trip back to town and found still others standing idle, and he asked them why they had not gone to work for someone; and they responded, 'because no one hired us,' and he said, 'you too get in the back of the truck,' and he carried them back to the field with him at around 5:00 P.M. and they were able to work for about an hour.

"At 6:00 P.M. crew chiefs gathered their men and began counting tools and putting away equipment when the owner drove up and began calling everyone forward to receive their wages. He began with those who were hired last—near the end of the day and paid them for 12 hours. Others standing around were shocked at his generosity and expected to receive more, but they also each received 12 hours pay for the 12 hours labor that they had agreed to. However; these same laborers began complaining about the fact that they had blistered their backs during the long heat of the day while these 'Johnny come latelies' had been out less than an hour and only after the evening winds began to pick up."

"And you've made them equal to us," they grumbled.

"But the farmer answered and said, "Men, I'm doing you no injustice, for we agreed for an hourly rate. Take your money and go on, but I wish to give to this last group the same as you. Am I breaking the law for doing as I wish with my own money? Look at yourselves, you're seething green because of my generosity. For this reason, those at the end will be up front and those in the front placed in the rear."

This lesson set Peter and John back on their stools as they sipped the last of the coffee and considered a kingdom that was run on principles that were totally unfamiliar to them.

"It's all about the heart when it's all said and done, isn't it, Jesus? I mean that's what the settling of the accounts is all about, isn't it?" John asked. "Everything will be considered: values, secrets, motives, everything will be dissected and laid bare for examination."

"That's right, John," said Jesus, "and again, make this part of your operating capital, many in front will be moved to the rear, while those in the rear will be brought up front."

John grew in wisdom of the Lord that evening and recorded in his journal before bed that Jesus had used the strongest, perhaps even the most offensive terms available to describe the quality of intimacy he desired for each of his followers as well as defining kingdom rank and preference in a way that caught both he and Peter off guard. It began to sound like the old but familiar, 'he who is greatest will be your private,' but with a new twist; not everyone who serves from daylight to dark—beginning to end, can be counted on for doing it with the right motives, which in this new kingdom means everything.

Chapter 14

Students at the University of Wisconsin were on Spring break and Jesus took the opportunity to arrange for a three day retreat for the many followers who had been begging the twelve to persuade him to spend more time with them. Many of Jesus' closest and most devoted followers hadn't seen him in months. His itinerant plans for the region were not complete and before a final visit to Milwaukee, where he had been on two other occasions over the Winter months, he wished also to spend time in Madison. Bart, Robbie and Carol were the experts at lining up meetings and booking appropriate places of assembly. Earlier in the year, the three sat down and mapped out a one week teaching stint by Jesus, which would include a visit to the University. There were nearly 2,000 men and women on hand and arrangements were made to utilize the cafeteria for food service. All of the collections for room and board were handled by the programming team who were able to cut everyone an affordable deal thanks to the University's generosity. As was often the case, when people learned that Jesus was out in the open and available, they flocked to hear him. And while the leadership wished to keep crowds to a manageable size, it seldom worked out that way. Accommodations were limited at the University to 800 registrants because of renovations being carried out on several of the larger halls. As a result, all of the overflow stayed around town, or slept in vans and travel trailers.

One key lecture by Jesus each morning was followed by seminars led by the twelve who were stationed in smaller classrooms or dorm lobbies. Jesus wanted to give the twelve some first hand experience teaching subjects that he himself had been preparing them for over the winter months. Following the disciplines of a good coach, Jesus was beginning to supervise his crop of interns and was generally pleased with their development and grasp of kingdom concepts.

Matthew was a financial wizard and found his element lecturing smaller crowds in the wise stewardship of material resources. His seminar entitled: 'Your Money Matters,' was drawn and recounted from an entire lecture he mentally transcribed from Jesus around a fire one evening at the cottage.

"Three individuals were entrusted with different amounts of money based upon their ability," Matthew began with Jesus reclining in the back of the room and smiling at a man who had learned to hate greed, and who was beginning to pay attention to the careful management of God's property. Matthew talked on in a conversational and interactive teaching style over the next 50 minutes to a group of Jews ranging in age who were eager to learn what they perceived to be of imminent importance to Jesus. Matthew was drawn to the seminar material based upon his own encounter with Jesus; and although he was degreed and well experienced in financial concepts and book-keeping jargon, he nevertheless broke it all down and placed it on the level of a story which the simplest minds could understand. Before the time expired, Jesus quietly excused himself and walked outside to the water's edge.

Evidence that geese had pastured the area lay all over the grass in abundance. The campus looked to have been aerated leaving finger length plugs that waited to be melted back into the soil at next rain. A large flock of Wild Canadian walked a distant bank while others sat on

Lake Mendota, bobbing with the gentle waves. Goslings were already hatching and a mother escorting her brood watched traffic while the little ones dunked for soft grass which lay submerged near the lake's edge. Seasonal rains had lifted the water levels providing fresh aquatic items to the menu. Jesus found a quiet place to pray and although he forbade his followers to attract attention to themselves by outward acts of piety, it was difficult not to be conspicuous sitting on the open banks of the campus. Peter, James and John approached him from a distance and waited upon him, for they realized he was meditating and praying as was his habit. After several more minutes, Jesus invited the three to join him along with many others.

"Jesus," James asked, "will you teach us to pray the way Jack taught his disciples?"

"This would be an appropriate time," Jesus said, and he invited everyone to find a place to be seated. "When you pray," Jesus began with his hands folded together in a loose golf grip, "Say, 'Father, your very name is holy.' Don't go on with your prayer until you are sure you mean it and your heart begins to be humbled under the weight and beauty of that truth. Petition your Dad in heaven to bring his kingdom and wishes to bear here on earth just as they are carried out in heaven. Each of you have personal desires and needs for daily sustenance; be sure to tell him about all of this and lay your concerns before him. He already knows, but you need to spell it out so that your abandoned-control trust will have opportunity to develop. As you pray, ask God to forgive your sins as well as anyone who has violated you. God will not forgive you so long as you are unwilling to forgive others for their debts. Always conclude your prayer with a request that God protect you from evil and deliver you from temptation. Your adversary is a roaring lion and he is always scouting someone to devour. Your prayer to God in these important areas is an admission that you are not sufficient in and of yourselves. God is pleased with the broken hearted and failures who seek his mercies and restoration. Blessed are those who realize that they are bankrupt in spirit for theirs is the kingdom of God."

A woman near the front asked Jesus, "Is it really O.K. to call God 'daddy;' I mean will he hear us in the middle of the night and during times of crisis?" Jesus answered the woman's question with a story.

"Say for instance, that one of you is fortunate enough to have a faithful friend, and you go to her in your time of need because other friends of yours have arrived unexpectedly and you don't get paid until next week. Groceries are at their normal low for this time of the month and you don't have a thing to fix. How ridiculous do you think it would be for your faithful friend to offer you poor excuses like: "Don't bother me now because you couldn't have called at a more inconvenient time; I've got kids to pick up from a ball game in just minutes, or I'm going to miss my hair appointment if I don't leave right now; or Bill and I have an appointment on the greens across town in less than 30 minutes."

Someone shouted from the crowd, "I don't know where you're going with this story but that 'T' time sounds pretty legit!" The older gentleman's humor was rewarded with a good laugh and even Jesus saluted the possibility with two fingers and smiled before going on.

"But who would believe such weak excuses delivered to a friend in need? Obviously, the very notion is outrageous and amusing. You see, the faithful friend might be called upon at the most inconvenient of times; but because of the relationship she bears, the inherent trust and sense of honor she carries on her shoulders like an awesome mantle, will cause her to stop what she's doing and find a way to 'make it happen' as they say. In the same way, your Heavenly Father can be counted on to come through for you for such is his character and 'daddy–caring' nature. If human failures like yourselves come through for one another regularly in such menial ways, how much more will God pay attention to your requests when you call upon him whether in crisis or daily need? Just speak up and he will give it to you, look around carefully and you will find it, ring the door bell and it will be opened for you. Friends, I assure you that everyone who asks will find themselves on the receiving end, she who seeks will locate what's most desired and the one who rings, well the door will swing wide open because God's honor requires it for his own name's sake."

Thomas, who sat near the front, was physically and verbally abused by his father and ultimately abandoned while still a young boy. He was emotionally stirred to the point of tears by Jesus' story because he struggled with the character traits of a loving father just laid out for everyone's consideration. Jesus saw the tears streaming down Thomas' cheeks and felt compassion for a man who privately pulled them away with the cuff of his hands. Jesus wondered how many times as a small boy he might have done the same thing during a scolding at the dinner table, or for some other minor slip up that displeased his stern pedagogue. For the way Thomas drew wet palms to his side and dried them mutely upon the legs of his slacks looked terribly learned.

Jesus pushed his foot forward unnoticed and let it rest gently upon the calf of Thomas' leg that was turned beneath him, then said, "What father after all, if he is really deserving of that title would think of giving his son a ring of razors when asked for the keys to the car or a glass of strychnine when asked for a cool drink? If you morally corrupt individuals understand how to give good things to your children, how much more will your caring daddy give good things to those who ask him?" Jesus rose from his place and would have dismissed others for lunch, but an old woman trembling with fear approached him with her adult son who couldn't talk and had remained under her care for the many years. With scarcely a word of her own, for she was terrified to be in front of people and hardly had the courage to approach Jesus, she presented her son in hopes of receiving a merciful touch. She had heard of Jesus' special abilities to heal, but never understood the blanket invitation until the day's message.

Glen's mother gave Jesus his name and stood beside him to see what would happen. Jesus opened his hand and ran it along Glen's jaw and throat. He looked at something inside the man for it was obvious he wasn't speaking to Glen, then said, "Come out of him you dumb spirit!" The man's throat enlarged and convulsed and while some stepped aside fearing what might be projected, Jesus helped Glen be seated as his tongue was loosed and he was overcome with ecstatic joy and wonder all mixed with unspeakable gratitude. Glen appeared to be doing a combination of traditional sit-ups and stomach crunches, sobbing uncontrollably while his mother sought in vain to hold him still. Glen was over 40 years old and though he never uttered a syllable in his entire life, he was speaking fluently with a wonderful range of vocabulary. The crowd was astonished for he was a local man and many people knew he and his mother as regular members of their synagogue.

No sooner than Jesus regained his stance, a small element in the crowd from a strict Jewish sect who had traveled all the way over from a synagogue in Minneapolis stood up and challenged Jesus' use of authority as well as its source. Men like these were always nearby when Jesus was public and they were constantly seeking ways to discredit his teachings.

"He casts out demons by the authority of the ruler of demons," they shouted, while others of their company demanded that he perform a sign.

Peter yelled back over the crowd, "Why don't you goons crawl up here and have a word with a sign—his name is Glen and he would be pleased to talk your leg off." Both John and James thought the move was pretty gutsy, but it wasn't countenanced by Jesus who began a fresh diatribe directed at the visitors for he was aggravated at their hardness of heart and overt blasphemy.

"No kingdom that suffers civil war can stand and when a fortress is divided against itself, it too will collapse. And if Satan is splintered among his cohorts, how can his kingdom remain? For you insist that I cast out demons by the ruler of demons. It's interesting to consider by what power your sons cast them out. They will be your judges! But if I'm casting out demons by the power of God, then the kingdom of God has pounced upon you. A well defended fortress is protected and those who live within its walls dwell there securely. But when someone stronger scales the wall, removes the fortifications and overpowers the guards, he will parcel out everything inside. If you are not with me, you are against me and whoever doesn't lend me his hand is one with him who destroys," said Jesus.

"Where do demons go after they have been removed?" someone asked.

"When an unclean spirit departs, it moves through dry places looking for a home and not finding any it will return to its previous residence; however, when he arrives back and finds the place cleaned up and organized, he brings along a full set of spirits more wicked than himself and they come and dwell there and the final condition of the man is worse than the first," Jesus replied.

At that moment a woman in the audience who was overcome with excitement shouted, "How wonderful the woman who bore you and nursed you as a child!"

"On the contrary," Jesus said, "specially regarded is the person who hears God's word and does what it says." More and more people were streaming down to the lake front and Jesus walked the edge in order to position himself where the greatest possible number could hear. He then began another speech directed at the entire audience. "The people living at this time and place in history are evil," Jesus said. "They want everything posted on a bulletin board, but no sign is going to be offered them except the billboard featuring the prophet Jonah; for just as he was three days and three nights in the gut of a huge fish, so will the son of man be three days and nights in the belly of the earth. Great men and women will rise up at the judgment and condemn this generation because they came from hundreds of miles around to hear the wisdom of Solomon and yet someone greater than Solomon is here. Likewise, the people of Nineveh where Jonah preached will rise up at the judgment and condemn this generation because they repented after hearing his message and yet one greater than Jonah is here." The crowds were astonished at Jesus' teaching style. Some felt sorely rebuked because their inner motives were being exposed while others were drinking in the refreshing springs and worshiping God for long awaited answers to prayer. Jesus dismissed the crowds for boxed lunches that were being served on the grounds when one of the religious leaders from Minneapolis invited Jesus to join him for a meal off campus.

A strict legalist hollered over at Jesus, "Take the address from my courier. Join me for lunch at Gino's on State Street." The office assistant returned to Druker after the short errand.

Jesus didn't hesitate and yelled back, "I'll meet you there at 1:00 P.M." Ronald Druker departed while Jesus collared Thomas before he could follow the larger crowd back to the serving lines.

"Thomas, let's walk for a few minutes before lunch," Jesus said. 'Let's walk,' was a phrase Jesus coined to let his followers know that he had something important or up close and personal for them to hear and understand. Thomas was appreciative of the private appointment with

Jesus but really didn't know what was up; maybe instructions to follow-up something Jesus wanted cared for. The two men stopped after distancing themselves several meters away from the crowd. Thomas could tell Jesus didn't have appointments or the next day's schedule on his mind. In fact, Jesus' only business was his Father's and it included as a priority caring for the immediate sheep of his fold.

"Thomas, the years are fleeting," said Jesus, "and you've not yet grieved the terrible losses of your childhood."

"Oh, that back there," referring to the tears he assumed Jesus must have noticed with his radar like perception, "I was just touched by the way you were sharing as I thought about a friend who could have really used that encouragement." Thomas' words were pushed back into his face by a caring sigh from his mentor. Jesus had a worn face that made him appear much older than his real age. Lines across his forehead, eyes and mouth traced the story of a man who had laughed hard and regularly throughout life, but there were other lines that revealed long sets of anguishing prayer and intercession that could only have been etched through lengthy periods of facial fixation. When it lay relaxed, only his eyes seemed to move, and they, looking out from a distance of another world entirely. Jesus might have on other occasions respected the privacy, but he knew the moment was right to explore the heart of a young man who needed to develop a voice of his own. Thomas was not one to invite others into his private world.

Jesus was wearing his usual retreat uniform—worn denim, polo shirt and boat shoes. He lowered his head in a respectful manner and asked, "What's your friend's name, Tommy?" His voice inflection mixing with a concern that was richly felt ordered flood gates to open on a dam that held back a deep reservoir of tears. Thomas began heaving and sobbing like a small child. Jesus caught him around the waist and stabilized his footing. The embrace appeared utterly pathetic, but Jesus cradled Thomas' head upon his shoulder and held him there until the sobbing subsided.

"Some things we lose can't be found," Jesus whispered into his ear, "but other things are too important not to recover. Thomas, you need to go back and walk him through the trauma, lost years, loneliness, rejection and abandonment. The rage you offer others isn't going to dissipate until you do." Thomas was offended by the suggestion that he was somehow an angry person because he worked very hard to mask the defect and present himself as a model husband, employee and friend.

"What do you mean—rage?" Thomas asked while retreating to his own personal space.

"It shows up in everything you say and do Thomas." Jesus was first serious, then sought to entice Thomas with another approach. "The way you manage rage, your environment, your friends—nearly everything about you says, 'I'm too sanitary to touch.' But it's really the fragility isn't it? No one gets to experience you, Thomas, because you've been harmed and now you have walled yourself off so that it will never happen again. As a result, you are harming others, you deprive us by only offering us the same stale daily routine that has come to define who you are. Thomas, look at me, friend. You're so polite, spring flowers must bloom two weeks early at the scent of your stocking feet tiptoeing before their bulb beds. There are really only three fine French writers of etiquette presently living and I'll bet you receive birthday cards from two of them." Thomas rolled his lips and turned up the corner in one eye but couldn't break a smile before a man trying desperately to help hold a mirror in front of his darting personality. One minute he was there and the next minute he had drawn his head back inside. "And you're the epitome of kindness, Thomas," Jesus said with a friendly dash of sarcasm. "How many people have you helped already today? Let me see, early this morning when you arrived, you put extra change in a meter for the little lady that was a few coins short on a parking meter; at breakfast you carried plates to the table for two elderly people. During your presentation, you basically apologized all the way through it for your lack of anecdotes as well as the countless phrases, 'now Jesus would say it this way.' After we arrived at the lake, you changed your seating three different times to accommodate others. Thomas, I have a little homework for you that is to be kept between you and me because fools would never understand; and I want you to carry it out to the best of your ability. You're dismissed from this conference and I don't want to see you over in Milwaukee later this week when the rest of us arrive. Put away your vitamins and this month's issue of the health journal; buy a couple quarts of chocolate milk, go back to the cottage and find one of Peter's finest cigars. You have my permission. Then strip down to your briefs, sit on the back deck; belch, drop ashes where you please, eat plenty of red meat, leave the dishes, sleep on the lawn, chip golf balls into the lake and if you get sick and vomit, I want you to roll in it. Get mean with a grin. Bury a large piece of furniture on the beach and scream until the Coast Guard comes to pick you up. Any questions?" Thomas was utterly dumbfounded and couldn't think of a thing to say, when Jesus who hadn't blinked said, "Thomas, I'm going to check up on every piece of this prescription, and it's going to get a lot uglier if I have to walk you through it."

Jesus left Thomas in a daze and the poor man was still wondering if he had in fact heard Jesus correctly as he wandered back to the main campus and found his car. Jesus arrived at Gino's at 1:00 P.M. Druker had waited patiently in the foyer with an attorney friend, going over a list of questions and checking it twice. The three men were guided to a booth by a waitress and while Jesus sat down to look at a menu, both Druker and the attorney, Joel Feinstein, went to the lavatory to wash their hands and prepare for the meal. After they returned, Druker began complaining about the overall poor condition of the rest room and continued drying his hands on a white towel that he carried with him at all times.

"Joel," Druker asked in Jesus' hearing, "did you direct my accountant to send along the large gifts to the charities I indicated?"

"Oh, yes sir, Mr. Druker," said the younger attorney, "everything has been cared for as you requested. The checks were cut yesterday."

Just as the waitress arrived for drink orders with pen and pad in hand, Jesus waved her off and said, "You strict, obsessive, bigots for tradition are quick to clean the outside of anything you touch, but inside you are full of extortion and evil doings. Did it ever occur to you hypocrites that the one who created the shell made the meat inside?" Jesus said while staring at a shallow bowl of fresh oysters on a nearby table. "You people are so careful to care for outward appearances and somehow think that the glossy veneer hides the sinful motives of your hearts." Both men were highly insulted and placed their menus on the table as Jesus continued, "A day of reckoning is just around the corner. You tithe to the nth degree and could squeeze milk from a buckeye, but all the while you disregard justice, the love of God and the weightier matters of the law. All of this you should have done without neglecting the rest. Yes, and how you love to be greeted as reverend." Jesus had to stop for he always weighed his words carefully, "and absolutely no human being is worthy of that title!" He shouted while reseating himself. "And how you love the most prominent seats in the synagogue. You people are no different than the manhole covers people walk over in the streets. How often do people stop and consider the sewage that passes beneath the road."

The young attorney just couldn't sit still for Jesus' berating barrage and said in defense of his profession, "Teacher, you also indict us with those words." He shouldn't have been so welcoming, for Jesus asked the waitress to return in a few minutes and began exposing the methods of lawyers.

"The way you treat common folks is wretched and cruel but you're proud of your craft. You heap heavy loads upon others, but you have skillfully arranged not to be touched by them. You build the tombs for the prophets, men like Jack, and you take care of all the paper work. You're just like your fathers, whose criminal acts you endorse. And because you approve of it, all the blood of the righteous will be laid at the feet of this sinful generation. You lawyers—look at yourselves, you've so corrupted the paths of understanding. You weren't traveling them and you have now hampered those who would." Jesus excused himself from the meal, "I'll need a hot bath after spending time with the likes of you. Now stay out of my way!" The two men followed Jesus to the parking lot and others of the same Jewish sect sitting at opposite tables were quick to get up and join them.

The men were enraged by his harsh treatment of them and unflinching reprimand. "Wait a minute, Jesus," one of the men shouted. "You just can't walk away like that," for they wished to justify themselves and find opportunity to catch him in a contradiction.

Joel Feinstein was so angry he could hardly talk but was able to blurt out, "By what authority are you doing these things and who authorized you to interpret the law?"

Jesus stopped near the door of his van and said, "I will ask you but one question and if you can answer me, then I will answer you. Quid pro quo, Joel. What was the source of Jack's baptism; was it from heaven or the fabrication of man?" Seven men began consulting one another right there in the parking lot—defense attorneys standing before a grand jury.

"If we say from heaven," one observed, "then he will say, 'then why didn't you believe him.'"

"Yes," said another, "and if we say from men, the entire city will be on our backs because they think Jack was a bona fide prophet."

In a moment Feinstein turned and said, "We are not sure."

Jesus replied from the dock, "and neither will I tell you by what authority I operate." Before he got into his vehicle, Jesus asked the men, "What do you think about this vignette? A man had two sons and he told one of them to go to the shop and finish packing a supply order. The boy said, 'O.K. dad,' but he didn't follow through with his father's directive. Later he found his other son and told him the same thing. This boy told his father that he wouldn't go, but later he felt remorse and got up and went. Which of the two, Ronald, obeyed the father?"

"Well obviously, the latter," he said.

"I'm telling you in the most solemn terms, that harlots and those with notorious reputations will enter the kingdom of God before you because Jack presented himself in the way of righteousness and you rejected him while the ungodly believed. Even after witnessing this, you didn't feel sorry or have a change of mind." Feinstein wanted the group to beat Jesus, but other patrons were busily passing in and out of the parking lot. Jesus backed out of his space and pulled away under their wrathful scowl.

* * * *

Meanwhile, F.B.I. Special Agents Charlie Moore and Art Keller joined Dr. Leonard Geiger for lunch at Printer's Row on South Dearborn, downtown Chicago. Geiger had invited the men to be his guests, although they initiated the follow-up based upon an earlier phone conversation in which Geiger alluded to possible ties between the Chicago bombings and a disgruntled militant of the Jews for Freedom which was an organization of his own fabrication but considered extremely secret because so little was known about them. Geiger's real objective was to find out how much the F.B.I. knew and who they were presently pursuing. The 'whole cloth' Geiger was knitting had to be flawless and the more he knew about their understandings and findings, the better positioned he would be to interface, supply evidence and make their conclusions collaborate with his own.

"Good morning, Dr. Geiger," said Moore. Geiger tipped his head as he took his seat.

"Rabbi," said Art in a professional gesture of welcome.

Both Charlie and Art had been with the Bureau over 25 years apiece. The two men had worked on intricate cases of mail fraud, Interstate theft, bank robbery cases galore, serial killers and about everything in between; but the present unraveling of the twisted mind behind the bombings that nearly leveled two hospitals and claimed 342 lives including physicians and patients was only equaled to unbending the mass of braided concrete and steel at both bombing sites. It would be too late before the careful agents discovered that the animal they sought sat inches away from them, thumbing through an expensive wine list with crooked claws; a well respected professor at one of the most prestigious Universities in the world. Everyone was a suspect, but not Leonard Geiger, who made regular house calls to the homes of victims still emotionally hemorrhaging from the concussive, mind ripping news of the blast subsequently delivered to their families.

Typical of Geiger's therapy was his visit to the Lambert's home just weeks after the bombing. Mark and Joyce lost their twin sons in the blast at the Crippled Children's Hospital. Both boys had suffered from joint disease but were recently outfitted with synthetic devices and were hopeful of leading fully productive lives. The blast at Shriners as well as the one at the Veteran's hospital, were both detonated after midnight and it added to the horror of parents and rescue crews who worked feverishly sifting rubble and tunneling through layers of debris to connect with faint cries of those pinned under the blanket of night fall and concrete.

Geiger replayed the visit in his depraved mind while the waitress brought appetizers to the table. He knew the day of his visit that undercover agents were parked out front of the Lambert's home less than a block away as part of their routine follow-up work. It wasn't uncommon for a criminal with a history of unstable mental health with a profile like the suspect police sought, to walk the sidewalk in front of a victim's home the way a pyromaniac reappears at the scene of a fire. An off the wall tip led investigators to believe that the Lambert's residence might yield a lead on such a fiend. Officers watched Geiger approach the Lambert's front door with loaves of fresh oven baked bread and remarked at what a kind gesture it was for a man of Geiger's caliber to pull away from his busy schedules to pay a pastoral visit to a hurting family. Of course, this is exactly what Geiger wanted the stake to believe.

"Mark and Joyce, thank you for affording me this errand of mercy and intrusion into the sanctuary of your home. I have come bearing the very bowels of compassion of God." As soon as his voice waves bounced off the microphone tucked behind the exterior porch lamp, the agents returned to their coffee and paper. Geiger had spent several nights sitting up in a reading chair in his bedroom rehearsing the conversation on a voice recording device, not unlike the one he was presently wearing in the presence of the detectives. After he was sure of just the right voice inflection, all the necessary nonverbal communication, pauses and false stammering for words, he would memorize the pericope and play it back before the unsuspecting like a performance that he had auditioned for that would win him an acting award.

The Lamberts invited Geiger into their home, and he feigned tears which was a learned specialty while handling portraits and reminiscing the lives of the two young five year olds. While sitting in the company of their living room, he ran his eyes over the soft cheeks of the boy's faces and examined their blonde locks rather than listen to anything the Lamberts had to say. It had been just days prior to the blast that the Rabbi had paid visits to the boys and fondled each of them. Joyce was still sedated in those early days with medication but was able to thank the Rabbi for his involvement with the funeral eulogy which won him the love and respect of so many non-Jews.

"Never has anyone offered us such words of consolation, Rabbi," Joyce said. "You are obviously a man who lives in the very presence of God and we would not be able to go on with our lives except for your prayers and the many Jewish synagogues around the city who also offered prayers by your suggestion."

"Yes," Mark agreed, "we and many of our friends are taking steps to leave the World Wide Hub and convert to Judaism." Geiger actually blushed at the thought, he was so accomplished at his trade. He was also so consumed with hypocrisy, that he reeked but so polished and lamb like that even his most discerning critics conceded the authenticity of his deep religious commitment to piety.

"Joyce," Geiger said, "allow me to place these loaves in the cupboard. My lovely wife, Ann, baked them fresh this morning; and we just wanted to offer them to you as a gesture of God's kindness." Geiger had picked the loaves up at a local Jewish deli before driving over and lied again when he said, "I have already blessed the loaves with the Hebrew prayer of thanks. Please enjoy them as a token of God's bounty such as is found in all of his creation. Seth and Sean cannot come back to you, but you will go to be with them," Geiger prayed before leaving and quoting from the words of David.

"Rabbi Geiger, as tragic as our loss has been, God has already begun to redeem it by allowing our paths to cross and exposing us to the nature of God through you."

"Perhaps God is still working through the lads' lives." Geiger said. "It's a tender and sacred thought, but God works in mysterious ways. Nevertheless, the heartless Nazis…" Geiger fell to one knee bawling uncontrollably. After gaining his composure, he continued, "their day of recompense is dawning and," Geiger changed the person and number of the pronoun, "he will be nailed for the crime." Mark and Joyce were both deeply touched by the Rabbi's apparent heart felt anguish and even apologized for the emotional trauma that he was experiencing. They both thanked the Rabbi for the mental and emotional anguish that he accepted from God as his special calling in life in order that others might benefit from a little happiness. The approach of a waiter brought the Rabbi back to the table and business at hand.

"Gentlemen, I am satisfied that two choice agents like yourselves have a long day ahead of you, and I would be terribly disappointed if you don't take full advantage of my treat and help yourselves to the finest entrees on the menu."

Both agent's were hungry and swimming with anticipation. Though highly dignified and crack professionals, Charlie warned Art, "You better idle back on the mushrooms before you slap your brains out with your tongue." Geiger played along with their fun although he didn't understand the joke Charlie had made.

"Gentlemen," Geiger asked while picking through a most delectable salad as though it were somehow contaminated, "many of the families we are seeking to counsel and console will never be able to bring closure to this dastardly and inexplicable tragedy until they are confident that the ring leader to this atrocity has been placed behind bars to await execution. Has the Bureau made any further progress in terms of narrowing their list of probable suspects?"

"Rabbi," Charlie took the lead, "obviously everything we know to date is strictly confidential and has been compartmentalized even at the highest levels. Art and I report directly to the Attorney General. He hand picked us for this operation and we debrief with him weekly in Washington. Now, there is no one on the planet privy to conversations conducted in his inner chambers; but because of the enormous personal investment of time and the obvious passion which you yourself have demonstrated toward this case, Art and I have agreed to invite you in on some of what we know and strictly off the record."

"Dr. Geiger, we know of your crypto logical clearance issued by NSA, and of course the background and history files under your name are impeccable," added Art; "however, this is an investigation of the highest level of importance and one that touches issues of national security unlike anything that has ever occurred in our history as a nation. Terrorism of this…" Rabbi Geiger raised his hand in a manner that led the special agents to believe that he was nauseated with recounting the details of the blast.

"Special Agent Keller," Geiger said, "the Attorney General, Washington, indeed the entire Country owes both of you men a debt of gratitude for your valiant and untiring efforts. You have devoted yourselves to this investigation in a way that is legendary and I myself have already appealed to the Attorney General's office with lengthy signed petitions by women and men of enormous prominence in this city and even the nation's capital to wit: distinguished honors and awards are due you for the lightening like speed with which you apprehended the first wave of suspects. Twelve hours to round up felons of this rank—it is absolutely mind boggling how you achieved that record. This meal as I said is simply a small token of thanks for how I personally feel about your professionalism and commitment to the Bureau's highest levels of excellence."

Geiger was never successful at placing anyone on the inside of the Attorney General's office, and running wire taps on F.B.I. agents was more risky than Geiger's present needs warranted. On the other hand, Geiger had worked more difficult angles before; and if he could just posit in their minds a link or two, he would be content to let the present status of events momentarily rest. The F.B.I. had considered Jesus and his following early in their investigation but never had even remotely sufficient reason to bring him or any of his followers in for questioning. Geiger didn't want to place Jesus in their hands personally, that would be stooping far too low for a man of his expertise. He only worked with thicker plots; and though time was running out, he at least wanted to involve Judas whom he would string along in hopes of having him carry out his plan. Geiger didn't mind attending to the most insignificant details, both for security purposes as well as to ensure there were no slip ups by an underling; however, it was a personal boast of his own, and to himself alone, that he had never nor would he ever be traced or linked to a personal killing of any kind. That he would find utterly defiling. He was the mastermind, but others with rubber gloves were paid to transport drums, bodies or anything else he considered a natural contaminant.

"You know, gentlemen, I've been spending some time on my own with Judas," Geiger said as he pushed a small file across the table with a few select notes and dates as well as the reminder of Judas' alleged involvement with the burning of a synagogue which was a highly profiled investigation in its own right. Both of the agents were familiar with Judas, but he had been ruled out early on for a number of conflicting reasons mostly involving known alibis they didn't have to even question. "No, Judas is not smart enough, and if I might add, courageous enough to have put together these mammoth bombings," said Geiger in a serious tone of contemplation. "I do believe on the other hand that he has connections with the mad man whose finger pushed the button on the detonating device." Both agents drew cloth napkins to their mouths and note pads from their coat pockets. "No, no," Geiger said, "I don't mean to have names and hard evidence; I'm just aware of how this man operates and if you will just give me a little more time to win his trust, it is my firm opinion that he will deliver the, 'mother of all terrorists' into our hands."

"Well, Dr. Geiger, what do you need from us?" asked Charlie?

"Nothing at this time. Maybe one thing. Give me some space and don't call upon me for any reason. I will contact your offices with information as I receive it. Judas is wiser than you might give him credit and the last thing we need is for him to get skittish or back away. Just give me a few more months—I assure you it will be worth the long process in the end. Both of you will be handsomely rewarded for bringing him into custody," Geiger almost called his name for his rage often overrode his better sense of judgment, "the most notorious, heinous criminal since Nazi Germany."

"Look, Dr. Geiger," said Special Agent Keller, "we've got enough goods on this Judas to fill a room. There's nothing in this file that we don't already know. By the way, where did you get some of these documents?" Keller looked closer at a file that he said he would have to confiscate, which is exactly what Geiger wanted to happen. While the agent dug deeper, Geiger accepted another cup of coffee and checked it with the tip of his finger for temperature.

"What do you know about this Internet address?" asked Keller. Geiger had created the site himself and monitored visits to the page or created his own dialogues with phantom guests as part of his special contribution to the investigation.

"I've been keeping a close eye on the number of people who visit the Web Page created by Judas. Perhaps I can generate some leads by using a noose he has tied for himself." At the end of the day, Geiger simply wanted Judas' file to rest on the top of somebody's desk so that when a specific series of events were revealed and unfolded, his name would already be familiar and attached to the briefs.

"O.K., Dr. Geiger," said Keller, "but we're taking this file along and intend to monitor his activities for ourselves." This fit perfectly into Geiger's plan which could now be manipulated to feed the Attorney General's office with timely information emailed by Geiger but expunged from a mock network of underground sources.

Following lunch both agents thanked Dr. Geiger for a profitable visit and wonderful meal. "Please keep us informed, Dr. Geiger," said Special Agent Moore.

"I assure you, I will," promised Geiger and the special agents returned to their offices. As soon as the men left the luxurious restaurant, Geiger moved to a different table and was joined by three journeymen who carried blueprints for an intricate die that would be used to extrude all the necessary timing and events the way alloys are poured and drawn through a cast mold. Geiger handed each of the men fresh leaves for their files and verbally communicated that the agents he had just visited with were wary of Dr. Geiger and the three men who presently sat before him.

"Dr. Geiger, how can that be?" asked Fritz, "Lame-Vet," which was a code name for the Chicago blasts, "was as clean and well swept an operation as anything we have ever done for you. We followed your instructions unequivocally and there were absolutely no errors."

"Yes, gentlemen, you impressed even me," said Geiger, and he had never before offered them verbal appreciation for anything, "The agents just have their suspicions," Geiger continued, "This is all the more reason for us to work with the greatest possible care. Memorize, scrutinize, live, sleep, drink and eat every detail of these files and instructions. For if the young Rabbi....," again Geiger nearly lost emotional control and the men were deathly afraid of his rage, "... if he isn't executed next year on the day of Passover, I will personally expose the three of you as the masterminds to the entire Lame Vet operation. Gentlemen, are we clear?" Rueben's knees were knocking beneath the table and the other men trembled as well when they saw something flash in Geiger's eyes that made them think they might prefer lethal injection over whatever their master was contemplating for those who would fail him. Stories circulated in their tight nexus of an individual who had trifled in Geiger's presence about a mistake made on an assignment handed him by Geiger. His body was found later with its skin surgically removed having been dipped in bleach baths until the life expired.

"Yes, Dr. Geiger," Rueben spoke for Fritz and Mr. Milgram, "your intentions are understood and will be carried out invisibly with our greatest care. There will be no mistakes, and the blood you desire will be spilled on the date you've indicated. Geiger's closest associates were as infuriated with Jesus as Geiger himself, not because of anything personal, but because their lease on life was dependent upon their success of his downfall.

Chapter 15

Set-up crews had been working throughout the night preparing sound and staging equipment for County Stadium downtown Milwaukee. The Brewers were away on a long visiting trip which provided a few days window of opportunity for Jesus' crew to set up for two nights, tear-down and clean up before their return. A sizeable space was reserved for Jesus around the area of the pitcher's mound and additional speakers were installed at strategic points for improved P.A. performance. Jesus arrived with his road team Sunday afternoon, and they walked the grounds surrounding the stadium while considering the opportunity before them. It had been recommended earlier that they scope out a larger stadium size facility because of the growing interest their work had attracted over the past couple of years. Although a large number of Jews were drawn from local ranks, far and away, the larger percentage were being bussed in from greater distances around the Great Lake's region.

Interest in Jesus' message had not grown appreciably beyond the Jewish populace; and for that matter, it hadn't been directed to anyone else. Besides the few major world religions, most American non-Jews who had any spiritual interest were involved in Eastern mysticism, New Age philosophy and a variety of self-discovery belief systems. The

World Wide Hub embraced all gods of every nation; and while their national headquarters is in Wheaton, Illinois, The Roman Pantheon, which is an enormous edifice that enshrines the many religious icons representing the various religions, is located on The Mall in Washington D.C. American religious leaders boast of their tolerance of the many and varied religions represented by their countrymen; and while pluralism is promoted as a humanistic ideal, these same architects really desire religious homogeneity and have little patience for dogma or those who single themselves out as unique or exclusive. Monotheistic Judaism was always on the outs for this reason. Theirs has always been the one religion that insisted on serving the one true God who had performed miraculous works of wonder and deliverance for his people since ancient times. Adherents of Judaism were admitted on the basis of race at birth and could not co-join other religions or accept their pagan practices. A Jew is loyal to God because of his selection of them as a people. And precisely because of their peculiarity and unwillingness to co-mingle with other faiths, they were often hated and misunderstood. Some in their ranks, however, savored their status as a select people, and instead of following Moses' directive to tutor the nations, they instead grew arrogant and despised those of inferior religious status. And because there was often little dispute about the nature and historic relevance of their faith including powerful acts by the Supreme Deity, the snub was all the more deeply felt; and it created a dividing wall of partition between themselves and all non-Jews.

Peter, James and John rose from what would have been some terrific seats on game day, right along the first base line and close to the plate. Jesus stepped out of the bullpen where he had been praying and joined them on their walk to the van leaving workers on the field to care for the remaining details before tomorrow's message to a crowd anticipated to range between 15–20 thousand. On their way through the gate, followers brought a woman to Jesus who had insisted upon seeing him. Kathy was a young thirty-year-old and it was obvious that she was of mixed race—Caucasian and Afro-American. Upon seeing Jesus, the woman ran toward him as though she was being chased. Falling at his feet she began begging him to order a wicked spirit to leave her nine-year-old daughter.

Jesus wasn't the well dressed, flagrantly silly, audacious male who sought a mass following for the sake of notoriety. And there was never a heady, power-thirsty aura about his person that sent "lesser life's" diving for his feet like a stolen base. Jesus was a man who had a reputation for being kind and gracious, but there was also a certain sternness about his demeanor that was tough on sin. Like a good umpire, he wasn't afraid to make the difficult calls.

While Kathy groveled there in the grass, her cries were touching those present who had the sense that she had spent many sleepless nights with the child and was constantly consumed with her personal needs. Jesus' followers waited patiently as they always did due to the gravity and intense personal anguish of the situation. Between sobs that Jesus was presently being unresponsive to, sirens could be heard in the distance as Kathy cried and asked him to come to her home and cast the demon from her daughter, Phoenicia.

Jesus continued waiting until it grew uncomfortable for those standing near him, then he said, "You must wait until my kids are first satisfied and content. It wouldn't be right to take their sandwiches and pitch it before a pack of hounds." Kathy sat up from a prone position, turned her face to Jesus but did not open her eyes which were still filled with tears. She appeared to be gathering her thoughts for a speech. Franticly scribbling with her tongue, she searched desperately for the wisest words she could possibly gather—words powerful enough to persuade a Governor to grant immunity or stay an execution—she was no quitter. Kathy continued mumbling and pulling sod from it's roots realizing that the clock was running out. She looked to be searching the interior walls of her heart for something—a gift, a weapon or a word. Jesus leaned with his body and began to step away when Kathy's desire, thread without syntax, poured from her heart and mixed with words.

"Yes! Stop! Sir, I agree," she blurted out in a stream of uncontrollable sobbing, "Your purpose and plan must be respected. Do you also ignore hounds that lay beneath your table—aren't they allowed to have the scraps that hit the floor?"

Jesus raised his head revealing a grin as broad as his face. The woman stole home with me standing right here on the mound with the ball in my hand, Jesus mused inside of himself. "She's safe! Go on home and find your daughter," Jesus shouted while throwing back his head. He sounded just like a song breaking into my favorite chorus. "Because of your answer, the demon has been ejected." Still trembling, Kathy embraced Jesus ankles with her hands and kissed his feet before rising and running off wildly in the direction of her home.

Jesus sent John ahead and told him to trail Kathy to her house and call Siva on the cellular when he located her. About twenty minutes later, John called in on a cellular phone and informed Siva of Kathy's residence number. Jesus directed Siva to ask John several specific questions about the demographics and possible number of children in the area. Jesus was spending some of his last life savings in those days and sent Matthew who was a bargain shopper along with Thad and Philip, to a supermarket to buy several food items including hot dogs, cut up fryers, marshmallows, chips, pop, condiments, light tins, baked beans and something in the form of a salad from the deli.

"Meet us at Jackson Park in the next hour," Jesus said as the men departed with grocery list in hand. Barb and Siva joined Jesus and Peter in his truck while several others with aching bellies followed along in a small caravan down Stadium Freeway before jogging over to 43rd and on to the park. Some of the men gathered a volleyball net that was always in close reach along with portable uprights while others broke out Frisbees and nine laundry baskets for a game of golf. Those who had been with Jesus on trips like this already knew the strategy and everyone pitched in to help prepare for an unexpected afternoon of fun, food and games for all the area neighborhood kids that they could round up and car pool over. Jesus had never targeted a non-Jewish quarter before, but everyone was excited for what lay ahead, especially the food!

Around 11:30 A.M., Peter gave the signal and John approached Kathy and others on her street to invite them to a Bar-B-Que in their honor. Kathy was still very much in a state of shock when John's knock at the door sent the dog barking, and she immediately recognized a Jewish man who had been with Jesus at the stadium earlier. Kathy had been cradling her daughter and carrying on in a conversation unlike any the mother and daughter had ever had. The little girl had been diagnosed as a textbook case of schizophrenia, but was also anti-social and would often experience fits of rage, grinding of teeth and episodes that left her body limp and catatonic. Kathy sat in her bentwood rocker stroking her daughter's head, still wondering who she found when she returned home from the stadium. A new girl had been brought into her life. Her daughter's voice, general behavioral characteristics and facial appearance had all changed, "she was a different person," Kathy thought to herself, "but she's my daughter, my new daughter!"

"Hello, Kathy," John yelled, as he peeked inside from the outer screen door and could view her straight through the large open front room to the kitchen at the rear of the house. Kathy's home was a monster for maintenance. The old two story would have been a mansion in another era. Tall twelve foot ceilings accented with beautiful crown molding that was balanced with elegant base and jamb casings resting upon rich hardwood floors would be prohibitive for anyone but some of the most affluent to purchase in today's market. Homes like Kathy's had been abandoned years ago as part of the flight many families made to run to the suburbs when less desirable ethnic groups encroached upon their choice neighborhoods. There were very few poor whites still living in her area, maybe a scant handful in their entire quadrant.

Kathy came to the door not suspiciously but certainly curious as to what the visit might mean.

"Hello," she said quietly with Phoenicia at her side. The wooden porch creaked with aching sounds that went entirely unnoticed by the tenants. Smells from inside told of nearly a century of oils that had passed through her galleys. One might wonder how many layers of paper lay beneath the dated flower pattern of harvest gold that hung upon walls in the front room. Heat and return air registers painted the familiar brown, were grates that hung over storm drains which had barred many a child over the years from retrieving a lost marble, brooch or new coin.

"Kathy, I was just with you at the stadium when you met Jesus. Is this your daughter?" John asked.

"Yes, this is Phoenicia Renee," Kathy said and she was controlling some emotion that wanted to surface, "she's been found," and the tears started down her brown cheeks again.

"Listen, Kathy," John began in an understanding manner, "we're trying to pull together all the children we can from your neighborhood and treat them to some games and food over at Jackson Park. Will you and Phoenicia be our guests?" Kathy didn't have a thing in the house to fix for lunch and was in fact wondering how and where they were going to eat for the next week before food stamps were issued again.

"Oh, mommy, can we?" asked Phoenicia with the most beautiful smile and in a tone that Kathy had only previously heard from other children or a movie on television, for Phoenicia had never desired to do anything before.

"She's gorgeous," John flattered them both with a smile, "she'll be a real heartbreaker."

"Thanks," said Kathy who was feeling a little confused and still wondering about crumbs from beneath tables and the like, "let me grab my purse and maybe we could ride over with you."

"That would be great. By the way, how can we round up more kids and mom's who work at home?" Kathy caught the question and having not thought to invite John in, she began dialing into a chain of friends that produced over fifty including moms, kids and a few grandparents. And with the exception of Kathy, none of them had ever heard of Jesus, The Way, and neither did they have a clue as to what might be in store for them.

John arrived back just after noon and people began trickling in immediately until the crowd swelled to nearly one hundred by the time all of Jesus' team arrived. Matthew got grills fired up at five different locations and deputized chefs on command. Spirits were generally always high; but when smells of food were in the air and Jesus was the host, well, it just shot everything up an extra mark or two. Several volunteers began introducing themselves and involving little ones in a little pre-lunch activity as a warm-up for the game day that was coming. Kathy approached Jesus with kindness in her eyes and wondered how she and some of her friends could assist. Siva heard the offer before Jesus could say beans, and had a manner about her that could recruit a sales staff to market snowballs in Anchorage on New Years day. One of the locals opened the doors on an old Buick Electra and tuned into Motown, which brought big grins to the twelve who were trying their best to be neighbors.

"Who thought to bring a can opener for these beans?" Matthew asked. He had already laid out several tins prepared for another open charcoal grill but didn't have a tool to remove the metal lids.

"Here you go," said Jesus, "Joey calls it a 'John Wayne,'" and he pitched Matthew his key ring which held a small folded can opener that was standard issue to military personnel.

Matthew turned into his work and whispered to Thad who was assisting him, "why doesn't he ever do the presto thing on difficult stuff like opening cans and starting reluctant charcoal fires," and they had a private laugh.

Meanwhile, Jesus began pouring gook into another tin that would become the sauce for the chickens. A Frisbee issued by Phoenicia got away and found the back of Jesus' head before deflecting to the ground. Jesus turned and complimented her for her range and accuracy before sending her a field to retrieve it again. Kathy looked on with pride at her daughter who had begun to live afresh. She was overcome with emotion as she thought about how the home would never be the same with late night vigils, always living with the unexpected, suicide attempts and just the numbness that comes as the result of years committed to hopelessness. Siva pulled up along side of Kathy who she surmised was daydreaming; and while she never behaved as a mother or made others feel awkwardly indebted, that's exactly what she was to so many adult-children. She was a shepherdess right after the pattern of her Lord with just the right common sense and tender touch that so many people required.

"What do you call that concoction, Jesus?" asked Peter.

"This stuff here is guaranteed to set you free, Peter," said John looking in over Jesus' shoulder. He had been treated to the Bar-B-Q sauce before, and was salivating at the thought of eating chicken parts basted with the stuff.

Jesus just placed the tin up over hot coals and told his apprentice, "watch and learn." He then poured in a full quart of white vinegar, bottle of lemon juice, liquid smoke, bag of brown sugar, tomato sauce, garlic, stick of margarine, red and black pepper, salt, and some 'what's-this-here' sauce for something too difficult for Peter to spell. It was John who made the verbal jab while reminding Peter about his need to build a vocabulary before he got too old to pick up a heavy dictionary.

"Peter, you have no idea of the many principle palpitations of profundity that go right over your head on a daily basis because you are too hard headed or shall I say too cool to continue learning." John said with purposed verbosity. Peter picked up a meat fork and began barbing his palm with it while making hideous noises of torturous pain mimicking the groans of one gouged to death with tooth picks. John was a little out of character for the day. Perhaps the ethnic mix and activity tripped a switch inside, but he decided to play Peter's hand and so continued taunting him with his own style of torture.

John pulled his bottom lip up under his upper teeth in a tight stretch forcing a buck-teeth look, then began bowing his head repeatedly while mimicking an Eastern gentleman, "Oh, ha, ha. You funny man," he said after the character he saw in a kung fu movie, "You big and dumb and have very small brain—Oh, ha, ha. You think little forking tool will harm great stud like me, Oh, ha, ha." Jesus did a double take to ensure it was actually John standing behind him taunting Peter, who himself could hardly hold a straight face.

"What do you think, Jesus?" asked Peter, "has the little fellah just been up too long? I've been reading a book that contains several multi-syllable words recently and have discovered that long periods of stress without adequate rest can result in neurosis, and without treatment can lapse into possible psychosis which often results in a rare form of locust sweat showing up in one's ameotesis theses. I would say by looking at the facial distortions manifested in this patient that we are definitely dealing with a manic episode in its four-fold advanced state with a depressed master ego searching for some new experiences in modal aspects outside of his present temporal reality." Peter slipped past Jesus gently, but John saw it all coming and he ran from Peter's grip the way a wide receiver goes out for a long bomb. Following the little ruckus that brought hoots from some of the elderly who sat along the tables, Jesus stooped down and picked up Peter's new thesaurus that had fallen from his pocket.

"There's no way you would tell him about this, is there, Jesus?" Peter ordered while snatching his book from Jesus' hand. Jesus returned to his stir, while Peter followed him around almost nose to nose, sidestepping the grill for an affirmative.

"Peter," Jesus said with a wry grin, "I'd just as soon take a dog by his ears as get between you and John. No need to worry about me meddling with that strife."

"So that means 'mum,' right?" demanded Peter.

The first dogs were being served up by Matthew and his crew while Jean, Marion and other volunteers directed the kids to drinks and places at the tables. Jesus offered a word of thanksgiving for all of God's provision and little hands moved across plates like hedge clippers sampling everything before them. Chicken was promised to everyone willing to wait the extra cooking time, but the time passed quickly as neighbors breathed in hickory, caught up on local talk, schools and many who wished to see their children's fathers again. Jesus was aware of the plight, cultural dynamics and realized that there were no simple solutions in a world driven by principles of upward mobility. He had been teaching his followers about values that were diametrically opposed to the prevailing trends of the day, but it would take longer cooking time for these to baste before distributing them to a world hungry for a taste of heaven on earth.

Following the meal, some of the elderly took naps and those who had to leave were encouraged to take the perishables back to their homes. The remainder of the kids took part in what Jesus called a 'Dog Party.' The conversation earlier with Kathy, and the memory of a book Mary used to read when he was a child about dogs sitting in the top of a tree at a great picnic, made him coin the name. Four teams of eight were drawn for water balloons, a variety of relay races, hoop scores with rod and reel, modified croquet scored by strokes needed to make goal and the finale—a watermelon eating contest.

The Red Team led by Tom and Angie won the competition easing out the Green Team by a foot or two during the seed spitting contest introduced new this year by Peter. Kathy had joined in all of the day's events and still could not hardly believe that the encounter with Jesus could possibly have led to such a rich experience with old friends and new acquaintances.

"Jesus," Kathy said, "this is the first time some of these children have been around any men for over a year. I know you're someone special and we'll never forget your visit here today. I hope your meeting at the stadium tomorrow will rekindle as much hope in your people's lives as it has done for me and my Phoenicia."

"The helpless and dependent find God. Your stepping-off-the-ledge trust has dumped you into a vast ocean of acceptance. Go on, Kathy—just try to swim its breadth! Enjoy the peace of God which is his gift to you." Most everyone from the community were gone when Kathy and Phoenicia hugged Jesus' neck, declined a ride home and chose rather to walk and talk about plans for tomorrow.

The meeting at County Stadium the next day was nearly passed over by local media who pared down the numbers of those who attended the event by under-reporting more than 40 per cent. Jesus wasn't concerned about the number of people attracted to the event and cautioned his followers to be sure to avoid that evil themselves. Jesus wasn't committing himself to the masses for he knew what was in their hearts, and that group followings could be rallied by most anyone who had a little charisma and something novel to peddle. On the other hand, Jesus didn't discourage the masses for he often described the crowds as weighed down and discouraged like sheep without a shepherd. Although there was no risk of filling County Stadium, the numbers Bart and Thad reported exceeded the 20,000 they had anticipated as an upper end.

Jesus spoke on in an enlivened manner from a hot mic for well over an hour. He began with a warning to the audience about the strict religious legalists who were steeped in hypocrisy. He exhorted the great crowd to give themselves to the kingdom of God and to work hard at building authentic relationships where honor is a high priority. He described the hypocrisy of the strict religious legalists as leaven. He warned them in no uncertain terms about how this evil, once begun, would work itself into a person's very life and personality until they were overcome by it and it came to characterize their very person.

"And because of their blindness," he said, "they will be the last to find out how corrupt they have become by it." Jesus then quoted an extended portion from Proverbs to underline his teaching, a portion that speaks of one who hates another but disguises the hatred with his lips. The proverb described one who lays up deceit in his heart. Jesus knew that the multitudes were afraid of their religious leaders who afflicted them with harsh treatment, guilt, coercion and demanded their unwavering loyalty. "Don't be afraid," Jesus would say repeatedly, "the hairs of your head are all catalogued." While on the subject of appraising the religious elite, Jesus said that everyone who spoke unkind and even blasphemous words against him, would be forgiven; but if they leveled this same accusation against the Holy Spirit, the sin would not be forgiven them in this life or the next. The notion of the Holy Spirit, while not entirely foreign to the Jews who were familiar with the Psalms, was receiving additional revelation and instruction regarding his character and special work in the lives of believers. Jesus promised on other occasions that he would reveal more about Him at a future date.

After setting aside an obviously important matter, Jesus began teaching the audience in Milwaukee similar message material as that which he had taught other crowds in Chicago, including issues of anxiety over food, clothing and shelter. Again, Jesus reminded the masses that if the birds are fed and the grasses are clothed, how much more should they count on God to care for their necessary and important material needs. In the end, however; he exhorted the crowd to seek first God's kingdom and his righteousness, promising that all the things that occupy their worrisome minds would be added to them as well.

He was well into his message when his eyes met with two men in the audience who had earlier sought his judgment in the settlement of an estate left them by their father. The men were seated right out in front of him. Jesus wanted to address the issue because similar calls had been brought to him, and he was aware that covetousness ruled the hearts of men and women. Right in the middle of the lecture, Jesus cut into the disease with a scalpel by telling the story of a man who had grown wealthy and accumulated so many vehicles, water sports equipment, motor homes, cycles and other large possessions that he had to add a 5,000 square foot auxiliary heated garage just to house the expensive toys.

The man in the story said to himself, "Bubba, you've got it made in the shade and more toys than you can play with in three life times. Kick back, eat, drink and enjoy it all—isn't life great."

But Jesus interjected a word into the story that came to the man from God, "You fool! Today your time is up and you will die. Who will end up with all this stuff? Jesus concluded his story by saying, "that's the way it will be for those who are not rich toward God in their interests." Returning to an earlier motif, Jesus tied up several loose ends by encouraging people to lay up wealth in heaven where it will not deteriorate, "for where your wealth is," Jesus said, "there will the interests of your heart be focused as well."

Jesus wrapped up his message with a stirring sentence or two that peeked the interest of his closest followers especially. He returned to material that they had longed to understand more about—a future time when the son of man would return to the earth. Jesus' followers had scarcely digested the news that he would somehow be executed, a thought that was really not embraced at all since no one could conceive of such a thing. Nevertheless, any mention of events associated with the end times drew curious question marks on the faces of everyone listening. The upshot of Jesus' words was, "be found faithful when I return because the temptation will be to become weary and begin abusing one another." Those in leadership positions were held to a higher standard of expectation because they were responsible for caring for the crowd's spiritual needs. Jesus likened it to one who directs a boarding school.

"Singled out for special treatment will be the one whom I find faithfully tending to the needs of the children when I return," said Jesus. "On the other hand, if the director says to himself, 'the superintendent will never drop by,' and they begin getting drunk, caring only for themselves and abusing my kids, I'll come when they least expect it and it won't be pretty I assure you. Be on your guard," Jesus concluded, "for the son of man is coming at a moment that you do not expect. You will be overjoyed to be found faithful."

* * * *

Followers of The Way finished packing and completed rental returns Friday morning and made a return trip to Door County the same afternoon. Jesus and several others went ahead of them and arrived at Nick & Beulah's cottage back at Egg Harbor by 4:00 P.M. Everyone was ready to get out of the vehicles and stretch their legs. Thomas stepped out of one of the back bedrooms unshaven and about half dressed, which everyone thought was a bit odd, for Thomas was never seen with even a wrinkle in a sports shirt. He was always starched, cleaned and pressed and to find him with disheveled hair and a 'fetch it yourself' look on his face made others feel a little nervous.

Peter stepped into the living room to look out the slider onto the bay when he noticed marks left in the rug by a piece of furniture that used to sit in that spot.

"Hey, who ripped off the recliner?" he asked.

"Somebody probably moved it to the game room," said John.

"Well, I'd like to see it brought back," Peter said for he was fond of napping in it. Thomas ignored the discussion and had no intentions of revealing where the leather chair lay, for it was tattered and torn by his hands before he lay it to rest beneath six feet of pea gravel and sand. Jesus too acted disinterested but assured those present that he would personally settle up with Nick for anything damaged or stolen for he was aware that Jude had already lifted an article or two.

The twelve were joined that evening by several volunteers who made a surprise visit to the cottage. Siva and Barb occupied Jesus inside with half truths about a relational problem between themselves for which they needed his counsel while others hung lights and decorated the back lot in order to spring a surprise birthday party on Jesus. No one knew his birthday and the attempts made to lift it from the Secretary of State or simply snatch his wallet and read it from his license all proved futile.

"The date is not important," he would always say, then close with a phrase about his death that always sounded extremely important but a little cryptic. Anyway, his followers had about all the ambiguity and run-a-rounds they wanted, and so they decided to mark the hard and successful work in Milwaukee with a little celebration in Jesus' honor. Since they didn't know his birthday, they decided to just make it up.

Siva was sobbing at the kitchen table and Barb clung to Jesus the way a defendant holds on to her attorney in a heated court battle. Both women put on performances worthy of Oscars and since James and John were cued into their vice, they made occasional passes into the kitchen to eavesdrop on a man who was being mentally stretched by the polarizing and conflicting data he was being given to mediate.

After another minute or two, Jesus stood up and declared, "you're both liars," without a clue about what was going on outside.

Just when he began to qualify the remark with some words aimed at adjusting their characters, both women leaped from their chairs and praised him for his terrific insights, compassionate manner, profound wisdom and then ran outside saying, "we're just going to take a walk and work through the rest of this on our own." Jesus was caught off guard by their abrupt change in attitude and wondered why more men didn't choose to remain single, then he turned around to find nearly forty men and women singing him a happy birthday wish! Siva and Barb crossed one another's shoulders with their arms in a gesture of peace while Allegretti presented the cake for Jesus to blow out the candles. With a huff and a puff, Jesus leaned into the cake and extinguished all 32 candles which he had admitted to but without a date. Following cake and coffee, the volleyball net awaited all comers and though everyone was emotionally spent, failure to beat the ball could not be tolerated. Thomas laid down three spiked sets in a row at Peter's feet which had never occurred before, and there was some private discussion in the rear about the possibility that he had been experimenting with some form of narcotic.

The hours always seemed to careen by when the ball was in flight. Slowly, as the night wore on, most everyone left including several of the 12 who went back to Chicago to see their families. Jesus intended to follow them shortly but remain out of the public's eye until the timing was right for a shift in events.

Just before midnight, Jesus walked out to the bay where Thomas stood gazing into the sky. As he approached him he stepped over a rise in the sand and he pressed it down with his foot for emphasis.

"So, you completed your homework?" Jesus asked.

"Happy Birthday, Jesus," Thomas said. "Yes, I followed your words to the letter, but I'm not sure the Coast Guard patrols these waters for I'd surely have raised them."

"Peter's going to miss the chair, of course, but we'll find Nick another one. Thomas, you're looking better than I've ever seen you," Jesus said, and there was no question but that he meant it.

"Thanks to you, Jesus. By the way, why do you recommend all the bazaar stuff?"

"Thomas," Jesus responded, "you still have no idea what a death grip control can have on a person's life, but I think you're getting a glimpse. People like you set standards for yourselves that I can't keep," Jesus said.

"I think I know what you mean Jesus, because it has nothing to do with your ability."

"Yes, Thomas, and it also has nothing to do with what's important. Just remember, when you're scared and everything feels black around you, and you don't know where to go or turn, it will always feel easier to go back to familiar patterns of lifeless control, turning on the flood lights rather than behaving as a god, walking in the darkness and trusting God to provide you with light of his own."

"You know, Jesus, the night we were on the bay and you came walking out to those of us in the boat? Well, I'd like to try it again," Thomas admitted. Jesus understood from Thomas' words that he wasn't interested in playing a game for the sake of walking on water as Peter had done nor putting Jesus to a senseless test. Rather, he had the conviction that here was a man who had never been up on skis, one who had tried repeatedly and failed but now was ready to try again. Jesus took Thomas by the hand and walked him out into the bay several meters until they could not be seen from shore under the dark skies.

"Thomas, you have to trust me," Jesus said, "and not doubt."

"O.K., I think I'm ready." With knees bent slightly like one trying to balance himself on a floating device, he released Jesus' hand and flipped immediately into the water.

Jesus noodled around just beneath the surface and retrieved his floundering mariner and raised him to his side and asked, "Why did you doubt?" Surprisingly, Thomas was not angry or embarrassed, just a little more experienced and thought he might try it again. Jesus shared with him that their walk on the waves was not a skill to attain but rather involved an abandoned-control trust that needed development. Something, Thomas would need to pursue in his private devotional times and prayer.

The next morning, Jesus turned down the hot water heater's thermostat, double checked locks and his team's attention to the details of laundry, house cleaning and squaring away the garage and outdoor facilities. Nick and Beulah had been kind to loan out their cottage and Jesus was always sure to show appreciation by leaving it in better condition than what he found it. He was completing a note card at the kitchen bar when the last of the men went to the van with their bags of personals. The card was placed on the table along with a colorful vase Jesus thought Beulah would enjoy. He then took a last look around at a cottage he would likely never revisit.

"Father," Jesus prayed quietly, "this is eternal life, that they find you, the only true God through me. They are already beginning to know that the things I give them are directly from you. The words that you gave to me, I've passed on to them and they have accepted them and have come to believe that I came from you and was sent by you. Father, keep them under the care of your name."

* * * *

The Mayor of Chicago had been planning an important fund raiser for his wealthy constituents for the last several months. Harry loved to charm, host dinners and provide rich entertainment for the people who admired and feared him. Many people in high position want their own personal circle of cult members made up of men and women who live to be in their presence. No different than his arch enemy, Harry had predilections of his own; but he never tried to hide them from his inner fold who would do absolutely anything he directed. Tonight's formal ceremony was being billed as a fund raiser to help replenish an account that would help fuel a paper campaign for his upcoming reelection bid. But since there were no serious Republican candidates on the horizon, Harry used the opportunity to further cultivate and improve the poll's favor of the construction of an airport which seemed to consume all of the Mayor's energies.

It's true, Harry was relentlessly pursuing ground work for Chicago's next regional airport in spite of cries from Aldermen in southern wards—men and women to whom he had previously promised to yield. He had just arrived back earlier in the week from a three day visit to Washington where he continued meeting with House Appropriations subcommittees as well as officials working for the Country's Department of Ways and Means. Little did Harry realize but Leonard Geiger had already been working well in advance removing what had always appeared to be insurmountable financial and planning obstacles. Geiger knew the airport would never be built; but if he could lead Harry to believe that it was achievable and that he himself was behind Harry's efforts, it would pave the way for obtaining the Mayor's cooperation later on when his scheme to bring Jesus down reached the final days of his carefully mapped timetable.

It was difficult enough to persuade residents of lower Cook County to move out of the way of an approaching 747 jumbo-jet, but Washington was impossible. No one at the Capitol even believed there was sufficient need for an additional airport and because politicians knew about Harry's appetite for paving rich farm soil or established neighborhoods with asphalt, he received little attention from those who controlled the nation's budget. Of course, Harry had been down on his luck before and was in fact standard operating procedure to begin at a subterranean level and work up through official ranks until he got what he wanted. Harry wasn't a mole, but he had several who worked for him, not the least of which was the Illinois State Governor and another he would have never counted on; but then, Geiger always generously rewarded himself for his work.

Look Mr. P., just calm down," said Harry, speaking into a telephone receiver. "I know the thought of actually saying something you mean terrifies you. After all someone might begin to take you seriously and you'd have to stand up, wipe that cheap grin off your face and make some decisions—decisions that actually belong to you, drawn from plans that you yourself cast after careful consideration of all the risks." Although Harry could hardly speak to the Governor without richly coating his words with sarcasm, he did in the back of his mind have a mild concern for the man as a fellow male and couldn't stand to see the way he was ordered around by his wife as though he was some kind of yard servant. "By the way, Mr. P., when do you intend to move over and let the Mrs. run the State?" asked Harry. "I mean it must be awfully difficult just getting in and out of the bathroom with the two of you constantly bumping heads."

Everyone close to both the Governor and Mayor knew the intense hatred between Mayor Harry and Treep, the Governor's wife. Although the Governor didn't care for his wife any more than Harry, it was beneficial to remain married so long as he stayed out of her path. Treep was a feminist of the most rigorous stamp and had authored a number of well publicized magazine and journal articles which addressed issues she found loathsome and the product of her male dominated society. Much of her theses were often on target, but the cyanide with which she laced her sentences was enough to poison populations that far exceeded her readership. Because of some gross misunderstandings about Jesus and his methods of leadership development, edited and placed on her desk in written form by Geiger's people, Treep found it convenient to make castigating attacks aimed at destroying his credibility, and men in general. And the more she wrote and went after Jesus the more her passions as an assassin came alive until she took another carefully aimed shot in the form of a new article for publication. Topics of feminism Treep discussed were written on such high academic levels and so thoroughly nuanced that even people who didn't respect Jesus, if they knew who he was, largely ignored the written diatribes directed at him because they either didn't understand them or they were indifferent to their relevance. In the end, Treep viewed him as an easy, indefensible male representative that she could direct some hate towards without fear of retaliation.

Harry had a different opinion entirely and didn't interpret Jesus' apparent unwillingness to enter the ring with Treep a specific weakness in him. Harry had a keen eye for wimps and much of his political success was due to his ability to separate men from boys on the basis of experience and performance. Since he ranked Jesus high in both of these categories, growing political fears mounted because of how Jesus might one day be groomed to run as an independent candidate for Mayor. Both Harry and Treep had a common enemy and this was always generously fueled by Geiger who was seldom seen but heard from in the form of timely and well posited rumor. Mr. P. on the other hand didn't have any real personal investment in the ongoing vendetta, he just wanted to follow the wishes of his wife.

The Governor was a paper tiger—a good man with no fight. His incredible finesse and starry optimism were his tickets to success in life. His associates nicknamed him, 'the eternal optimist,' among themselves and not because of his brilliant outlook to the future but because of his unique ability to stand ankle deep in water on the deck of a sinking ship and assure everyone that the great hole in the hull was simply imaginary and that the ship was indestructible. He hid behind many false facades, not the least of which was the impression given to his associates that he was a visionary. In reality, Mr. P. was a frightened little boy who never grew up. But speaking of finesse, he always seemed to know what side of a conversation to be on, what topic to take up, who to quote and what name to drop with whom, while in the solitary confines of his home at the end of the day—he was a weak man with the dumb smile of a stick horse.

Mr. P. had an amazing ability to keep everything at status quo and even keel until he left an assignment, then everything fell apart. He credited himself with an uncanny ability to manage chaos; but in reality, all that he ever accomplished was appeasing the disgruntled like one who keeps the draft low on a freshly stoked furnace. When the door opened and he moved on, everything burned to the ground behind him because of his inability to take issues by the horns and deal with tough choices. As a result, everybody around him worked in a confused bewildering tunnel of wind, being constantly jerked this way or that depending upon what arrived in the day's mail or who Mr. P. spoke with in the last 24 hours or a book recently read. And Mr. P. loved to read; it was his one great escape. He hid behind a mountainous library and always had a book in hand or was talking to someone about one he just finished. Mr. P. knew all about running the State, that's what got him elected. He was a polished orator and could talk his way through any problem, but that's all it ever amounted to—talk. He could never seem to work his way through a problem even after recommending reasonable solutions. His office, campaign and financial managers resigned with such regularity, it would make the door spin, but he attributed their dissatisfaction to sloth, unwillingness to go forward, or an inability to perform. When Mr. P. was under fire from various sectors to get things done, he would often book meetings with his cabinet or those who served his office and find ways in the conversation to politely relate how people he had hired in the past did superior work in less time and supervision. Mr. P. was strictly an idea man, in fact, that's how he came to be known as 'Pilot,' for he was always trying to float a new idea before his advisors. He was committed to positive thinking and if ever caught red handed for breaking policy he himself had set in the presence of his colleagues, he would make small insignificant admissions as a pittance of the real harm done to others.

When challenged by his team, or if it was ever inferred that he might be the problem, Mr. P. would remove his glasses, put on a pasted humble look, false with exasperation and with his arms extended, resting upon the sides of his chair and fanned away from his body with palms laying limp, he would ask, "Margaret, what do you suggest?" Mr. P. could weigh the vote in any meeting and always come down on the side of those with the strongest voice. If decisions meant losing a quality staff, they were replaced without regret and the new plan was underway driven by fresh legs, who would have to discover for themselves the lightweight for whom they worked. By the time they learned, they were too tired and confused to care. Resignation was always easier than fighting a system or expending energy exposing someone so deeply and impenetrably hidden beneath many layers of namby-pamby cowardice. But for everything Mr. P. lacked in the area of backbone, his wife could compensate the office with bulging abs of steel. She could cuss with the best of them and most folks were genuinely afraid of her. But not Harry. Treep was one woman he would enjoy meeting in a dark alley. He often entertained his closer associates with demeaning talk about how he would publicly humiliate her by making her crawl on her hands and knees down Michigan Avenue while bawling like a pet goat. Afterwards he would load her into a sea going crate marked: Genuine Fire Breathing Dragon, with enough postage for Hong Kong.

"Taz-Creep would be so hot by the time they opened that box," Harry reveled among his associates, "she'd swim home by a team of sharks in the same day!"

"Harry, I've already told you," said Mr. P., "I'm done making speeches for you and there is no way I can be on hand for the May fund raiser this memo describes." Harry laughed on the other end of the line—a defensive linebacker holding the car keys above his head and out of the reach of his 110 pound wife beating his massive chest like a small child crying to go to the mall. Distance was the one great friend of Mr. P. when it came to his relationship with Harry. For if Harry were closer to Springfield, the Governor would certainly be reduced to a water boy on his own major league team. On the other hand and given the real distances, Harry tried to play by the rules and respect the notion that all the clout is wrapped up in titles no matter who they are ascribed to and because Mr. P. was the Governor, he was therefore useful to Harry and needed to be courted accordingly.

"O.K. Mr. P., I understand how you must feel like you've got time for everyone but yourself," said Harry trying another approach. "I'm sympathetic to your living situation and that's why I was so willing to surrender the pictures and negatives back there after you helped me out a little with what I needed." Mr. P. was curling his toes on the other end of the line and because of the kind of man he was without an ounce of courage, he couldn't bring himself to hang up and so he listened as he was being penciled into yet another column on Harry's expenditure ledger and marked paid. "That's better, Mr. P.," said Harry who was sensing that the Governor was already feeling rushed with the usual black trance that always came over him when he entered the twilight zone under Harry's hypnotic control. "Now the stakes have been raised since you last addressed the audience here in Chicago; and since I know you follow our City's great newspapers, you are fully aware of how far we have advanced in our crusade for the disenfranchised in the south who are overdue for an airport in their region close to home which will provide even more jobs."

Harry broke into another laugh that touched his gut when he related to Mr. P. that the unemployment rate was already so negligible that Chicago was sucking new hires from all over the country and even expected the next census to show appreciable population growth because of his efforts as the City's Mayor. "What do you think, buddy?" asked Harry who had lost himself momentarily to a childhood memory in paths carved in mud and talking to a stick man about a new road system he intended to bring through his clay village.

"I've got a doctor's appointment in ten minutes, Harry. Helen or Bob will call up for the slate—goodbye." Mr. P.'s voice was so unusually deflated that Harry made a point to check in on him later in the day. Of course flowers were sent downstate from his entire staff, thanking Mr. P. for his great leadership ability and some other remarks that always brought him back around like smelling salt after a knock down.

Chapter 16

James laid aside the sport's section, then kicked a waste paper basket that sailed across the room and came to rest against Jesus' leg who was talking with someone on the other end of the phone. He was thoroughly incensed by another loss.

"Relax," said Peter, "the Cubs don't have any pitchers, no hitters and the whole team is owned indirectly by that guy in Texas—the same guy who owns the Detroit Red Wings—you know the guy with the satellite. Federation wrestling, baseball, it's all the same—an act! The managers get together at the end of the season and decide who will win the pennant races and who will make it to the world series the following year. It's all rigged for idiots who collect picture cards and can't read—right John? And because the Texas guy has the most money, his Red Wings get all the national air time selling his sponsor's products. We drink their beer which helps us forget it's all stacked and scream our lungs out like we're really going to pull the outcome."

"Shut up, Peter," said James, "You don't know hockey from shuffle board. If he would have just brought in Harpenau to pitch hit in the eighth and lefthander Windmill Woody to throw relief in the bottom of the ninth, we could have pulled it out and taken the lead in this series.

But oh no, Harrelson's got to show the whole world what the Coliseum was built for—to put the Cubs on stage as the laughing stock of major league baseball. I wish they'd send him to the American league, maybe Toledo to manage the Mudhens or some other farm club. Now that would be excellent, let him manage major feeder systems and screw up the entire American League in just a few short years. You know how cancer cells work, feed young upstarts through his system and in just a short while the whole American League is corrupted. Then when they trade players back to the National League we clean them up, debug all their bad habits and suit them up in a real uniform. Our day is coming. We're out of the Coliseum and back at Wrigley tonight—we've just got to be patient," said James staring out the window without a thought for the others in the room.

John, who was a baseball buff in his own right mentioned, "Yeah, but I wouldn't hold my breath. They haven't been there for fifty years and you won't see Hank Sauer or Banks traded back in this life."

Jesus hung up the phone and said, "and maybe not in the one to come! Hey, what's with all the grief while I'm on the phone?"

"James is still steaming because his little Cubbies took a beating last night at the hands of the Pirates," said Peter.

"What do you think, Jesus," James asked seriously, "you seem to be able to predict the future about other things. Will the Cubs ever win a World Series?"

"Does it matter?" asked Jesus.

James threw his arms in the air with disgust saying, "can you ever get a straight answer from this guy?"

"James, how many double plays do you have to see thrown with perfect precision before it's enough? How many home runs, steals, pick-offs at first, catches on the warning track or even an occasional no-hitter; when is it ever enough?"

"For crying out loud Jesus, I just asked a simple question about a stupid ball game," yelled James as he snatched his blue windbreaker from the back of a chair, "and now you have to go off on me too!" James left the room pretty angry and there was silence for a moment or two except for the movements of John who was marking his page in a recent novel he had purchased to read. Everyone realized how easy it is to get caught up in sports and the joy one experiences when the home team is on a roll, but sometimes they don't perform to our level of expectation and the disappointment is hard to bear, especially for men.

"Like vapors of emptiness," Jesus reminded Peter and John, "are hopes in a man grasped by the hand."

"Yeah, but it's just a game, Jesus," said Peter, "whoever wins the World Series isn't going to change the way I behave. I think James just got a little carried away over their loss last night; it was a close game."

"Well, Peter, I didn't intend to go there, but since you brought it up, try telling all that to the several hundred women who were battered in this city after the Cub's loss." Jesus didn't reveal the confidence, but he had already confronted James for a brush, as he called it, with his wife Diane, that left her jaw swollen for a few days. None of Jesus' followers came to him in mint condition; and although Jesus didn't tolerate abuse of any form, he was sympathetic to the human condition but committed to eradicating deep seated patterns of self-centeredness from each of them. Jesus had never rejected anyone for their harmful relational styles, but some stopped following him because of his uncompromising stand against sin, similar to the way one calls off a root canal after considering the cost.

"Yeah, O.K.," Peter said, "I can see your point, it's like we put too much of ourselves into it or something."

"Jesus," John asked, "doesn't it also have something to do with the concept of glory you spoke to us about?"

"Go on, John," said Jesus.

"Well, I can see according to the way you said we're wired up—well, I could see where a man might get all caught up in the game, maybe identify with a pitcher or place himself in the game as the leading scorer and then to have it all fizzle would be like another glory shattered. We want heaven on earth and for our lives, our teams, our plans to work out the way we want. And when something frustrates an important goal or gets in our way, we get mad and possibly even harm the people we love."

"That's not a bad analysis," Jesus admitted.

"Let's take that a step further, what do you think Jesus—now come on, don't put me off because you ask me the same thing all of the time, so what do you think; is it possible to get along in life, sample some of the fleeting pleasures, maybe buy a ball cap, take in a game with the family or are the Separatists who stay on our tails 24 and 7 right after all? I mean, if you don't watch ball games or give your soul to anything but God, you can't be all wrong can you? They're not filled with rage too are they?" asked Peter.

"Fundamentalists are sometimes militant and yes, they burn with rage, but not all of them. Many have allowed the form of their religion to become the very substance. Separatists I have in mind have so contractulized their covenant with God that it has become nothing more than a hyphen. They are unable to give their souls to anything but the piles of codified, printed legal documents they stand behind. Relationships terrify them unless they're in complete control. Don't ever forget what I've said—get this through your heads for sure—man looks on the outward appearance and by that standard the Separatist looks like a sterling model of righteousness, but God looks on the heart and from his vantage point, he is full of rottenness and all uncleanness. You see a separatist, legalist, fundamentalist, pick your pronoun—he will never place his soul at a vulnerable level of human interaction, a place where he might actually fail but grow through fresh experiences with God and his fellow man. He lives with a fortress mentality; and though he prays diligently and attends dutifully to many spiritual disciplines, he never stops to consider how God might feel about the dry, empty routine. Here's a question for you to consider: can anyone relate to God privately with any more authenticity and depth than that which he is able to offer another human being?"

"Do you mean it's possible to be a spiritual schizophrenic?" asked John.

"Many people so compartmentalize their perfunctory duties—and make no mistake, it can't properly be called faith because it doesn't even come close to abandoned-control trust. It's just duty—a job! They honestly believe they can treat their brother with contempt one moment and walk into their prayer closet the next, do the Dr. Jekhel—Mr. Hyde shift and be pleasing to God because they break their backs with religious rigors. The reception on transmissions of this kind are real poor from God's standpoint, and I tell you the truth, they will never enter my rest."

"So that's why all the gloom and doom," said Peter, "but if their religion is really that empty how do they stay motivated to press on?"

"They thrive on script fit only for manikins and love the challenge of asceticism for punishment's sake. Their spiritual high, if you will, comes from cultivating an attitude of superiority because of what they believe to be an impeccable track record of obedience and spiritual suffrage for what they deny themselves. They have placed dozens of things off limits to themselves—things I intended for them to fully enjoy. Their outrageously arrogant rationale says, "I'm going to be more righteous than God!" The tragedy of course is the myriad of proselytes that follow them down that path.

I should tell you what a soul in their condition smells like to God. A couple of years ago I wanted to get some personal time with Jack, and so I agreed to help clean out a couple of barn stalls on a warm day in May. In those days, before his arrest, you'll remember that he was living in a tenant arrangement with the Strassfeld family out west of here several miles. Anyway, Al, who owned the farm backed a manure spreader into the barn and Jack and I loaded it up so it could be spread over a garden area they were preparing to plant. I'd say the temperature inside the barn after lunch was about 90—110 degrees under the hot tin roof. Jack and I were freshly tanked up with some of the finest home cooking available on the planet; and as the afternoon wore on, I noticed Jack was becoming greener and greener. The warm manure being turned up from 12—18 inches down was ripe, fermented and yellow in color, you could taste the smell in the air and because there was no ventilation, both Jack and I were full of the rotting, gangrenous, decomposed grasses mixed with animal urine that would gag a maggot."

"Jesus are you about to conclude?" asked John who set a donut aside and was feeling a little squeamish by just listening to Jesus recount the graphic details.

"Almost, John. You see, the strict religious legalists are much like that beautifully painted barn nestled in a lovely pastoral setting that's pretty enough to frame. But nice pictures and smiling faces don't always tell the whole story. Open the doors on the barn and find something to hold on to because when you step off into a side stall of one of these corpses' soul compartments the gas will take your breath away. And that's what God finds when he inspects their private chambers."

"Well, I guess the moral of the story is 'put on a gas mask and haul out the manure,' right Jesus?" asked Peter.

"That would be great," Jesus admitted, "but most of the folks I have in mind have no intention of going to work on these stubborn areas because they are too blind to see manure when they're standing knee deep in it—they can't even smell it because they've grown accustomed to the scent of a barn lot. In the end, it's all useful to them because they are able to gain a lot of mileage in terms of respect from others who admire their self-inflicted martyrdom."

"Then how can we be holy, Jesus?" asked Peter, "Like the song says, 'if a man's gonna eat fried chicken, he's gotta get greasy.'"

"Involve yourselves in the world in a critical manner, either use your heads and common sense with an eye on my word, or else drift into one of two extremes, both of which will render you useless for kingdom endeavors. Listen, if you separate yourselves from the world, you will never be the light and salty savor they desperately need; on the other hand, if you totally immerse yourself in all the godless festivities the same is true. Always be prepared to offer others a taste of God's limitless supply of favor and truth. I'm talking about meaningful participation without contamination—it's not an impossible walk, but you must ruthlessly endeavor to be authentic. Array all your efforts and will to destroy sanctimony on the one hand and the temptation that whispers capitulation on the other. This is the 'finger-licking' walk I expect from you."

James made his way back into an office Jesus called home, a drawing room on the top floor of the Fine Arts Building with an apologetic look on his face. Because James had missed an important lecture, Jesus looked at the three and repeated a command that they had heard dozens of times, "be your brother's keeper," and then added, "sometimes it means going in with a pitch fork and hauling out a little manure. Do it for my sake."

After a moment of consideration John asked, "What's on the agenda for the rest of the day?"

"I think we should call everybody we know and meet out front of Wrigley Field for their next game with the Pirates tonight," said Jesus.

"Alright!" shouted the three as Jesus drew a stack of tickets from his pocket thick enough to choke a horse.

"Whoa, these are awesome seats," said James snatching them from Jesus' hands, "right on the third base line and low, low, low!"

"Yeah, who did you know this time, Jesus?" asked Peter.

"That was Jenkins, the Cub's owner, on the phone a moment ago, he called to ensure that the tickets were in hand and that everything was in order. And because he's a generous man, he's invited the first twenty that came to my mind to join him for dinner at Grappa's for some of the finest Italian dishes in the city."

Peter and John rose from their seats and John hugged Jesus for his thoughtfulness, "thanks for the cool evening you've planned for us," he said, "Grappa's has got to be one of the best!"

"O.K. John, down boy," said Peter who was also overjoyed but too cool handed to express himself.

*   *   *   *

It was just after 9:00 A.M. when Jesus looked at his watch and he urged the three to join him out front where they caught the 'L' at Van Buren and traveled up to a neighborhood off McCormick Boulevard between Skokie and Evanston for a message he planned to deliver. Jesus had recently dumped his van and turned over his title to a local salvage yard after blowing a head gasket. Because the body was just about gone and the engine past repair with 240,000 miles, he opted to pass over costly repairs and make greater use of city transit and lifts from his followers.

Rueben and Fritz, two of Geiger's closest associates met Milgram, their counterpart, at the salvage yard in South Chicago and posing as F.B.I. agents with all the necessary credentials, directed the owner to move the van to lock up storage until they called for it. While on site, Geiger's men busted out the front windshield, lifted vin numbers from the van in order to leave the appearance that the numbers and documents were purposely expunged and falsified. Fritz asked to see the salvage title while in the office and with slight of hand returned a similar Illinois State title which had been altered. In addition, a carefully detailed planner with worn fringe pages, coffee spills, head hairs and flakes from Jesus scalp taken from an earlier break in to his van were sprinkled onto the pages, closed up with city maps that included points of explosive material transfer—the very ones used by Geiger, then placed beneath the driver's seat between the cushion and springs to give the appearance of having been left or forgotten. Also, a small stash of cocaine and explosive paraphernalia were wrapped and stowed up under the driver side dash.

"Vince, just leave the vehicle in lock-up, see that nothing is tampered with and we'll call to have it removed when we're ready," said Rueben.

"No problem," said Vince who owned the salvage yard, "by the way, does this have anything to do with the Chicago bombings?"

"It's too early to say," said Fritz who could tell that Vince was awfully proud to have some of the chief evidence resting on his property. "Just be sure to keep everything locked down tight until you hear from us."

"No problem," said Vince for a second time while pushing his tongue through a gate made by the extraction of his two front teeth, then added, "I've got some new dogs just brought in last week and there ain't nothing safe inside that fence after 10:00 P.M. Well "thitz," I won't even go in there with food, and they recognize me! It'll be here when you need it, you can be "dath" sure of that."

Jesus and the three closest to him stepped off the 'L' when a television reporter accompanied by a cam operator approached him with a tablet of notes and asked, "Sir, we've learned from others that you're terribly exclusive about who you enroll in your organization. Can you tell us; are there just a handful that are being saved?" The question was previously gathered from those standing by in the crowd who had heard that Jesus was coming to Skokie on today's date.

The reporter didn't understand the question he was asking, but Jesus turned from him and addressed the crowd, "Set aside everything that encumbers you and make every effort to enter at the narrow passage, for I'm telling you the truth, many will seek to get in but will not be able. You see, after the lights are out, the master will go to bed and security will immediately make their rounds to ensure that his dwelling is locked up tight. Then you will shout from the street and beat on the door and insist that it be opened; but he will reply, 'I don't know where you are from.' In desperation you will remind him that you used to be drinking buddies and that he taught in your neighborhoods, but before turning in he will shout from the window, 'I'm telling you, I have no idea where you are from, now get off my property you wicked beasts!' Friends, beware! You'll be an emotional basket case when you see the great Patriarchs and Prophets in the kingdom of God while you yourselves are thrown out. People will come in from all directions and dine in the kingdom of heaven, but remember some who are last will be first and some who are first last."

While Jesus was still speaking, some Hasidic Jews approached him and shouted from a distance, "get out of Chicago while you can—Harry wants to have you killed."

"Go tell Mr. Cunning that I'm not done with cures and deliverances, but on the third day all will be accomplished. For the time being, I must keep traveling and I'll revisit the city when the time comes for it just wouldn't be right for a prophet to die outside the great City. O my people, my people, those who murder the prophets and execute those sent to you! I can't tell you the times I wished to just gather you around my apron with snacks, the way a mother does her little ones, but you didn't want anything to do with me. Listen up," Jesus shouted with more volume than usual, "Your house is being abandoned and I won't be back around until you can say, "Singled out and specially regarded by God is he who comes representing the Lord." Jesus moved off the street after healing several people of various afflictions and entered the house of a retired couple who had invited him to their community.

Jacob and Chess were God-fearing Jews who were looking for the kingdom of God and believed that Jack was God's special emissary who had paved the way for Jesus' unique pronouncements. Like a few others who were confessing their belief in Jesus as the awaited Messiah, they too had been ostracized from their synagogue and warned never to return. Their own children had stood up in the assembly beside other religious leaders when their expulsion was announced. Anyone who was confessing Jesus was singled out and labeled an apostate Jew and everyone was held accountable not to even associate with them—they were to be treated as a non-Jew. Chess wiped tears from her eyes through most of the conversation with Jesus while Jacob related some of the more serious harm done to them by families with whom they had grown old. "Blindness is the only word I can think to explain their haughty attitudes which prevent them from even comparing notes with us about the prophecies and writings we believe point to you," said Jacob.

"Blessed are your eyes, Jacob and Chess, for what you see; and I continue to thank my Father that these precious truths have been concealed from the wise and intelligent but revealed to those with childlike trust."

"Lord, what will we do?" asked Chess, "everyone has deserted us and we are shunned in our community."

"Welcome to the New Community," Jesus said as he raised from his seat and extended his arms in a gesture to embrace them all as his select fold. "You've made some tough decisions and paid a price to follow me and this will not be overlooked in the resurrection. Also, the love you've demonstrated in response to God's forgiveness is remarkable. I know you're loneliness feels overpowering at times, but you've burned a bridge behind you that you need never to regret. And though I will not be around much longer, I am with you always even to the end of time. So don't fear those who can destroy your bodies and after that nothing more can be done, rather continue your honorable regard for him who is able to destroy both soul and body in eternal junk yards where cars are never scrapped for steel and in constant need of repair."

"I thought there would be cars in hell," James soberly remarked.

"Jacob and Chess, I've told my followers on more than one occasion that though they might forsake family, friends and businesses in this life, for my sake—it will all be added back—your relationships and lands," again Jesus pointed to his followers indicating their brotherhood, "and in the time to come —eternal life."

Jesus spent the morning and early afternoon with Jewish families in Skokie who were slow to approach the house for fear of being seen by others. Those who braved the ban were rewarded with powerful parabolic stories and as many as were afflicted, he healed with the touch of his hand.

"Jesus, our leaders hate you for healing on the Sabbath," said Gregory. And we are not allowed to come back to our synagogue because we were sympathetic to the healing you performed upon our friend Agnes."

"Yes," said Gregory's wife, Ruth, she has been my friend since college and for years she has just not been able to get out of bed because her body had been nearly doubled over. Physicians were unable to help her and when you touched her and released her from that terrible bondage, we thought everyone would rejoice with her, but we got the surprise of our lives when our leaders turned and verbally attacked you."

"The irony is absolutely astounding. The hypocrites think nothing of walking their dog on the Sabbath and filling up the car with gas is considered just a trifle; but when this daughter of Abraham is released from her stocks-a painful bondage of eighteen years, the only morbid thing that they can think about is what fraction of the law was violated," shouted Jesus. "And remember, the Sabbath is a gift to man! Moses said the law shall be your wisdom before the nations, not your sheriff. Man is not to get all tangled in knots on account of the Sabbath. Getting this reversed is no different than living with a military mentality, poised and in a constant state of readiness for battle. Of course, the military have pledged themselves to your protection and vigilantly await the day, but God never intended for your entire life to revolve around the Sabbath—poised for next Saturday! No, it's a shadow of something greater—an eternal rest, but one that can be entered upon today!"

"The entire picture looks to be about a half a bubble off plumb," said Peter. "Here Jesus have another cup of coffee."

Others smiled at Peter's sense of humor which prompted another short round, "What I mean to say is that they're about one brick shy of a load—you know, their elevator doesn't go to the top floor. Definitely not the sharpest tool in the shed."

"Alright," said the law-giver, who wished to maintain the gravity for a moment longer, "it was never God's intention for people to shrink wrap and vacuum seal his gift so that it could never be enjoyed by those to whom it was given. Open it up and follow its wise design."

"Thanks for the reassurance," said Gregory, "what you've shared is truly comforting."

"Friends, let me leave you with something to ponder," Jesus said rising from his chair to leave, "I'm going to give you a little advance notice for something you'll have the wisdom to piece together later. Don't think for a minute that I've come to mutilate the law and the prophets, I've not come to mutilate but to fulfill them. Watch for the fulfillment—it's coming just as the Scriptures predicted. You see, those outside search the Scriptures because they think that they will find eternal life in them; but it is these very autographs, sacred as they are, that tell all about me.

"Ruth, thank you for your wonderful hospitality, but now we must be going." Gregory and the others hugged Jesus roundly and promised to hold steady through whatever trials were ahead of them. Peter and James grabbed refills from the coffee urn and followed Jesus back outside and over to McNally Park on foot.

"Jesus," John began as they walked along, "what then is our relationship to the law? What will we teach others? I feel like I just passed though a mirage back there; everything we have been taught since childhood just seemed to vanish when we crossed through some mysterious chasm."

"Jesus, I have to admit, I had the same reaction," said James.

“Go ahead, fill them in, Jesus,” said Peter as he took a fresh gulp of coffee which rendered his mouth timely shut for his own advantage.

“Men don’t you remember our visit to the top of 333 Whacker? Listen to your hearts. What do you think that exercise was about, to have a birds eye view of the Chicago River? The Torah has played an important role in redemptive history. It highlighted the wantonness of an unrestrained generation and it remained a taskmaster to tutor God’s people until abandoned-control trust should come. The law was never intended to overwrite the promise God made to Abraham. On the contrary, it strains to show the necessity of the promise; for no one can keep the law and if one fails by a single breech, he is guilty of it all!”

“For crying out loud sir, how will people ever come to learn of God’s moral demands and things like his righteousness if we can’t appeal to the law?” asked Peter.

“I have much to say to you, but you cannot bear to receive it all now. But when the Counselor comes he will guide you into all truth, for he will take truths from me and disclose them to you.”

“Wait a minute, Jesus, you’re treating us like we’re the crowd. Give up the goods! We can handle whatever you’ve got to tell us—right guys?” said Peter.

“Well, get strapped in; you asked for warp drive,” said Jesus who then continued, “we’re standing on the threshold of a new age—an age in which people will no longer look back to Torah as a standard of God’s righteousness nor the benchmark of his moral demands. An act of obedience in time and space is about to occur in which God’s righteousness will be forever and indisputably grounded. And regarding this event, all of the law and prophets concur. You’ve heard this before, but God’s heart is turned over within him. He is presently in the throughs of a great dilemma, but one that was prepared for before the world began…"

"Whoa, wait a minute, time out, put some time back on the clock," said James. "This is all sounding way off any planetary charts we know anything about."

"Hold your questions, James, and each of you listen up," said Jesus. "God's holiness and hatred for sin will not be compromised, neither will his great love for man. A new covenant is about to be enacted upon better promises. You will no longer need commandments engraved in stone because they are soon to be written on your hearts. Reread the prophecy of Jeremiah—God will be merciful toward iniquity and he will not bring your sins to remembrance because they will be covered forever."

"Jesus, I think you've been clear enough on all the aspects of atonement and forgiveness, but how about going a little deeper with the question I asked earlier about an objective code to which we can appeal," said Peter.

"Peter," John said somewhat exasperated and wanting Jesus to move on, "how many bricks shy of a load? The Voice from above the building, 'this is my beloved son—listen to him.'" Peter changed lanes, eased John off the sidewalk and pulled up along Jesus looking like the next wreck in a demolition derby.

"He's squared up, plumbed and nailed down on all sides, Peter," said Jesus grinning with pleasure. "Let me add, however, that the Comforter is coming after my departure and he will convict the world of sin, God's righteousness and the penalties that await the disobedient. He is man's regulator for conduct—this is no situational ethics we're playing with because he will bear witness with each conscience on the last day; for he will lay every soul bare before the eyes of him with whom each of you will have to meet. The standard is my Word. And whatever does not stem from abandoned-control trust is sin!"

"Lord, it sounds like some things are being carried over and some things are being left behind with you sitting behind the desk of a huge clearing house."

"That's right, James, a new league is already underway; it's still baseball but a different way of managing the team. Think of it in terms of continuity versus discontinuity. You're standing on the shoulders of Judaism, but you're also an entirely separate faith in terms of how you relate to God. Much of the theological structure is the same and although the new age of faith is linked to the old, it's also breaking out of the old mechanical system and moving toward something more pneumatic. Think of my message as fresh pads on a new ABS system that has come in place of the old which is definitely being superseded. Men, it's obsolete." Jesus spent the afternoon praying and walking the park with Peter, James and John who were becoming true leaders and gaining confidence day by day.

About two hours before the game, Jesus and twenty men and women sat down at Grappa's and were presented with a wine list and menu savorous enough to eat as an appetizer in its own right. Mr. Jenkins, the Cubs' owner sat at one end of the table and Jesus about midway down on the side. The folks at Grappa's were considerate to join tables and accommodate everyone at the same place. Jesus' followers began filing in, many of whom had never been in a fine restaurant and had little idea why there were extra glasses and silverware at each place setting. Seats by Jesus and Mr. Jenkins filled up first where a few tried their dignified best to wrest others from chairs they perceived to bear their names. As usual, Jesus was looking for fresh teaching material and the perfect context to speak to those who would carry his message into the next generation.

Jesus was often very blunt in his communication style, but that's all anyone had experienced from him and so it wasn't thought obtrusive when he began, "Only the host knows who is on the invitation list of great banquets, weddings and other formal occasions. When you are invited, don't break your neck getting to a seat of honor because someone more distinguished might be on that list and although the host invited you both, he might come and ask you to switch seats. Can you imagine the humiliation one would feel in front of the guests? But, when you are invited go to the last place, perhaps you will be called up—at least, you won't be demoted! And if you are called up, you will be honored by all. You see, whoever lifts himself up will be humiliated and whoever humbles himself will be lifted up." Then Jesus turned his eyes toward Mr. Jenkins and honored him by using him as an example to follow. "And when you hold a banquet, don't invite only your family, friends and wealthy neighbors, because they are likely to invite you in return for the kind gesture and you will be repaid. Rather, when you give a reception invite the poor, the lame and afflicted and you will be specially regarded by God since they don't have the means to repay you. Your reward will be conferred in the resurrection of the righteous."

One of the men sitting at the table offered a toast and said, "specially regarded indeed is everyone who eats at the banquet in the kingdom of God."

"Yes," Jesus said, "but oh, the excuses people give!" After entrees were ordered and appetizers were flowing freely, everyone listened to Jesus' story except for an occasional whisper from a waitress wishing to fill a glass. "There was a man who provided a huge banquet and mailed out many invitations asking each of them to R.S.V.P. Just a week before the special event, he directed his secretary to follow up with a phone call and see about the many regrets. Each one of them had a commitment and asked to be excused. One said I've just purchased a farm out on the edge of town and I need to go have a look at it."

"What?" said Matthew, "what investor in his right mind would buy a farm without first looking at it—what a lame excuse!"

"Yes, Matthew, and we'll come back to the place of the lame in just a moment." Then Jesus continued, "Another woman said, 'I've just purchased floor and wall coverings for my new house and I must be sure they coordinate."

"Good grief," said Thad, nudging Matthew, "are these two husband and wife, she's definitely got the same wicked case of 'buy now—compare later.'"

Jesus concluded the vignette by saying, "Yet another man said, 'please consider me excused because I've just married and I cannot come.'"

Peter caught that between bites and said, "who are these people kidding; have you ever known a woman to turn down a dinner she didn't have to cook? I guarantee the husband isn't skipping out on her account!"

"Let me tell you what happened when all these flimsy excuses came back to the office. The owner told his secretary to trash the guest list, go out in the streets and gather the poor, lame and blind. The secretary knowing the heart of her employer said, 'but sir, this has already been handled and there is all kinds of room left.' Then he said, 'go then to the bridge underpasses and drive over to cardboard town, bring them all in until the hall is full. Because none of the original invitees will taste my banquet!'"

Those with their backs to the floor at Grappa's didn't notice a larger crowd that had gathered around Jesus' table. Entrees were arriving and there was scarcely room for the servers to maneuver. Someone in the lurch identified Jesus and word spread around the place that he sat with his followers and the Cub's owner in the open floor.

While others ate, Jesus looked up and said to the crowd, "No one will be scouted by my league who does not hate his own family, spouse and children, yes, and even his own life! Unless you strap your self-centeredness into an electric chair and throw the switch the first thing every morning, you can't be on my team." Sherri leaned over and told her friend Nancy to ask Jesus if he felt those at the table could survive his Spring training. Jesus responded by saying, "Which one of you, when you decide to build that dream house does not first break out the calculator and see if you've got enough money to complete the job? Obviously, if you get the foundation poured and a few walls up and then run out of money and have to stop, the neighbors will laugh their heads off, 'look over here,' they will say, 'William thought to build a house—well, well, well.' The same is true of military exploits. What President and Congress in their right mind when waging war doesn't first sit down with their commanders and advisors to see if they have the strength to prevail against an army double their size? If they can't, then terms of indemnity must be sought to preserve peace. In the same way, therefore, no one can join my road team who doesn't give up ownership for the sake of ownership." Jesus took up the salt container and began shaking it liberally over a vegetable side dish and concluded, "This salt is good; but if it becomes tasteless, how will it regain flavor? Obviously, it can't and might as well be thrown onto the lot outside for winter snow melt. Get on your headphones, those of you who can hear!"

That evening several car loads of fans began parking along Addison and making their way to Wrigley Field. "Man it's been great since they brought in the lights. I think residents have pretty much gotten used to them, too," said Thad.

"Yep, nothing like a night game at Wrigley. Anybody seen a program?" asked James. Nancy and Sherri always came prepared and flashed one before his eyes along with Cubs pennants attached to slender dowels.

"James, we're here just for you," said Nancy. "We heard you fell out of bed last night after our loss to the Pirates."

"Yeah," said Sherri, put some pillows down on the floor; it will soften the blow."

"Yeah, and leave 'em down for the season, they're turning this losing thing into a habit," said Nancy who could feel a little heat rising from the top of James' head.

"Well, time to go root for our Cubs," said Sherri departing. "Maybe we could call some college subs down from Northwestern if we get desperate."

"Sherri," asked Nancy, "what do the Cubs have in common with an opossum?"

"I don't have a clue," Sherri replied over the noise

"They play dead at home and get killed on the road," Nancy yelled in the direction of James.

"That does it!" James shouted after the two women who were already running off and laughing uproariously.

Jesus looked up to see about all the flutter, when James yelled overhead to his reassurance, "just playing along Jesus—this game means nothing to me." As soon as Jesus turned back to seek directions from those who stood near him, James drew a pen from his pocket and began managing the entire game before it even got under way.

Once inside, everyone found seats and were early enough to take in a little pregame batting practice. James stood close to the fence with his face away from Jesus shouting words of advice to those visiting the cage. Several threats later a new batter spit tobacco juice on James' tennis shoes and he melded away along the fence as inconspicuously as possible before resurfacing with the others at their designated seats.

"Well, did you straighten them out, James," asked Jesus, "everything in order, bullpen ready?"

"We are ready to play ball," James said with a friendly bite and program in hand, but it's just not the same without Harry leading the seventh inning stretch."

"Yeah, I guess," said Jesus, "but Stone offers a great play by play and has a definite voice for the game." The stadium began to fill with people and calls for peanuts and beer while messages from sponsors lit up the big board. Kyle, a five-year-old sat in front of Jesus with his dad while Jesus' back was lined with corporates who stayed over late from their downtown offices to take in the game. All ten men resembled a religious order with their Chicago starched whites, dark suits and yuppie eyewear. They were reasonably calm during the opening innings, but as the game wore on so did the alcohol; and by the seventh inning stretch, one of the men fell forward into Jesus' lap, three sheets to the wind and bobbing.

"Whoa big fellow," said Jesus who tried to help him to an upright position and back to his seat. One of the man's associates was already angry that the Cubs were trailing the Pirates by two runs and because he thought his friend was drug across the seats, he began spitting out some abusive language of a sexual nature that was offensive to some of the women who accompanied Jesus. Peter thought the disturbance might correct itself and since they had encountered this kind of thing before, he knew Jesus would let it go and get back in the game. However, on this occasion, garbage continued spewing from a he-man who was obviously way over the legal limit.

Peter had about all he could take and so turned and said, " Look Tarzan," for the man had already stripped off his shirt as part of an earlier war cry to raise past powers that rest in the soil of Wrigley Field, "stay in your part of the jungle because you have no idea who you're messing with." Others who shared his limb opened a new barrage, but Peter warned them that one more swing from the vine into their territory would result in a terrible crash between the slats up against a tree.

"Go stick it up your nose, boy," shouted one of the men to Peter.

"Did you say, 'Roy' or something about an 'Almond Joy?' Punk, I've walked over bigger guys than you just to get to a fight!" One of the ten was tickled by the remark and began laughing so uncontrollably that it caught on like fire. Cups of beer were poured over Peter's head and it was met with a fresh volley of pop and beer from their section. No fists were thrown because everyone was laughing too hard and seeing threes of everyone in Jesus' company. Security arrived about the time the inning was getting back under way and Peter insisted that the ruckus makers be allowed to finish the game, for it was clear from the securities standpoint where the trouble had originated. Several of the men fell asleep before the bottom of the eighth while those who remained awake entertained Jesus and his followers with sporadic laughs about boy, Roy, and Almond Joys.

"I hope they've got a designated driver," said John.

"Yeah, they were drunker than a three legged goose when they walked in tonight," said James, looking over his shoulder and still nervous about the outcome of the game.

At the bottom of the ninth, the Cubs had two men in scoring position, tied ball game with no outs. Everyone was sure the Cubs could pull it out at home and move ahead of the Pirates with a hit, but hopes were doused when their power hitter, Tim Keller hit a scalding line drive to short stop which produced a double play when Kolar stepped on the bag at second daring the runner on third to go home. A cry went up from the stadium that made the pitcher show his teeth. Ortiz, the Cubs left fielder, was stranded on third while, Cousino from the middle of the order stood in against one of the finest finishers in baseball—Toulouse who could keep a knuckle ball within a two foot pattern, and tumbling across the plate like a derailed train. All a batter could hope to do is swing at the dancing load in hopes of connecting before it burrowed into the catchers mitt. Toulouse dug around on the mound mostly for play, picking at the rosin bag, watching third and popping signs off his cap while spitting at appropriate times. Cousino was faced with two balls and two strikes when James sat down and waited for the final nail in the coffin.

"C'mon, James," said Jesus, it's just a game. This will be good for you. Stand up here with us and watch the outcome." Cousino swung at another zinger and snatched enough of the ball to foul it back to the section where Jesus and his crowd were sitting. All heads watched the ball come to rest in shark filled waters during a feeding frenzy. Everyone in a huge radius was snatching at the ball as though it were a round of white meat. Drunks from above fumbled the ball and it dumped into James' hands after several more attempts to snatch it from the air. James was smiling from ear to ear and gripping the ball for dear life.

"Wow, how about that James!" shouted Jesus who tried as hard as anyone to catch it on the way down.

"Yes! Now this is where real life begins," said James, who began to grow strangely uncomfortable with the words that came from his own lips.

"Great catch, James," said Jesus.

"Way to go, James," winked Nancy and Sherri in a sincere gesture with two thumbs up. Everyone in the stadium remained on their feet for the last pitch and more out of honor than anything else. Toulouse was tamping down the mound with his spikes and it was clear that he was carrying on a monologue with himself, toying with the batter and fans. He sent a slow change up down the middle and Cousino who was standing on his toes gouged the face of the ball sending it over the head of the second baseman who leaped and nearly caught the missile which rolled to the wall and provided the game winning RBI. The crowd at Wrigley went nuts and even those in a stupor rose to salute their warriors. Everyone was so overjoyed to hoot and boo Toulouse off the mound that only one other person witnessed the exchange by James when he handed off his prize ball to five-year-old Kyle while wrapping the boys little hands around it's autograph—"Go Cubs. Win Kingdom!—a man in the park." Jimmy held the ball in his glove like gold that glowed when it had been fired in the furnace seven times, but something more precious glowed in another man's heart—a glow that would shine before others for years to come. Jesus marveled at the sight and couldn't speak right away when someone nearby slapped him on the back and congratulated everyone at home for the win. Though pitifully silly to some, Jesus knew for James to give up the ball was the sign of a man growing up on the inside and transferring his allegiance to a score card with more important X's and O's. Peter was aware of Jesus' response because there was some obvious emotion in his face and tears swept from his cheeks; and while he thought it was all about a game won, Jesus was savoring a more important victory that would have eternal ramifications.

"C'mon you guys, you're coming with us," Jesus said motioning to ten business men who had driven over from a nearby consulting firm. "You guys couldn't find the seat of your pants with both hands," offering them a modified version of something he heard Joey say on an occasion when recounting a story from the Corps. Jesus was able to evict three sets of car keys from men who were not entirely objectionable, then assigned drivers heading to the suburbs who could ensure that they made it home safely.

"Where are you going, Jesus," asked his followers. "I'm going away for a few hours," which generally meant that he was going to find a place of solitude and pray until he was ready to be seen again.

Chapter 17

It wasn't as though the other followers were less interested in Jesus, but John was still single and had a more flexible job than most of them. He kept up the rent at the apartment on Cove after Jesus moved out, and it provided a room for three other men who were young in their careers and grateful for a place to call home. John had saved the larger percentage of his income over the past several months and recently purchased a one year old Saab which was the first car that he owned. Following the memorable game at Wrigley, he drove his fiancé, Lynn home and then swung over to Belmont Harbor where he thought he might find Jesus. John knew that Jesus spent a good bit of private time praying and meditating on the land mass separating the harbor from the Lake. On this night under the light of the moon, John watched Jesus walk the lakeside, lifting his arms in gestures of intercession, sometimes stopping for long periods of time, kneeling and then walking on again. John loved Jesus deeply, the way a man loves his good friend—with a love that sticks closer than a brother. He seemed to know from the beginning that Jesus was no ordinary man. He wondered at his words and memorized his facial expressions and considered Jesus a unique body of literature, like a word from God that had become flesh to live among men. Reading this man was John's greatest joy. Each night he journaled and recorded insights from the day's adventure as well as specific interpretations of scripture that Jesus offered in his own rabbinic style.

John fell asleep in his car which wasn't terribly comfortable, but he awakened just as the sun broke over the lake to signal a new day. He fumbled for a radio station to catch a brief news update, but somebody sounded as though they were dying of a wasting disease on the country station the radio self-scanned and he shut it off just before the cowboy's life expired. John stepped out of his car for a stretch, then walked out and met Jesus who was still wide awake having never gone to sleep. It hit John for the first time why Jesus' face, so laden with lines of sin sorrowing sad heartedness could be so deeply etched. Frequent all nighters in a bar shedding tears in glasses of beer was a certain sadness of regret, but the impressions in Jesus' face favored the frequent all nighters of a man wrestling with God to grant repentance for those too blind to know the difference. Men who live with regrets remain captives of the bottle, while those who find repentance are taken captive by God and given back as gifts to men.

"Boker tov, Rabbi," said John. Jesus embraced John and they slapped one another on the back for friendship sake.

"Good morning to you, John," Jesus said in return.

"Say, Jesus, what do you get when you play country music backwards?"

"Well, I don't suppose I've ever considered that John—so what do you get?"

"Well," John said, "you get your pick up truck back, your wife back, your dog back…" Jesus' laughter cut him off and he asked, "so how do they fish all of that back up from the bottom of a glass of draft?"

"Hey, that's good, Jesus, I'll remember that one."

"And John," Jesus asked testing his perception, "what does a believer get when he reads God's word backward?"

"Now I've never tried that for sure, but I'd be interested to know."

"Just think of it, John, you get your disease back, your burden, sickness and greed…"

"O.K. Jesus," said John, "how about if we don't go fishing there?"

"Nope, not me, John. Think of God's forgiveness in terms of the Dead Sea. The lowest body of water on the planet, several hundred feet below sea level, with no outlet. Didn't Micah say that God has cast all of your sins into the depths of the sea?" Jesus was aware that John had a very sensitive conscience and was often plagued with feelings of unworthiness over past deeds of immorality. "John, your loving Father has not only cast your sins into the depths of that black hole, but he's also placed a sign on the bank—'No fishing!' You see, God delights himself in his own unchanging love."

"You know what I like about you, Jesus? I never know where you are going to go with a simple joke or question."

"John, you are already washed up and spanking clean because of the word I spoke to you." Jesus extended his hand and allowed a low lying branch from a nearby tree to rest in his palm. "There are many lessons we could draw from a branch and one I'd like for you to remember is the fact that I'm the vine and my followers are branches. If you stay vitally connected to me, then I will remain vitally connected to you. In this type of relationship you may ask whatever you wish and it will be done for you. My Father will be glorified by the fruit you bear. Obviously, a branch cannot bear fruit by itself—it is wholly dependent upon the vine for nutrients."

"I'll remember the branch, Lord. Thanks too for reminding me again that there isn't tackle available to draw my past stuff up from the bottom of the gook pit."

"That's right, John, but how people try. The adversary roams those banks for he loves the smell of raw sewage. Be on your guard, for he's a master at conning people into deep sea fishing in spite of the truths I've just related. He is successful because people's shame is so deeply felt. Guilt is one thing. It's the legitimate response of a healthy conscience that has been morally violated. This is how God has designed a soul. And if one will simply confess the transgression, he can get right back on track with God for he is faithful in character to forgive sin and wash away all of a person's unrighteousness. Shame on the other hand is something people like to tinker with; however, the experiment is no different than a novice trying to defuse a bomb—it will always go off in his face. When a person feels shame, they have the option of dredging up cancerous mutations filled with bleeding tumors or dining at my Father's table, which is always spread with the choicest fillets, breads and wine. Folks who are unwilling to repent and accept God's provision, dwell upon their sin, 'I'm no good,' and generally find a way to appease their conscience with human works that amount to payments. Their inner thought is, 'if I can just beat myself up long enough for the screw up, I'll pay for the misdeed and be back on track with God.' Self-punishment is no substitute for repentance and spiritual credit slips that folks talk about at the Hub have never been issued from heaven. They're just one of many man made systems designed to sidestep the atonement and perpetuate the madness. Repentance is not regret, rather it's a person's admission that he is helplessly depraved and in need of pardon; pardon rich enough to forgive the entire debt load. It's a difficult concept for man to embrace because he thinks enough goodness resides in his heart to appease God. However, God's standard for acceptance is perfection. As I've said before, unless your credentials exceeds that of the strict religious legalists, you cannot enter the kingdom of God. But again, God's favor cannot be earned by human effort based upon some kind of installment plan. Good works are the result of receiving God's favor, but they are never the cause. Man's propensity is to constantly get this reversed and so his soul has no rest because he has no way of determining how many good works are needed.

"Satan is delighted to sign people up in this kind of race. Unfortunately, it's unwinable—a devilish marathon hatched in the depths of hell itself. It will be a day of rude awakening when they appear before God and offer weak explanations for why they rejected rest and eternal life as a free gift and opted instead for the tread mill. Many of the bumper stickers you read around the city betray their inner gripe, 'Life's a wash, then you die.' The one liner is a succinct commentary of their lives, but they indict themselves with their own words. An individual's own foolishness ruins his life, but his heart roars back with rage against God. They have said in effect that God is not good and his offer of eternal life cannot be trusted. They have judged themselves unworthy of eternal life. John, I tell you most solemnly, all that the Father confers to me will come to me and the one who steps over to me need not fear being bounced back. Again, the one who hears my word and trusts him who sent me has everlasting life and will not be brought before the tribunal, for he has passed out of death into life."

"Jesus, it sounds like there are three basic categories of people: those who are broken, spiritually worn out and tired of the race; runners who think they can finish the marathon, but have no idea of the infinite distance to the finish line; and then the more obvious who sport bumper stickers like 'screw guilt,' 'live and let die,' 'better me than you,' and a few others."

"That's right, John, that last category you mentioned are proud to understand that only idiots put themselves through spiritual rigors when there is so much interesting vice available to explore. But they're also runners, they've just been too caught up in their own whirlwind to realize they've finished the triple crown. People of that category I've personally sought to persuade, flick me off and verbalize their desire to ultimately end up in hell. They say, 'I want to be with my friends.' It takes a great deal of prayer and persistence to win this kind over, but a soul has eternal worth and so the cultivation and labor is an honorable enterprise. Like the proverb says, 'The one who catches souls is a true heavy weight.' God's love is boundless, John. That's why he tirelessly pursues sinners who populate a pint size planet in a little known galaxy located way off the back side of an expanse that has no ends."

The time with John passed quickly and others of Jesus' followers began to appear including several children who wanted to see Jesus. As the little ones approached him, they and their parents were rebuffed by Jesus' followers, who insisted that he not be bothered by children. Jesus told his men not to hamper the kids, "For I'm telling you straight up, unless you receive the kingdom of God like a little child, you cannot get in at all," and he welcomed them into his arms and related a story drawn from the book of Ecclesiastes which taught that their passage in life would be safer if they traveled with a friend. Jesus picked up a branch from the ground and asked if anyone in his audience of children could break it in two with their hands. All of the boy's hands shot up immediately, each one of them hoping to be selected to demonstrate how stout their tawny little arms had grown. Jesus handed the stick to Caleb, who looked to be the oldest of the group and was sitting near the front flexing his arms. "What is your name?" Jesus asked looking into his eyes.

"My name is Caleb," said the eleven-year-old, "would you like for me to break the stick?"

"Yes, Caleb, why don't you stand here next to me and show the others how you are able to snap it in two." Caleb rose to his feet and quickly snatched the stick from Jesus hand and with a little effort rendered it double and it snapped with a pop."

"Nice job, Caleb," said Peter.

"Yes indeed," said Jesus. Caleb began to recover his seat when Jesus said, "Oh, we're not done yet Caleb," and he invited him to stay by his side. Jesus then gathered three sticks of nearly equal thickness and length and asked Caleb to exert himself a second time and snap all three bundled. Caleb's little sister and a cousin sat near him and were cheering for their muscle man as he took the branches into his hands. "O.K. Caleb," Jesus encouraged him, "now flex with all your might and break the three branches!" Caleb bore down on the branches with his body weight and stomach strength but was unable to break them in two even after attempting to pull them against his knee. He was awfully determined and after he was physically exhausted from the exercise, he returned the sticks to Jesus' hand. All the adults cheered while Caleb's little friends looked on with dismay for they fully believed that he would snap three as easily as one. Jesus used the physical exercise to illustrate a truth he wished to communicate to the children. "How many of you think that Caleb could break the three sticks if he handled them one at a time?" All of the children agreed that Caleb could easily break them one by one. Jesus rewarded their astute response by saying, "Yes, Caleb is a strong young man and could break single sticks all day until blisters formed. But what happened when he tried to break the three?"

"He couldn't do it!" they all shouted, then looked to their parents for the nod.

"That's right," said Jesus, "and in the same way, you are safer from the evil one when you bind together and help one another, for a bundle of three sticks is difficult to snap in two." One of the mothers sensitive, to Jesus' schedule, gathered the children and moved them away but not before he touched them and spoke words into them individually. He asked one girl her name and told her its meaning with a view of growing into it; another he embraced and complimented his smile, while others were similarly encouraged with words or strokes on the head while admonishing them to remember his words.

While the little ones were being escorted away from Jesus' lap, he began teaching his followers by saying, "Without question, stumbling blocks are going to come, but miserable indeed it will be for the one who plants the stick. Why, it would be better if a transit bus were attached to his neck and he be thrown into this lake than that he should cause one of these little ones to fall."

"Jesus," James asked, "what do you mean by 'planting the stick?' What on earth is a stumbling block anyway?" Jesus again took up a stick from the grass and snapped ends of the twig until he created a short two-pronged fork at the top.

"This is a stumbling block," Jesus illustrated. "Prop up one end of a baited box with this stick, tie a string to it and then let out several yards and conceal yourself until your prey happens along and falls beneath it when tripped. Stumbling blocks come packaged in all shapes and sizes, but they all have one purpose—entrapment. Be on guard for yourselves and by all means don't even think of laying out one of these for others—the lake is deep. Men, if your hand causes you to sin, sever it and pitch it away from you, for it would be better to enter life missing a limb or two than to enter the eternal fires all in one piece. The same could be said for your eyes as well!" While looking into bewildered faces, he said, "Don't despise the little ones, for their guardians behold the face of my Father who is in heaven. C'mon, put it together, this has to do with you; if one of you lose an important article of clothing, maybe that expensive wool sweater or leather jacket, will you not forget about all your other clothes until it is found? And how do you feel when you find it? Listen, men, it is not God's will that any of these little ones should be lost and forgotten." Jesus' followers didn't fully grasp his instruction, for he was using children as an illustration about men.

More and more sailboats were moving out of the harbor, their pilots wishing to take advantage of the breeze whispering in from the land side. Jesus walked further north along the lake where he found a broader place to spread out with a crowd that was amassing itself.

"Jesus," Matthew asked, "What should we do if we observe this 'stumbling block' behavior in one of our brothers?"

"All of you listen carefully to me because this is likely to be one of the most difficult assignments you will ever receive. If your brother sins against you, don't go off and tell the whole world about it! Zip it up and keep the problem between the two of you, but go to that individual and confront him in private. If he agrees with you and turns, you have saved your brother."

"O.K. Lord," said Matthew, "but what if he doesn't want to discuss it and finds ways to avoid you?"

"Take two or three of your friends along who can validate the behavior; and if he still won't listen or treats you with disregard, then tell it to the church, and if he won't listen to the church, then treat him as a hypocritical fraud."

Showing more restraint than usual, Peter raised his hand in a gesture to get Jesus' attention when James leaned over in his direction and said, "let me save you some embarrassment—I just know you're not going to ask him, 'now who is my brother?'" Peter was as much a numbers man as anyone could be and was interested to learn how many times a day Jesus required one to forgive a brother.

Jesus turned in Peter's direction who then asked, "O.K. Jesus, so how many times do we go through this process with someone like you've just described? Seven seems like a biblically significant number; is that enough times?"

"It doesn't come close, Peter. You'll need to raise the power, for I'm telling you to be ready to forgive 7 X 70 if necessary. Calculate that in numbers of years and you will begin to understand man's inabilities and the grand forbearance of God.

Because of the enormity of the issue, Jesus motioned for those standing to be seated which generally meant a story was going to follow. "God's expectation in the area of forgiveness is huge! Perhaps a story will help you envision the broad parameters I'm describing," Jesus began. "The kingdom of heaven is not unlike a collection's agent who received a letter from his client describing an account which was in serious arrears. Porter owed something like $1.6 million and had absolutely no means to repay the debt. As a result, collection agents from a firm with a ruthless reputation accosted Porter at his home and threatened to ruin his life and make him forfeit everything he owned—his wife and children would ultimately leave him. But the man fell on his face and pleaded for mercy confessing he was broke having lived many years way above his means. The creditors felt strangely compassionate for Porter. Before them lay a grown man sobbing—a man accustomed to luxury and wealth, had humbled himself before their eyes. After reconsidering the vast debt and Porter's inability to repay even a fraction, they decided to write it off as bad credit."

"Good grief," someone yelled from a distance, "that's more money than I make in a month!" Jesus was just setting the stage for some instruction about moral indebtedness, man's inability to repay and how this should affect the way we treat others.

"There's more," Jesus said. "This debtor who had just been released from an incalculable debt got on his shoes as soon as the agents left his house and marched down the street to his friend's place, kicked down the door, put a gun to his head and insisted that he be paid a two thousand dollar debt in full. Charlie begged for his life while staring down the barrel of a pistol, but it was no use for Porter had no intention of showing mercy. Porter hauled Charlie into small claims court and succeeded in having him imprisoned until his wages could be garnished and hasty means of repayment established. A neighbor, Mark who was a ware of the details of the recent transaction was also in court the day hard-hearted Porter drug Charlie before the judge. Mark knew them both and was horrified at how slightly impacted Porter had been in view of the extreme leniency shown to him. Mark ran to the collection's agency which released Porter and outlined the entire story. Creditors showed up at the jail a few days later where Charlie was serving a thirty day sentence. They took his deposition and hurried back to the home of Porter who they had previously forgiven an enormous debt. The agents seized Porter with cuffs and hustled him off to court where he was ultimately given a life prison sentence for embezzlement. Hear this all of you," said Jesus concluding, "my Father will do the same thing to each of you if you do not release your brother from the dungeon of your heart!"

It was nearly lunch time when Jesus dismissed the crowds, many of which had moored nearby to listen to him lecture. He then sent several of his followers ahead of him with instructions to rendezvous around 6:00 P.M. in front of Navy Pier. Peter, James and John followed Jesus on foot through the crowd which was reluctant to disperse. He healed many who were afflicted with various diseases and stopped to spend time with some of the elderly who could scarcely talk or hear. The men eventually reached the parking lot and drove out to Rolling Meadows for a plate lunch at Ritzy's on Algonquin Road. Jesus ordered his usual soup of the day with tossed salad, while Peter launched into something that was more suited as a dinner for two. While the four men ate, Jesus discussed plans to remain more or less remote going into the upcoming winter with specific plans for the Spring and Passover, 2000. Jesus generally planned about six months in advance on a very loose slate that was subject to change without too much notice. He directed his men to use their heads but to remain sensitive to the Holy Spirit's promptings in their individual lives which sometimes meant shelving plans or charting a new course based upon his directives and personal interaction through prayer.

Following the meal, Jesus stepped into the back lot to reboard Peter's vehicle when they were approached by nine Jewish men and a middle aged Korean who was a convert to Judaism, all of whom looked to be suffering from A.I.D.S. The men lived together and cared for one another's medical needs but were seldom seen in public due to their physical weakness and the fact that they were societally eschewed.

The men wouldn't come near but stood by their vehicle shouting at Jesus from a distance, "Jesus, Master of disease, have mercy on us!"

Jesus responded by saying, "Go to your synagogue and present yourselves to the Rabbi. He will tell you what to do. The men had heard reports about Jesus' miraculous powers from others and didn't hesitate to obey him. As the ten began climbing back inside the van, an unusual and surprising thing happened. Their skin returned to baby like color and texture and the nauseousness that they each lived with passed away in a moment. Sores that had been opened on their bodies or caused by bed bruises or disease disappeared, and the men were overcome with a sense of victory. They shouted for Ronnie once but without waiting any longer, they drove off leaving him in the parking lot with his eyes still fixed on Jesus. Ronnie felt like a failure. He immediately got down on his knees and crawled over fifty feet before finding Jesus' soles and weeping there with thanksgiving for he was filled with gratitude. Ronnie felt like a man who had just been released from a life sentence where he was destined to waste away in a prison cell. As he lay on his face, he lost all consciousness of those standing around except for the one who granted his petition. Ronnie was overcome with feelings of personal freedom and the worship due his new master.

To those standing by, Jesus asked rhetorically, "didn't I heal ten men? But where are the other nine? Could none of them take time to give God honor except this outsider?" Jesus helped the man to his feet and said, "go on now, your abandoned-control trust has made you well." Jesus spent the afternoon counseling the three closest to him, while Geiger in another section of town began to fine tune his scheme to deliver Jesus up to the authorities as the most notorious criminal of the Century.

* * * *

It seemed as though everyone who was in a position of authority wanted Jesus out of the way. His methods of leadership and uncompromising attitude toward injustices on every hand, coupled with the fact that he had never succumbed to the status quo for popular support, and turning down lucrative bribes offered by lobbyists, made him obnoxious to those who controlled the Country at higher echelons of political power. Mayor Harry wanted Jesus moved out of his City due to the tremendous political threat he perceived Jesus to be, while Mr. P. wanted him extradited for his wife's purposes. But it was Geiger who was clearly the most maddening about his very existence. Geiger was deeply troubled at a core level about Jesus' true identity and while he came close on occasion to admitting it to himself, he could hardly breathe the name Jesus and take in all that name stood for without flying into a violent and rageful fit. Geiger was so overcome by rage on one occasion that he lost consciousness while alone in his home and nearly swallowed his tongue. Something tripped inside his psyche and left him physically debilitated for the better part of an afternoon. When he awakened, his mouth was still filled with white foam, thick with mucus that had to be pulled from his mouth and sponged away with a cloth. He no longer had the ability to level with himself. Geiger had lost that sense long ago; and though he could no longer see, he was adept at flying by critically calibrated instruments through dark clouds and wind storms that had become his normal operating environment.

Geiger's plan would soon kick into gear and was in fact so important that it be run flawlessly and with the greatest secrecy that he took a one year sabbatical from the University in order to superintend operations from his home. He was a careful man, but this score required his greatest efforts of concentration and focus. Several maps lined his personal drawing room which was part of the square footage enveloped by his hidden laboratory of files and electronic surveillance equipment. Against the wall in front of his 'L' shaped desk were detailed schematics, calendars, names, phone numbers and city plats that were detailed right down to the street frontage of housing lots. Each of the wall hangings were flow maps, whether calendars, people, roadways or events, Geiger had spooled out a comprehensive net that was woven tighter than a widow's web and certainly more toxic.

Near the bottom of the maps, just above Geiger's desk, he placed a graphic to indicate the place, timing and means of Jesus' execution. Each of the documents and information ledgers were treated as prominent terrain features on a military map. Geiger charted his position and the timing of events by reading the back-azimuth of each of his compass shots and scribing intersecting lines that led back to a point of destination. Timing was everything, for Geiger wished to have Jesus executed, and make no mistake, imprisonment was never an option as far as Geiger was concerned; and so he worked along meticulously while keeping the pot stirred and leaving nothing to chance. A form letter to the families of bombing victims here, a little crumb or two for the F.B.I. there, another meeting with the Mayor on this date and one with the Governor's wife on another. Everything was proceeding according to plan and Geiger was happier than many had known him to be in recent years. Even his wife, Ann, felt strangely affectionate from time to time and the two of them shared a drink at her dining quarters before parting for their individual beds on a recent occasion.

Jude had never been to Dr. Geiger's residence; in fact, he didn't even know exactly where he lived. It would be a very rare occasion that Geiger would invite anyone into the privacy of his home; but during this special season of planning, it required lengthy discussions with Jude whom he needed to keep on the front lines and available for deployment.

"Welcome, Judas," said Dr. Geiger as he opened the door of his home to his guest.

"Thank you for the special invitation, Rabbi Geiger—you have a beautiful home." Ann was an interior design fanatic and had redesigned portions of the upper level three times in twenty years at a cost of nearly $150,000 per conversion. The front foyer was twenty feet wide with door side lights and transom that allowed light to touch the soft pink marble floor. Oak hardwood joined the marble in a dining area on one side and lush carpets on another that ran out before French doors into passages that were lost in turns and corridors lit with ornate sconce and costly paper. Ceilings were accented with crown that consisted of at least five individual pieces to complete the beautifully painted bulwark. Utter elegance exuded from every corner, but it was such an apparent oddity to visit with Geiger or his wife, Ann, against such a backdrop. The contrast was so glaring—like water damage on the legs of an otherwise beautiful antique walnut chest of drawers. 'What a shame one would admit,' while considering the layers of buckled veneer.

Geiger took Jude's jacket from him and placed it on a suspension and then led him to the Florida room where aromatic coffee and Danish were prepared on etched glass.

"Tell me, Judas," Geiger began, "where has the imposter been spending his time of late?" Judas had not yet had breakfast but was petrified to ask Geiger for a cup of coffee or sweet roll. His eyes were still locked onto the cheese Danish when Geiger lifted the plate to Jude's side but didn't repeat the question.

"Well, Dr. Geiger, as I've said, he spends most of his time with the same three that I've told you about before. Since giving up his car, he's been spending more time around the city but seldom in public. He lives in a studio of sorts on the top floor of the Fine Arts Building in a drawing room owned by a friend and uses the city transit or one of the men will give him a lift here or there."

"Judas, I have some information you might find surprising. What I'm about to confide in you has not been made privy to anyone else and even the F.B.I. are unaware of the complete contents of this file." Geiger lifted an accordion file from the side of his chair and removed two or three select files for Jude's perusal. "Go ahead, Judas, have a careful look at the dates, movements and speeches by this man and you tell me if we are not dealing with an extraordinary psycho-path of mammoth—no, monstrous proportions!" Jude laid the files out side by side with the help of Dr. Geiger who was now pouring him a second cup of coffee, something he had never done for anyone before in his entire life, then scooted a little closer like one sincerely interested to learn the interpretations of his young apprentice.

"Dr. Geiger, how did you piece this together, I mean sir, this outlay is incredibly accurate."

"Your interpretation, Judas," Geiger said.

"Well, sir this is uncanny. You see, I was right there with him for most of this, but I guess I was just too blind to put all of this together. So this man I've been following around like a zombie is the one they're looking for. I can't believe it—I've been right by the side of the one who pushed the button—this is incredible! Yes, Dr. Geiger, it's definitely him." Jude wasn't especially offended by the blasts, and in fact thought it was a class act, the killing of the innocent notwithstanding. Jude could understand the deceptive practices of the young rabbi and wasn't surprised that he had everyone fooled, but something he couldn't understand was Jesus' talk about ultimately dying. None of his followers understood those lessons and they were becoming more and more frequent.

"Dr. Geiger," Jude asked, "how do you account for the fact that Jesus seems to be engineering his own death. He has no fear of political powers and speaks boldly and openly whenever and wherever he pleases." Geiger lowered his head and picked at the nap of the carpet which was a clear signal to Jude who had seen this behavior a few times before in other contexts, that he had just crossed a boundary by believing reports, thus tacitly ascribing authority to one Geiger lived to destroy.

"Judas," Geiger miraculously kept a lid on a boiling pressure cooker as he opened new instruction, "we have revisited this man's techniques of deception dozens of times" Geiger's voice began to grow, "he's a master of deception because he is controlled by Beelzebub himself; and it should be no small wonder that he is able to lead a motley crew of uneducated half wits around the world if that be his intention. Now, we won't return to the primal character deficits of this thing again—whatever it is. And now Judas," Geiger was screaming, "what is your ultimate conclusion based upon this material?" Jude was standing on his feet with cup in hand when Geiger took the cup into his shaking hands, gestured for Jude to be seated and regained his composure. "Judas, I've lost a great deal of sleep in recent months trying to console families, assisting the F.B.I. with their investigation, serving regularly at the synagogue and keeping pace with the many social demands that hang over me related to the University or other civic responsibilities. Now, this man will pay for his crime and everything will be cared for in time. You are the very key to the success of his ultimate capture and judgment; however, the timing is not right just now. I've talked with special agents Moore and Keller who agreed to allow me some time to work with you in preparation to spring a trap."

"The F.B.I.?" exclaimed Jude.

"The multitudes are utterly deceived about who this man is," Geiger continued, "and it is our duty as citizens as well as those committed to preserving pure Zionism, to purge ourselves of this adulterating influence and further eliminate the effects of his presence from this land. Clean up following the aftermath of his arrest and incarceration will be as physically and emotionally demanding as his expulsion. It might take years to eliminate all the poison he's poured into the minds of the ignorant."

"Dr. Geiger, I want to help in anyway possible. I just need a little time to digest it all."

Jude was reeling inside from the shock wave that just rolled over him after reading the findings by Dr. Geiger. Jude was angry on the one hand that he had been deceived; but on the other hand, he still couldn't fully extricate himself from something that gripped his soul regarding the authenticity of Jesus' claims. Without question, no one taught in the authoritative manner that was characteristic of Jesus; and if there were areas of incongruence, they were certainly not being comprehended by even the most astute. This all left Jude very confused but he wouldn't dare express his doubt in Geiger's hearing, but he wondered how one individual could be so incredibly clever to lead such an immaculate double life.

"Judas, our time is up," said Geiger who rose for a final word with Jude. "I have something to pass on to you, Judas. Today you have taken a step forward in your personalized training, and I want to present you with a little token of reward for your diligent efforts and commitment to secrecy. You see, Judas, you yourself have been the subject of investigation since our trouble with this man began, and you would not have heard from me a second time if you could not have been trusted implicitly. You have demonstrated remarkable resilience at many of my canned outbursts which were staged to test your mental stamina. I want you to know that the F.B.I. wire taps to your home as well as the surveillance devices attached to your car were removed this morning while you visited with me. Judas, you are being extended a welcome of fellowship today into an elite division of Zionists.

"Dr. Geiger, I don't know what to say," while rocking back on his heels with surprise, "I'm flattered, I'm overwhelmed, I just don't know what to say."

"Judas, are you worthy to wear the mantle and keep this secret code?" asked Geiger. "Are you willing to work the inside and give him up on my command?"

"Yes of course," said Jude, and although Geiger had bluffed about the F.B.I.'s involvement, Jude checked out and met Geiger's stringent requirements for the list of lies and half truths he would be feeding him in the days ahead. In that moment, three men stepped out of an adjacent inner room, greeted Jude and welcomed him into their circle of confidence.

"Hello, Judas," greeted Rueben, Mr. Milgram and Fritz. "Dr. Geiger has told us about you're zeal for Zion, tremendous patience, attention to detail and submission to authority," said Fritz.

"Judas, it's always a pleasure to work with another professional who performs as well as you and shares a deep concern for our objectives. We will go forward in a unified front until this enemy is destroyed. I'm very much looking forward to having you on the team. Dr. Geiger tells us that he is counting on you for some indispensable inside work. We are your honored associates and will assist you in every way we can," said Rueben, and each of the men nodded in agreement. Dr. Geiger then presented Judas with official credentials including his color portrait in a very prestigious and expensive embossed leather and $30,000 in cash advanced as reward money for taking down such an important score.

"Welcome to the brotherhood, Judas," said Rueben as he embraced him, and the others likewise warmly welcomed Judas before departing from Dr. Geiger's residence.

Jesus arrived at Navy Pier about a five-thirty and walked the length of the huge concrete mass slowly reminiscing nearly three full years of teaching, counseling and individually modeling the very essence of the Father before the eyes of his followers. He realized that the time was approaching and all that the law and prophets predicted or foreshadowed would soon find its fulfillment in his personal suffering and ultimate death as Adam's representative substitute in their stead. Jesus had already made up his mind how he would spend the remaining months based upon his prayer communion and intimate relationship with the Father. Tonight he would tell his faithful followers something of what the future holds and how to live discerning lives and not be led astray by the many false christs that were sure to arise in the generations to come.

Dunnewald and Stevens carpooled down with several other volunteers from Quest and were joined out front of Navy Pier by Siva, Patty and Maggie who had been working with crews most of the afternoon assembling box lunches for everyone to enjoy along the lakeside as Jesus spoke. Jesus was touched by their servant's hearts and stirred inside when he considered his fold and remembered a shortcut that was presented to him sometime ago on top of the Sears Tower that stood in the background. 'Yes,' Jesus thought to himself, 'he will see his kids, he will stretch out his days, and the good favor of the Lord will grow in his hand.'

"Hello, Jesus, great to see you again," said Dunnewald.

"Great to see you too! So how is the family, was Rachel able to make it?" asked Jesus.

"Oh sure, she's back there in the crowd catching up with friends, she'll be along. So, how can I help out; do you need this crowd moved from point 'A' to point 'B'? I can grab Peter, he doesn't need a megaphone."

"No, I think we're all set," said Jesus. "I intend to speak for a few minutes from right here after everyone has had time to find their place."

"O.K.," said Dunnewald, "but let me know if you need anything, I'll be right here on the side."

Jesus kept a clear record tucked away in the back of his mind of previous instruction given to audiences and like a good professor he wanted to fill out the curriculum for this crowd by telling them about future events that would follow sometime after his departure. Hundreds of people sat down on blankets or jackets spread over the cool concrete and Jesus began relating, "In the days ahead you are going to deeply desire a day like this with me in your midst teaching you of the kingdom of God, but you will not see it happen. Be on your guard because false Christs will arise and lead many astray saying, 'here he is or look there!' Don't follow them because when the Son of Man returns it will be apparent to everyone—just like when the lighting flashes from one end of the sky to the other. But before any of this happens he will first suffer and be rejected by the present population."

"What kind of sign will precede your return? What should we look for?" asked a man standing nearby.

"An ark is under construction," said Jesus, "but just like the days of Noah, people will go right on with their lives and mark the usual passages of marriage and the like until the moment the door shuts and the rains begin to fall. Or again, it will be like the days of Lot, folks were conducting their usual business, commerce was flowing briskly until the angels escorted Lot from the city, then fire fell from heaven and devastated the place. Things will be very much the same when the Son of Man is revealed from heaven. Listen, when the revelation is made, don't worry about packing a suitcase or running back in doors to turn off the stove—remember Lot's wife. Whoever pursues the preservation of their life will loose it and whoever forfeits their life for my sake will stay alive. On the night I'm describing, pairs of people will be caught up doing similar things, but one will be taken while another is left, whether asleep or working 2nd shift."

Someone in the crowd answered and said, "Where at sir?" And Jesus responded by asking, "don't friends hit their favorite diner?" Folks were already picking through their lunches when Jesus fielded another question about what to do in the meantime.

"Should we pursue business as usual as we await your return or move to Utah and sit on our hands?" someone asked.

"Be faithful and above all else remain in prayer and don't grow discouraged. Let me tell you a story to illustrate God's kindness and keen sense of hearing." Jesus began, "Imagine a jurisdiction over which a dishonest judge presides. The judge I'm describing isn't worthy of the title for he doesn't fear God which leaves him pretty much at a loss for dispensing justice. Neither does he fear man which creates a certain high headedness and disregard for anyone to whom he might have to answer. In this city lived a widow who pestered him with letters and phone calls seeking legal protection from someone wishing to evict her from the family farm. For a long time the judge was unwilling to give her a hearing since he didn't fear God or man, but it occurred to him late one evening after another long conversation with the woman that she would soon wear him out if he didn't comply. For this reason alone the judge said to himself, 'I will satisfy her wishes.' Ponder what the unrighteous judge said. By contrast don't you think God will bring about justice for his select people who cry to him day and night? Do you think he will sit on his hands and make a mockery of justice! No way, in fact, he will move swiftly and will be sure to render judgment for them. But let me ask you a question, those of you sincerely interested about how to occupy yourselves; when the Son of Man comes, will he find any abandoned-control trust on the planet?"

Night had already fallen upon the city and the air was a little cool on the lake front, but Jesus looked at his watch and the hungry faces before him and decided to shift gears and move into another short discourse before dismissing the crowds. The strict religious legalists who often hounded Jesus and his followers were driven by a sense of self righteousness that resulted in a very definite sense of disdain for others. This same religious arrogance sometimes showed up in seed form among Jesus' close followers; and because of the mixed audience, Jesus began a new story by describing a man who trusted in his own righteousness and beheld others with contempt.

"Two men approached the wall to pray. One was a social outcast and the other was a strict religious legalist. Listen into their private prayers:

The strict religious legalist prayed to himself, 'God, I thank you that I'm not like all the others: a crook, sex addict, someone without a sense of justice, or even like this social outcast standing behind me.' The strict religious legalist drew in a deep breath, sighed, then concluded by reminding God that he fasted two times a week and tithed from everything he received. The social outcast on the other hand who was unwilling to put his face to the wall, lifted his eyes to heaven and while beating his chest as an expression of repentance offered words commensurate with his outward action, 'God, be merciful to me, I'm the sinner!' I tell you in the most solemn terms, this man went away from the wall justified rather than the strict religious legalist because everyone who raises themselves up will be thrown down and whoever throws themselves down will be raised up and honored.

"Look, it's already late and many of you will be pasting on cosmetics as you roll down the Kennedy tomorrow bright and early," and he winked at his friend Barb. "Let's be dismissed with a word of thanks to God. Father, thank you that we have confidence to pray and that you always hear our cries for help. We are comforted to realize that you are not a capricious God whose opinions of us change with the wind, rather your lovingkindness is constant and without change. Forgive some here who have had slight regard for you this day or an ungrateful attitude. Strengthen the weak and encourage those who live with doubts about your goodness, provide for our daily needs just as you have promised, amen."

Jesus was one of the last to leave the massive concrete pavilion and was surrounded by friends who just wanted to be near him. Up ahead a blind man had ventured near the pier and was trying to get a straight answer from those walking by about all the confusion, for the man was dependent upon sounds and he could tell that a large audience was passing before him not unlike the crowds that used to throw him coins as he begged outside Soldier Field.

"What's all the commotion about?" Lasher asked. Someone told him that Jesus, the one who worked signs and wonders would be passing by in front of him in a moment. Lasher took pause and considered deeply in his heart what this once in a lifetime opportunity might mean for he had heard about this Jesus and his extraordinary powers.

Lasher couldn't control his excitement and the thought that he might never be this close to Jesus again in his life—it was now or never and maybe a once in a lifetime opportunity—made him begin shouting, "Jesus, Son of David have compassion for me, Jesus, Son of David, won't you stop for me." But the crowds were sternly warning him to shut up and not bother Jesus for it was late; but he cried out with all the more volume, loosing his balance, falling and then screaming again—"Jesus, son of David, have mercy on me!" Jesus stopped the procession and told those in the crowd to bring him over. And although Chicago is a large city, Lasher was recognized by many as a legitimate blind beggar who frequented ball parks and the pier for enough money to get a few extras in life—maybe an occasional pair of new shoes.

When Lasher was brought near, Jesus asked him, "What do you want me to do?"

Without hesitation he said, "Sir, I want to be able to see!"

Jesus paused momentarily and considered the gift and accountability sight would bring once restored, then rewarded his fierce seeking with the words, "Receive your sight; your abandoned-control trust has healed you." Lasher's eyes were immediately opened and he began crying aloud and running about examining colorful garments under the pier lights and seeing stars he had only previously heard about. He refused to blink. He thanked Jesus profusely and lay at his feet until he was physically wrested from his ankles but permitted to follow him. Everyone on hand began glorifying God for his generosity, awesome power and supreme mercy.

"Matthew, I don't know about you but I'm pooped." said Peter as the crowd began to disperse, "These late nights and growing crowds make me feel like it's about time for another mini breakaway to the lake. What do you say, we snatch Jesus up the first thing in the morning and head out somewhere in the sloop?"

"I've already told you Peter," chattered Matthew while extending both arms with palms ninety degrees to the deck, "you're not about to get me out on the water again—ever, and especially if Jesus is coming along! And that's that! Don't be kidding around about stuff like that—I still have nightmares."

"O.K., O.K. big guy," Peter laughed and slapping him on the back, "No more boating with Jesus. See you tomorrow Matthew." While walking away, Peter turned and concluded, "On the pavement and no waves!"

* * * *

The Jewish Feast of Booths was approaching and as was Jesus habit, he retreated with the twelve and observed the feast with friends outside the city. Winter months were devoted to intense upper level training for the core group; and while Jesus' movements were carefully monitored by his enemies, they chose not to harass him but were content to wait out the calendar until the upcoming Passover.

Chapter 18

It was late March when Jesus emerged from a beach residence in north Glencoe. Signs still lingered of the new millennial celebration and could be seen in the form of loose ribbons, confetti and spiral papier-mâché that survived clean-up and had not yet deteriorated back into the soil. Bradford pears were some of the first to evidence buds and they lined the boulevard Jesus was presently strolling along with his followers. Up ahead a crowd had already assembled and were waiting to just get a close up glimpse of Jesus as he made his way over to the beautiful architecturally designed Temple of North Shore Congregation Israel. As Jesus and his followers neared the crowd, a conspicuous form of a man could be seen saddled upon the street sign marking Sycamore which was subsequently abandoned by the local street department. The small man lifted himself up from the hood of a nearby car and climbed the remaining height to the top of the pole. Clinging to the sign with one hand and a camera in the other, the little man strained to see, Jesus.

"What do you think Jesus," asked James as they approached, "have your ratings with the Mayor just reached a new high, and has he sent out photographers to obtain a keepsake of his beloved rival?"

"No," said Jesus, "that's not one of Harry's underlings; this guy's clothed and appears to be sober." Jesus had to stop the procession at the front end of the crowd because they had the entire sidewalk and a portion of the street blocked off like a winter herd of cattle waiting for someone to break the bales.

Before Jesus could ask the man on top of the sign to identify himself, Matthew burst into laughter and shouted, "Zack! I don't believe it—Zack is that you?" Matthew had not seen his mentor in many years, but there was no question in his mind that the man clinging to the sign was none other than Zack who was widely know by the nickname—'Zack-the-Bat,' which had been shortened over the years from, 'Zack, the financial acrobat.' Zack's C.P.A. firm would make Matthew's previous operation an IRS example to the world. He was an absolute wizard in the area of electronic theft and was also conferred magna cum laude degrees by his associates in the disciplines of money laundering, rigging audits, stacking books, rolling pensions, and shaping the lucrative financial careers of dozens who rewarded him handsomely. Zack may have been a man of small stature, that's why he was above the crowd on this important day; but he stood on a pile of gold that placed him head and shoulders above even many of his wealthiest clients. Zack's reputation grew like fire, after he rescued a well known pharmaceutical company that was under scrutiny from the IRS and owing the Federal Government over eighty million dollars in back taxes and penalties. This exposure led to another investigation by outside labor attorneys who uncovered the mismanagement of the employees' retirement fund which was also showing a multi-million dollar deficit in payments. Zack-the-Bat was regularly featured in both Chicago newspapers and miraculously saved the floundering vessel from nearly capsizing by a number of ingenious financial maneuvers that spared the company bankruptcy, satisfied the IRS and tidied up a retirement account that previous investigators only thought was corrupted. Auditors over at one of the local Big Six still scratch their heads and believe they were misled, but Zack made the numbers jive and when the papers changed their story venue, the company's problems slowly went away as though there was never any story there in the first place.

"Zack," Jesus shouted, "get down from that sign. I'm inviting myself to your house for a bite to eat." Zack slung the camera strap over his head, swung away from the crowd and jumped to the ground. Upon gaining his balance, he shook Jesus' hand and led him on foot over to his home which was less than a quarter of a mile away. The crowds were disturbed that 'The Bat' swept Jesus from their company for they had already prepared a wonderful reception inside the synagogue and were anxious to hear from the famous young rabbi that had stirred their city. Jesus was aware of the crowd's intentions and generally found the Q & A time spent with their kind about as interesting as washing dishes; and so upon finding one of sincere interest dangling from a sign, he broke the engagement and joined Zack at his place in order to follow-up an investment God had apparently opened up to the man. The crowd began to hurl abusive speech at Jesus when he turned on the sidewalk and chose a new bearing.

"Go ahead, Jesus," they all shouted, "you must be just like him—that's all you've known—to dine with sinners and riffraff." Thomas, feeling a little over zealous with his new freedom, sort of "mooned" the crowd, not quite, and had to be verbally reeled in by Jesus who made it plain that his followers were not to return evil for evil but rather overcome evil with good. Others of Jesus' followers waited until his head turned and then slapped Thomas on the back and congratulated him for the timely display. With the exception of one or two, all of Jesus followers were in their mid to late twenties and had plenty to learn about growing up and taking on the important responsibilities that would soon be placed in their laps.

While on their way over, Zack took Jesus' arm and spoke to him with the same humility and brokenness that so many in the past had demonstrated before him during times of moral crisis. Zack was just one more sinner at the end of his rope and looking for mercy.

"Lord," Zack began, "I want to give half of everything I own to the poor; and to everyone that I've personally defrauded, I will pay back four times as much!"

Jesus stopped on the walkway of Zack's lawn and said, "Do you see this house? Eternal life has come to this place, for Zack is also a son of Abraham." Matthew was a big teddy bear on the inside and was overcome with emotion and began weeping with joy over the outward display of Zack's repentance. He could identify with a man who had given his life to get rich only to be suffocated with the responsibilities of managing the horde and staying another step ahead of the hounds. Matthew had laid all that down and now his life mentor was also making a dramatic turn in his life orientation, and it created an overflow of joy that couldn't be contained. Hasidic Jews from another area were on hand this day and flanking Jesus step for step when he stopped and asked them, "Do you men want a short and concise statement of my mission—here it is: 'The Son of Man has come to apprehend and rescue people who are wandering around lost.'"

"Yes," said one leading the opposition, "and you all appear to be lost! The crook you're dining with should be imprisoned."

"I tell you the truth," said Jesus, "he has been released from his chains. Now, there is one other thing I want you scoffers to note carefully; and if you've got a pen and pad write this down—be dumbfounded and waste away, for I'm doing something right before your eyes that you will never believe even though someone should take you aside and draw you a picture."

Once inside his mansion, Zack directed his two lifetime chefs to assist him with a spread that would feed a platoon. He then got on the phone and invited several of his friends to join him; and of the dozen or so invitees, seven others dropped in for a private reception in honor of Jesus and his followers. Zack was literally panting from all the activity and so pumped with emotion that when Peter remarked about the lovely engraved walnut mantle above the fire place, Zack ran to storage, retrieved a pry bar, pulled it from the wall and threw it into the hearth along with a rosebud antique chair to kindle all that he intended to burn before their eyes. Peter and John nearly dove from their seats to clear an area where Zack was furiously dismantling fine furniture and placing carved limbs over lit gas logs. Jesus was aware that he was beside himself and stepped up as he was going for another decorative stacked table set imported from China, embraced him around the waist and held Zack as he sobbed uncontrollably with remorse for all his terrible thefts and business mishandlings. None of the twelve thought the outburst strange, for Zack's response was pretty typical of others whether something as dramatic as the Maggies picked up from gravel lots, or the quiet sobs of a John resting on a pillow before going to sleep. When people were touched at the core of their being by God's penetrating compassions, it left the object of his love woefully unraveled. While one lays sprawled out in that condition, God secretly opens his very womb, strange as it all seems, and cuddles the broken hearted in that place with cords of love that are utterly otherworldly, but can be the possession of anyone who earnestly seeks his acceptance. Jesus pried Zack's hands from his body and the two of them faced the fire box, now hurling with flame; he wiped his eyes and invited Jesus to offer a prayer of thanks for the lavish spread of food before insisting that everyone feast heartily.

Jude was at the front of the food line and like everyone else liberally sampling the delicacies and piling his plate high. He made his way between waves of men and found a place near the interior colonnade where he thought Jesus might choose to lecture, which was almost a given. Jude furtively worked the inside of his jacket to ensure that the recording device was ready and on pause, then turned to his meal and enjoyed some conversation with those reentering the room with food. Zack remained single, following a divorce ten years previous, and lived in a home that was large enough to accommodate three or four families comfortably. The great room was wonderfully designed with vaulted ceilings that looked massive with unique depths and coffered cuts of cherry that had darkened considerably with age. After several minutes, others found their seats and Jesus had already consumed his portion before the last person was seated.

Conversations among Jesus' followers with Zack and his friends made the room rumble with a definite hum of baritone, but it quieted to a hush when Jude, with tape in gear, asked, "Lord, will the kingdom of God appear today?" Everyone was greatly anticipating the moment Jesus would disclose the timing of this remarkable event and James tapped Jude's foot with his own and nodded with an expression of appreciation for bringing up the matter. The concept of the kingdom of God or kingdom of heaven, which Jesus seemed to use synonymously and interchangeably, occupied the bulk of his teaching; and everyone had the sense that he would at anytime reveal the exact moment it would be put in full force. Peter, James and John had been talking with one another as early as yesterday about their Lord's intention to go back to the city proper and they could only conclude that the kingdom was at hand. All of the men were excited to be a part of this unusual calling and couldn't wait to see the faces of Romish American Bulls when their pseudo-democratic model of tyranny toppled and was driven under foot of the everlasting reign of God's coming kingdom. Jesus' followers had a difficult time piecing together the important and multifaceted aspects of God's kingdom even though Jesus spent far and away much more time teaching on this subject than any other. He had taught them previously that the kingdom of God was here but not in it's full form, that it would soon be inaugurated, but not entirely consummated, that it worked like leaven, while bringing noticeable change, that it could be entered now as well as later and that it was in their midst as well as something more concrete to be experienced at a later time. In spite of all the nuance, or perhaps because of it, the followers of Jesus were left in a bit of a blur about the whole picture and would have to revisit his teachings and compare them with the prophets before finally catching the 'aha!'

Jesus pulled a chair from the side of the room and stationed it beneath an arch where he could be seen by everyone. At that moment, Jude settled into a new position and Jesus began a story that was applicable to the guests Zack invited as well as anyone else who wished to make wise kingdom investments with their time, talents and treasures. Jesus summarily described this important interim of time with the phrase, 'now and not yet.'

"A certain politician who happened to be a man of terrific honor was invited to Washington and elevated to a special appointment and commissioned to an advisory board that had tremendous and far reaching authority. Before he left his home town, he put his private business in order and assigned ten of his choice employees to manage his corporate assets while he was away. He gave them power of attorney and their signatures were accepted at each of the financial institutions where he did business. Each of the ten were given resources of equal value and directed to conduct business until he returned, at which time he would settle accounts with them." Zack and his guests busily worked on plates of food and drank freely of the wine but stayed tuned to the nomenclature of a message that was familiar enough for them to finish Jesus' sentences. Jesus continued, "No sooner had the man left for Washington than the citizens of that community sent a delegation after him, who petitioned outside the Whitehouse, urging the President not to authorize this man, 'We don't want this guy representing us,' they said. The appointment was made in spite of their pleas and a couple of years later, the gentleman returned to his home and caught up with those who cared for his business. One by one he called them into his office. The first woman laid a spread sheet before him and said, 'sir, the hundred thousand dollars you entrusted to me is still on deposit; and if you will examine this column, you will note that sales I've brokered have earned you an additional hundred thousand.'

'Great job, Jane,' said her employer, 'and because you've been faithful in a very small thing, I'm placing you in charge of accounts in ten cities.' As soon as she left, Herb came out of the waiting room and proudly displayed his portfolio which showed that he had a 50% growth on investments he made in his employer's absence.

"Great job, Herb,' congratulated his boss, 'you've been faithful in a small thing and now I'm giving you the oversight of five more accounts!' Next, Mort was invited in, but his countenance wasn't very bright and his employer could tell that he was steaming about something. In a moment he lifted one hundred-thousand dollars cash from an envelope tucked inside his shirt and laid it on the desk before his employer and said, 'Here is your money that you left with me—you can count it—it's all there. You see I've kept it all tucked away since the day you handed it to me because I was afraid of your methods. Others may be ignorant, but I know that you've accumulated wealth by ripping people off, skimming accounts and turning over investments based upon inside trade.' His employer raised from his seat, pushed the intercom for security and said to the worthless employee, 'I'm going to air you out and size you up by your own words. So you knew all this trash talk about me; then why didn't you at least put my money in the bank and let it accumulate interest?' Then he told those who had arrived in attendance to gather the hundred thousand and give it to Jane who doubled his money while away. And those who heard it said, 'but sir, she already has huge assets!'

'That's right,' the boss said, 'and to everyone who has made a return—more be given, but to the one who doesn't have, even what he thinks he has will be snatched from him. And now those wicked citizens who didn't want me to represent them, round them up and arraign them in my presence."

Jesus was silently praying the way he did after concluding every message, imploring God to open deaf ears to insights that could only be granted by him. Although there were plenty of question marks on the faces of some, several others appeared to be piecing together a message that described a spiritual kingdom; though it was as real as anything could possibly be; it would nevertheless, one day become even more tangible, in certain respects when abandoned-control trust gives way to sight. In the meantime, there appeared to be work to do that would require the wise stewardship of the talents God has given to each individual. Matthew who was assisting Zack with refills spoke to the others present during a short lull and invited them back for more food. Some got up from their seats for food while others approached Jesus with follow-up questions to his message or other issues that were important to them. Jude stood in a circle of six around Jesus and took pride in asking what some of Zack's friends perceived to be some very insightful questions about the nature of the kingdom of God. Everything was brand new to them and of great interest; however, they didn't realize that he was baiting Jesus with lead questions and seeking to catch him in a blatant admission that he himself was seeking high political office.

"So, Jesus," Jude asked with syrupy sincerity, "when this kingdom comes, if it ever does, will you run things differently than past presidents or Monarchs?"

"Jude," Jesus answered his question with a question in a sincere effort to redirect his soul but to also admonish him without embarrassing him unduly before the others. "Why do you think the nations are presently in such an uproar and devising vain plans? Yes, Jude, the kingdom is coming just as I have promised; and though they threaten to kill me, they will be aghast when my wrath is revealed. The rulers need to take heed and worship the Lord with reverence and do homage to the son, for his wrath may soon be ignited, but specially regarded indeed are all those who seek safe harbor in me."

"So you freely admit to what the Jewish leaders have alleged—you yourself are God's one and only unique son, therefore, making yourself equal with God?" asked Jude, for he was on hand nearly a year previous when some of the strict religious legalist who take genealogy most seriously, took up bottles and bats to kill him for making a similar confession.

"Gentlemen," Jesus said, addressing Jude and all of those standing before him, "Hear the scripture, 'The Lord is at your right hand and he will make sample ballistics of presidents and rulers on the day of his wrath. He will render judgment among the nations, line them with dead bodies and the leading men over an entire country will suffer concussions. He will drink from the stream along the way and be refreshed.'" Jude was absolutely pumped inside at Jesus' words and was smiling from ear to ear to have heard right from Jesus' own mouth some of the most specific predictions of revolution ever uttered by him. Jude was more confused than ever about who to trust and follow. Jesus appeared to have the real power and authority; but if Dr. Geiger's assessment was correct, then it was all just talk and Jesus would soon be pushed aside. Jude withheld the recording from Geiger for the time being even though he was later questioned specifically about what transpired in Zack's home on that date. Jude had played two hands before; and although Dr. Geiger was a man to be careful with, he felt that some time could be bought as he waited just a little longer to see if the kingdom Jesus spoke about would soon manifest itself from heaven and rule the world just as the prophet Daniel had predicted.

It was nearly 2:00 P.M. when Jesus excused himself, having asked Zack earlier if he could grab a nap before it got too late. Jesus seldom gave himself over five or six hours of sleep, but lately he had been averaging far less and so an afternoon cat nap on a bus in transit or catching a few 'Z's' sitting on a park bench was not uncommon. Jesus' followers didn't know where he slipped off to and Zack was asked to keep the confidence; so one by one, all of Zack's guests departed and he himself collapsed in an easy chair before coals that were still warm from an earlier blaze. The grandfather clock tolled 8:00 P.M. and although Zack was seldom conscious of the sound, it ordered him from his nap and he was shocked to realize what time it was. All the emotional exertion sapped him of something or else relaxed something inside that had been wound tighter than that time piece when weights were up, and for many years. Zack got up from his chair and walked upstairs to the east wing where he found a bedroom door wide open and Jesus still sleeping soundly.

"Jesus," Zack said as he nudged his body, "Jesus, it's well past the time you asked me to raise you." Jesus began to stir and opened his eyes to see a man who had only hours before been medivacted from a blazing inferno where he ostensibly died and was brought back to life by the word of Jesus.

"Thanks, Zack," Jesus said, "that's got to be the best nap I've had in months. What is this a feather mattress?"

"Yes, indeed it is sir and from now on it's your feather mattress—anytime!"

Zack drew an entry key from his wallet and offered it to Jesus, who kindly declined and remarked, "I'll be leaving soon Zack. I appreciate your generosity; maybe you will offer shelter to others who need a man like you in their lives."

"I'll keep my eyes and ears open for that opportunity," he promised Jesus.

"Zack," Jesus said, still groggy from the deep sleep, I had the most wonderful dream as I lay here in your house," then broke into laughter.

"Well, tell me Jesus, what did you dream?"

"Well, I'm sure it had something to do with the way you were tearing into the furniture earlier," and now they were both laughing real hard.

"So how about the dream; what was it about?"

"There was a wonderful and gorgeous woman in this dream." Jesus sat back against the headboard and pulled his knees under his chin and continued. "She was running along a soft sand dune with a crystal of dark red wine in her hand and fresh cut roses in another. She had the charm of an older woman but the behavior and giddiness of a much younger girl." Jesus smiled as he remembered the face and said, "There were soft love songs flowing out the window of a beach house and it must have been the west coast because the sun was setting on the ocean behind her."

"Was she alone, Sir?" asked Zack.

"No Zack," Jesus said, and he seemed to be reliving an experience that ran very deep because mist formed in his eyes, "she was being pursued by a prince on a swift and muscular steed. He overtook her at the crest of the dune and with his great arm, swung her to his lap and the two embraced in a kiss that was absolutely glorious—just the way it was meant to be."

"Wow, Jesus, I mean I haven't seen, heard or felt anything like that in years. Is there more?"

"Yes," Jesus said, "they folded into a hammock on the ocean side and that's when I remember hearing you call my name."

"Awwh," said Zack, "I love happy endings. So, did you know her name?"

"Yes, Zack, her name is Lucy and I'm sorry to inform you that she's happily married."

"Hey, what is this," Zack said crashing Jesus' head with a pillow, "you're just trying to rile me up. Well, let me tell you something, I was quite the ladies man in my day, back before all this money started coming to me."

"You mean your money mistress," Jesus said, returning the feathers. The two men nearly broke the bed down as they jumped from floor to corners and over end furniture in a hilarious battle of pillows which Jesus lost hands down.

"C'mon, Jesus," Zack said, offering him a hand, we've got a whole mess of leftovers to attack after expending all this energy!"

Jesus left Zack's place about 10:00 P.M. and walked the Lakeshore south throughout the night in prayer. Passover was just weeks away and Jesus could feel the coalescing of all history wrapping its cords around his person and drawing him to a destination that he himself was mysteriously orchestrating. The Chicago side of the lake was not particularly clean except for the man-made beaches, and the smell of marine life was not exactly faint. Lights peppered the near north shore-line and muffled horns from distant ocean going vessels could be heard in the distance. Jesus' face when lifted toward the water shown in the light cast by the moon like a beam from a lighthouse making its revolutions. Many great men and women had preceded Jesus and many more would follow. Jesus mused upon the vessels and human lives—pilots adrift upon the waves of relativism in which any nautical navigation was acceptable while the map of the heavens and properly calibrated compass were discarded.

"How many will reef or remain lost in uncharted waters?" Jesus whispered to himself. To all of those who felt themselves adrift or presently shipwrecked, he had previously urged, "come to me if you are weighted down with burdens and I will give you the fair haven you seek. Stroke with me—our ores in hand, for I am a gentle skipper and you will find safe harbors for your souls, for my pace is easy and my duties light."

It was the middle of the night as Jesus walked the base of a bluff and the water's edge, when someone above who had been following him and wearing a mask shouted down, "let the fool pay," and then laughed hysterically. Geiger had never been drunk in his life, but a late night drink at his home after completing some work associated with files to be delivered to the F.B.I., left him in the mood for another which led to others and before he knew it he was thoroughly intoxicated and feeling mean. Geiger didn't want to confront Jesus personally; but he did enjoy taunting him; and since the day of reckoning was just around the corner, he thought to have some personal fun before the authorities put him away, never to be seen again.

"So, Jesus, you heard from Jack lately? Any letters out of Seagoville? They tell me he lost his head at a party one night. Hey, Jesus, I mean I think he might have really lost his head," yelled Geiger who was laughing sarcastically. "He was a good ole boy and will be sorely missed, don't you agree? By the way, authorities have been out snooping around Prophetstown and the salvage yard, and I don't think they like the picture they're piecing together. I mean the way Mr. Madden tells it, you were pretty fast and furious about the way you swept away evidence of little Jack's cottage, and the stuff found on board your Chevy is convincing enough to persuade your own mother that you pushed the button. What did you think, Jesus, that you'd just waltz into the city and dazzle a few uneducated half-wits with your slight of hand and take over the world?" The far fetched phantasm mixed with Geiger's own rage and he began yelping violently until he lost his footage and slid down the slope of the cliff and tumbled to the pea gravel below. Jesus climbed the bank and was nearly half way up when Geiger passed him on the way down. Jesus walked south along Sheridan Road near Winnetka while Geiger spent the better part of the early morning trying to find his way up a steep bank and back to his car. The little man had lost a slipper worth more than eight hundred dollars and the expensive wool European suit he was wearing was so frayed by the end of his ordeal with the cliff that it too had to be discarded for rags.

* * * *

Jesus was no longer walking about publicly because of the many serious threats being made by the Jews to kill him. One week before Passover, Geiger convened a special meeting with leading Jews, who were infuriated with Jesus and felt that he would eventually jeopardize their good standing with the American government and its citizenry should he continue his self proclaimed political advances as they understood him. They were equally incensed that the whole world was going after him and so they were conspiring to have him put to death. Geiger had the entire Chicago theater staged for the most dramatic act in its history and was methodically tying up loose ends with all the necessary liaison so that his goals could be achieved without mistakes. Caiaphas who was a Jewish high priest after a pre-exilic order that had been largely corrupted through twisted political bouts during the reign of a distant Hasmonean family was present at the meeting with Geiger and spoke prophetically, though unwittingly of Jesus' imminent death. He gained their attention during a debate over Jesus' influence and said, "It is for our benefit that one man should die for the people so that our nation not be swallowed up. Now let's tend to the business at hand and lay out the specific plan of attack. Dr. Geiger, you obviously have invested the most time and energy and we are all indebted to you for your tireless efforts; lead us in a discussion of the brief you shared with me earlier for none of the men present have any idea of the complexity of this 'Jesus plot' to destroy Judaism.

"Thank you, Caiaphas," said Geiger in a most solemn and professional manner. Gentlemen, I earlier had the distasteful, but shall I say, patriotic privilege to lay before Caiaphas and his select counsel some of the most sordid and cunning trails of an apparent psycho-path that has ever stepped onto God's holy soil. I am happy to report further that he has also graciously given him into our hands. This imposter who has been parading about our city for the last three-and-a-half years, born right here in the suburbs, is nothing more than a mortal man," Geiger dipped his chin in a gesture of humility for some of the men present regarded him as the messiah who would shortly reveal himself. Then rolling his expensive fountain pen between fingers of both hands continued, "But because he is a master of deception, he has succeeded in drawing away a large portion of the populace. Gentlemen, as those God will hold accountable to guard his sacred possession, our blessed heritage and nation, we will not be found milling around in a cowardly reactive posture while this...," Geiger lost emotional control and began raving and he could feel the foam forming again in his mouth. Several seconds passed before he gained control and moved on with his speech, addressed to those sitting with him at the table. Everyone felt utterly humiliated when they compared their feeble efforts to dissuade Jesus' followers with the long and arduous labors of Dr. Geiger who pursued his enemy like it was his chief employment. Geiger drew a handkerchief from his pocket, turned from the men and cleared his throat before continuing with his disclosures. "Gentlemen," Geiger tried to restart, but applause rose around him and everyone but Caiaphas bowed and genuflected in oblations of what could only be described as some form of worship. Geiger motioned with his hands and everyone returned to their seats. "I am only doing that which would be expected. As I said, we are under obligation to rid ourselves of this thing and our zeal for the Law will compel us!"

"Yes, Lord Geiger!" said Jude who sat nearby in the closed and highly confidential meeting.

Geiger took the opportunity to single Jude out for everyone's inspection and was pleased to notice the glee that grew in his eyes when he related, "Judas is key to the success of this entire plan. When I give Judas the signal Thursday night of Passover, he will lead the National Guard right to his den." Geiger pointed on a map to Belmont Harbor where Jesus spent a great deal of private time especially at night, "and there he will be brought before a crowd angry enough to…" Geiger was recounting steps he had memorized, digested, slept with and played back repeatedly in his mind and caught himself before revealing his ultimate intention, "what I mean to say, is that some of our leading citizens will want to examine him personally. This will, of course, be handled in a careful clandestine manner before handing him over to the authorities for proper judicial procedure." He would never reveal it to anyone, but Geiger knew the exact moment when tempers would flare, restraints snap and every learned civility would be cast aside in favor of unleashing pent up fury that would render Jesus isolated and prepared for execution in the streets.

Following Dr. Geiger's briefing, everyone flowed out of the basement beneath the Federal Building on Adams and back to their respective posts. Geiger had a great deal of work ahead of him and was facing a week of intense pressure that would push both his mental tenacity and physical stamina to their limits.

Late Saturday afternoon, Jesus boarded transit in Winnetka and made his way down to Cicero where he stayed with Lazarus, Mary and Martha who had moved from their previous address in Wheeling. The last time Jesus saw his friends was on the occasion when he raised Lazarus from the dead. The fact of the miracle was not disputed by Jesus' enemies, but they had intentions of killing Lazarus because many Jews were becoming believers on account of his experience and they wanted to put a stop to the flow. Lazarus was thrown from a horse several months ago and the fall broke his neck and he was instantly killed. Jesus was not in the vicinity, but news was sent to him while Lazarus' sisters permitted him to lie in state an extra day before finally placing him in an above ground crypt at the mausoleum. Jesus finally arrived four days after the death and sought to comfort Mary and Martha who were emotionally devastated. He vividly remembered his conversation with Martha on the front lawn as she sobbed uncontrollably and insisted that her brother would not have died had Jesus been with them. Jesus smiled again as he remembered her abandoned-control trust, 'even now I know God will grant whatever you ask.' It was in response to her words that Jesus assured her that her brother would rise again, but Martha thought Jesus was referring to the general resurrection he often taught about. Before entering her house on this day, he repeated the words he offered to her just before raising Lazarus up, "I am the lift and the life; the one who believes in me will lift up even if he dies, and everyone who lifts up and trusts in me will never suffer decay. Martha, do you believe what I'm telling you?" Martha's simple trust touched Jesus as he recalled her words, 'Yes, Lord, I've already settled on who you are—the Christ, the son of God who comes into the world.'

Jesus knocked on the patio door and Mary nearly flew through the screen before sliding it aside at the sight of him. "Jesus, you're back!" she squealed, "Oh, is it good to see you, hurry, hurry, get in here where we can all see you!" She pulled Jesus into the kitchen where he was met by two more sets of flaying arms looking to embrace his neck.

"Alright!" said Lazarus, "put on some more coffee, Mary." Lazarus hugged Jesus then stepped back with a handshake just to have a closer look at the man he loved.

Jesus let his forefinger rest on Lazarus' wrist and then asked him, "How are you feeling these days my friend?" The gesture was a joke a mortician once played on Jesus when he shook his hand while counting his pulse.

"No, you're getting the coffee," Mary said, and she escorted Jesus into the living room for a visit. Martha dropped a dish towel and turned in quick pursuit.

"Be right there, Jesus," said Lazarus, "I know just how you like your coffee." The morning flew by as the four of them caught up on all the events and stories that they had heard about through the integrated grapevine; and before they all knew it, they were seated around the dinette set for a bite of evening dinner that consisted of fruit tea, breads, raw vegetables and a selection of cheese.

Many of Jesus' close followers arrived throughout the day when they learned where he was staying; and while some of them visited around the table, Mary drew a very expensive bottle of perfume that had never been used from her personals and poured it out on Jesus' feet while wiping them with her long dark hair.

Several from the living room peeked in to see where the rich aroma was emanating when Jude raised up the empty bottle and said, "Good grief, this stuff is costly as all get out, why wasn't it sold and the money distributed to the poor?" Jude had little interest in the poor and was just looking for further monetary donations that he could skim.

Jesus spoke before some of the others who were suspicious of Jude's poor money management and said, "Leave her alone. Now keep it for the day of my burial. The poor are always around and in need if you'd like to help them, but you will not always have me."

The evening closed out with some wonderful singing and clapping that poured into the back yard. The following day many more Jews arrived at the single's residence because they were anxious to see Jesus, as well as Lazarus whom he had raised from the dead. Jesus stood at the porch with Lazarus at his side while he fielded several questions from onlookers. He was aware of another element who had no interest in truth but were on hand to criticize his work and controvert his message. Since the critics were in the minority, Peter strolled about the lawn and whispered threats into their ears, insisting that they move along and take their goons with them. Peter wasn't a hulk by anyone's estimate; but with a day's growth, little sleep and a cigar tucked between his cheek and gum, it made his threats appear fearsome. James walked the perimeter with him like a good Secret Service Agent with the result that the afternoon and evening remained reasonably calm. In fact, it was a bit eerie the way the crowds left that evening, like birds roosting before a storm.

Someone commented, "Gee, this place was bustling just minutes ago; where did they all go?"

"Yeah," said Maggie, "we were driving through Kansas one evening on our bikes when all of a sudden the wind laid down and everything got really quiet, like everything was being sucked into that black funnel that jumped out of the sky. Plenty of noise followed, let me tell you! It sounded like a freight train rolling across that wheat field and she was sure billowing the smoke." No one standing around Jesus knew anything about the tremendous vortex that was presently gathering itself somewhere between the powers of heaven and hell. A horrific week was ahead for some and an altogether glorious one for others, but both sides had it all misinterpreted when their care for hermeneutics was most crucial.

CHAPTER 19

The phone rang at Geiger's residence on the lower level. It was his secure line and only a select number of individuals knew the dialing code and number. "Leonard Geiger," he said, picking up the receiver.

"Good morning, Dr. Geiger, this is the Attorney General's office in Washington please hold for the transfer."

"Dr. Geiger, Max Randolph speaking."

"Good morning, Attorney General," said Geiger.

"My office has continued pouring over files you've forwarded over past months," Randolph began, "and as I related to you last week, we intend to wrap up this investigation in the next 72 hours. I'll have transport on the ground at O'Hare within the hour and would like to invite you to my office as an overnight guest. Actually, this could turn into an extra day—are you able to pull things together and make the trip on this short notice? You know we could extract the information another way, but the work you've already done correlates perfectly with evidence the F.B.I. and A.T.F. have assembled, and we just want to tie up every loose end before we take this public."

"No inconvenience at all," said Geiger, "and I will look forward to our visit."

"Dr. Geiger, we are sending out a limo to your home and arrangements have been made for you to meet with federal agents and myself at thirteen hundred. We'll debrief through late lunch and cover the remaining details tomorrow after my advisors and I have at least a day to sit on this. Everything has been cared for on this end—all deluxe accommodations of course—I'll see you at Camp David as before." Geiger turned from the phone and gathered another file or two before retrieving an overnight clothing bag that contained several articles that always stood ready for immediate flight. Although Geiger seldom traveled, the bag remained ready in any event and was seasonally rearranged with various weights depending upon the climate.

Geiger drew his umbrella from the tall vase in the foyer and placed it along with his personals on the front porch for pick up by the livery. He then stepped back inside and walked over to the Florida room to catch morning feed from CNN while he drank his lukewarm coffee and ate his cold bagel half. Cameramen and reporters on location in Cicero were pretty much standing around in a holding pattern as they waited for Jesus to make his move and lead a procession down Ogden Avenue. Talk on the street revealed that he would be traveling downtown with his followers in some kind of a parade formation and holding a rally near the fountain at Grant Park. Geiger set his bagel aside when a reporter asked one of Jesus' followers if they were pursuing revolutionary ideals that were purposefully being kept from the American public.

Andrew stepped in front of a camera since he was the most comfortable and experienced as a front man and said, "Revolution is not a word we would choose to describe the quiet spiritual awakening that we are spearheading. 'Let Justice Rain Down,' has always been our banner of nonviolence. Our leader has lectured openly since the inception of this special work and I guess we're a little surprised by all the late interest from the press." Andrew stepped away from the mic when he saw Jesus step out the front door of the singles' home. Most of the crowd who arrived had been on hand Sunday and brought others back to see Lazarus as well as the miracle worker who raised him from the dead.

Geiger held his tongue in the privacy of his own home until reporters panned Jesus and began making remarks about the alleged raising of a dead man. At this, Geiger exploded in a hot rage, hurling bitter speech at the television crews as well as those in the electronic frame of the camera. Geiger had important work ahead of him and he clicked the remote and walked to the door just before further footage was offered about Jesus' means of transportation to the Park.

Two of Jesus' followers had been previously directed to bring over a Dodge Colt parked next door in Berwyn, a brand new one that had never been owned was placed there by a Chrysler dealer who was a friend of Jesus.

James and John arrived in Berwyn and found the little pickup just as Jesus said; but as they began to unlock it, a man standing nearby asked, "What is your business with that truck?"

"The Lord sent us over—said he needed it today," replied John. And so he gave them permission. Arriving back with the vehicle, they placed a stool in the bed up against the cab where Jesus was invited to sit. The crowds grew and so did the hysteria as they made their procession down Ogden Avenue. Many believed that the kingdom of God would appear at any moment, not the least anxious was Jude who kept a hand on the front fender and walked along its side.

Others in the crowd began placing their jackets and small tree limbs on the road before the vehicle and singing, "Wonderful and renowned is the King who comes in the name of the Lord; peace in heaven and praise to God!"

An Hasidic Jew jumped up on the side of the bed of the slow moving vehicle and demanded that Jesus rebuke his followers; but before Peter helped him back to the ground, Jesus said, "You have to understand, if these people are silenced, the very pavement will cry out!"

Other Hasidic Jews pulled out of the crowd and said, "Forget it! It's no use, the whole world has gone after him." The procession stopped just below California Avenue when Jesus rapped on the roof of the truck but couldn't speak because he was overcome by tears as he considered the songs of peace among the crowds and gazed at the City. For he was amazed at the Jews' blindness and how hungry they were for any form of new hype. After a moment, he gathered himself emotionally and hollered out to everyone within earshot, "Even at this late hour, had you people only known what makes for peace! But now it has been hidden from your eyes. And because you have not recognized the day of your visitation, your enemies will soon surround you, wall you off and level your communities to the ground. Not one stone will be left standing upon another!"

Jude watched carefully and wondered if Jesus would not at last make a pronouncement that he had been waiting for, but Jesus and his immediate company drove into the City and ended up at Grant Park which was his favorite spot to lecture. The ever present bounty hunters were on the fringe looking for additional evidence to incriminate Jesus, but the crowds were hanging onto his every word.

The Attorney General, Max Randolph, entered a secure conference room at a Camp David compound which was surrounded by armed Marines who were on rotation from TBS, Quantico, Virginia. Dr. Geiger and federal agents rose to their feet when he quickly ordered them to dispense with the formalities while they were together. The Attorney

General singled out Dr. Geiger and offered him wonderful words of praise before his federal associates.

"Dr. Geiger, throughout my tenure in the legislature as well as my present political appointment, I've not yet run across another human being with the specific talents and gifts of investigation that you bring to the task. I speak on behalf of everyone in this room when I say to you that the American people salute you because our national security is owing to your heroic efforts and the superhuman drive with which you've pursued this criminal." Mr. Randolph positioned a tall file in front of him for everyone's consideration and continued, "Only the federal agents sitting at this table with us today after years of experience and rigorous training have been able to duplicate this standard of work."

"That's right, Dr. Geiger," said Special Agent Moore. "If the seat is ever vacated you'd get my vote for Directorship of the Bureau."

The present Director himself offered Dr. Geiger a wry smile and said, "Outstanding work, Dr. Geiger."

"Before we hear Mr. Goodman's report from the A.T.F., let me relate to you what we know at this stage of the investigation as well as what we're prepared to do based upon our findings. First, a word of personal warning. Gentlemen, we are dealing with an individual of incredible psychological prowess; his strengths of charisma and ability to delude the masses ranks right up there with the likes of Jim Jones and other wacko, self-proclaimed, religious fanatics. Don't think for a moment that we've underestimated his personality profile. On the contrary, our experts have given this aspect of the investigation their most careful scrutiny. Their composites are before you for your perusal."

"Max," said Fred Tucker, head of the F.B.I., "we think he might actually be plotting fresh sabotage based upon some recent clandestine meetings our own coverts have monitored as part of our surveillance along the City's lake front."

"We're way ahead of him, Fred, no need to worry, all the goods are here and he's not going anywhere anyway. He is so deluded about his own personal majesty that he can't stay away from all the media and attention. He'll be right there on location when we want him, I assure you. I've directed everyone not to harass the young rabbi in any way, and I've taken a cue or two from Dr. Geiger here since I want to honor the personal interest he has in waiting until their sacred Passover before we reel him in. Dr. Geiger, the timing will actually be perfect based upon how our investigation has proceeded, it's uncanny, almost like someone planned it that way." Leonard scarcely contained a sigh of victory on account of the remark. One of his chief goals had been to carefully manage the timing of Jesus' capture while leaving authorities with the impression that the time table had always been in their hands.

"Since we've arrived at this juncture, allow me to relate that Dr. Geiger himself will pull the string on this trap. Judas, our prime subvert is an extension of Dr. Geiger's hand, and Leonard will give us the nod at the precise time we are to move in and apprehend him."

"Gentlemen," said Dr. Geiger, "it is crucial that the masses be contained. He has deceived thousands and they follow him in rank. His apprehension needs to be handled as discreetly as something of this nature will permit. If I may make a suggestion, in my humble opinion, a deep sense of fear needs to be immediately instilled. His close followers will disperse at the sight of an armed force of our respected National Guard. A well disciplined, crack unit trained in riot control might be just the means to inoculate a possible outbreak. After all, the Veteran's Hospital was one of his targets and the populace will have a more sympathetic feeling if soldiers escort him to custody rather than a police swat team after word is out and the connection drawn. The last thing we need is for the zealots close to him to become violent and begin burning and looting the city—a lot of innocent people could get injured." Geiger had never stopped managing his own plans for Jesus' execution—not for an instant. The moment Jesus' arrest makes news, he will already be counting on hundreds of angry survivors and families of victims to surface, people he would previously alert by guise who would agitate the military and crowds until justice stumbled in the street and pent up emotions and tempers tripped mayhem at the moment Geiger pulls the cord.

"That's a brilliant observation, Dr. Geiger. I'll bring that before my advisors," said Max. "My suspicion is that they will find it a wise line of operation. A small unit just to back up and show some presence. Yes indeed, Dr. Geiger, with fixed bayonets even the most zealous won't be crossing any boundaries."

"Mr. Randolph, I happen to know the local Commander personally," said ATF Director Goodman. "I'd be happy to coordinate your wishes and carry classified messages back to him."

"Excellent," Max said, "my advisors will follow-up with you after we conclude tomorrow's meeting."

"But returning now to my earlier remarks, this Jesus has a very definite political agenda and has been pushing it rather aggressively since the day he appeared on location. Besides this, he has an apparent ability to create delusional apparitions that have drugged the masses. These signs and wonders as they have been variously described have been his chief means of recruitment and self promotion. His followers believe that they attest or authenticate the fact that he is deity in human flesh." Geiger began to excuse himself from the room, for the very suggestion that this young rabbi was one with God most high sent him into a downward spiral of rage that was genuinely felt both emotionally and in his physical being. Fred Tucker, who had perhaps the greatest admiration for Dr. Geiger stepped aside to assist him for he had not made it out of the room and fallen to one knee, gagging into a handkerchief.

"Dr. Geiger, can I assist you?" asked Fred. "Dr. Geiger," but he still could not talk and Fred could tell that the lengthy investigative process had taken a toll on the Doctor's physical and emotional health. After a moment longer, Dr. Geiger rose to his feet as though nothing had happened and apologized for the interruption of a most important meeting. Everyone interpreted the mild convulsion in the same way and so there were no further words offered that might embarrass the kind doctor. He repositioned himself in his chair with his face still red with blood flow but was able to refocus his thoughts when the Attorney General mentioned his name.

"According to Dr. Geiger, the young rabbi feigns involvement in orthodox religious practices with mocking pretense and will be celebrating the annual Jewish Passover with his followers this Thursday evening at a location not yet disclosed.

"Let me remind you that we have surveillance all over this," said Mr. Tucker while rubbing Dr. Geiger's shoulder.

The Attorney General nodded approvingly and continued. "In fact Dr. Geiger has already related to me that Judas will single him out for the soldier's identification immediately after the meal. This will most likely be carried out at his lair near Belmont when he returns there with the others, but we're watching the area of Humboldt Park as well," as he indicated locations on a Chicago city map with an electronic hand laser. "Dr. Geiger, for the benefit of the uninitiated," said Max smiling, "maybe you could take a moment to cue us into the meaning and purpose of Passover. We might be better advised in terms of knowing what to expect, especially if a communal meal like this should trigger other militant acts."

"Well, of course, gentlemen," said Dr. Geiger who hadn't fully recovered. "As you know, many of the more noted acts of God have already been put into motion pictures—stories that are well attested both archaeologically and historically. The God we serve," Geiger stopped momentarily to bless his name as part of a rabbinic ritual that he had learned as part of his training, "is the everlasting God and it is true that he will one day send the Messiah just as his servant Moses predicted. But when he comes, there will be no question about his origins," Geiger said sarcastically, for many Hasidic and Orthodox Jews often made jokes about the fact that Jesus had been born a bastard and really never had a father, "nor any mystery about his agenda. As far as this man goes, no one knows where he comes from; and his agenda, as we have seen, is anything but savoring to God."

"Yes, Dr. Geiger, and the Passover?" asked Mr. Randolph who wished to tacitly draw him back to the principle issue.

"The Passover is the most sacred of the Jewish feasts. For on the night our people left the captivity of Egypt—on that terrible night, a death angel moved through the enemy camp and struck down the first born male of every house. God made a distinction on that important night between the sacred and the profane, and he led out a host of over two million by the hand of Moses. Since that time the Jews celebrate the deliverance by sharing a Passover meal together in which an unblemished lamb is selected. In fact, it would be selected today since Passover is this Thursday night." Geiger paused but for a moment to wonder about the possible allusion the young rabbi had been making on this day with his presentation to the people as the Passover lamb of some kind. For Geiger knew that Jesus often referred to himself as the Lamb of God who would take away the sins of the world.

Everyone at the table was taking notes since the Jewish cult and ritual surrounding the meal was always a mystery to them, and they were hearing descriptions directly from the mouth of a Jewish scholar and Rabbi who many other conservatives considered to be the Messiah.

"Well, the meal sounds harmless enough," said Max, "and nothing too difficult. Let's ensure that we pull this off without a single shot being fired. Mr. Goodman, I'll have some personal words for the Commander, but I'm counting on you to reinforce what I've said in everyone's hearing—absolutely no shots—all we need is another dead civilian from an errant round. I don't want any glitches, gentlemen. Phyllis, you'll brief the President and keep him apprised of our efforts. Everyone else, when you return to your respective offices, be sure to debrief at levels of confidence appropriate to your subordinate's clearances, and remain on standby for commencement of codeword: 'Street Sweep.'"

A knock on the door alerted the Attorney General that lunch was served, and chefs pushed trays to the inside walls and served plates from behind. After everyone arrived back at the table, Max invited Dr. Geiger to offer a word of thanks for the delicacies and then directed A.T.F. Director Goodman to follow with specific data, including dates, movements, motive and circumstantial evidence that pointed to Jesus as the man all the Country had been pursuing.

With a nod to the A.T.F. Director, Mr. Goodman rose to his feet and invited those present to open their files and follow him through some abbreviated remarks about all that they knew or had assembled to date. "As you know, the bombings of both the Crippled Children's Hospital as well as the Veteran's Hospital each occurred on the same night; but equally significant for our purposes is the information Dr. Geiger supplied because of a concurrent investigation he himself was conducting as a safeguard for the preservation of Judaism of which he perceived the young rabbi to be eroding. Dr. Geiger's notes mark Jesus' departure from Chicago within the same twenty-four hour period in which the bombings occurred. Dr. Geiger, without this single piece of evidence, which we've since corroborated with our own information, there is little reason to believe that our present investigation would not be stalled indefinitely; and again, we are all wonderfully indebted to you." Dr. Geiger nodded with appreciation, then burst into tears as he envisioned the culpability shifting from his conscience to Jesus. He was equally aroused by his own iniquity which he flattered in his own eyes. Transgression was shouting at him from within; but since there was no fear of God before his eyes, the cries were muffled beneath words of wickedness and deceit that he constantly rehearsed. Geiger was a dangerous comic with a seared conscience that never smiled. Others in the room laughed the way a parent smiles at a small child who has shown unusual humility, for they had totally misread the deceiver's eyes.

While everyone enjoyed their meal, Mr. Goodman continued. "Another important link that came to us through Leonard, involved the hidden location of this Jack fellow," as he skipped a black and white photo across the table top. "As you know, he was ritually bathing proselytes in the DesPlaines River during those early days; and as it turns out, he had been living on the back side of a farm owned by a Strassfeld family out west of here until his relief showed up. At any rate, the Strassfeld family checks out—nothing there, he apparently had them all fooled. They insist to their graves that he was an honorable man and would never have involved himself in something so vile and notorious as the beast we've alleged. I shelled out the usual profiles of his kind who eat at your table while they fondle your kids; but it was no use, he kept them totally in the dark. Anyway, the neighbor, a guy named Madden, says he witnessed a lot of strange behavior by this Jesus who had been on the property more than once. Madden lives in the next house over, 25 feet from the Strassfeld's front door and is nosier than an ant eater. The guy interrupted my Agents three times while trying to gather information just to tell them detailed stories about a neighbor who happened by, or an incident of local significance that he knew everything about. Madden will do a fine job on the witness stand."

"Now what else do you have, Mr. Goodman?" asked Max.

"Well, before I leave this Madden fellow, let me just say that we were able to later verify the fact that this Jack give-you-a-bath guy, lost his place of residence following his incarceration due to the fact that Jesus dropped by unexpectedly one day with the Strassfelds on vacation, tears down his lean-to, burns up all the evidence and reseeds both bare areas before returning to Chicago. Now somebody tell me what that's about? Next, a cash purchase of diesel was made at a local station, I've got the hard copy. And several tons of ammonia nitrate were lifted from a rail car on the night indicated in your files. This all seemed real suspicious but as random as other leads until we compared notes with the F.B.I. A spokesperson for the local seed and fertilizer company reported a large quantity of nitrate stolen—several tons from rail—right there in Erie which is next door to Prophetstown. In addition, Jesus' van turned up abandoned at a salvage yard in South Chicago. The F.B.I. have since moved it to their own storage and forensic teams have been pouring over it since the day it arrived. Traces of both diesel and ammonia nitrate were found in the vehicle. It's all before you as well as detonating caps and the crown jewels—the maps you've all heard about which mark the timing of events and chemical transfers by his associates including some high test aviation fuel. Forensic teams did a marvelous job, the handwriting compares favorably enough with receipts signed by him…"

"O.K.…," Max said.

Then Mr. Goodman went on a second longer in his excitement, "We've got house addresses, names, witnesses—everything squares right down to the confessions from his own lips about bombshells, birth pangs and his preoccupation with his personal governing authority which he promises to invoke at a very near date. In addition, when you compile all this with the sworn affidavits from the Indian woman and automobile mechanic out near Tulsa together with a paper trail stretching all the way to Phoenix and back, where he hid in the desert…"

"Mr. Goodman," Max said, "your analysis is only equaled by your superb commentary. Allow me to round out our time with some remarks and specific instructions for each of you before we adjourn." The Attorney General held the meeting spellbound for another fifteen minutes before concluding by saying, "and Dr. Geiger, you might be pleased to take one last look around the room because following the arraignment of this man, you will see us all again when you are invited back to Washington to receive a prestigious award from the hands of …well, let me keep that compartmentalized and a special surprise to you. We will please be excused."

Jesus lectured throughout the afternoon at Grant Park, interspersing his time with specific interpretive visits with the twelve closest to him as well as extended opportunities for those seeking the healing touch of his hands. Shortly before dusk Jesus offered some words leveled at reinforcing in their minds the fact that he himself would shortly be summarily executed. This startling pronouncement came as a response to an inquiry made by several non-Jews who were seriously interested in a deeper understanding of God. Philip brought their request to Andrew who in turn brought them before Jesus.

When he saw them, Jesus said, "The time has arrived for the Son of Man to be glorified. I tell you in the most solemn terms that unless a grain of wheat falls into the soil and rots, it will remain alone as it is; but if it decomposes, it will bring a great yield."

The twelve were within his reach and one of them asked, "Tell us, Lord, how specifically does that apply?"

Jesus responded to the question by saying, "I've related to you before, but it bears repeating, life preservers lose, and people who drown themselves to this world win eternally. If you're interested in serving me, then follow me; and wherever I moor, there will be slips for you also. Be sure of this, whoever serves me will be honored by my Father." Others who had taken a break for a bite to eat or who were on the fringe milling around were brought to attention when Jesus continued, "I'm deeply troubled right now in my soul. Should I therefore petition the Father to save me from what's about to happen? No, for it is because of what will soon transpire that I've come into the world. Father," Jesus cried out in a resigned manner, "magnify your name!"

To everyone's complete amazement, a voice dropped down out of heaven and said, "I've indeed already completely overloaded it with weight, and I'm going to do it again!" The crowd was stirred by the wonderful phenomenon and while some said it thundered, others insisted that an angel had spoken to him. But Jesus said, "This voice is for your benefit, not mine. Judgment rests upon this world right now and even as I speak, the ruler of this world is cast out. Now listen carefully," Jesus turned his gaze to the Non-Jews who were also present, "if my feet are lifted up from the earth by execution, then I will draw all men to myself." Jesus spoke prophetically indicating the kind of death he would suffer.

A spokesperson in the crowd shouted, "we've been taught from the law that the Christ will remain forever, so how can you speak of lynching and murder?"

Jesus paced around in the grass and concluded his message by saying, "You will have the light in your midst for just a little longer—walk in it so that the darkness doesn't envelope you. Whoever is surrounded by darkness has no idea where he is going. While you have the shining brillance, believe in it so that you can become sons of the shining brillance." Jesus stepped aside and was assisted by those closest to him as he managed his way through the crowds to a remote place.

Jude was devastated by Jesus' remarks and resolved on that day to turn evidence in whatever form that he deemed useful to investigators. As far as Jude was concerned, time was running out and this, 'would be messiah,' whoever he was, had just issued his own death warrant. The crowds were also mixed up and even though Jesus had performed many signs before them, they remained in a state of unbelief.

Jesus left the city at dusk and caught a ride back to the home of Lazarus, Mary and Martha who had provided him a bed and private bath in their basement. Some of Jesus' closest followers were befuddled about his unwillingness to step forward and make something happen, while a select few others thought perhaps he would do exactly that, and very soon, but were unsure just how it would unfold.

It was nearly 1:00 A.M. when John arrived back at his apartment. He left the park after the crowds dispersed and sat in Due's Pizzeria on Wabash sipping a stout and nibbling a personal pepperoni thick enough with cheese to plug a hole in the moon. John was fond of good pizza and only literature surpassed his penchant for the 'round Italian grocery discs,' as he would refer to them. Between his elbows rest a worn cowhide binder filled with notes scribbled upon loose leaf paper. John had been recently memorizing a portion of scripture taken from the prophet Isaiah because Jesus had persuaded him to make scripture memorization a regular habit. As he considered the day's events, he was struck by how accurately Isaiah could have been describing the crowds at Grant Park last evening when he wrote, 'Lord, who has put any stock in our message? And to whom has the strength of the Lord been revealed?'

"No wonder these people are not believing," John thought to himself when he recalled another passage that said, 'He has blindfolded their eyes and poured cement into their hearts.' John recorded later that Isaiah was able to speak in that manner because he saw the glory of Christ's day and spoke of him. In spite of the hardness of the masses who were mostly out for thrills and personal healings, several even of the Jewish leadership were believing in him; but they weren't about to say anything publicly since they would then be excommunicated from the synagogue. Sadly, they relished the favor of men more than the favor of God. John completed his notes with his usual written prayer, pushed aside a generous tip and wondered about what tomorrow would bring as he made his way out of the city and back to Mount Prospect.

Chapter 20

Jesus rose before daylight as he often did and walked over to Hawthorne Race Track to pray. With the exception of a change of clothes and a small package of personal items, he placed everything he owned into two shallow cardboard boxes about 24 inches in length and tied in a manner that provided a hand hold on each. These he deposited on his way over at the door of a poor family he had previously observed. John showed up at the pre-arranged location at 5:45 A.M. and others trickled in shortly after. Jude had excused himself for the day even though Jesus forbade him and chose instead to sit by his phone and await a return call from Rabbi Geiger.

It had been a damp night. Fog hadn't begun to lift from the area of the track when Jesus and his followers stepped out from the concealment of a block wall and wandered the perimeter of the track with Jesus walking point. From a distance, the veteran squad resembled a reconnaissance team crawling out of a carved hole in the bush before first light, without words, slight with gear, and moving in a decisive, orderly manner towards the next forward observation post. And like a fire team cut-off atop a hill in southeast Asia by an NVA force of overwhelming size, these men had no idea their Platoon Sergeant would soon run into the face of automatic fire on their behalf and fall mortally wounded, nevertheless staving off enemy attack and buying precious seconds for his men to take evasive measures. It was going to get hot, and only Jesus fully understood the cost and reward. A recurring word of encouragement that he turned over in his mind was a scripture that motivated him to press on, 'He will see his kids, he will stretch out his days, and the satisfying grin of the Lord will bloom right in his hand.' Jesus considered his men on this morning and grew strong with the realization that he had trained them well and fully revealed the Father to them in human flesh. Jesus would soon be awarded the Medal of Honor posthumously by those who loved him, complete with citation; but surprisingly, he would personally hand it all back after three days with the promise of something greater.

Before leaving the track, Jesus, who had not had any breakfast, stepped away from his men and approached a small apple tree that was covered with blossoms. Because he found no apples, he cursed the tree in the hearing of the others who had joined him by now and said, "May no one ever eat apples from you again!"

The incident humored Peter who said, "Gee, Lord, I can pick up some donuts and coffee; you don't have to go off on the tree just because you're a little ticked. Shoot, fruit won't be due on this thing for another two or three months."

Jesus responded to Peter saying, "and I've waited on this people for two or three millennia."

Immediately following the episode with the tree, everyone piled into vehicles by Jesus' direction and made their way back to Grant Park for another day with the crowds. Jesus told Peter to take the lead and make preparations ahead of them and that he would ride alone with John. The men were well ahead of rush hour; and when John pulled in to grab coffee and rolls, Jesus tucked a small package of personals beneath his passenger side seat. Everyone arrived at the lake front bright and early but not before Siva and a horde of volunteers from Quest who made it their highest priority to assist Jesus and his men on every hand. Siva quickly removed a Styrofoam cup from Jesus' hands and replaced it with a fresh cup of her own blend in an attractive clay mug.

"Siva," Jesus said, "what will the world do without you when you grow old?"

"How old do you have to be to retire on your team?" she asked.

Jesus smiled, having been caught by the spry remark and matched it by saying, "I know of a little lady outside Calcutta who served well past two of your life times before her batteries were up."

"O.K.. Jesus," Siva said hugging his neck, "you win as usual." Siva was very slow to release Jesus because of a deep sense she had in her spirit that she would not have him much longer. It was a long embrace, but Jesus didn't seek her release. Instead he stroked her head the way a mother nurtures a small child.

"Thanks, Jesus," Siva said while toweling tears onto his collar, "please be careful—O.K.?"

"Siva, you're breaking my heart as the others. I've come into the world to accomplish the work given to me by my Father. I'll be with you a while longer and where I'm going you cannot come just yet. You've been serving faithfully—keep up the good work. But I'm going away to prepare a place for you so that where I am, someday my friends will be too. You see, Siva, I'm no longer addressing you and the others as servants, because servants often have little idea about what there boss is doing. I've called you friends because everything that I have received from my Father, I've made known to you." Peter and James sandwiched Siva's face between a kiss by them on each cheek, then grabbed Jesus by the arm and ushered him away to the fountain where they were anxious to hear fresh teaching for the day.

A half circle shaped area in front of the fountain had been scribed by the position of Jesus' followers as in previous visits to Grant Park. Immediately, Jesus startled everyone by removing his belt and diving into the face of vendors who had set up makeshift umbrellas and booths to market their wares.

"Stop gouging the poor with this garbage!" Jesus shouted. "You're turning the place of my Father's work into a carnival stand." Jesus whipped the adults with his belt and overturned tables that showcased air paints and laser-printed 'T' shirts. Raffle tickets blew in the air as Peter jumped into the fray to assist Jesus, but James and John were shouting at him to get off an elderly man while pulling Jesus apart before mounted police showed up.

"I'm just getting started," Jesus screamed, "I won't stand for their commercialization of the special message I've brought—Judaism ought to be known as a house of prayer for all the nations, but these are turning it into a robber's den."

Feed of the outbreak went directly to mobile dish COM 2 and was reported to the Attorney General who kept a watchful eye but felt it was premature to throw the net. Meanwhile, Geiger was in the air and in route back to Chicago when the same word reached his first class cabin by his associates standing in Grant Park. WGN moved in for a closer look while Geiger directed his associates to join Mr. Holdheim, Caiaphas and himself along with Judas at a secret place of meeting.

At 4:00 P.M. Tuesday afternoon everyone sat quietly as Caiaphas offered an opening prayer of blessing for the plans that would follow. Jude placed a thin file on the conference table top and slid it in the direction of Dr. Geiger. Jude's reports were generally the transcriptions of recordings he obtained from private meetings with Jesus and his close followers. Geiger immediately noticed some lapses of reporting and surmised that Judas had been vacillating about his allegiances. Geiger left the file open while listening to Caiaphas vent some rage about all the destructive undermining of Rabbinic Judaism brought on by the young self-taught leader of The Way. Geiger didn't particularly like Caiaphas, but he was useful since he was the puppet high priest and respected by all the Jews. Actually any animosity that could be generated toward Jesus was pleasing to Geiger, so he bade his time until the meeting should be turned over to him. There were ten men in attendance, each sworn to secrecy and willing to lay down their lives for the posterity of Zion. Geiger simply guided discussions and often allowed the men to make decisions they felt were their own based upon his coaching and agreement after leading them there the way a parent lets children make choices they've already decided upon.

"Judas, where are you at today?" asked Geiger with a lethal verbal grip. Jude knew immediately what Geiger meant to ask and so he launched into an explanation that everyone found satisfying. Others in the room were willing to extend the novice some understanding as an undercover agent who had a foot in two worlds for too long; pretty soon one begins to look and think like the loaths under investigation. For this reason, Geiger secretly hated Jude, for he considered his very clothes adulterated and tainted with unfamiliar smells. He already made up his mind to be rid of Jude in a very definite sense as soon as he was done with him.

Jude was disturbed inside and growing with anxiety. On one hand, he clung to deeply held passions for Zion's prosperity that were not coming to fruition through Jesus; on the other hand, he believed Jesus to be kind and harmless, but a misdirected man, who was orchestrating his own death. He resented having wasted so much time following Jesus only to have his hopes for revolution dashed before his eyes. And since

Geiger's ruthless pursuit of purging Judaism of impurities was looking more and more realistic, he threw in his entire lot unreservedly on this round and didn't intend to look back.

The men spent over four hours without breaking for lunch as Dr. Geiger related classified material of a top secret nature to individuals who had no classified clearances and little interest in the national security of the United States.

Near the end of their discussions, Dr. Geiger, in a rare moment of praise, if it could be called that, turned to Jude and reaffirmed him by saying, "Judas in a short time you have picked up some fundamentals that will serve our people well. There have been some interruptions to the flow and an unfortunate misplacement or two," Geiger spoke on like a comptroller offering a quarterly report to the board about a shaky commodity he was sure would increase in value, "but the bottom line is what's important; and since the weight of our success rests upon your shoulders, we're all counting on you, Judas. I want you to consider yourself fully re-instated to the brotherhood of the code." Jude smiled with appreciation and drank in the expressions of approval that he was receiving from others in the room. Dr. Geiger excused Jude from the meeting and everyone rose as a matter of salute.

"Judas, get the rest you will need for the event this Thursday night. We've put you through a lot and this will all be a closed case very soon thanks to you."

"Good night, Dr. Geiger, gentlemen, and thanks for this opportunity to prove myself—the man is a lunatic and deceiver. I'll be on time Thursday for the final details and can be reached at these new numbers." Jude had recently changed apartments and unlisted numbers, but Geiger already had the information in hand before Jude passed him the corrections.

Jude was escorted from the room and driven by one of Geiger's closest associates out of a parking garage and was not unblindfolded until they reached the Kennedy expressway. Following his dismissal, everyone broke open notebooks and Geiger began running down an agenda that was so tight it squeaked.

"Fritz, give up your previous post and stay a step ahead of Judas until this is all over. Mr. Holdheim and myself will monitor everything from the suite upstairs. Caiaphas has already agreed to be available all day Friday. 'Kite,' as Caiaphas was often referred to, it's imperative that we rendezvous with you back at Point Crown immediately after his arrest. There are a number of leading Jews who have already waited too long to get a look at this man, and I'm planning something real close up and personal for their viewing pleasure. Following their examination, Harry and Mr. P., who is in town this week, will want to see the face of him who launched a thousand emergency vehicles."

"What about your relationship with the Mayor, Leonard?" asked Caiaphas.

"Harry's been bending over backwards to get a look at this man since the day he made his presence known. I cut a deal with him in return for a helo-lift Friday and a phone call to the chief of police urging them to move very slowly once the operation is put in motion. The chief is a retired soldier and needed very little persuasion following a short review of the death toll at both hospitals," said Geiger. "Harry is due a favor by me but only after he agreed to speak to the chief of police on our behalf."

Leonard rose from his chair and spoke in chain-linked syllables the exact procession Jesus' route on foot should take between his holding cell at Cook County Jail and the Federal Courts Building on Friday morning.

"At this place," Geiger relished, "on this slab of concrete at 8:00 A.M., the imposter will be surrounded by ravenous Gentiles and led away for execution." Geiger smiled and everyone lifted their eyes to a rare sight when he concluded by saying, "Josephus describes in the 'Antiquities of the Jews,' the only fit means of death for a blasphemous imposter of this sort…" Geiger had rubbed the carved form that he carried in his pocket for so long that it had become slick with wear, "and all the world will owe us a debt of gratitude for hanging him there."

Loose ends were as much a pleasure for Geiger to tie up as laying out the big picture. He would take each one in turn, tease out the fray and meld it into another with seamless perfection before weaving the combed huck into a wrap thick enough to absorb any potential leaks.

"Gentlemen, let us now turn our attention to the body. It will decompose. Afterwards, I want to see the skeleton before it's ground to ashes. Milgram, I'll have documents from the Commander's hand when you need them. There will be no argument by the time I'm done speaking with the Attorney General. Secure the tomb, wherever they lay him and ensure that nobody is allowed access. The last thing we need is for someone to make off with the body and announce that he has risen as he predicted. The last deception will be greater than the first."

"Dr. Geiger, where will this execution actually take place?"

"That is all being cared for as we speak, Kite. In addition, Fritz and Rueben will be among the crowd and seeking to corral things the best they can. The formation needs to stay tight, gentlemen. Let Herzl and I worry about outside interference. Citizens of this pitiful republic are so disgusted with the pansy judicial system that lets criminals walk through their courts like a revolving door—gentlemen, it's over. The people's patience has worn so thin that thought of another mass murderer remaining alive for several years while many of the survivors die before seeing justice served is just more than they will be able to endure when these sentiments are murmured among the crowds. Matters will be taken into their own hands when color photos never before released are distributed in mass. The execution itself must be moved outside the city, so that our home not be defiled. My best estimate is that you will drive out the Stevenson, get off at Route 20 and arrive above Justice before 9:00 A.M. Materials will be on site and can be picked up near the railroad track and sanitary ditch. He will be pressed until he can no longer walk before placing him on the upright."

Geiger's description of his precision quartz solicited a raft of fresh questions by sober minded students who were furiously recording nomenclature and movement of the works being dictated by their esteemed master jeweler. After another hour, Geiger sat down for he had been standing since Jude left, offered another prayer of blessing and placed everyone under oath before departing.

Chapter 21

The events of a new day kicked off again at the race track in Cicero before moving downtown to Grant Park.

"John, have a look at this," said James who was standing along side with Peter.

"Well, what do you make of it, Peter?" asked John.

"Don't expect anyone will be eating apples from this tree again," he said.

"Yeah, right," said John, who was looking for a little deeper spiritual commentary.

"C'mon, John, don't look so beleaguered, he'd probably explain it to his favorite if you'd just ask," said Peter. John often bore the brunt of inside jokes directed at him because of Jesus' apparent favoritism.

"Yeah, well maybe I will," said John as he continued wondering about a tree that was beautifully in bloom just yesterday at this same time.

A shout from the corner of the lot said it was time to make route to the City. As Peter, James and John walked away from the tree, Peter tripped John from behind but he caught his balance before falling to the ground.

John returned the favor with a literary remark that nearly sent Peter skidding on his palms as well. "Peter, I'm only beleaguered when I'm bludgeoned by people like you with boring boneheaded remarks they mistake for refined intellectual discourse. Do you think you could dispense with your nude, adolescent remarks while in my company and save it for obdurates of your kind who find it entertaining?" Peter ignored a question he was unable to decipher but was able to put together enough pieces like bonehead and boring to determine that John's ramblings were not exactly praises. James stepped into Peter purposefully on accident as his little brother slipped by his grip and ran to the car, where he locked himself before the big man could lay hands on him. John should have been done, but he made a face Peter had seen only one other time at a park in Milwaukee. The other men were laughing so hard that they staggered, but Peter wasn't finished and drew a wire from the back of his truck and slipped a lock before John could start the engine.

"Well, the coyote finally did catch the road runner," Philip said. John squealed aloud like a rabbit being drawn from a homemade box set out overnight with bait. Peter held John in a head-lock and administered a knuckle-rub that made the others wince.

"Yep, the dog feces have definitely hit the oscillating fan; haven't they little buddy?" said Peter before others delivered John's head from the terrible vice.

Jesus was still recovering from a belly laugh when he said, "Any chance of the two of you getting with the program and joining us downtown—we've got a lot of work ahead of us and little time for horse play." Peter's palms met one another coming and going as he gave his hands a quick up and down slap indicating a job completed. John didn't feel like 'horse play' quite described the fire just lit to his crown but wasn't in any mood to argue about it. Peter threw his keys to James and joined John in the front seat of his Saab while giving Jesus a facial expression that said, 'I'll make up with the little fellow on the way downtown.' Everyone found a seat including Jude who happened to be on hand. Peter pestered John all the way to Grant Park by keeping the radio tuned to country favorites that were squalling at a volume loud enough for the world to hear.

The men walked into Grant Park from Balbo and were confronted by Jewish scholars alert to their arrival who had come over from Judaica. Always concerned for where Jesus obtained his authority, since he wasn't a graduate or pedigreed by their institutions, the Jewish leaders castigated him and his followers and demanded explanations for Jesus' continued defiance of the strict observance of Jewish law.

Jesus stopped near the crowds and addressed the aristocracy by saying, "I've told you before that if you can tell me if Jack's baptism came from heaven or whether it was a product of man's own concoction, I'd be more specific about where I derive authority." The Jewish leaders were silent because of their fear of the crowds and so Jesus addressed the entire audience with a story. "A man out in the middle of this corn belt poured a round concrete foundation and erected a continuous flow dryer that was easily accessible for his many grain trucks that moved it to world markets. The owner leased the entire farm that was subsequently drilled with corn and left the country for he had business to care for overseas. Around September he sent over a trusted broker to collect his percentage, but they beat him up pretty badly and told him to get along before something worse happened. He sent another associate the same week, but they hit him in the head with a ball bat and shamed him mercilessly. The next week he sent another of his trusted employees who sought to collect his employer's rightful cut, but they killed him and hid his body. And so this cycle continued; they beat some and killed others. The owner had one more emissary, a beloved son; he sent him after the others saying, 'they will show respect to my son.' But those tenants conspired among themselves and said, 'This is the one who will inherit the farm, let's kill him—then the title will pass to us!' Yes, you guessed it, they killed the son and threw his body off the farm. Let me ask you a question," Jesus paused, "what do you think the owner of the farm will do in response to this utter disregard? I'll tell you what he will do—he will come and execute those tenants and give the farm to others. By the way have you not read: 'The stone which the builders threw out, this became the crucial corner for bearings;' this came about from the Lord and it is so great to behold?"

"Some of the strict religious legalists who were standing nearby said, "Away with you and your talk of a kingdom; your doctrine is contemptuous!"

"That's why, the kingdom of God will be ripped away from you and given to a nation producing the crop of it," said Jesus. As the Jewish leaders were walking away wagging their heads, Jesus called after them saying, "The one who lands on this stone will be broken into bits and pieces, but upon whoever it lands, it will pulverize him like ground powder."

Jesus taught the crowds throughout the morning and early afternoon. His closest followers sat close to the front for better reception and to ensure that the over zealous not cross boundaries and ascend the stage. John sat a distance away under the shade of a tree and appeared to be painting with water colors as he laid down sentences in a notebook. Soft pastels on a paperboard. John was personally discouraged on this particular day and not because of all the harassment Peter and the others had shelled out. The apple tree and the spiritual bareness of the masses was a connection he could not put out of his mind, and it pained him to wonder how his leader could continue speaking so passionately to those he perceived to be on hand for entirely wrong motives. In that same moment, John recalled a phrase uttered in the past year by Jesus that helped him put things in perspective and grow in his understanding of Jesus' mission: 'I feel deep heart stirs for all the people because they are mere sheep—stressed out and exhausted without a shepherd.' Jesus was certainly a shepherd above all else and John would be forever marked by that characteristic.

As evening neared, the crowds grew in size as usual since many who wanted to hear from Jesus, or venture approaching him for healing, were constrained until now because of work schedules. Jesus always made himself available for that audience and sometimes repeated nearly verbatim a message he had delivered to a different crowd earlier in the same day. Shortly after 7:00 P.M., Jesus motioned for Bart which always meant for him to pull his team together and provide him with passage to a vehicle. Jesus communicated with his men to join him at Humboldt Park—they knew the flower garden—"join me within the hour."

James and John approached Jesus in the garden and could tell that he was more emotionally distressed than usual. They sat along side of him as they often did and quietly prayed after him until he should break the solemn observance with words of instruction. Peter and others arrived and took up positions of prayer without speaking to one another. After nearly forty minutes, Jesus rose from his knees and began quietly unraveling a sub sandwich which was the only food he had taken on this day as far as John knew. When he was sure others had concluded, he began with personal questions of interest the way a shepherd inspects his flock, checking up on sleep patterns, priorities for those married, and personal time with God. These moments were cherished by most all of the men since a question directed at one person would often inspire others to consider it for themselves; and before you knew it, everyone had been drawn into some quality reflection on life and meaningful applications for themselves individually.

More than once Jesus gave others permission to take the lead and expose particular issues needing to be addressed. 'Kill it before it multiplies,' was an expression used by everyone, which adequately capsulated their commitment to stamp out harmful relational styles before they grew into something uncontrollable. No one felt especially embarrassed to be singled out on these occasions. In fact, several of Jesus' followers secretly wished to be placed on the 'hot seat' and grilled with penetrating questions unlike they were ever asked before in their lives. Adult men who were genuinely concerned for one another probed deeply into one another's souls with the hope of exposing harmful styles of relating that had been learned over a long period of time. These relational styles that seemed as natural to humans as climbing is to squirrels—styles that had been developed over a lifetime to either insulate one or perhaps gain an advantage for another were all carefully learned, deeply imbedded, habitually practiced, as natural as instinct and had to be skillfully hunted down and killed. Obviously, this was not the kind of aim and trigger pull a man could make on himself while standing down range at the same time.

Metal tops popped as canned drinks were passed from a small cooler. The crinkle of sandwich wrap could be heard like leaves beneath the feet of one entering the wood and creeping stealthily toward his prey with a Browning semi-automatic 12 gauge: 30 inch ventilated ribbed barrel, full choke, and chambered with high brass field loads. Movement was observed in the bough of a distant hickory, but it would require a great deal of caution to reach its base without being noticed by the wary fox squirrel busily shopping the day's select produce. After hand picking his favorites with the most discriminating care and dropping them to the ground below, the red patron lissomely descended the broad steps of shag bark and gathered food stuffs to be carried home.

When and where death occurs is an unfamiliar intersection on a local map. Without warning and while least expected, the barrel dark with blue, its receiver resting snugly in an artistically carved stock of poplar moist with linseed hangs parallel like a new branch from the trunk of a tree, then faint and quiet as a shadow cast by a small cloud making leave of the sun; the bead finds the soft hairs of his fine garment, trimmed with tailored cuts by an expert couturier. One last glance at life and the safety slips on the decorative piece at the moment his cheek touches grain and the bore opens its mouth with terrific muzzle velocity at close range ripping a gaping hole in one's abdomen the size of a man's fist and spilling out all of his guts. Back in the wood, a moment is taken to absorb the recoil and steady a piece that has already chambered another round. The smell of powder cleared out about the same time as the flutter of fur relaxed itself at the base of the tree. Everything that creeps went into hiding momentarily, as thunder echoed back and sent birds to flight. But like critters that cannot count, other hairy red ones were back within the hour ready to trade their birth right for a casual nut. The invisible hunter sat among the leaves on a nearby stump, camouflaged, smooth and properly scented. He patiently awaited his next kill. Brilliant yellow monarchs playfully ascended and descended just above his head.

Jude was front and center on this occasion. His smile and cool manner like nothing ever mattered was ridden with deceit. He was still single after 34 years and did exactly as he wished with his time and money; and if anything had surfaced in their few years together, all of the men would agree—Jude was totally uncommitted. He was a guy who kept all of his options open and never made a decision that didn't put his own needs above everyone else's. This attitude precipitated heated exchange on more than one occasion when phone calls by others were not returned or he would show late for meetings, or not show at all only to later lie about his whereabouts while everyone else was held in the lurch waiting on him.

It was Jude's relationships with women that was most obnoxious. He often referred to them in shorthand as 'bitches in britches' and the like. On one occasion, Jude told members of this small group about his decision to room with a female associate while in Florida. Several employees at Jude's place of employment had won the free trip based upon sales over the past quarter. Jude laid out his plans for critique by the others who resembled a hungry hunting party desperate to blow away everything fleshly and pick over his bones in an effort to hold him accountable for his decisions and immoral behavior.

Prior to meeting Jesus, these men had never had a meaningful conversation with another man outside of sports or a new scheme to make money. Most of their wives and girl friends had been kept in the dark as the bulk of other women regarding man, his make up and imminent goal to remain anonymous. 'That's just the way guys are,' most women figured, but Jesus was never terribly tolerant of prevailing world views, opinions about man's make up, and he generally pushed the envelope to the limit and demanded the most ruthless personal inventory of his followers. 'Man's heart is a dense and twisted pathological mess,' he would often remark, 'who can see through it?' Some of Jesus' followers were still scared to death to allow another human being to get to know them at more than a cliché level of communication. Bad relational experiences had taught them to keep people at arms length. 'I've been hurt and rejected before and I don't intend to take any more risks,' was a common sentiment. This poor justification was discarded right out of hand by Jesus, and he seldom allowed one of his followers to even finish a statement if he sensed that they were traveling down that path.

"Jude," Peter began, while toking on a fresh Cuban hand wrap passed along by a friend recently in from Montreal, "so you intend to fly down with Lisa, spend the weekend with her, sleep in the same bed and you want us to somehow believe that nothing's going to happen—strictly economics and sharing costs?"

"Yeah, that's basically it," said Jude smiling. "I'll be cool. Besides, Lisa's a professional and doesn't mix sex with work."

"Can a man dump white-hot charcoal into his lap and not get bar-b-qued?" asked Drew who was citing a proverb he felt was relevant to the discussion.

"Jude," Matthew cut into the conversation, "just for arguments sake, let's say we all checked our brain at the entrance to the Park on our way in this evening. Now is there anything you're not telling us? I mean is the bed outfitted with stocks for your hands and feet, is there a sheet of plexi-glass a half inch thick standing upright and separating your bodies as you lay in this bed you've described?"

"No, nothing like that," said Jude who loved the play and sense of shock he derived from the exchange with the others. "It's just as I've said, we're mature. We're friends and work associate, just sharing costs."

"Let's move on to the next screen," said Bart who had little patience with Jude and his usual ramblings and questions that undermined Jesus' standard lessons about morality. "We've been here before and there is no way to persuade someone who is deceived about who they are." Jude, who sat next to Jesus, began laughing at Bart and the others as though they were still green and afraid to enter the real world of risks and adventure. Jesus remained silent as James began a fresh line of interrogation directed at Jude.

"C'mon, Jude, you can't be serious about this poodle-poop because that's all it is—a crock full of it!"

"Ah, you guys are just jealous. We've entered a new millennium," Jude continued, "nobody lives by the letter anymore—right Jesus? I mean even you have said that all that stuff has been abolished. It's up to us to choose for ourselves given the situation." Jesus again remained silent while the circle erupted with eleven other muzzles of various gauge that had already drawn a bead on Jude's gross misinterpretation of Jesus' words regarding the law.

After most of the clamor subsided, John, who as a literary analyst realized every sentence has a context, gained the floor, looked into Jude's eyes and said, "Let me take you back to that discussion. Jesus said that he didn't come to throw away the law and prophets, but to complete them. He is the new law giver, for he is greater than Moses and the prophets, right Peter? I mean 333 Wacker and the voice from heaven, 'this is my beloved son, listen to him.'" Jude continued staring back at John with a glazed disinterested look for he despised John's youthfulness and regarded him as a sniveling, blood sucking parasite who couldn't live apart from Jesus.

Everyone read Jude's expression when Thad concluded by saying, "It's in the book, 'a fool is more keen in his own estimate of himself than seven men who can offer razor sharp advice.' Jesus often let truth rest without always forcing a confrontation. His personal humility respected an individual's choice. Accounts would be settled at a later time; and as a result, he seldom coerced opinions or obedience. Besides, whether Jude realized it or not, he had just been riddled with buckshot by men who genuinely loved him in spite of his bullheadedness. John was puzzled by Jesus' silence and lack of intervention and later while leafing back through several pages of notes, his eyes fell upon a sentence recorded nearly two years earlier, 'don't give pit bulls things that belong on the top shelf and don't throw what is precious before hogs, lest they rip them to shreds and turn to maul you.'

Matthew, was feeling a little uncomfortable since the interaction between the men was a little hotter than normal. He broke some ice by turning everyone's attention to the city's skyline as the sun cast a wonderful orange hue across its face.

"The buildings really shine on an evening like this," Matthew remarked.

"Yes," Jude agreed, "incredible feats of human achievement."

Jesus rose from his own abstractedness and entered the conversation by saying, "As for these beautiful buildings, one day there will not be left one stone stacked upon another that will not be pulled down." Everyone knew Jesus was filling in with another installment of what could be expected during the last days.

"Teacher," James asked, "how will we know when all of these things are about to pop?"

"Remember what I've said before. Many will come along after me and proclaim that, 'I am he,' or 'now is the time.' Ignore them. And if you hear about military conflicts or even get caught up in world wars, don't be rattled because the end is not yet; and all of these things must first take place. Countries will wage war with one another, earthquakes, famines and disease epidemics will visit various sectors—there will even be huge signs from heaven. But before all this happens, they will be cruel towards you, judging you in both the synagogue and civil courts. Some of you will even be imprisoned and brought before governors and presidents for my name's sake. It will provide for you a place to stand up and tell your story. Settle the matter right now—don't worry about how to defend yourselves or what you will say because those words will be given to you when you need them. My words through you will not be refuted or resisted by them whoever they are. Brace yourselves because you will be hated by everyone on account of my name. Even your parents and blood relatives will betray you and put some of you to death. Hang in there under trial and you will win your souls—it is as I've said, not a single hair from your head will perish."

"Should we still expect all of this to happen when the great city is surrounded by military machines of destruction?" asked John.

"Yes," Jesus said, "her destruction will follow in that moment. There will also be signs in the sky, both day and night and dreadful wonder among all the peoples of the earth because of the churning of the seas and tidal waves."

"Whoa," said Drew who had a special fear of storms, "I get anxious just thinking about those pictures."

"Grown men will faint, Drew. They will be gripped with fear for the shear expectation of all the calamity about to fall upon them," said Jesus, "for the powers of heaven of which you have had but a taste will all be shaken. Then they will see the Son of Man coming in a cloud with tremendous power and weight. When you see the sign, get your head out from between your legs and stand up because your redemption has arrived."

"Jesus," Drew asked, "are you now teaching with a story or is this literally the way things will shape up?"

"My stories and figures are truth-pictures of what you can expect. Consider a tree of any variety, even these late pin oaks over here, as soon as they begin to leaf, you notice it right away and realize that Summer is just around the corner. In the same way, Drew, you must realize that as soon as the things I've described begin to dawn—you must know that the kingdom of God in its fullness is near. I'm telling you straight up, that generation will not turn over until all these things take place. Heaven and earth will turn over but my words will not be overturned."

"Lord, will you give us some kind of signal besides this—maybe an early warning siren or something?" asked Bart.

"Be watchful and pray," said Jesus, "for what I've described will come upon everyone who lives on the earth. Don't allow yourselves to be blind-sighted with worries or dull with drugs so that the day will sneak up on you like a hunter in the wood. Pray that you may escape and be able to stand before the Son of Man unashamed."

Philip and Bart had fallen off to sleep on the fringe while others excused themselves to go home. It was apparent that Jesus was done lecturing; however, Peter, James and John remained on hand and visited with Jesus until after midnight when he excused himself to walk the park in prayer. Peter shook Bart from a sound sleep and Philip was also awakened and wondering about the time. Five men put their heads together for several minutes more talking through preparations and responsibilities for the Passover meal next evening.

Chapter 22

Mary removed the saucepan from the cook-top and found tongs to draw boiled eggs from water still rolling with heat. A delicate stamp of memorial light flickered from the dining room sideboard and winking at the stir she made by several trips carrying dishes and service for the evening celebration of Unleavened Bread. Sarah, Jimmy and their spouses would be on hand tonight with their children as well as two single women from the synagogue who were Mary's close friends. After arranging place settings and two handmade lazy-susans by Joey at each end of the table, she made a mental list of food items still needed before stepping out to the market. Mary always rolled her own matzah and ran a redel over it until evenly perforated. As soon as it comes out of the oven, she would be off to the store the same way she had many Passovers before to purchase horseradish, romaine lettuce and enough ingredients to complete her special recipe of charoset.

"Hello," Mary said, picking up the portable phone while handling a hot tray fresh out of the oven.

"Mom, you're as beautiful as your voice," Jesus said, speaking from a pay phone downtown. "Now let me guess. The eggs are cooling, table is set, wine is chilled, you're beginning to bake matzah and probably still need to make a trip to the store." Mary was silent on the other end and unconsciously found a stool while pushing her glasses in place with a finger white with flour that left evidence on her forehead. Tiny seconds were falling from the kitchen clock mounted there in the corner. The little black specks could scarcely be heard hitting the hardwood below and beginning to mound. But the room was deathly still and they could be heard, each one of them lopped off by the stroke and cast down.

Mary cradled the receiver, held her boy close to her ear and said, "you're just a kid." Several seconds passed before she continued, "I was a kid once. It's hard to believe we were ever that young. The years have flown. I can still remember standing with Joey's parents down at the bus station when he threw that big green bag over his shoulder. I told him I loved him and to be careful and not do anything foolish. But you know Joey. He flicked that eagle, globe and anchor pinned to his cap and said, 'we're needed in Vietnam, and don't wait up.' Jesus," Mary continued reminiscing, "Joey never told anyone that he was awarded the Silver Star for heroism. I didn't see him for twelve full months and I prayed for him every day. God brought him back, Jesus—even after placing himself in harms way and at great personal risk."

Mary couldn't bring herself to ask the question of Jesus and his audible sighs on the other end were felt in a way that let her know he understood. "Mom, one does not know what a day may bring forth. I'll be throwing a heavy tote over my shoulder soon enough." Jesus let his thoughts wander during another moment of silence by his mother. "Sometimes I wish this could be Omaha Beach or a tank battle in North Africa," he thought to himself. "None of their commanders past or present have seen anything like what is presently being arrayed for this attack. Hoards of horsemen, strong bulls of Bashan, trounce in the dark valley and speak wantonly of victory. Their horses scoff at war, snorting and lifting dust from the floor of the great basin which rises like fog as high as their bridles. Yellowish gaunt light, sick with muke green, layers over them and is swept around by battle axes and clubs wielded by torturers with massive iron arms."

Sound of the 'L' passing overhead brought Jesus back to the moment. "I've sent the men ahead of me to prepare for Passover. I wanted to have this meal with them alone. We'll be on an upper floor at the Holiday Inn adjacent to the Mart."

"You're in my heart as always, son."

"I love you, Mom, and it won't be twelve months—I promise."

Jesus fed the phone a few more coins to satisfy the operator before rejoining John who waited along side in his car. "By the way, John," Jesus asked, "why are you selling your car?" 'For Sale' signs were recently taped to both rear side windows of the late model Saab complete with phone numbers and asking price. "You've only had this for a few months. Having mechanical problems? Payments have you strapped?"

"No, nothing like that. Actually, it's been a great car and it's paid for. I've been looking at an older economy model and couldn't trade without taking a hit so I'm doing this on my own."

"I guess I'm a little surprised. This Saab is the model you spent so much time researching and everything."

"Well, I'm selling it and that's that!" said John with a surprising amount of energy. "Jude said he might be running a little late tonight," John continued while changing the subject. Jesus let it go and directed him to drive over to Belmont Harbor where he wished to spend time with the three. Peter and James were leaning over the hood of Peter's utility vehicle when Jesus and John arrived. Peter who was making special efforts to encourage John was surprised to see the sale sign on his vehicle after just praising the car to him less than three days ago.

"John-John, what's with the sale signs?" asked Peter. "I mean that's one great car and definitely the best sound system I've ever heard on wheels. You're not serious about getting rid of it are you? Didn't you tell me it was paid for?"

"Actually I've already got a buyer. He's picking it up Saturday," John said while skirting the question. James felt something stir in his own gut when a new Lincoln Town car pulled in next to an older well worn make just beyond them where John stood next to Jesus.

"Let's get moving," Jesus said. "We've got plenty of work ahead of us and I've got some important information I want to pass along to each of you while there is still time. James popped his brother on his back side as the three followed Jesus over to a grove of trees at lake side where they found a comfortable place to sit down and relax.

"The Evil One...," Jesus began to speak when he was interrupted by Peter.

"You mean the E.B.O.," and he quickly reminded him of the short-hand everyone approved at an earlier time of meeting." Peter of course was responsible for supplying the 'B' and occasionally shouted it out for everyone's benefit.

"The E.B.O. wants you to feel worthless, isolated and utterly confused about life and your ability to lead," Jesus began afresh and let his words out slowly the way a man trolls the Lake with baits. "Look at yourselves! You behave like zombies—what the dogs drug in and the cats wouldn't eat. You're alive—you've got a pulse and you each have a simmering energy that wants to boil—to overflow for God's glory. I want you to begin spending periods of solitude in order to explore what prevents you from coming out and engaging other people. It will take some time, but ask yourselves the question, 'How do others experience me?' Pay attention to what you journal. Chances are good you'll discover techniques you've honed to keep people at a distance and anything worthwhile about yourself safely out of sight. As sure as you breathe, you resonate with the eternal—it's part of the way you were designed. Identify the glory you live for and be sure of this, the E.B.O. doesn't want you to walk paths that lead to a deeper sense of honor. Being a man frustrates his purposes by sending electrical surges back to his area of operations atop utility poles where he tinkers with transformers. That kind of counter surge travels back and swells into a blast leaving him covered with black suet and ash. He doesn't want you to be a man—to live after God. He carefully recruits men and convinces them that they will never be regarded by God as anything more than pitiful 'wanna-bees.' The E.B.O. is man's constant accuser and you will definitely grow in shades of darkness if you listen to him and buy into his appraisal. He wants to convince you that you walk with him, that you're his—just another hopeless case of abuse, or an actual abuser or both, then you're derailed and off the track of honor."

April wisps of fresh laundered breeze swirled gently about the cove lifting cuffs and parting hair before stepping aside to consider the cut and clipping again. It was a gorgeous day and great to be alive: speaking leisurely with Jesus, no demanding schedules in sight, favorite hot drink and sitting on a piece of lake side they had come to consider their own.

"Is he doing this right now?" John asked. "I mean how do we know when it's him? Didn't you tell us before that our hearts are also desperately sick?"

"I'll come around to that, John," Jesus said as he spoke casually with his good friends, cup in hand and forearms resting upon his knees. "Man was created for worship and obedience. He was also created for relationship—to give love and receive love. Unfortunately, worship often gets sidelined for something perfunctory while obedience is swallowed up in placid forms of duty. One of the E.B.O.'s chief aims is to destroy communion. God wants you to pray so that a relationship of trust can be developed between him and yourselves. He wants to relate with you through prayer even when you feel emotionally devastated—especially during those dark times. And if you're too low to find your own words, then pray the Psalms of David—now there is a man who spelled out his feelings. The E.B.O., on the other hand, wants you to grow cold and offer God the same silent treatment you offer others. You don't relate to God any differently than you do your own spouses or significant others so snap out of that delusion and come clean with yourselves."

"Speaking of being honest," said John, "God often seems distant and silent as well."

"Especially during times when life's on a terrible skid," injected James.

"Yes," Jesus replied, "and man often interprets God's silence as indifference. Man begins to think that God is just like him. God's silence is often his patience. 'You involved yourself in all that stuff and I didn't say a word, you thought I was just like you.'" Jesus rapped his cup against the trunk of a small tree and motioned with his eyes for Peter to give him a refill from the thermos. Jesus continued, "Of course the E.B.O. leans into man's self-centeredness and whispers that silence is good, silence is strength—you can get along on your own. But isolation and independence have a way of making people mean and destructive. As a result, you begin to assault one another and now you really are isolated and independent. 'I may not have any friends,' Jesus raised his voice, 'but I'm strong!' Rage wells up inside a man after he figures out how he's being used by the E.B.O. It crawls up the back side of his throat and he swallows the acerbic spit as though it were gasoline feeding a terrible inferno in his belly. Then the smoke billows out, 'I'll be stronger! I'll build towers! I'll climb above the others!' But the E.B.O. is the mother of all abusers. He whispers threats, warns you to stay a brick ahead, then turns right around and tells you that you're just a babbler—too empty and weak to involve yourself with others and enjoy any sense of community down below."

"How can we combat that kind of spiritual yo-yo assault?" asked John who was intensely interested.

"Unfortunately, most men have to be known for their achievements rather than who they are—whose image they bear. The thought of offering others their unadorned selves—no prefixes or suffixes attached to the mailing label is terrifying—they feel naked. But who ever told man that he was naked? Man agrees with the lie because he knows there's been plenty of exposure in his personal past to back up the E.B.O.'s claims. Man says in effect, 'everyone can see right through me yes, I'm unreachable, I'm no good, I'm naked, I really am a coward....'"

"What are you talking about?" Peter blurted out. "Just the other day I beat the face of some of those idiots down at the Park who were peddling their wares!"

Jesus continued, "The E.B.O. deceives men into thinking they're strong by the things they do, then he moves to the next section of his electrical manual subtitled: Polarity." Although his teaching was applicable to others, Jesus was aware that two of the men sitting in the small circle had been seriously abused as young boys and had only begun to untangle a web of issues that had been thrown over them like a net, preventing them from flying the way they were designed. "One day you opened a compartment in your heart called desire. You saw an individual as someone you could connect with—someone you admired, but they took advantage of the relationship and trampled trust like a heifer loose in a flower bed. A few days later the E.B.O. came along wearing bib overalls and while looking for his stray, places his chin upon stacked fists on top of a fence post, pulls a straw from his mouth and says, 'you're just too easy to break in on—you really are weak! Why didn't you use a stronger mesh?' Man becomes a cave dweller at this stage and pretty much gives up. His heart is hard, his thoughts cynical and his words are manipulative: God doesn't see, God doesn't care, he can't feel and he's hidden himself. He abandoned me when I needed him most. I'm going to begin relating to him in the same way! And so man decides to remain distant, silent and alone. But this is just the front end of the E.B.O.'s strategy. The thing he's really working toward like a licensed electrician is totally screwing up your circuitry and cutting off the house lights."

"O.K.," asked Peter, "So what does his electrical code call for? And get your pen ready, John."

"His plan calls for pulling people through a miserable conduit—people who have already suffered profound rejection. The E.B.O. runs them through repeated experiences of abandonment until they are left feeling blackballed and ignored. He normally uses your friends to accomplish this. After awhile, people begin to feel like alternating current in this kind of circuit. One day they feel like a victim and the next they feel like there's enough rage surging through their veins to kill someone. The E.B.O. has to get closer in order to make the connection, so he drops down from the utility pole, enters your basement, opens the main panel and creates a dead short by tying up wires marked: trust, acceptance and fraternal with horrific feelings of utter unloveliness. Circuits begin to trip and one enters an emotional twilight zone where sparks fly and overloaded panels melt with heat. In effect, you are being emotionally and spiritually electrocuted. 'Not only are you weak,' he whispers, 'but you're hopeless. Get out of the house!" Jesus screamed to the top of his lungs, "I said get out of the house! Move away! Buy down! You're deviant, hideous and perverse—drive your junker to some dark hole on the other side of the planet and bury you're face! There's nothing attractive or lovely about you—even you're best friend knows this!'"

John pulled up to the trunk of a tree and thought to let out a sigh, but like mild abdominal gas it was merely the prelude to an explosion of emotional diarrhea that caught two of the other men totally off guard. Both Peter and James were seriously concerned for their brother who was nearly convulsing with deep groans and sobbing. Jesus was sitting with his legs crossed and heels pulled up beneath his thighs. He leaned forward in a gesture more powerful than words and waited for the quaking in John's chest to subside.

"Can you manage some words, John?" Jesus asked.

"No, not right now, but I will soon." He admitted with a soft inflec tion that issued from a heart that felt like ground chuck. Peter and James also felt deeply impacted and pleaded with Jesus like starved men seeking bread to go on and teach them further about their souls.

"John," Jesus said, but addressing all three, "the reason the E.B.O. wants you isolated is because he hates community and he wants to stamp out networks of giving before they can reciprocate. Consequently, the gift of receiving also gets circumvented and so no one ever feels touched by another human or worthy. You see men, the heavy 60 amp breakers he really wants to disconnect are abandoned-control trust and hope. Stay on your guard, for the Accuser will tell you that no one can be trusted, that you have no friends and certainly no advocate. He wants you to lead a life of derision in which abandoned-control trust becomes a joke. Abandoned-control trust ever lives to watch the sea part down the middle and it yearns for another more significant redemptive act," (a phrase which splashed over their heads), "but if abandoned-control trust is destroyed, you will never receive; if hope is lost, you will never step out of the cave and take the hand of another, and that my friends is how the E.B.O. cuts off love which is the 200 amp main that feeds everything else in the house and keeps the lights burning. You are left in the dark with a disengaged soul—a cave dweller—lost in oblivion, numb, mean and cold. David once prayed from the mouth of a cave and his cries were heard. He had to be delivered from his persecutors because they were too strong for him. Don't go toe to toe with the E.B.O. A lid will be placed over him at the appointed time. Ask God to deliver your soul from prison and always be ready to assist others seeking light from the inside of a dark cavern."

"His strategy seems simple enough," said James. "The E.B.O. gets us interested in assisting him with a wiring project only to learn after it's too late that it's an electric chair with our name on it; and before it's all over, we're willing to lay down and throw the switch ourselves."

"That's right, James, the digression described in the first Psalm explains how you departed from innocence. Reverse the pattern, crawl out of the huddle with the scoffers, stand up and walk away from it—you'll begin to flourish like a well watered tree. If you don't make this passage, then you're left with feelings of self-hatred which flow through conduits and on out to a variety of other-centered contempt receptacles that have people's names on them. In reality, this is nothing more than a selfish effort to escape from dealing with your feelings of worthlessness, sense of isolation and twisted circuitry. People as you said lay on the gurney and their souls will tell you flat out, 'Don't appeal to the Governor—I'm going down!' You see, self-hatred conforms to the E.B.O.'s electrical code. Yes, you've all committed crimes worthy of death, but you didn't light the Chicago fire—it wasn't Auschwitz for crying out loud! You need pardon and I tell you the truth, one greater than the Governor is here."

James cut in, "You know, Jesus, I was feeling like that gurney thing wasn't such a bad idea a few weeks ago. Diane was trying to offer me some understanding following a blow-out we had, but I told her I had to have some space and so I took a long walk—I can't talk to her about this kind of stuff.

"It's sabotage, James. And it generally comes on the heels of some significant spiritual breakthroughs or personal enrichments," Jesus began. "Wasn't Abram promised the Land? But a famine provided him opportunity to quench the thrill—it just seemed too wonderful! So he passed right through the promise on his way to Egypt where he prostituted his wife to a stranger for the safety of his own hide. Elijah is another sterling example of male testosterone and strength. He slaughtered the prophets of Baal, then turned tail and ran to a cave after a few verbal threats made by Jezebel. Obstacles that could otherwise be conquered by an abandoned-control trust grow like giants of terror in a man's soul—Canaanites eyeballing your every move—preventing you from moving in a good direction or else standing firm. You know you have to make a choice but you don't like God's options; instead of humbling yourself and waiting upon his light, you take angry control and lead on with a man-made torch right into a foreign land with your platinum credit card or else a nearby cave that offers cheap relief in the form of lurid video. All the while, you rationalize and convince yourself that you're playing by the rules, improvising where you can, doing God all kinds of favors and that he should be proud to have you on his team. God owes you something huge; doesn't he? Listen men," Jesus paused while looking into the sky, then briefly surveyed the harbor and continued softly but with a detectable firmness, "God is not owing to anyone; nevertheless, he's obligated to pay for everyone."

"That sounds like a glaring contradiction." John observed, "How can God be free and obligated at the same time?"

"You heard right, John. God's justice and love are bolted together more tightly than boiler plate on a tank and nothing can vibrate them apart." Jesus continued without further qualification, "But that's not all. Everyone he purchased will also be developed. God is growing up souls that will last for eternity. He's building oak trees not squash—it takes a lifetime not six months. If you men only knew the investment of time, care and the high priority God places upon every individual soul! It would change your minds about a lot of childishness." Fire flashed in Jesus' eyes. "Job eventually got it right. You young Jobbers don't even know the right questions to ask of the physical side of the universe that you can see and touch, but you've got all the moral answers to the spiritual side that is hidden from your eyes.

"James, let me just say it out loud: your withdrawal from Diane is another way of saying, 'I hate you.' Yeah, the words you use are, 'I'm tired,' or 'I'm going out,' when in reality you believe you deserve better and so you continue denying your wife involvement and basically abort your marriage. You treat God the same way when something important like a Cubs loss throws you into a tail spin."

Peter whispered with a guttural grunt of his own making, "Don't let him get away, Jesus—the boy is trying to weasel out of your grip."

"C'mon, Jesus," James said while ignoring Peter, "how can that be sabotage—I sometimes just need some space."

"Because you're quitting at the precise moment in which some beauty is about to birth between the two of you. You walk out in hopes that Diane will feel sorry for you and conclude that she's the entire problem."

"Crystal clear," James said to Jesus.

"Well, see if this helps," Jesus said. "Your past personal rejection is useful to you. You could take steps to grow up emotionally and be the man Diane needs but then something rich and exquisite would have to be released—your grateful response for God's forgiveness and his pursuit of you. Isolation is useful to you because then you get to flagellate yourself and rehearse all the many legitimate reasons why you don't have to be a man for Diane. Or to put it another way, keep shoveling manure: walk in it, stand in it, and sit down in it. Revisit Psalm 1. You don't have to get up and be a man, because you agree with the E.B.O.—you're the very worm he has been describing. Hard work with a shovel always feels less difficult than walking toward glory. Self-contempt is a refusal to acknowledge that I might offer others a good gift. You never have to raise a sweat. James, let me take you back to the time spent with the others that night after the game at Wrigley Field. Do you remember how cool you were toward your friends and how you responded to me when I complimented the way you gave little Randy the ball? Everything about you said, 'Don't come any closer—you won't like what you find. Besides, I'm too cold and empty to have a relationship with you.' You ruined a great evening for yourself."

"O.K." said James with sincerity, "I guess I've never thought about it that way. I'll see if I can stay engaged next time around and not abort a good thing."

"Each of you stay engaged. Always. And don't leave your brother even if the E.B.O. has locked onto you with a heat seeking missile staring up your vulnerables. You need one another and if you fail to give your heart to anyone, you're simply filling your pockets with ordinance, drawing a target on your backs, marking your position with flares in clear view of the enemy, while shouting to the top of your lungs, 'Hit me. Over here! Hit me!' If you don't do anything else, be your brother's keeper."

"Jesus, do you want to know the truth? I mean just between us girls—I usually pick up a six pack when it gets that bad," Peter said to the others while rising up from laying on his side.

"Well of course you're not weak," Jesus said with a stoic look. "Pop a top. I'm not worthy to be shown such promise,'" Jesus continued as he cited a cripple. "Pop a top, Simon. 'And why show mercy to a dead dog like me?' Pop a top, Simon. But even though he ate regularly at David's table he denied the king when it appeared his fortunes had turned. Pop a top, Simon. Peter, a lot of people drink more than they should. Pop a top. That leaves one in the ring for the drive home. Go ahead," Jesus concluded while shaking his head with disgust, "might as well pop a top."

"I said I'm not weak, Jesus," Peter said tortuously.

"A guy on the radio said we pursue addictions in order to fill an emptiness inside," said John.

"No sir, the soul is much more desperate than that," Jesus said to them. "People do those things in order to siphon off rich levels of glory that have risen too high. People want to feel like scum so they can control Yom Kippur and keep God at a comfortable distance. Again, self-hatred is high octane. People think if they can manage the atonement, they won't have to grow up. 'I'm too wicked to forgive,' they admit, which in some twisted way makes God responsible for their hardness of heart. Only the gospel: pardon, unconditional acceptance and reinstatement, can shatter a soul in that condition.

"Think of the ways people mar beauty, cut their souls, stamp out a vine before it can climb and thrive on all sorts of self-inflicted abuse. In effect, people kill something inside the soul that was made to thrive, not die. Souls hunger to sit down and eat at a table in heaven that is not accessible to them today. Understandably, this produces sorrow and when my select community—the Church is sufficiently ready, she will begin to pray for the kingdom to come in place of all this trouble. In the meantime, addictions look attractive, but they are nothing more than fuel for the fugue. People wake up one day and wonder what they did with their lives. Like I've told you before, sit with yourselves and mourn—it will not go unnoticed. You will be singled out, and comforted for the Servant of Yahweh is also a man often saddened, acquainted with disappointment."

"You're basically telling us that we don't have to get drunk in order to be somebody..."

"Alright, James," said Peter, cutting him off, "let me hear the rest of this."

"You will be somebody, yes and one to be reckoned with when you stand up, face crisis and speak with a confidence that is derived from outside of yourselves. So get ready and brace yourselves for it will require all the courage you can muster when others begin to take you seriously," said Jesus.

"Men, I want you to grow comfortable with a sense of mystery. Life is a collection of impossible likelihood's because God is near and personal. Don't run from confusion. Let it flirt with your faith. Have proper regard for the past and examine what has happened to your souls. Treat the future like a blank canvas—paint a beautiful winter snow scape with a glistening frozen lake and leap into it. Friends, you have two options, either sit on the bench and grumble or lace up your skates and try your splendor out. When you grasp paradox, life can become a dance on ice. This is when you will make the good news known to a confused world that spins on an axis of ambivalence.

After a moment of interlude, John who had been mostly silent, lifted his eyes and asked Jesus, "So how do we get rewired—I mean those of us who have been pulled through the wrong conduit?"

"Create the surge," Jesus said. "You each have it within you. Keep turning from darkness to light—from anything that trips your circuit breakers or anyone else's. Begin living with a view to wiring light in others. Isn't it a drag to live in the cave? If you're involved in turning on lights, then you've struck upon something big. C'mon Flintstone, it's a new day. Lose your life to gain it. It's O.K. to have a life, the path is just paradoxical. For instance, you call me the Manager and you're right, but I've moved among you as the water boy."

"O.K., Jesus, but how about boundaries—time for ourselves?" Peter asked. " I mean we've been nearly overrun on more than one occasion."

"Truth-tellers need no such limits," Jesus responded. "When you speak the truth in love some people will move toward you while others will fall away. If you can demonstrate a little understanding with gentleness, keep your lips from flattery and are not afraid to call a spade a spade, you'll never have a problem with people stampeding your door. Boundaries are something crowd-pleasers use to fence people out after all the hysteria and swoon has worn off. They justify their segregation by saying, 'I'm burned out and need some space.' The wicked egotists have no concern for the sheep. The only thing they're concerned for is next month's accounting and how many people passed through the turnstiles to be entertained by their personal promotional antics. These will receive the greater judgment.

Honor one another men. And keep up your daily time with God in the Word—it's a source of direct current since you normally roll out of bed and start the day with low batteries and set on a path of dishonor. You've heard it said, 'the ordinary will create availability for the extraordinary.' Reversing the polarity begins with a spark of aspiration which changes your affections."

"Lord, teach us to repent at deeper levels," said James.

"Repentance is ultimately a gift but can be jump-started through periods of meditation as you consider God's character. When you invite his loveliness to break into those deep recesses of your heart, the shadows will be chased away and all your craft can be easily tagged. Don't confuse repentance with the Hub's self-mortification variety pack which they use to appease the conscience and sidestep their need for atonement. Reread Isaiah. The whole head is sick. Stop repenting over what you've done—that's symptomatic—repent over what you are. James, when your soul wails, and you find yourself seeking God by verbalizing you're own depravity, then you're deeper than the harm done to you. Man has a greater problem than his pain—never forget my priority for the soul of the paralytic who was lowered in the atrium of the hotel on a stretcher. When you get in touch at that core level, then you're standing down at the bottom, several floors below deck next to the ship's boiler with a good light and tools in hand. You'll find words because voice comes from desire."

"Yeah, I get the picture," said Peter, "sort of like Robin Williams in the 'Dead Poet's Society,' he placed his hand over the kid's eyes and drew out his voice." John and James looked at Peter with a smile for bagging the largest goose."

"Yes," Jesus added, "groan inwardly, wait expectantly and take back your voice. Did I not say that you are gods?"

"Is getting turned around the goal?" asked James.

"It's part of it, but let the hunger take you home. Don't settle for the simple 'do better moralism' that works so hard to be different. Go home and get the necessary refreshment so that you're willing to take risks with your life. The bad son came to his senses, but it was God who gave him the means to get home. You have no energy to approve others until you've had the sense that you have been singled out and are specially regarded by God. Step up on the lawn—you'll know when you've arrived home. Then invite others to the Bar-B-Que. Tell others who are bad or ugly about a good God who only eats with Davids—adulterers and murderers. These are the only people he welcomes to the party. The reaching-others process should not include an R.S.V.P. Live the celebration in spite of everything that's wrong around you. Others will catch wind of the sweet hickory smoke and make their way to the Bar-B-Que. Now you've got a context for sharing the kind of determined love that found you out and remains committed to you unconditionally. This quality of love says to others, 'I want to offer to you what I've been given.' It fits back into the notion of being singled out and specially regarded by God. Confess to those you've offended that you're undeserving of God's love, that you're murderous and bent on prostituting yourselves."

"You make us sound like dangerous killer-whales," said Peter.

"That you were dangerous." Jesus said as he fastened his hand over both of his eyes. "But killer-whores. Yes, and can you believe that God eats and drinks with the likes of David?"

"Do you recommend that we make vows or promises once we get home based upon what we want to be like?" asked James.

"Just stay in community, James. Keep checking your style of relating and grooming your brothers. Back your nose off from the broad side of the barn so that you can read what your brother's advertising. Now you can have a look. And stop keeping people at a distance; it's your angry control that says, 'if I can't have heaven on earth then I'll see that no one else does either.' On the other hand stop obligating people to stay in relationship—you'll know the difference. The E.B.O. will set aside important projects in favor of managing losers and he's always standing on the side line with a list of techniques for helping you fumble the ball—all kinds of head fakes to ensure that you don't score—that you remain independent and not contribute to community. He whispers defensive game plays from the side—all kinds of options to help you distract people from your soul. Fake left and boot leg right—the same method you use to anger people. If you're not in the starting lineup just sit on the bench and show people that you don't amount to much—don't expect too much from me.' The E.B.O. then flips the strategy card to the back side and tells the offensive line: 'Protect the quarterback at all costs—he'll be devastated if he loses more yardage; Quarterback, don't move out of the pocket—shame the line, family or anyone else within earshot during huddle, obligate them with whatever threats come to mind; Wide receivers, keep running until you blow out your knees—you'll of course keep the trophies; Kickers, miss a simple ten yard field goal from time to time—the crowd will sense that you're helpless. Cower back to the locker room, grovel around the office and explain that you can't survive without the team's reaffirmation.'

Peter chuckled, "C'mon, Jesus, you don't know football from tennis—right James! Besides, real men don't carry on like sissies and listen to all those signals from the E.B.O. in the first place. Can we get back to the electrical discussion?"

"God is not interested in rewiring your souls or the style you use to get people close, but not close enough. God's real purpose is not to change your style of relating but to use it. He will use even the most twisted circuitry to create voltage—to glorify himself. The goal is not to hit the top in this life—you'll never become state of the art. God works with blown fuses. He shatters those he uses. Yes, the E.B.O. will tell you it's weak, but Peter, Weak is the crucial finish section in God's collection of schematics labeled, Strong.'"

Fritz reached Geiger on his mobile while in route with Rueben to Point Crown and related from his observation post that there had been no apparent movement by Jesus on the lake front. Geiger sat in the back seat of Rueben' Mercedes, spinning his umbrella with one hand with its tip to the floor while holding the receiver with the other.

"Just stay out of sight and only alert me of anything unusual. I expect he will lay low today and gather the rest of his pathetic entourage by early evening. Fritz and I will be with Kite through most of the afternoon and we're waiting to hear from Judas—confirmation about a lead we received indicating they will be at the Holiday Inn at Mart Plaza around 8:00 P.M. Geiger disconnected without regard and dialed a private owned press, directing him to place several reams of color prints out at the front counter for courier pick-up.

"They're all here, Dr. Geiger," said Drexler. "Tell your man I'll take cash only and remember, these graphics didn't come from here. By the way, who was the heartless animal that shot these for you? Are they still undergoing therapy for emotional recovery? Some of these decapitations and gut shots are worse than anything I've seen since those two Italian guys who literally had their brains beaten out with tire irons. Hello, Hello." Geiger was pleasantly warmed by the news and jogged his mind ahead like a conveyor to the next shelf of stock.

Brenda had the day off and Marie Pierce took the incoming call on a scrambled secure line. Before she could identify the Mayor's office, Geiger reeled off a couple of crisp commands in a stern academic tone, "Geiger here. Dial Harry and place him on hold while you conference in the Chief of Police. Move on it, the Attorney General is awaiting word in Washington."

Harry excused reporters who were sensitively laying out sentences for an upcoming cover story that would showcase the Mayor's plans for

'Southgate,' Chicago's newest and most expensive airport. The mammoth design would swallow O'Hare and probably not even tap its full potential before much of it grew obsolete. Congressmen and women around the Country laughed behind Harry's back over the outrageous proposal, but Harry would build or die; and one of the most powerful men in the country, an enemy recently turned coat who had promised special personal conditions of involvement and plans for national indemnity, was holding for him on the phone.

Harry picked up the line which connected two wharfs of the same muridae family, one black and the other albino. Harry hadn't seen or heard from Geiger in months; then recently confidential files began to grow in his desk vault with incriminating evidence that would remove Jesus from the scene once and forever. Harry enjoyed being Mayor more than food or sex because the post facilitated his personal plans for the city's growth. As a result he was extremely paranoid about young upstarts who might gain a percentage of the vote. Republicans and Independents were never a serious threat in Chicago, but Harry was so insecure about being unseated that he even had a woman murdered who he learned intended to make a bid as a Democratic candidate. Removing Jesus would help him rest more soundly and maybe, he thought, even chase a ghost from the Harrison that showed up on occasion following the grisly night. Harry left dinner and was escorted home early one night due to a delusional episode in which he swore a decapitated man walked the center aisle of the grand ballroom. Paramedics assisted Harry out front as he lay on the sidewalk and those close to the Mayor reported the incident as a reaction to prescription cold medication. Harry demanded to be interviewed back on the job with stogy in hand the following day.

The click of magnets preceded the voice of Ivan Cox, the City of Chicago's Chief of Police. "Greetings, gentlemen," said Ivan in a somber tone, "line secure, Harry?"

"Everything's fine Ivan. Dr. Geiger whom you've worked with before is attending this call."

"Mr. Cox," came Geiger's voice in a manner of greeting. "Gentlemen," he continued, "codeword: 'Street Sweep' will enunciate at my signal in less than 12 hours. Mr. Cox, you will join Commander Colonel McBride with his troops at Humboldt Park at my command. Use the bus route we discussed, place him in chains and disband his following with any means you see fit short of live rounds. The Governor and his wife are staying at the Ritz. We've rehearsed this before, but he will verbally give up any thought of clemency even after things are out of his hands. I want the condemnation of this criminal and public nuisance official."

"Mr. P. and I are both looking forward to seeing this Jesus and don't worry, Mr. P. is clay in my hands," said Harry. "Anything else you need from the Governor, Dr. Geiger?"

"Stay away from the media, out of sight, out of mind and let them draw their own conclusions; it will be apparent enough. When interviewed, obviously, it is to be regretted that matters were taken into the public's hands." Rueben pulled into Point Crown and waited upon Dr. Geiger to pull together loose ends with two key players.

Before meeting with Kite, Geiger produced an electronic rolodex and double checked it for the name of anyone who may have been overlooked. In exactly five minutes, a computer would dial out a fresh recorded message to survivors and families of victims of the terrible city bombings. Geiger's words would describe more recent evidence that was pointing to a young rabbi who was growing a reputation in Chicago and adjoining suburbs as one sent from God. Geiger included all the necessary inflammatory remarks and embellished quotations regarding his claim as a supremacist and political insurgent. Geiger's message was replete with punishing remarks about sharing race with one responsible for the atrocity of apocalyptic proportions and the attendant shame his people must bear for the Star of David was invoked.

Kite, who was the high priest, welcomed Geiger and Rueben into a borrowed office at Ida Center about the same time Jesus departed from Belmont Harbor with his men.

As they were leaving the harbor parking lot Jesus said, "Peter and John, drive over to the Merchandise Mart where the others are waiting to help with tonight's supper."

"Well, where do you want us to make preparations?"

"Look, when you arrive at the Plaza, you'll see a man unloading bottled water, follow him inside and tell the manager that I've sent you and he will take you up to a large furnished room. Prepare it there." Peter joined John and hopped downtown and found everything just as Jesus described. They followed behind a man pushing a cart load of natural spring water into the Holiday Inn and spoke with the manager who was standing in the lobby supervising his staff. Siva recognized John's Saab and alerted the others to bring in racks from the van. Special arrangements had been made with hotel staff to cater the meal and Siva was way ahead of the program along with Gary, Darlene and others who were finding ways to be useful. Preparations for food by Allegretti, soft music, seating arrangements outlined by Jesus and every detail was carefully cared for and carried Quest volunteers into the early evening before they completed preparations.

James joined Jesus in Peter's vehicle. They caught Fritz looking who got confused on passengers and ended up following Peter and John downtown before he discovered that Jesus had passed through his fingers.

"Surveillance is up, Dr. Geiger," said Fritz with intrepidation in his voice. "He gave me the slip at Belmont and I'm watching two of his men right now walking into the Holiday Inn you marked."

"Hold your position," Geiger said, "and let me know as soon as he shows." Fritz was shocked not to have been blasted with vehemence for bundling a job, but Geiger knew things were getting far too late to worry about anything being significantly jeopardized. Meanwhile, Jesus pulled in at Point Crown and parked with the driver's side facing a dark Mercedes sedan. Jesus listened to James speak about suggestions he had for an upcoming fishing trip. After an hour, Dr. Geiger walked out of the building with Kite and Rueben on each side and making their way to the vehicle in order to grab a late lunch.

"Boy, get a load of this," James said, nudging Jesus on the leg and pointing with his head in the direction of the building, "now are they styling or what?"

"Just cocks in a barn lot," Jesus sighed, not moving his head.

"Good night, that's Caiaphas himself," James said excitedly, "Who are the men with him?"

"The one closest to us is Geiger from the University of Chicago."

"Geiger?" James asked quizzically, "I thought, well you said to—hey what's up with us being here anyway?"

"Just trading baseball cards, James, besides we've never met, and Geiger wouldn't recognize his own mother. At some point in our brief conversation ask him if he can be reached for an interview near the sanitary ditch above Justice or if we should look for him at his office."

"Huh?" James shrugged to Jesus, but was ready for the game. Geiger stopped at the rear door of the car ignoring passengers in a vehicle next to him and concluded another conversation with Fritz by snapping the cellular shut.

"Fritz is down at Mart Plaza," Geiger said in open air for the benefit of his associates, then stood looking over the roof of Fritz's car in a direction away from Jesus and James. "He says he was given the slip, but he's found the rest of them." Geiger was utterly cool on the outside, but his mind was swapping files, 64 bits a hit at nano-speed. "Don't worry, gentlemen," he said aloud and reassuring himself before the others.

"Gentlemen," Jesus said weighing the appellation and drawing their attention, "word on the street has it that an informant is about to spill his guts."

Geiger often placed the point of his umbrella between his feet when lecturing. "Look," Geiger said to the two men in the utility vehicle, 'you tell you're editor back at the Tribune that I don't know where he's getting these outlandish ideas but rumors fill a city of this size. Everybody wants a piece of this story and you'll have the whole truth in your hands very soon."

James leaned over and asked Geiger, "Dr. Leonard Geiger, now how do you spell that?" Jesus inconspicuously pressed James' shoulder back against the seat to prevent them from seeing his teeth. "G-e," Geiger began with exasperation in his voice, "no wonder the papers are filled with errors."

"No," James stopped Geiger momentarily, "'Leonard'—how do you spell 'Leonard' and is that an acrostic or some metabolic numeral for something worse—the chief editor will want to know. Geiger warmed up a little slower than usual to the fact that he was being toyed with but before he could formulate a retort James said, "The chief also wants to know where you can be reached for a personal interview in the next 24 hours. Should we meet you at the sanitary ditch above Justice or will you be at your office?" Geiger thought to poke James in the eye with the point of his umbrella, but he lost grip of it as the electric window rose and it fell beneath the tires and was crushed as Jesus and James pulled away from Point Crown.

"There's a dangerous leak," Geiger shouted, while jumping around the lot like a small child throwing a tantrum, "damn that rookie!"

"Doctor, it couldn't have been him. Jude was never privy to the location." said Rueben. Geiger picked up his crumpled umbrella and threw it to the ground when something inside pressed F5 to print. "He was sitting right here behind a pair of cheap sunglasses while a junior grub asked me to spell my own name!"

"No way," said Kite, "not in a million years would he show up here." Geiger said not another word about the mysterious interview. The three men climbed in their car and made passage downtown to a command post at a secret suite in view of Grant Park.

Emotional fires began to burn by late evening fanned by poignant printed rhetoric being distributed as a first wave by Geiger's associates. People had already begun to amass downtown in order to hold an all night vigil insisting that the criminal who had brazenly walked their streets peddling good news be brought to justice. Bull horns sounded around Grant Park with reminders about courts and a lackadaisical judicial system led by men and women who were soft on criminals and more interested in media hype and seeing their names in the paper than bringing criminals to justice and helping families cope with loss. Jesus had already joined others at the Holiday Inn for the Passover meal. Everyone in the room had spent the afternoon preparing their hearts for the special annual celebration and were oblivious to the growing unrest down near Grant Park. Stories of a death angel and blood sprinkled upon the lintels of Jewish homes were being recounted in Jewish homes all around the City while Jesus and his twelve closest followers sat down for their own private celebration of the Exodus.

No sooner than the meal had begun and everyone looked to Jesus for the traditional retelling, he surprised them by saying, "I have looked forward to this meal with great anticipation, but I tell you most assuredly, one of you will betray me!"

Each of the twelve who had been hand picked and given a special commission nearly dropped their flatware defending themselves saying, "Surely you're not thinking of me, Lord."

Then Jesus said, "The one who dipped his hand with me in the bowl is the one who will betray me."

'Just this morning,' John thought to himself, 'I read the passage from the book of poems where David wrote, 'He who eats my bread has lifted up his heal against me.'"

While the men were still grumbling among themselves and looking at one another with accusatory eyes that led to a debate about who was the greatest among them, Jesus said, "The Son of Man will go just exactly as it has been previously written of him; but sorry indeed will be the man by whom he is betrayed. That man would have been better off not to have been born." Jude sat directly across from Jesus at the table and in his typical deceitful style asked, "surely you don't think I would do such a thing."

While others were still squabbling, Jesus said to him, "Judas, you have said it yourself. Get on with what you've determined and move on it." And because gifts were collected before the meal for the poor, others felt that Jesus must have excused Jude to carry a gift over to a nearby street shelter for the poor. Jude slammed his fist into the elevator panel while shouting at the ceiling all the way to the lobby where he entered the dark streets.

After Jude had departed, Jesus began a conversational lecture that was intimate but disturbing. "Now is the Son of Man set ablaze in lights," he began, "and God is set ablaze in him." Jesus spoke for several minutes describing the special relationship each of them enjoyed with God, but the commensurate persecution they could expect from the world in which they lived and for them not to be surprised. The men were most impressed with recent word about the Holy Spirit whom Jesus described as a comforter, teacher and guide—one who would come in Jesus' stead following his departure. The room was quiet and still as the clock climbed toward 10:00 P.M. Jesus stood and offered a prayer on their behalf that astonished them all, for he prayed for their literal oneness with God himself. Jesus' words were so intertwined and convoluted that his followers were lost but gloriously trapped in a mirror maze of words that reverently reflected God with us and us with God.

Following the meal, Jesus broke matzah and distributed it to his followers saying, "This is my body which is given in your place; repeat this in order to remember me. Afterwards and with nearly the same words he took a large glass of wine and told the men to share it among themselves saying, "This is the new covenant in my blood—a glass being poured out for you—I won't be drinking from vintage again until I drink it brand new with you in the kingdom of God."

Peter received the glass from John who was invited to sit next to Jesus and said, "He means—you're basic maintenance agreement little fellow—fresh pads on new ground rotors that won't wear out—now that's a warranty I want."

"Not now," John said to Peter. He appreciated Peter's insights and ability to grab the big picture and break it down, but there was something going on at the table that Peter and the others seemed oblivious to and it didn't set well with John.

Jesus led the men in familiar hymns of blessing and thanks; then they met in the lobby before loading up and heading over to Humboldt Park where he wished to spend extended time in prayer. Everyone unloaded from their vehicles at the edge of the park, and Jesus told them that they would all run away on account of him tonight; then citing the prophet he said, "'I will strike down the leader, and the team will be scattered.' After I have been raised, I will go ahead of you to the lake side."

The air was a bit cool and Jesus pulled a cotton hooded sweater given to him by his mother over his head when Peter said with certain gravity and respect, "Look, Lord, I don't know who you have in mind, but even if the rest desert you—you can count on me—even if I die with you and each of the men nodded and repeated pretty much the same thing. Jesus felt compassion for the children who stood before him—little guys with wooden poles, plastic arsenal and war belts ready to engage an imaginary enemy lurking among hog weed and patches of broom sage on the back side of the old Roby farm.

Jesus, not needing anymore time, loosed his watch after setting the alarm and said to the boy with the biggest stick, "Peter, place this on your wrist. Before you hear the alarm, you will have denied me tonight three times."

"I'll hold it for you," Peter said to Jesus, ignoring his lack of confidence and he strapped it on his bare wrist for feel. By the time he looked up, others had walked in the direction of the flower garden and he had to run to catch up having lost time because of his fascination with the watch.

Jesus directed the men to take up positions of prayer while taking Peter and Zeb's, two sons, a distance away to pray. Jesus was deeply grieved in his soul and asked the three to keep watch with him for he knew his hour was at hand. After a moment, he walked a distance even beyond the three closest to him, fell to the ground and prayed, "My Father, allow this death-drink to pass from my lips. Father, but according to your will." After several more minutes, wrestling with God in prayer, Jesus returned to his followers who were sleeping. "Peter," Jesus asked while nudging him awake, "what time does that time piece say?" Before he could focus his vision, Jesus asked, "Can't you three stay awake and watch for just one hour?" Jesus went away as before to pray while Peter, James and John tried to get back on their knees. After several minutes in prayer, Jesus again cried out in desperation, "Father, if the only way is straight up the middle, then I will drink the glass full to satisfy your good will." He returned to his men with new resolve and found each of them sleeping again for their eyes were too heavy to stay awake. After scolding them, he went away to pray yet a third time. John was sitting near Jesus when he made his last entry and was sure he saw beads of blood on the tops of his hands and forehead. Minutes later, Jesus returned and found his men in a stupor and said, "Are you still taking your rest? Let's go—time's up—the Son of Man is being sold out—right into the hands of sinners. Look," Jesus concluded and pointing in the direction of the sound of air brakes, "the one blowing the whistle has arrived." Peter raised his head and shook off his sleep with a fight brewing and walked out of the garden area at Jesus' side. Jesus reached the remaining eight about the same time Judas arrived with soldiers from the National Guard in platoon formation. They were accompanied by A.T.F. agents who carried warrants along with Fritz and Mr. Milgram who represented the Jewish High Priest carrying warrants of their own.

"Ferret him out, Judas," ordered Colonel McBride. And Judas stepped forward without hesitation and kissed Jesus on the cheek and greeted him with some such pleasantry typical of his hypocrisy."

Jesus said to Judas, "Friend, do what you've purposed to do." Soldiers stepped forward with a belt and wrist chains while Peter pulled a blade from his pocket and dove into the mix cutting off one of Fritz's ears.

A young corporal swung at Peter's head with the butt of his rifle, when Jesus shouted authoritatively which stopped everyone, "Enough of this! Put the blade away." Jesus stooped down with fettered hands and lifted an ear from the grass and put it back in place on Fritz's head where it remained. Then looking with disheartedness at followers slow to believe, said, "Don't you know that I can dial up my Father even now and he will immediately place at my disposal twelve battalions of angels? How then will the scriptures be sewn up and tied together unless it should happen just this way?"

"Enough of these bald remarks," said Judas as he stared at Jesus' cuffed hands. The shouts by Jesus' followers cursing Jude and deriding the soldiers as a bunch of authoritarian Franco pigs was cut off when the Army Commander told his platoon for the first time that they held in custody the ring leader of the terrible city bombings. Outrage erupted from both sides on the heals of that incredible accusation or revelation depending upon what side of the line they were standing. Colonel McBride quickly stepped his men back in formation and shouted out a command of port arms which was unfamiliar and frightening to Jesus' followers. When the rifles snapped in open palms with a crack and unsheathed bayonets glistened in the night's light, each of Jesus' followers turned tail and ran in every direction out of their path and away from memories of Kent State. The swift mechanical like action by the soldiers instilled fear in Jesus' men, and no one wanted to wait around to have their brains sewn back into place for they were sure the rifle butt would open up a skull like a sledge to a ripe watermelon.

Jesus turned to the soldiers and Jewish leadership saying, "Have you come out here to apprehend me with rifles and brute force as though I'm some kind of criminal. I taught daily in the City at Grant Park and you didn't arrest me; but all this has happened so that the scriptures may be fulfilled." Abusive speech and profanity rose from the soldiers who were scarcely restrained by their officers because of the hatred they carried for the one responsible for bombing the V. A. Hospital, not to mention the cowardly attack upon the Crippled Children's Hospital.

"Awwwten—hut," shouted a Commander equally incensed but determined to harness the fury until the appropriate time.

A.T.F. agents were escorted out of Humboldt Park by the Guard while Jesus' followers ran to the perimeter like children running for their lives. Shouts by the Commander and movement by olive green military busses brought profound reality to the situation at hand. Unmarked cars left the park in route to Point Crown at the same time the Guard drove downtown with police escort. By now television networks were all on line and most of Jesus' followers were huddled around a tube to learn the story and public opinion from news anchors—a story that was brand new to them. James and John were furious with local authorities, Judas and whoever was behind the strategy to imprison Jesus. Mary was overcome with dread and collapsed in her living room as the monitor poured out data, and moment to moment updates. The entire Country was rejoicing over the capture of the notorious criminal. News of the report reached sportscasters at the Coliseum and over 200,000 fans broke into shouts of victory that could be heard in neighborhoods great distances away. No one close to Jesus believed a word of the allegations, but they were so seamlessly woven that they would be humanly impossible to unravel.

Live coverage of the lake front at 11:00 P.M. revealed large crowds that were growing in intensity. Little news had leaked out before this date. Now a hydrant was being opened. The entire story was being delivered and repeated on the half-hour for newcomers to the broadcast. Reviewed documentary from the bombing sites, including heart-torn mothers with their hands uplifted over rubble and fragmented body parts wailed afresh. The emotions were felt by the populace like it was the very first showing. Geiger's courier was on location with dozens of aids poised for pictorial leaflet distribution that would occur in mass at his command. Riot police and other units of the National Guard were brought into Grant Park to patrol the Pier and everything as far south as Meigs Field. The Attorney General was not interested in disbursing the crowds for he was convinced following Dr. Geiger's advice that much national healing could be achieved by allowing the crowds to experience the public release of pent up emotions while gently containing their parameters without dispersing them.

The media were led to believe that Jesus was escorted downtown for custody at the Cook County Jail, but Peter who was now wide awake kept a closer eye and followed cars to Point Crown where Jesus was pushed inside the facility by wicked men. Several federal agents stood in the foyer of the building, but everyone close to the vital center moved inside to a secure conference room. Peter stepped inside the exterior doors where others were crowding registers for a little heat to knock off the chill. Several of the Jewish leadership kept trying to force false evidence against Jesus even bringing back witnesses who were on hand when he delivered much of his more controversial teaching.

"He said that he would destroy Judaism and our places of worship and rebuild it in three days," said one witness reading from notes taken less than six weeks ago. Caiaphas was enraged as others for the way his teachings had turned Judaism on its ear and caused many to leave time honored orthodox practices as well as undermining the authority of the synagogue. Jewish leaders demanded that Jesus respond to the allegations, but he was as utterly mute through the entire deliberation.

Since no one could get their story straight and the Jews were being embarrassed, Caiaphas silenced everyone. As High Priest he placed Jesus under oath and insisted of him, "By the living God, I demand that you tell us if you are the Christ, the Son of God."

Jesus solemnly responded by saying, "Yes, I am. It has come from your own mouth; but listen carefully, afterwards you will see the Son of Man sitting at the right hand of power and coming on the clouds of the sky."

Caiaphas was so infuriated that he tore his vestments, saying, "He has blasphemed! What further need have we of evidence? What is the consensus?"

Everyone answered on cue, "He deserves to fry!"

In that moment, someone spit in his face while others slapped him with mocking taunts, blindfolded him and demanded he predict who would hit him next. Peter raised his head when the door to an inner room opened wide and Kite exited with his immediate associates. Jesus was in clear view and Peter could scarcely take in the sight of his leader strapped to a chair and beaten mercilessly by thuds who had been hired for that very purpose.

Rage was welting up in Peter's chest when he was approached by a woman who often accompanied others in pursuit of gathering information about Jesus. She asked, "You are his close friend aren't you? I've seen you with him many times." Others in the closed circle turned to see who Rhonda was addressing, when Peter adamantly insisted that she was mistaken about his identity. Peter stepped away from the crowd and began walking down the sidewalk when he was met by Rhonda's friend, Beverley, who also identified him as one of Jesus' inner circle.

"I swear I don't know the man, I'm just up here like the others to get a look at the guy—you've got me mixed up with someone else," Peter said to her. Because of the suspicion being stirred, he thought he would loiter a little longer. But the more time others had to consider him, the more they were convinced that he was the big one who crashed vendors a few days ago in the park.

In a moment some of the men standing by approached him and said, "You are definitely one of his followers, you even sound like one of those weaklings."

"What in the squat do you people want—flipping papers? A double-frosted flabber finking passport I.D.; I've already told you that I don't even know the man!" Immediately the watch on Peter's wrist began chiming and one of those standing by asked if it was not 1:00 A.M. Peter walked away in rage and found his vehicle in a nearby lot. He sat down and slammed his fist into the driver's side window which shattered the glass. Peter crumbled at the wheel and began weeping bitterly.

Chapter 23

Geiger found several hours of good rest during the night while Maggie and others gathered around Jesus' mother at her home to watch and pray. Peter, James and John weren't talking with one another and each found an isolated place to hide and be alone. During the night Jesus was transferred from Point Crown over to Cook County Jail where he was being held without bond. Geiger's alarm sounded at an early hour. He shaved while watching CNN and was out the door before 4:00 A.M. with a new umbrella in hand.

Mr. P. who was known by his enemies as 'Pilot,' because of his many ideas and prototypes that were never executed, was picked up in front of the Ritz-Carlton by a limo and driven over to City Hall where he would join the Mayor and Chief of Police, Ivan Cox. His wife called to him from her bed without rising and, though she hated Jesus, warned her husband to have nothing to do with him because of a disturbing dream she had suffered about him during the night. But Treep was not the last person Mr. P. would speak to prior to Jesus' arraignment. And true to his character, the governor always turned downstream wherever the greater current directed.

The weatherman promised a wonderful picture book spring day for the entire Midwest and excitement was carried along the loft of air as Kenny entered the feeder side of the family owned dairy farm to fill troughs for young Jerseys that would become the next generation to fill milk trucks. Pasted to an outside panel of the stainless cupboard where veterinarian supplies and vitamins for the cattle were kept hung a poem entitled 'Ragged Scarf' given to him by a man named, Danger who had picked him up several months ago and offered him a shuv home. Kenny's dad entered the breezeway without his usual work clothes and cast down a small package to the counter.

"Happy Birthday, Kenny," said his dad, while gripping the back of his son's neck. The small package was obviously wrapped by Dad. None of the corners and flaps were even or very well tucked. Kenny's pursed lips and bent brows offered thanks for a gift received, then pulling off the lid he was amazed to find several hand made flys.

"Dad, these are beautiful," Kenny said, "but I'm still saving for the rod." Two of Kenny's uncles arrived at the door of the barn and when Kenny turned to greet the unlikely guests he stood face to face with a brand new fly rod outfit and waders that he had previously circled in an outdoor magazine. The men graciously drove Kenny and their brother from the barn while assuring them that the milking would be carried out with all the attention and care their own herds received. The father and son caught a cooler from the lady of the house who blew a kiss as they jumped in the farm truck and headed out to a local stream to try their luck casting for an early morning mess of brown trout.

Thousands of demonstrators still remained in Grant Park having camped there over night and were chanting for their governor to fulfill their wishes to condemn the recently captured criminal. Reporters for CNN were spooling more video than they could use with live feed issuing from key locations including the steps of City Hall where several hundred angry citizens awaited word from the Governor who was expected to surface at any moment. Most of Chicago was just getting out of bed while a secret screening was being carried out behind closed doors and away from pesky news agencies. Inside City Hall, the Governor was accompanied by the Mayor and a few select Jewish leaders who were well recognized in the community. Specific questions were leveled at Jesus regarding the bombings and interspersed with interrogation by religious leaders who wanted to hear from Jesus' own lips if he considered himself to be 'the King of the Jews.' Although he was vehemently accused by Jewish leaders, he remained silent throughout the entire crossfire.

Pilot had seen enough of Jesus' distorted face, maimed by the blows of hateful fists and because he surmised that a riot was brewing outside, looked to the Mayor in typical fashion and said, "We're getting nowhere with this, but what can we do? I don't want to put my head in the sand, but we can't very well police these religious squabbles either. I'm washing my hands of this. The courts will hear you soon enough," he told the Jewish leaders, "see to those infractions yourselves—I'm innocent of this man's blood."

All the Jewish leaders said, "We'll take responsibility for his blood—both we and our children!" While Harry said not a word to Jesus, it was obvious that he was pleased with the direction of things and was more patient than usual to allow the timing of events to work themselves out by the clock. Pilot was as cool as ever and wearing the same photogenic smile that had become his trademark, but these were not typical reporters yapping at his skirt, but rather hungry crocks ruthless enough to chew the tile from beneath his feet.

"Governor," said a leading Jewish spokesperson, "you will need to make a more decisive stand on this one. News of your indecision will not fair well in Washington not to mention the reaction of these crowds—there is serious threat that the city will be burned to the ground. You'd be wise to deny all forms of amnesty related to the death sentence before you are even questioned about it. Look, Governor, even though premature, the citizens of this City will interpret it as leadership. Something you've been running low on."

"He's right," Harry agreed in an uncommon show of support, "this is too big not to stay a step ahead of the hounds. The whole world knows he must die—better lead the pack or stay on the porch." Harry stepped back, squared shoulders with the Governor and drew from his cigar as he awaited a response. Pilot could feel diarrhea mounting. Harry had not blinked.

"So what's next?" Pilot asked the Jews.

"Get behind a push for immediate execution—within the year—we want to be done with this!" they shouted. Pilot had run-ins with this strain of Jew before and was aware of their jealous motives. He was equally unsure without a proper hearing if the man sitting before him had the ability to carry out such a dastardly act. Jesus was handed off by the Governor to authorities, his facial features marred more than any man with swollen lips and a great deal of dried blood upon his hooded sweater. One of his eyes was nearly shut from repeated blows and his scalp loosened above the left ear where his hair was also matted with blood, but still oozing with plasma. The Governor was squeamish but did his best to be a man before Harry who was thoroughly enjoying the mock proceedings. Between the two, they became good friends that day—two men who were previously enemies now joined in a common cause.

"Ladies and Gentlemen," Mr. P. began from the front of the building. "Your assembly here this morning on the steps of our City's Trust have been duly noted by the entire American public who have followed the unfolding of this story with great interest. You have each modeled extreme restraint and are to be commended for the example you've set for the Nation. I've already pledged to do everything in my power not to allow anything to impede the swift execution of justice this case demands. The criminal responsible for the cowardly bombings in our great city will suffer the crucible of our courts, and be assigned judgment severe enough to fit the crime." Turning to the Chief of Police, he concluded, "Mr. Cox, do with him as you may, I'm not involving myself any further."

Following some brief Q & A on the steps of City Hall, the Governor and Mayor excused themselves back indoors where they conveniently exited the rear for breakfast and an early morning tee appointment.

In the meantime, Jesus was moved to another room and held by soldiers of the National Guard who made sport of him and repeated the same physical abuse that he had received during the night from the hands of the Jews. Deference was extended the Guard by other Federal authorities who allowed them to punish Jesus thus vicariously representing all military personal who were shamed by the bombing of the Veterans Hospital. The officer in charge, a veteran of the Gulf War ordered one of his men to pull a spoke hubcap from a car out back and bring him a tire iron. Once inside, the men used wire pliers to spread the spokes and arrange the barbs to penetrate Jesus' scalp where it was forcefully driven in place.

Several of the men took turns rapping the hubcap while mocking him as King of the Jews, bowing and repeating, "Hooray Jesus, King of the Jews!" They then spat on him and exchanged turns rapping his head with a tire iron they had given him as a scepter until fresh blood flowed freely. Some of the men were already drunk in celebration of the criminal's capture and were looking forward to moving him to the street where cameras could get a closer look at how terrorists are handled in their Country—the obvious beating notwithstanding, for word had already circulated on the street that he resisted arrest and threatened to call angels from heaven to assist him.

Judas stood along side the soldiers through Kite's midnight court at Point Crown; but as the beatings resumed without superintendence and no indication on Jesus' part that he was going to throw off his enemies; he was filled with an overwhelming sense of defeat. Everything from here on out would be the same song and dance in the courts that he had seen in the past. Jesus would receive a life sentence or more likely the death penalty. Although Jude didn't know who pushed the button, he was sure who orchestrated it from beginning to end, and it couldn't have been Jesus. Feeling remorse about the entire betrayal, and that he had been used as a mole, Jude excused himself to the restroom, and drove over instead to Point Crown where he confronted Kite and others still cleaning up from the night before.

"Jude, what are you doing here?" asked Fritz.

"I've sinned by giving up an innocent man," Judas exclaimed, "here take this filth!" And Judas threw all $30,000 down the corridor and ran from the building shaking his fists. Jews at Point Crown could not accept the money back into their coffers since it was money used to stage an execution. After some time of counsel among themselves, Fritz suggested that it be used to purchase a few burial plots for strangers. The idea was taken up and grave plots were subsequently purchased at a nearby cemetery and named Potter's Field, or some called it Field of Blood.

Roger and Lucy's flight arrived in San Diego during the night and they were somehow oblivious to the national event filling television screens across the country. Their drive down to the beach house in San

Clemente was leisurely and filled with memories of yesteryear while they listened to their favorite recorded music. The morning began with some time at the beach still dark where Roger left Lucy while he slipped away and returned on the bare back of a friend's white Arabian that had been arranged for weeks before. Lucy was up from the sand and thought to surprise Roger back at the house with something light for breakfast, but she was run down atop a dune and swept into his still powerful hands and swooned to the hammock after a bath of fresh fruit and wine. It was truly a late abode by the time they reached the satin shears and wrestled playfully with magnificent throws until they both lay pinned beneath a release that would not let them go.

Back in Chicago, Geiger exited the Stevenson at LaGrange and drove south until he crossed the sanitary ditch and rail that ran parallel along side the DesPlaines River. Geiger directed Rueben to park along the shoulder and he got out and walked a path along the tracks remarking, "this Friday is just too good to be true." At his feet lay several large timbers delivered earlier in the week by Fritz and Mr. Milgram. The pile included three heavy cross beams lifted from a trestle and an equal number of 14 foot square timbers from the same discarded stock already notched for fit and long enough to protrude 6-8 feet above the holes presently being dug by Geiger's associates several meters ahead on the rough path. Geiger walked the entire length of Jesus' upcoming journey and made a final notation in his arranger when his eyes fell upon several hand held sledges and rail spikes picked up from the tracks nearby, that had been laid aside after some recent repair work and collected by his men. Having cleared every obstacle, Geiger took one last look around at the passage, then rejoined Rueben who gave him a lift back to the suite near Grant Park.

Maggie who could handle a car as well as Andretti agreed against her better judgment to give Mary a lift downtown.

Siva caught her in flight on a cellular and screamed, "Everything is a mess down here—promise me you won't bring Mary along!" Mary forced a disconnect and insisted that Maggie drive or she would find another ride.

"Maggie, you've got to do this for me," Mary said in desperation, "he's my boy!" Maggie pulled tears from her cheeks remembering how she had inflicted blows similar to the ones Jesus was presently receiving, never giving a thought in an earlier day to leave a man or woman alike to bleed and die in a dark lot.

"O.K. Mary," Maggie said, with no interpretation needed, "that was for the liking, this one's for the Lord," and she forced the pedal to the metal and caught a gear she hadn't used since prior to meeting Jesus. She awakened the oversize V 8 that screamed from beneath the hood forcing G-60's to claw the asphalt like a greyhound loosed from the gate on race day. Slower drivers were ordered to the side by the flash of the old Eldorado that was still showing plenty of kick. Maggie drew in her chin—a mechanical foil seeking just the right tilt and looked only once at Mary who was petrified but securely fastened with a seatbelt and her fingernails firmly embedded in leather upholstery. Unusual winds poured in from the open sunroof while invisible fingers pulled back hair from two courageous faces far more stately and resolute than the presidential pillars staring out from Mt. Rushmore; however, they could not be frozen in salt for they passed on swiftly and never looked back.

Mary arrived at the fringe of the crowd at City Hall the very moment Jesus was drawn outside by federal escort.

Overwhelming grief seized her. As soon as the crowd idled down she blurted out as loud as she could shout, "kid run!" Her voice carried over a street that Jesus had often crossed with his men—one that is still known by Jesus' followers as the Kidron Valley to this day because of

Mary's anguish. Jesus looked in the direction of his mother and acknowledged the woman by raising his head—a woman who had nurtured and protected him in life, still unwilling to give up her love and fight for his survival.

Angry crowds stood outside City Hall demanding further audience with the Governor who had already departed. "We want verbal assurances that this criminal will be properly disposed of and in short order!" cried the crowds. Jews in the audience wailed with similar lament demanding that they be rid of the king imposter, "We have no ruler but the President of the United States!" they shouted. And again, "You're no friend of the President and a traitor to our Nation if you don't move quickly to deny any possible appeals before they are even filed!"

Jesus was surrounded by U.S. Marshals who nearly lifted him from the steps in their effort to move him back to a holding cell at Cook County; but like a bullet totally unexpected from an assassin's arm, five men aided by a wave of over zealous National Guardsmen, fueled by a crowd mad with rage and mixed fear still holding color photographs of their torn slain, snatched Jesus from custody on video in broad daylight and forced him into a white Bronco driven by a coward wishing to prove himself before Geiger's associates. Jesus was thrust to the back seat and wedged between two guardsmen. Network reporters were running and panting with cameras in hand trying desperately to stay a step ahead of a mob who had just learned in that moment that Jesus had been wrenched from the hands of authorities. Mayhem spilled into the streets in utter chaos as political and police authorities who were 'in the know' threw their arms up in frustration with facial gestures that said everything was out of their control. The driver of the Bronco—Howard, who was a native of the city, drove furiously while striking Jesus' legs with a fist free from the wheel. Those outside nearly overturned the truck in an effort to fasten their hands on Jesus before he could be drug away by wild dogs stealing meat from other violent predators of the Serengeti. A convoy of vehicles stretched out of the city while Jesus' remaining eleven followers watched color monitors in disbelief, away in the confines of their homes. News of the outbreak filled radio waves as thousands of citizens stopped their vehicles on overpasses and along side the shoulder of the Stevenson Expressway to applaud his capture and cheer on what reporters were describing as a mob lynching in progress.

Geiger left operations at the secluded suite after the momentum swung to his favor. He then boarded a city owned chopper at Grant Park and was flown over head following the convoy out of the city while hovering above the Stevenson. The ride out to the site was cleared by police escort who provided shoulder passage when necessary and an even clip of over 60 miles per hour. Geiger controlled the escort's movements from the air and transmitted that they should exit the Stevenson at LaGrange and drive south to a location above the community of Justice where they would be directed by Mr. Milgram from the ground.

Jesus never lost consciousness though he had already lost about a pint of blood and was running on very little sleep and food. His undershirt was blood soaked and every nod of his head that indicated possible blackout was met by another flurry of fists that lifted his face and renewed his determination to persevere. One of the soldiers took a gulp from a pint of bourbon then placed his arm around Jesus' shoulder and sponged away blood seeping from his eye while preparing him for the upcoming round. "Now you've done real good up till now 'Rocky,'" his manager snickered, "you show the same courage in the 15th and you'll take home the heavy weight belt."

"Better let him rest while we can," said Mr. Milgram, "and remove his chains. Dr. Geiger has a little obstacle course for you to cross," and laughing aloud with the others about his play on words.

When the convoy arrived at the sanitary ditch, there were no less than twenty vehicles who were able to remain in the pack and follow the others who exited at LaGrange. Everything that followed was simply horrifying to watch and a step back into antiquity when criminals were hung upon trees and left for the birds to pick out their eyes while their corpses rotted with maggots. Indeed torture took on a new definition after this day. Men powerful from lifting iron with huge arms and bulging abs forced Jesus along with blows as they followed Mr. Milgram along to a prearranged place of execution. After about 300 meters, Jesus fell to the ground for a second time under the weight of the primary upright he had been saddled with upon his arrival.

"Mr. Milgram," one of the soldiers said, "maybe we should remove that hub cap and give him a little water before going further."

"Not a chance," said Milgram who had an eye to the chopper over head and knew that a single glitch would result in his joining Jesus on the tree.

"Well, he isn't going much further unless you want us to drag him," another soldier agreed, "and we aren't too interested in raising a sweat out here today." Milgram was getting a little nervous with the chopper circling overhead and realizing that everything was on a time schedule that had to be satisfied with meticulous care. Geiger was more critical than a skilled machinist when it came to precision.

During closed planning sessions when others were perspiring under unreasonable demands, he would often squash their objections regarding tolerances too close to hold by saying, 'It's all math, gentlemen, and just as easy for us to hit the mark as to miss it; and we will of course hit it.'

"O.K., hold up," said Milgram, "look, the rest of you take these two ahead and get them ready," pointing to two jewel thieves who were captured following a major heist. They had since been singled out as co-conspirators of the city bombings and brought along to accent the day's crowning event. "Wilkinson, run down there and see who that is coming this way. Maybe it's one of the lunatic's followers creeping around the outskirts like a coward." Wilkinson ran down the tracks holding an M-16 across his chest and ordered a civilian hiking in from downstate to come along and help bear the main post. In the meantime, other soldiers led the two men who had been conveniently sprung from jail and named as Jesus' accomplices along the same path. Mike and Benny were partners in crime—mostly felony theft, but railroaded onto this track by crafty politicians and police officials who were desperate three-and-a-half years ago to pin the bombing rap on somebody until the ring leader could be corralled.

Wilkinson returned to Mr. Milgram with a man named Sims who just arrived back from working out of state for several weeks and forced him to carry a heavy post the remainder of the distance while Jesus drug the smaller cross beam with a rope. As the procession got back underway, Geiger was still overhead and monitoring operations from a city owned chopper. He pulled a small wooden cross he had carried for months now slick with wear and flicked it into the open air where it was carried along by wind current until it fell to the ground below. Soldiers quickly assembled the timbers under Milgram's direction and stretched Jesus' bludgeoned body out on a beam that would support his weight. Men among the guard drove the spikes since they were under orders and would not be implicated nor religiously defiled. One held flat his limp palms while another stationed a sharp spike in the center and drove it home with forceful blows. Loud shouts of profanity followed orders directed at subordinates which helped relieve the pounding tensions bursting in their chests. Blood splattered onto their fatigues with each new blow. The men turned Jesus' ankles while holding them stacked upon one another in a vise-like grip. Another soldier slammed the powerful hammer down onto the head of the thick spike impaling him there. Screams by the victim were savored by his torturers who gazed at the puffy warm bloody flesh just penetrated by cold steel. Tissue foamed up around the spike in a strange embrace. Jesus' mother and others too hoarse to cry out any longer stood helplessly along side and watched as he was lifted above their heads for national view through the eye of an electronic lens that had been on site since the procession began. The moment the cross swung perpendicular it fell nearly three feet to the bottom of the hole that had been dug out to receive its butt. The impact sounded with a bass thud dislocating joints, but not a bone was broken. Jesus was still alive and experiencing all of the horrific searing pain that must have felt like thousands of sharp projectiles stabbing his gaunt body.

"This is not happening," is all Mary could manage through lips that draped from her shattered face.

The chief of police arrived with several units but had no intention of breaking up the frolic. He simply made his presence known and conveniently arrived by Geiger's cue after it was all over. The entire city was placed on a state of alert in the event that other terrorist should seek to save their leader.

Many more civilians arrived by now and walked by for a closer look at the one who murdered their loved ones while Jews taunted him with sarcastic words, "Release yourself and get down here—you delivered others!" Jesus had been beaten beyond recognition and scarcely had strength to hold his shoulders up and diaphragm open to receive oxygen.

The two thieves were hung on similar posts on either side of Jesus. One of the thieves noticed the inscription a soldier placed over Jesus' head which read: 'Jesus Christ—King of the Jews.'

"If you're the Christ," shouted one of the thieves, "then save us!"

He began hurling insults at Jesus, but Benny told his friend to knock it off. "We had something similar to this coming, but this man is innocent—just got on the wrong side of society. "Jesus," he said turning to him, "don't forget me when you cross the finish line—when you reach your kingdom."

Jesus promised him, "today you will join me in paradise."

From noon until 3:00 P.M., darkness moved in and covered the entire region. Geiger left the area because his job was done and a nasty storm appeared to be brewing.

"Dr. Geiger," said the helicopter pilot, "we can't stay up here much longer—we're pressing our luck not to get hit with an intense cross wind."

"Take us away," Geiger ordered, while goading the front of his seat with spurs. "Let the fool pay! We're done up here—now push this thing—I have some details to care for at home."

John parked his Saab along side of the others and followed in from the rear with his mind recklessly reeling from all that was happening. He fell to the ground and quickly got back on his feet. Everything had spun out of control. While walking over the path of a recent tornado he wondered at the force of the violent winds that had ripped off his roof and uprooted a stout green tree. Shirts, empty whisky bottles and loose tools were strewn in its wake. A putrid smell of human salt was in the air. John could hardly raise his eyes when he arrived at the site of execution where he joined Mary and the others. He was being provoked and simultaneously shouted down. Muscles in his face were twitching at the corners of his eyes and mouth. And there was little use in trying to control their distortive movements, for he had just stepped into an arena that nothing could have prepared him for—a killing room filled with utterly foreign moans from a familiar voice. Why is my friend hanging from that post half naked? Why have they mangled my leader's body? Why are these wicked jaws celebrating the capture and execution of the only lovely thing I've ever known—that has ever touched my life with any sense of beauty? John was overpowered by psychological pressures entering his blood in the form of a dreadful narcotic blend that left him emotionally debilitated. Any hope for tomorrow was dripping from Jesus' wounds and trickling to the base of the cross. John's sickened heart began convulsing and crying out to just vomit and purge itself of the hellishness.

While standing fast, he drifted away temporarily and entered what felt like a netherworld. He walked through acres of killing fields, frozen in time, featuring horrific sights too ghastly or inhuman to look upon. Near the end lay a small rocky parcel lined with trees which were named after neighbors who had stood heroically against the bloody onslaught. Beneath the shade of an elegantly twisted olive was the name, Jennifer Tiles who fairly represented the rest. Just beyond her name plate a stone stairway descended below grade to an enclosed room. Its elevation from the surface made the room nearly subterranean and feeling of a morgue. The entire volume of the room was softly aglow with five candles reflecting millions of individual flames in the face of staggered mirrors that had been carefully positioned to count each one.

An otherworldly voice spoke from somewhere within that cavern. Not happy or sad, but slowly, evenly and repeatedly reported, 'It was God's good pleasure to smash him, by assigning a sentence of grief, if he would volunteer himself as a substitute saddled with all guilt for the altar. My servant will make many sparkle and just, as he will carry their iniquities.' The smell of the supernatural filled that space.

Laughter by those standing by brought John up out of the hole. National Guardsmen had already stripped Jesus of his seamless hooded sweater and were presently throwing dice for the trophy as Mary wailed. Maggie wished for a knife and a pint of something strong, but a strange serenity let her drop the preparations, release her fists and wrap open palms around Jesus' mother. While blood dripped from a wire spoke wheel cover, soldiers continued arguing over who would keep Jesus' fine hooded sweater. Mary and John silently looked on while wondering at their man.

"Woman," Jesus said weakly, but audibly, "look at your son. And John, your mother." From that moment, John cared for Mary and took her into his own house. Soldiers were given strict orders not to do anything that would accelerate Jesus' death.

"Geiger wants this to be slow and painful," said Mr. Milgram. Turning his head to ensure no one important was eavesdropping he whispered to the soldiers near him, "the monster spent months researching torture and the most gruesome means of execution—too bad for these cons, he loved to read Josephus."

Jesus startled everyone in range when he yelled out in a foreign tongue from the cross, "My God, my God, why have you run out on me?" One of the Jews standing by thought he might be calling for Elijah the prophet to come and rescue him. He told a soldier to offer him a drink of his cheap wine sopped in a towel from the end of his rifle bayonet. Jesus cried out with a loud voice like one falling at the feet of a huge army and being trampled on a basin floor. Giving up his spirit, his last words were, "It's all done."

In that instant, something like a massive vault slammed shut in heaven and the thunder roared back over the entire expanse forcing every creature in that place to fall down in utter fear. The reverberation from above knocked Picasso's Guernica to the floor in Madrid's Prado Museum and it ripped from top to bottom. Blood that had flowed from the base of the cross entered into deep ruts and was carried away by a brief torrential down pour to a low stagnant pool in a nearby slough where no one ever fished.

Siva who had connections with just about everybody gained permission to remove Jesus' body from the cross. No ambulance service would assist and morticians were gravely threatened not to accept the body. "Let him rot!" the crowds shouted. At this, one of the guards who had witnessed the entire ordeal from up front pierced Jesus' side with a bayonet by the dare of another who accused him many times in the past of being a chicken. Water mixed with blood flowed from the wound and John overheard the young man remark, "this had to be the son of God." Others ridiculed their comrade's observation saying, "Let's get the boy out of here before he also gets converted," and laughter rang in the young man's red ears.

But Joseph Snyder, a rich man from the city who raised his own wealth as a wildcat in search of oil in the Ohio River Valley—a man who had little fear of anything and a righteous Jew—one who was looking for the kingdom of God showed up by Siva's request and without concern for their censorship carefully removed the heavy spikes and reverently handled the body of the deceased. Mr. Snyder had been a secret follower of Jesus; but when he was spit at by one of the soldiers for touching Jesus' body, he raised up and faced the officer without a word. A stare stepped out of Snyder's body like a phantom approaching the man as if to say—"you have no further assignment here."

Rigor mortis had already set in by the time they arrived at the mausoleum at Rosehill Cemetery where Mr. Snyder owned several private family burial chambers. All the Jews who were on hand made quick work lifting the body bag and placing it in the crypt with careful hands.

That evening Mr. P. and Harry joined one another for drinks above the Harrison while the Attorney General called an emergency meeting with his advisors to deal with the Chicago aftermath. Leonard Geiger declined special invitation to be with the Governor and Mayor choosing instead to go home and close a file that would become the crowning achievement of his entire life's pursuit. Geiger was strutting about with unusual vanity as he entered his vacant residence and walked floors that were off limits to his soles, talking to himself and rehearsing the days events; however, he would not allow himself sleep until he had sufficiently debriefed every thing to disk and placed it in closed-file lockup.

Leonard took gin from his wife's reserve without a trace of intrusion, gathered ice and a mix, then descended the stairs to his quarters. Opened upon Dr. Geiger's massive desk was his laptop still burning behind a screensaver. Geiger sat down while touching the pointer. The screen cleared revealing a large string of email addresses indicating the destinations of electronic files sent hours ago to eminent Regents of the University, prominent Jews in the communities of Chicago as well as several other influential citizens who were given back their lives in the form of email attachments—secret files that had been expunged from the computer's data base by a skilled hacker. A record of recipients was still highlighted along with an abundance of incriminating evidence that clearly linked Geiger as the mastermind of the entire operation that held Chicago's breath for over three years. Everything he regarded secret lay open as well as a carbon address of an overnight express letter destined to Max Randolph, the Attorney General of the United States.

Geiger thought the intruder might still be in his residence when he perceived that the secret passage to top secret files remained ajar, but his drink slipped from his hands and shattered on the floor when he turned and saw the silhouette of a man through sliding glass doors dangling by the neck from the upper deck of his home.

Geiger stepped over to the glass doors in disbelief. He could feel the marrow in his bones catching fire. Flicking on an exterior lamp revealed that it was Judas who had held a final trump card. Geiger's rage burned with such fury mixing with his own defeat that he expended his bowel and intestines while standing before the panes like a pit bull that lost a bout with a lesser breed. His master turned his head and the dog with nowhere else to go and no longer able to live with himself, he slowly lost consciousness and fell to the floor where he expired.

Geiger's wife had the home in the hands of a real estate agent the following day, but no one was permitted passage in or out until the F.B.I. thoroughly investigated every square inch of the premises. Geiger had not shredded anything nor deleted any electronic media. As a result news bulletins did an about face as new information began to leak out—word that agents refused to cover up. Many families were deeply remorseful for their involvement while others insisted that the new twist was a government cover up of some kind.

"It's obvious to any one blind wishing to investigate these files that an innocent man has been slain along side a couple of common jewel thieves," said Max Randolph who was presently standing in the lower level of Leonard Geiger's home where the F.B.I. and the coroner were taking care of different legal matters. The Attorney General himself had no intention of a cover up and would spend nearly a week in Chicago unraveling a twisted story and communicating it to an American public that was thoroughly confused about the events on Friday.

Many who participated remarked in hindsight that they felt like they had been caught up in a frenzy that was overpowering and quickly grew out of control. Many law abiding citizens without a hint of a police record, those responsible for hurling abuse and fists even members of the guard confessed to Jesus' true identity insisting that he had to have been God's son because of the way he died. All these were reeling emotionally and trying desperately to catch up from the jet-lag of the last several hours.

"It was all wrong," several admitted, "but we meant to do it and we'd do it again, but it was all wrong," shaking their heads, "look at us with blood on our hands."

All day Saturday, Jews who were furious about the revelations sought the Governor who wanted desperately to get out of the way and hurry back to Springfield. They caught up with the Governor about midday and demanded that he assign guards to the tomb.

"You know this man's popular influence," they shouted. "The sentiments of the masses are constantly shifting and already there is a growing hoax that he might rise from the dead. Move before they incite a riot and turn our city into an ash heap!" Mr. P. knew Jesus would be exonerated but was caught out alone with only his body guard and chauffeur. And since he couldn't make a judgment, he paused as though weighing the request, then reluctantly gave in while savoring the satisfaction of their praise and words of thanks for granting them their wishes. Stories were so controverted that none of Jesus' men dared venture out near the tomb for fear of being identified. Maggie and Mary, the sister of Martha sat alone in grief near the tomb at early evening before being driven away by guardsmen who arrived amidst the turmoil and conflicting reports.

Chapter 24

Saturday's headlines in newspapers all across the Country could be summarized with the phrase, 'Jewish Rabbi Exonerated!' The plot to place blame of the Chicago bombings on Jesus was uncovered and lucidly described by major presses and serious evening news commentators alike. Each hour more and more Americans were growing familiar with the intricacies and nuance of the investigation. Among files delivered by Judas were folders of information indicting Herzl Holdheim and at least three others of Geiger's closest associates. Regents and faculty at the University of Chicago were incredulous. The thought of Dr. Leonard Geiger mapping out a plan this sinister right under their nose while sipping coffee with him on weekdays or greeting him on the campus was just more than they could assimilate. The tomb at Rosehill Cemetery was still cordoned off—now by order of the Attorney General who also wanted assurances that the body not be disturbed.

John stood out in front of his apartment on Cove cleaning the glass on his Saab when Steve drove up to obtain the title and make the transfer. John was really in no mood to conduct this kind of business and only got out of bed because of the obligation. John had already relaxed his Sabbath habits as did many others of Jesus' followers, but the gloom and depression precipitated by yesterday's events still hung over him like a dark cloud, and he would have preferred on this day to just be alone. John had already removed the tags and was ready to sign the transfer when Steve extended his hand and said hello.

"So, John, you've kept it nice and polished right up to the time of sale. Did you remove all you're personal items?"

"Yeah, but maybe I should take another last look before I turn it over to you." John opened the trunk and interior compartments then poked his head beneath the passenger side seat and drew out a small package that he didn't recognize.

"Hey, a good thing you double checked—huh, John?"

"Yeah, I guess so," he replied.

Steve sat down in the car and surprised John by saying, "What is this for crying out loud—I thought you said this car had 14,000 miles on it—the odometer reads 40,000."

"No," John said to Steve, "that's what I've said all along—40,000."

"No way, the deal's off! I knew the ad was too good to be true—I thought I'd found a bargain."

"It is a bargain!" John insisted and I told you all along that the car had 40,000 miles on it—it's two years old; did you really think it had only 14,000?"

"Sorry, mister," said Steve departing, "she's your baby."

John ignored Steve's last remarks while he stared at the strange box. The wide gum band squeezed an old chocolates box with a piece of paper strapped to the outside that appeared to have been appended as an afterthought and simply read, 'John, full of solace and peace is the man who does not kick himself down in the things that he approves. Step out of the cave and shake off the ambivalence. By the way, did you keep the car?' Without even opening the box John pealed sale signs from the windows of his Saab. Back inside he called Peter's place but Jill said he was not taking any calls and she insisted that everyone give him some space for she feared he was on the verge of an emotional breakdown.

"John, he won't eat, he won't talk—all he does is stare at the wall and sleep," Jill wept.

Two of John's roommates agreed to buy out his equity in the unit on Cove. They spoke casually to one another to fill a void like the man who cut his grass on the day of his son's funeral surrounded by critical friends who just couldn't possibly understand. After setting provisional terms, he drove over to spend time with Mary and others who were desperately sickened that Jesus had died in vain. The mood at Mary's place was kind but surreptitiously subdued. Inside each heart the events from Thursday evening up to the present moment were being rehearsed like flash cards—events that had occurred in such a blink and caught everyone so off guard that it was humanly impossible to compute it all in one sitting.

John invited Mary out for a drive which turned into a mindless look at area homes that were open for inspection. The two of them consolidated their monies in order to purchase a comfortable tri-level with plenty of room for both John and Mary to entertain their friends and enjoy their own privacy when needed.

Later that afternoon, Peter ventured out of his house and drove over to the firm where he resigned three-and-a-half years earlier after meeting Jesus and hauling in a catch of stock that nearly tore his nets. He sat down at his old desk now occupied by an intern who was learning the ropes. Zeb drove by and having recognized the vehicle stopped in and spoke with Simon.

"The boys tell me you've all had a pretty rough week," said Zeb, still wondering if his previous employees had made the right decision but unwilling to bring up the matter. "Simon, like I told you before, the job is yours if you ever decide you might want to come back." Simon who always paid Zeb due respect and treated him like a father remained silent and never lifted his eyes. "Well, I'm heading out, Simon—can I do anything for you?"

After a moment he turned in his chair and simply said, "My name is Peter. Zeb, my name is Peter."

"O.K.," Zeb paused feeling awkward and wondered if Simon was taking prescription medication. "Peter, I'm going out now—you call me if you need me for anything." The door to the office closed and Peter drew his feet up on the desk and stared into the wall like he had done for hours at home until it frightened Jill. The office was now dark and the only sound was the tick of a clock that sounded an awful lot like the one Jill used in her kitchen to time bread that was rising. The phone rang and Peter picked it up more from impulse and the old surroundings than anything else.

"Yep, what do you need?" asked Peter.

"Thought you might be there—be right down," said John and he picked up James on the way over.

James and John walked into the office which felt more like a morgue than anything else and found Peter sitting at his old desk. "C'mon in, John. Hello, James," said Peter. His words sounded broken—not the syllables or pronunciation—just broken from something inside like a stick that had been snapped into several pieces.

Peter could hardly tend to his own needs but as he looked into the faces of his friends he felt compassion for them and remembered Jesus' encouragement to him just hours before the betrayal, "Simon, Satan has insisted that he be given permission to draw you through a sieve; but after you've pulled yourself back together, pick up your brothers." John set a hot deep-dish pizza at the center of the desk without his usual verbose spiel about groceries and discs, and both men took seats opposite Peter.

"It feels strange to eat our favorite pizza without Jesus," said John. Reservoir gates that had been managing flash floods burst open again at that suggestion and three men who had come through a typhoon that claimed the life of their Skipper now lay shipwrecked, unable to eat and marooned on an uncharted clump of sand in the middle of some hateful ocean.

Chapter 25

Maggie hadn't been back to the old snags in Hammond since the night she was carried out of there in the back of Jesus' van and transported to Long Grove for rehabilitation over two years ago. Folks at the many taverns and dens she used to frequent wouldn't recognize her anyway for Maggie had grown into someone beautiful beyond words. A femininity that used to hide behind a serious toughness began to come alive because of Siva's care and the unconditional personal acceptance shown to her by Jesus. And there was nothing cosmetic about it either. Maggie's beauty touched her home and work environment and was especially enjoyed by friends who were often serenaded by her guitar and lovely aesthetic style during their weekly prayer meetings in area homes that was coming in place of synagogue attendance.

One of the daily habits Maggie had cultivated over the many months was a regular early morning hour alone with God. She normally rose at 5:00 A.M., put on coffee and meditated on scripture before committing the day's events to him in prayer. Today she wanted to spend that time at Rosehill. Daily devotions felt more like life's greatest pleasure than a hollow discipline and so she hurriedly cut several roses from her own flower garden to save time before beginning a leisurely ride down to the cemetery. 'Hurry up and relax—be efficient to listen' was counsel she overheard Jesus offer to Martha on one occasion and Maggie was working on absorbing that same wisdom into her own life.

John rolled out of bed about the same time and sat quietly in his kitchen without awakening others who weren't due to be up for work schedules for another hour. John's usual journaling was generally carried out before bedtime; but having so much on his mind, he couldn't sleep and so he decided to rise early and write out some prayers. Not long into his sentences, John's thoughts were mysteriously sublimated and began to yield to something forcing its way into his consciousness that whispered, "he said he would rise." John pushed the notebook to the center of the counter and studied the thought or guess or hunch or whatever he was experiencing because it wouldn't let him go.

"Of course," John thought, "how could we be so blind—he said he would. And after three days! This is the third day," he mused further, "and any part of which according to my Jewish noodle being taken as a whole," he concluded with a shout that woke up the others—"It could happen today!"

"Hey, hey," said Frank running in from the back bedroom wearing only his briefs, "a thief break in—what's going on?"

"Sorry," John said to him, "I guess I got a little carried away." Frank was up for the day and so decided to mill around the kitchen and find something edible to nuke. While he scavenged refrigerator shelves mostly dumping molded items left behind by two other bachelors with food preserving habits just like his, John moved to the living room still trying desperately to recall the exact phrase Jesus used to describe his coming back.

"No.... maybe," his mind fumbled it again, "but how?" He continued searching and trying to make sense of the impossible when he dropped an eye contact onto the carpet which forced him to scour it's nap in hopes of recovering the indispensable illuminator. "He raised others, but can a dead man raise himself?" The fresh thought felt like something foreign pulling on a compass needle and away from John's gut that was oriented to true north.

"How about some eggs?" asked Frank who peeked in on John.

"No thanks, I've already had a muffin. I think I'll go out for a little run."

"Did you lose something?" Frank asked John.

"Yeah, it's right here, I'll find it." After a moment, John laced up his trainers and headed out onto the streets of Mount Prospect more determined to run down a thought than exercise.

It was a relief to Maggie when she arrived at Rosehill off of Western and determined that the National Guard had been called away from the hallowed site. The last thing she was in the mood for was a confrontation with belligerent soldiers doing their duty. Daylight was only beginning to grow and the air was as clean and crisp as she could ever remember. Easy listening was being supplied in natural stereo by morning doves on one side being answered by a lone whippoorwill from another direction. Rosehill Cemetery was as gorgeous as any of the city's parks. Its beautifully manicured grounds with paved passages too soft for concrete stretch out like fingers extending from palms laid open and resting upon the grass green apron of a woman's lap who cradles those who sleep there.

"The dead understand beauty," Maggie sang quietly through an arrangement she'd been working on, "so much hidden from the eyes of all living—concealed from the birds of the sky. Abaddon and death—yeah, they've heard the music."

Arriving at the mausoleum she was startled to find the heavy doors that always remained locked standing wide open and inviting her inspection. Maggie had been in dark caverns before and never had a second thought about venturing in and speaking with the curator. There was no movement inside nor sign of life.

"Hello," Maggie said, "Anyone here—hello." Suddenly she noticed the vault where Jesus' body had been laid pulled fully open with the thick body bag laid out in its entire length but empty with Jesus' burial clothes folded on top of it. Bristles and chills crawled up Maggie's spine as her shoulders pointed up and she stood on her toes like a cat backing its way out of a dog fight.

Tears filled her eyes and she screamed, "They've stolen my body! They've stolen my Jesus!" She dropped her roses and ran from the mausoleum out of Rosehill and past her car before she realized that she had over-shot her transportation. Returning to the Eldorado, she snatched the cellular with hands still shaking with anger as she tried three times to hit the right pads before successfully connecting with Peter's residence. Peter picked up the phone on his side of the bed; and before he could say hello, a blast of mixed verbiage—some not so clean came racing through fiber optic demanding that he and some men get down to Rosehill A.S.A.P. and figure out what happened to Jesus' body.

"Now you listen to me, mister—you better make like Peter Pan and get the rest of those men you call leaders down here before I dismantle this mausoleum and restack it in your back yard with eleven fresh corpses—I'll turn over every blasted stone and exhume every filthy rotten rich son-of-a-.... "Loud sobs cut off the woman's wrenching groans and there was no mistaking the voice. Either Janice recently rose or that was none other than Maggie probably suffering a flashback or some other delusional episode.

"There's no telling what still circulates in the poor woman's blood," Peter said to Jill as he pulled on pants and shoes. "I'm going down to get her—mind if I bring her back to spend the day with us?"

"Of course not, Peter, you don't have to ask—want me to come along? Mom can watch the boys."

"Yeah, sure," said Peter, "but let's get moving, that woman knows how to operate a D-9 CAT and as sure as we're standing here she'll rip up every inch of that place until she finds the body.

John stepped out of the shower and caught Peter and Jill on their cellular. "Peter, I've been thinking and I've got to run some ideas by you—this whole execution and death business isn't over."

"Well of course it's not over," Peter replied, "it'll be in the news for weeks. What are you talking about? Are the authorities looking for us?"

"No, nothing like that—I'm not sure what I mean exactly—I just think, well, I think the Lord might just..."

"John, do you need some fresh vocabulary—help with words—you think the Lord might what?"

"I'm being serious, Peter."

"O.K.," Peter said to him, "look, something's up with Maggie. Jill and I are on our way down to Rosehill right now. Maggie called from down there a few minutes ago and is hysterical that someone moved the body. She's fit to be tied and said she was going to tear into some walls if she doesn't locate the body. Anyway, I'm afraid she might get herself in big trouble and so we're going to see if we can cool her down."

"Is she armed?" asked John.

"No, no nothing like that," said Peter, "on the other hand, it might be better for whoever lifted the body if she were. Death would be quicker and a whole lot less painless from the muzzle of a .38 than falling under the tracks of a bull dozer. So what are you doing up so early? John? John are you there? Can you believe that," Peter said to Jill, "the little snapper hung up on me."

John jumped into his Saab and hurried to Rosehill while Peter and Jill pulled in for a quick cup of coffee just south of Evanston.

"Have we got time for this?" asked Jill.

"Well, not really, but after thinking about it, I've decided that I'm not much at hugging people and having them slobber all over me. I just thought we could buy a little time and let her cool off some."

"You guys have all the guts," said Jill who wasn't kidding.

"That's right baby and right now it's time to fill one and empty another."

"C'mon, Peter, hurry up, Maggie's really hurting." Peter took his time with a coffee purchase while wondering about women and their preoccupation with relationships.

John pulled in right behind Peter and the two of them walked briskly ahead of Jill before their steps turned into a run.

"What are you doing here, John?" Peter yelled. Without a word, John pulled ahead of Peter and out-ran him to the crypt. John stuck his head inside the door and saw the body bag and burial clothes, along with the linen cloth they placed over his face rolled up and set aside by itself but he didn't venture in. As soon as Peter arrived, he nodded at Maggie who was now more controlled and walked immediately inside to investigate the burial vault. The body bag was undisturbed and obviously empty, laying flat and fully zipped. John then entered along side of Peter and was amazed to find the seal they placed over the zipper on Friday unbroken. He saw and believed but still didn't understand the scripture that Jesus must rise from the dead.

Peter and John walked back outside to comfort Maggie who was already being consoled by Jill. "What do you think, dear?" Jill asked her husband.

"It doesn't figure. Guess I'll call Mr. Snyder and the County Coroner and see if I can find out what's going on. The guards are gone, but I don't think they had anything to do with moving the body—there's been no forced entry at these doors nor the vault; and according to what I saw Friday on CNN, I'm sure the soldiers are not in the habit of stacking clothing that neatly." John was so engrossed in his own interpretive maze that he totally failed to point out to Peter that the body bag had literally been undisturbed by human hands based upon evidence of the seal. "C'mon, Maggie," said Peter as he placed his arm around her, "let's get you something to eat. This is Sunday and I'll make some calls as soon as offices open around 9:00 A.M."

"No, I can't go," said Maggie. "I'm O.K. now and I'm sorry if I frightened you. I'd just like to be alone. I can drive and I promise I'll call you later this morning after I've had some time to think. I'll just spend some time and walk around the cemetery."

"Are you sure you wouldn't want me to stay and walk with you, Maggie?" asked Jill.

"No, I'm really fine," she said while urging them to go on without her, "and let me know if you find out anything."

"You'll be the first to know, Maggie," said John who turned to Peter and Jill and said, "I'll go ahead and see if I can relate this news as tactfully as possible to Mary."

"Yeah, O.K. John," Peter said to him, "Jill and I are going to hold back and keep an eye on Maggie—we'll catch up with you later." Peter was more puzzled than he was letting on and began to seriously wonder about what could possibly happen next. After several minutes he and Jill departed Rosehill.

Following a brief walk around the cemetery, Maggie returned to the crypt and thought to look back inside before making a more determined search of the grounds. While staring into the room her thoughts carried her back to an earlier day shortly after she met this wonderful man. Jesus had paid a special visit to her bedside following an attempted suicide. Maggie could scarcely deal with the shame she was experiencing in those days and Jesus told her the story of the 'Mercy Seat' that permanently changed her heart.

"Moses and the ark of the covenant," Maggie continued meditating upon a recollection of the Bible's description of two mirror image angels with outstretched wings overshadowing the lid of the ark—the Mercy Seat—the only authorized place of atonement where blood was sprinkled to cover the nation's sins. The sprinkled blood was familiar enough to Maggie, "sprinkled, splattered, what's it matter—we all bleed red," she remembered teasing with Jesus during her recovery as he laid down truths about innocence and substitution that were totally foreign to her.

"It's another important area of law that I've come to fulfill," she remembered him saying. Then before her eyes in a twinkling two angels appeared right there in the crypt and each one sitting at opposite ends of the body bag. Maggie was startled by their appearance and filled with wonder. She was overcome with joy months later when she put the whole picture together and wrote a song entitled, 'Recliner,' which became one of the house church favorites. Maggie's song described a sacrifice of infinite worth that provided sinners forgiveness and sitting room in the lap of mercy provided by terms of a new promise. John helped her edit it and encouraged her to think about changing the title and some of the bars to reflect a restful piece of furniture that is stationary rather than the soft saddle of a Harley 'Fat Boy' cruising down open road.

"Woman, what's troubling you?" asked one of the men.

"Someone has removed my Lord and I don't know what they've done with him." No sooner than the words were out of her mouth than she turned to the door at the sound of a soft step and saw Jesus standing there, but had no idea who it was because his skin was so different.

"Woman, why are you so upset? Are you looking for someone?" Jesus asked.

Maggie was sure the man could judge the dead and so asked him, "Sir, just tell me where you've moved him and I'll take him away." Jesus was touched by Maggie's love—love that would compel her to lift a body without giving a thought to the dead weight of a grown man and moving it by herself.

"Women." Jesus said, "semper fidelis."

"Say again, mister?" Maggie asked while returning her gaze to the angels that had mysteriously disappeared.

"Maggie!" Jesus said.

Maggie spun around in the floor at the unmistakable call of her name and shouted, "Professor!" which was a term of endearment she often used to refer to the Lord because of his penetrating teaching style.

"Maggie, Maggie loosen your grip, you're choking me," Jesus said, "and I've not yet ascended to the Father. Maggie, please let go! Run and tell all my followers that I'm ascending to my Father and your Father, to my God and your God." Maggie turned in circles while jumping on one foot and finding her direction was on her way in a flash and jubilant to share the news. "And watch the speed limit!" Jesus shouted behind her. But it was no use, even the old car seemed to have undergone a tune-up and as the powerful exhaust thrust began pushing a rust streak down the street on four wheels, Jesus uttered a brief prayer of intercession and two angels took up positions on bumpers of a fast moving Eldorado.

Jesus went up from Rosehill; and although it couldn't be heard in near galaxies, a shout of triumph shook all heaven at his arrival. One searches for words to describe such an outbreak and overflow of exuberant, inexpressible joy but sometimes events are just best left unexpressed since words would miserably fail to capture the rapture and color and movement and pageantry and effect and the myriad upon myriad of angels whose shouts couldn't be dampened even by serious warnings by Jesus who led captivity captive in grand procession.

"No, my son," he said from the center of the throne, "for if these are silent the very stars will cry out!" That word brought cries of welcome and intimacy by three of them and marked the beginning of a festival that has never stopped, the reverberations of which continue to bring shudders to those who dwell beneath the earth.

Without any luck on the cellular—Maggie arrived at Mary's place where John stood near his car in the driveway.

"It's no use, Maggie," John said as she passed him, "they think we're nuts." Maggie left the car running and ran inside without knocking and announced that she had seen the risen Lord. "What?" Mary asked, "You actually saw him?"

"Hold your foot on the clutch," Maggie shouted, "I not only saw him, but I spoke with him and touched him—just a few minutes ago right outside the mausoleum! Bart raised the newspaper again but Maggie snatched it from before his face and shredded it while screaming, "I'm not hallucinating!" Maggie got everyone on their feet and force marched them back to Rosehill against their wills.

A crowd of over thirty of Jesus' followers canvassed the cemetery under threat by Maggie who they all thought had flipped.

"Keep it up," Peter said to several standing by, "it's the least we can do. It'll be dark soon and we'll go on back home. Maggie wasn't angry at her friends and searched more diligently than the others—sifting every square inch of the cemetery hoping at any moment for Jesus to jump up from behind a tombstone and show himself alive. After several more minutes of politeness, Peter called everyone in and they drove to he and Jill's place for some coffee and discussion. Talk droned on for a couple of hours mostly people comparing stories of all that occurred over the past couple of days and speculating about what the authorities might do next. "Anybody attend Jude's funeral?" asked Thad.

"Not that I'm aware, but I did see the obituary in yesterday's Herald," said Bart. Others entered into a quiet conversation about Jude while Maggie chewed up fresh sticks of gum like ticker-tape. She sat in the corner nearly out of sight, but her fingernail filing on a slight emery pad sounded like a denim brad on a wash board and profaning the solemn presence. Peter looked over and shook his head at the sight. Maggie was grinning from ear to ear and looked to be holding the exact match to the State lottery. But of course, no one believed it; and of course, that's what made her smile which of course brought about the not so friendly scowl of all the others.

"I'll collect soon enough," Maggie said to herself.

Mary was helping Jill pour drinks for the search party when a shriek came from the living room that brought everyone to their feet. Jesus stood just inside a locked door upon the tiles of the entry foyer and said to them, "Peace be with you." And without further word, he kicked off his boat shoes and showed them his hands and his feet still imprinted with marks from the spikes. Everyone was speechless until Maggie broke the silence saying, "You can't keep a good man down!"

"Yes," Jesus said, "and I'm looking to enlist a few good men and women to carry that message to the nations beginning right here in this room, for just as the Father has sent me so I'm sending you." As soon as he said this, Jesus exhaled and said, "receive the Holy Spirit." Some of those present were frightened and thought they were seeing a ghost and so Jesus asked them, "Can a spirit eat food? Does a spirit have skin and bones? Touch me. And Martha, bring me something from the table to eat." Jesus' followers were astounded and utterly dumbfounded as they examined the scars and watched him eat food. Mary managed her way through close quarters, embraced Jesus and wept for joy. "I'm back as I promised," Jesus whispered to her, "and alive forevermore." After helping Mary to a seat, Jesus stationed himself in the middle of the floor and said, "Why are you so surprised? Isn't this exactly what I told you to expect? The law of Moses and all the predictions made by David and the prophets had to be fulfilled." Jesus then opened their minds to understand the Scriptures which indicate that the Christ would be severely abused and rise up on the third day. "Your mission is to announce the forgiveness of sins in my name to all the nations. That will include helping people get their lives turned around, baptizing them and teaching them everything that I've commanded you." Jesus commissioned each one of them as witnesses but told them to remain in the city until they should receive power from heaven. And without warning, he vanished from their sight.

Thomas was late getting in from a trip on Sunday night and drove over to Peter and Jill's place in response to a recorded message left at his home. Several men and women were still talking among themselves in the driveway when Thomas arrived and asked why all the urgency and commotion. Peter, James and John were now chewing gum and said, "You just missed the event of the Century!"

"What do you mean?—the millennium is just underway. Peter picked up the habit somewhere and began filing his fingernails right there before Thomas while looking into the stars and sighing about the fact that Jesus had just been standing in the front living room of his house less than twenty minutes ago. Everyone standing on the driveway pretty much looked like James who was drawing air through side teeth that had sandwiched the tip of his tongue, taking longer than usual blinks with their eyes and barely paying him any mind.

"That's just a bunch of poppycock!" said Thomas. "I wouldn't believe that in a million years! I'll tell you what I'll do. You go round up Jesus and when I place my fingers in the palms of his nail pierced hands and my whole hand into his side where that soldier ripped him open, then I'll believe."

"Goodnight everyone," said Maggie, "and Thomas, I hope you like a little crow with your salt and pepper, 'cause it's coming to ya in flocks!"

"I'm going inside to get something to eat. Isn't that Mary's car?" asked Thomas. "Now she'll tell me straight." As soon as Thomas opened the front door of the house, the entire room erupted with everyone talking over one another.

As others were departing and feeling like zombies that were desperate for sleep, Thomas' last words could be heard outdoors, "C'mon, the gig's up—they already gave me those looks outside. Here, Thad, let me borrow that file, I've got a hang nail."

Eight days later nearly forty of Jesus followers were behind locked doors at the home of James and Diane for word was rumored that Jewish authorities were searching for several of Jesus' key leaders who were leading people out of the synagogues. Thomas was sitting at the end of the sofa with only an end table between he and the wall and still spouting off about the ridiculous shenanigan pulled on him just over a week ago at Peter and Jill's place.

"You guys ought to get acting careers," Thomas said as he took a large slurp from his drink.

"Yeah, well I want to see how you act when Jesus taps you on the shoulder and says 'hello,'" said John. Thomas moved his arm to place his drink on a coaster when an arm reached through the wall and took the glass from his hand and began drinking from it. Air rushing down wind pipes all around the room sounded like back draft of a thirsty inferno sucking out all the available oxygen. Thomas looked like a little boy who just had the wits scared out of him and his knees were literally knocking for fear had gripped him.

Jesus tapped on Thomas' shoulder and said, "Hello, Thomas, reach here your finger and place them in my palms or here your hand and feel my side and leave no room for unbelief." Thomas said, "My Master and my God."

"Yes, Thomas, because you have seen you believe. Singled out and specially regarded, however, are those who have not seen and yet believe," said Jesus while winking at Maggie who was already beginning to 'caw' like a crow.

Many more things could be written about the signs that Jesus performed as well as comments on notes extracted from a box recovered from beneath the passenger seat of John's Saab, but these pages will be adequate witness for others yet to hear that Jesus is the Christ the unique Son of God—the only one of his kind and believing they might have eternal life in his name.

Epilogue

Mary and John each sold their respective properties and purchased the tri-level in Prospect Heights that they had made an offer on earlier in the year. John surprised everyone the first of June with news of his engagement to Lynn and they were wed in Peter and Jill's back yard on a colorful day in the middle of September. John's brother, James, was the best man and Lynn's life long friend, Patty was the Maid of Honor. During the reception, James lifted a glass of wine above John's head and proclaimed a toast saying, "Singled out and specially regarded is my brother." Everyone was silent and turned as though they were facing a national flag during a solemn observance. "Brother," James continued with misty eyes, "you are a pleasure to God and a gift to men. You are the one who sees. You saw the lad through muddy waters. You saw Christ ahead of the rest of us and I know that you will see more visions to write about," for word was leaking out that John had already begun compiling a monograph of Jesus' life. "Today, we celebrate your joy," and placing his hand on his shoulder concluded, "and may your heart never condemn you in the things that you approve." After that day John was nicknamed 'the Seer' after legends of old.

Peter never whispered a word not even to his wife, Jill, but he was still plagued with guilt resulting from the denials he made out front of Point Crown on the night of Jesus' betrayal and arrest. Some time after Jesus' last appearance, Peter went back to work for Zeb at the firm because he was going stir crazy sitting around the house counting bricks in the neighbor's chimney that was visible through rear windows of the house. Zeb was happy to have Simon back on payroll and several of the others followed him there including Zeb's sons—James and John. On one occasion, Peter stayed on at his desk and worked through the night rigging client files and refamiliarizing himself with computer software they used for fishing potential investments. Just as first light was growing over Lake Michigan, he pushed back from his desk and rehearsed again all of his cowardly remarks and behavior the night of Jesus' arrest. Peter's conscience would not be appeased and he found it profitable to beat himself with pummeling words. Then like hooded thuds with rubber hoses standing in shadows cast by a flood lamp hung over the culprit's head, someone would always call off the torture just before he lost consciousness.

Later that same morning following therapy, Peter was glued to the monitor when a call came in from an outside line inquiring about a line of stock. Peter didn't recognize the voice of the new client and was ready to obtain some fresh intake when the buyer asked him to first check the current price of a stock. Peter told him in short order that his was a respected brokerage firm and that if he wanted to throw dice he could call over to the pits on LaSalle and place everything he owned on pork bellies. After another moment and trying to keep his composure, Peter told the man for the third time that he didn't involve himself in grain futures.

"Look, mister," Peter told the man, when you're ready to buy stock come in and let's sit down and talk. We run a good business here and I'm sure we can find some safe investments for you." Peter shook his head following the disconnect and said to an intern who had entered the office, "Whew, what a kook. The guy said I wasn't dangerous enough."

"Well, said David, "some people think they own the cattle on a thousand hills—guess the man's got money to burn."

Peter went back to work but couldn't concentrate because of the voices laughing within and calling him a coward. He picked up pictures of Jill and the boys from his desk, considered his mortgage and decided to call over to the Board of Trade and place an enormous purchase of November wheat. A runner took the stamped trade to the pit where the bid was made. Right before Peter's eyes just minutes following the trade he was awarded several thousands of dollars which felt like another slot machine dispensed in his lap forcing him to his knees. The market rolled just like it had done on only one other occasion. He grabbed his jacket and ran out through the front doors of the office and saw a man he recognized standing by the pay phone across the street. Peter ran to his side, spilling over with tears and emotional regret and fell at his feet during mid-morning rush hour. Jesus helped his friend to his feet and told Peter to buy them each a sandwich and drink on their way over to the lake.

It was a long walk out to the locks where Jesus and Peter sat down beneath a tree by the water's edge. Peter had been doing most of the talking and relating to Jesus news of the market, status of the fledgling church and his joy to see him again. "So, Jesus are you going to continue making these dramatic and surprising reentries?" asked Peter. He knew Jesus heard the question but the only audible noise in the air was sea gulls angrily dipping nets and griping about the scarcity of smelt.

"Simon," Jesus finally asked, "do you love me more than these?" Peter thought the question was purposefully ambiguous and certainly comprehensive.

Peter responded with touching humility, "Yes, Lord. You know that I love you."

"Take care of my lambs," Jesus said to him. Then he asked him a second time, "Simon, son of John, do you love me?"

"Yes, Lord. You know that I do."

Jesus said to him, "Watch over my sheep." With little pause Jesus asked Peter for a third time, "Peter, do you love me?"

Peter was torn up inside because Jesus asked him the same question three times in a row but he responded by saying, "Lord, you know everything there is to know. You know how much I love you."

Jesus said to him, "Care for my sheep." Jesus turned and looked deeply into Peter's eyes. "You know, Peter, a few short years ago you carried on about life and pretty much did as you pleased, answered to no one, set you're own course and dared anyone to get in your way. A day is coming in which you will be harnessed by others and led into something unpleasant." Jesus related this to indicate the manner of death in which Peter would glorify God.

"Peter, I won't be back around in this sphere the way you are experiencing me today. I came to collect on my table you busted up back in our early days at Hinsdale. It's the only reason I'm here." Jesus said with complete soberness. "Now it's going to require some installments and by the time you get it paid up I'll see you again and we'll settle the account."

"Jesus, you're kidding—right?" Peter asked while laughing uncontrollably, "I mean it was just a worthless door. Look, I didn't know it was that important. Let's settle this nonsense right now."

"I am the door for the sheep, Peter. All that came before me were thieves and murderers. Bring the sheep along. All of them. And see that they pass through the door and find pasture—the joy is your wage," Jesus said, "and in that day we'll discuss the nonsense."

After this visit, Jesus said, "Follow me." Peter rose up and looked in the direction of the harbor and saw John walking toward them.

"What about John?" Peter asked, "Is he getting the same treatment?"

"What is that to you?" Jesus asked rhetorically while looking eastward, "What would it matter if he remained until I return in the end? You follow me!" Word circulated around the region that John would not die but that is not what Jesus said. He simply told Peter to mind his own business and deal with the door.

About the Author

My wife, Theresa and I have been married 21 years. Originally from western Kentucky, we've made our home in Atlanta as well as Chicago and now reside in southeast Michigan. We have three wonderful children: Nate, Sarah, and Stephen.

In the summer of 1984 we moved to Chicago from Atlanta where I pursued biblical and theological studies at Trinity College and Seminary. During this period I also spent three weeks of study in Israel. I received my Masters degree in 1991 and served as a pastor for more than 10 years in three different states.

I enjoy people and hearing their stories. I have many life experiences that cross both blue and white collar socio-economic fields. As a result, I have many stories of my own.

Printed in the United States
1855

9 780595 192045